The New Middle Ages

Series Editor

Bonnie Wheeler
English & Medieval Studies
Southern Methodist University
Dallas, Texas, USA

The New Middle Ages is a series dedicated to pluridisciplinary studies of medieval cultures, with particular emphasis on recuperating women's history and on feminist and gender analyses. This peer-reviewed series includes both scholarly monographs and essay collections.

More information about this series at
http://www.springer.com/series/14239

Tolkien, Self and Other: "This Queer Creature"

Jane Chance

Jane Chance
Andrew W. Mellon Distinguished
Professor Emerita of English
Rice University
jchance@rice.edu

The New Middle Ages
ISBN 978-1-137-39895-6 (hardcover)   ISBN 978-1-137-39896-3 (eBook)
ISBN 978-1-349-67986-7 (softcover)
DOI 10.1057/978-1-137-39896-3

Library of Congress Control Number: 2016950220

© The Editor(s) (if applicable) and The Author(s) 2016, First softcover printing 2019
This work is subject to copyright. All rights are solely and exclusively licensed by the Publisher, whether the whole or part of the material is concerned, specifically the rights of translation, reprinting, reuse of illustrations, recitation, broadcasting, reproduction on microfilms or in any other physical way, and transmission or information storage and retrieval, electronic adaptation, computer software, or by similar or dissimilar methodology now known or hereafter developed.
The use of general descriptive names, registered names, trademarks, service marks, etc. in this publication does not imply, even in the absence of a specific statement, that such names are exempt from the relevant protective laws and regulations and therefore free for general use.
The publisher, the authors and the editors are safe to assume that the advice and information in this book are believed to be true and accurate at the date of publication. Neither the publisher nor the authors or the editors give a warranty, express or implied, with respect to the material contained herein or for any errors or omissions that may have been made.

Cover image © Dennis Hallinan / Alamy Stock Photo

Printed on acid-free paper

This Palgrave Macmillan imprint is published by Springer Nature
The registered company is Nature America Inc. New York

For Joe, Rachel, and Arianna

"I do not think that I am frightfully important ... I am ... the most modest (or at any rate retiring) of men, whose instinct is to cloak such self-knowledge as he has, and such criticisms of life as he knows it, under mythical and legendary dress."—J.R.R. Tolkien, letter to W.H. Auden, 7 June 1955

Contents

Preface and Acknowledgments   xi

Abbreviations   xxi

Chronology of Composition and Publication Dates and Significant Events   xxiii

1   **Introduction: "This Queer Creature"**   1

2   **Forlorn and Abject: Tolkien and His Earliest Writing (1914–1924)**   19

3   **Bilbo as Sigurd in the Fairy-Story *Hobbit* (1920–1927)**   47

4   **Tolkien's Fairy-Story Beowulfs (1926–1940s)**   83

5   **"Queer Endings" After *Beowulf*: *The Fall of Arthur* (1931–1934)**   111

6   ***Apartheid* in Tolkien: Chaucer and *The Lord of the Rings*, Books 1–3 (1925–1943)**   133

7	"Usually Slighted": Gudrún, Other Medieval Women, and *The Lord of the Rings*, Book 3 (1925–1943)	177
8	The Failure of Masculinity: *The Homecoming of Beorhtnoth* (1920), *Sir Gawain* (1925), and *The Lord of the Rings*, Books 3–6 (1943–1948)	215
9	Conclusion: The Ennoblement of the Humble: The History of Middle-earth	241

Works Cited   249

Index   267

Preface and Acknowledgments

J.R.R. Tolkien, who was awarded highly coveted name professorships in Anglo-Saxon and Middle English at Oxford during his own lifetime, was much more forward-thinking than has previously been considered. Key are his humanism and his feminism—his sympathy for and toleration of those who are different, unimportant, or marginalized—the alien, the rustic, the commoner, the poor, the female, and the other. Conversely, Tolkien throughout his work and his letters expressed strong repugnance for the fascist, the despot, the master, and the king who exploit, abuse, or kill those who serve them.

I argue in this study that such empathy derived from a variety of causes: the loss of his parents during his early life, a lifelong shyness that made him uncomfortable among others (although he reveals in one letter that he can don the guise of affability as needed), the loss of close friends in World War I, and a consciousness of the injustice and violence in that war and World War II. As a result of his obligation to research and publishing in his field, propelled by his sense of abjection and diminution of self, Tolkien concealed aspects of the personal in his medieval adaptations, lectures, essays, and translations in relatively consistent ways. Tolkien's "queer" medieval begins with the study of Old and Middle English, Finnish, and Old Norse: his own early and scholarly interest in *Beowulf*, the *Kalevala*, the *Völsunga Saga*, Arthurian romance, Chaucer's *Canterbury Tales*, Sir

---

The original version of this book was revised. The version supplied here includes final author corrections.

Gawain and the Green Knight, and many other works. Among his most significant lectures and essays on the medieval are "Beowulf: The Monsters and the Critics," "On Fairy-Stories," "Sir Gawain and the Green Knight," and "A Secret Vice," along with his editions, translations, notes for, and adaptations of signal works (including, among others, the *Ancrene Riwle*, *The Battle of Maldon*, *Beowulf*, his *Sellic Spell*, the *Legend of Sigurd and Gudrún*, "The Story of Kullervo," *The Fall of Arthur*, and the poems of the *Gawain*-Poet).

These scholarly writings blend with and relate to his fictional writings in various ways depending on the moment at which he began teaching, translating, or editing a specific medieval work and, simultaneously, composing some poem, fantasy, or fairy-story. Especially significant in this analysis and comparison of works is the dating of each Tolkien work, by which I mean the date when he began reading, thinking about, and writing it, and when he last worked on it—not necessarily the date these works were published. This study progresses from a comparison of those scholarly works with his earliest fictional works and poems—some taken from *Unfinished Tales* and the *Book of Lost Tales*, along with *The Hobbit*, portions of *The Lord of the Rings*, and *The Silmarillion*. What Tolkien read and studied from the time before and during his college days at Exeter and continued researching until he died—primarily between 1910 and 1948—once detected, opens a door into understanding how he uniquely interpreted and repurposed the medieval in constructing fantasy.

In the introduction, titled "This Queer Creature" in reference to a "little man" Tolkien describes in an encounter in "A Secret Vice," I explore his use of this persona or doppelganger in terms of the concepts of alterity and the queer identified by theorists Lee Edelman, Alexander Doty, and medievalist Tison Pugh to identify what might be termed his aesthetic of a "queer medievalism."

Linked with this theoretical beginning is the second chapter, which is an exploration of the reasons for Tolkien's own sense of himself as different from others, queer—"Forlorn and Abject: Tolkien and His Earliest Writings (1914–1924)." Here, South African-born Tolkien emerges as a modest and unassuming author who never considered what he created as monumental. Orphaned at twelve, relatively slight in build, he made his way in his youth by means of mental acuity and male friendships, at King Edward's School and then at Exeter. A husband, father, and professor, all while fairly young, first, at Leeds, and then at Oxford, he found models for his characters in his fairy-stories and mythology in the medieval antihero. For these heroes he drew on Kullervo, Sigurd, Beowulf, the clerks in Chaucer's fabliaux, Sir Gawain, and others that he discovered as a student at King Edward's School in Birmingham and at Exeter College, some of whom he lectured on in his courses at Leeds and Oxford. In this chapter, Julia Kristeva's theory of the abject helps to unify Tolkien's early life, his poetry, and the issue of self-identity in the seemingly wide range of his different kinds of writing. Such embedding prompted his recreation of those medieval abject heroes—slightly queered as his own self-projections—in his own scholarly translations and commentaries on, and adaptations of, the works from which they originated.

In chapter 3, "Bilbo as Sigurd in the Fairy-Story *Hobbit* (1920–1927)," Tolkien composes *The Hobbit* as a fairy-story, in the light of his regard for Andrew Lang's paradigmatic Victorian fairy-story of the northern hero Sigurd. Fairies (=Elves) and the magic associated with them in this redacted fairy-story are based on the *Völsunga Saga*, which Tolkien recreated in his own *Legend of Sigurd*. Guided at least implicitly by his overarching and developing legendarium, he reshapes the Old Norse story of Sigurd in his own eucatastrophic *Hobbit* via his own definitions of the fairy-story: comic antihero Bilbo queers the tragic Sigurd while he engineers a cosmic and peaceful solution to the problem posed by the dragon Smaug and the enmity between Men and Dwarves.

In chapter 4, "Tolkien's Fairy-Story Beowulfs (1926 to 1940s)," just as Tolkien rewrote the harsh "Story of Sigurd" as a fairy-story in *The Hobbit*, here Tolkien's adaptations of *Beowulf* are explicitly marked by his desire to rewrite *Beowulf* as eucatastrophic, happily. While *Sellic Spell* and the lays differ in nature and style from his *Beowulf* course translation of 1926, they all share one feature: the omission of Beowulf's failure in the battle with the Dragon and his ultimate death as a result of his desire to prove finally heroic—in line with the necessity for a Tolkienian fairy-story. The chapter also compares his course notes and commentary on *Beowulf*, to emphasize his own repurposing of the original Anglo-Saxon in translations that similarly reflect the personal Tolkien, in line with his transformations of the epic in his fairy-story *Beowulf* adaptations. The latter, written in the early forties, after Tolkien had published both his famous *Beowulf* article, "Beowulf: The Monsters and the Critics" (1937), and *The Hobbit* (1937), was also written after his Andrew Lang Lecture in 1939.

Chapter 5, "'Queer Endings' After *Beowulf: The Fall of Arthur* (1931–1934)," emphasizes Tolkien's consciousness of the similar endings of both *Beowulf* and his own adaptation, *The Fall of Arthur*: the death of the hero and leader of his nation and his failure to secure his and its posterity by means of a legitimate heir and successor to the throne. What all three of Tolkien's original medieval poems (including the *Legend of Sigurd*) and his own translations or interpretations of them involve is the fall or death of a hero or king, in each case, one who has no legitimate heir to take his place and, as king of his nation, no guarantee of a future for his people. Tolkien's obsession with death mirrors Lee Edelman's understanding of the queer concept of "no future." That is, the Old English epic *Beowulf* would certainly have been in Tolkien's thoughts as he worked on *The Fall of Arthur* because of his teaching responsibilities at Leeds, and then at Oxford in 1925, which demanded that he lecture on it. Certainly his completed *Beowulf* translation existed beginning in 1926; he also wrote the unfinished poem *The Fall of Arthur* in Anglo-Saxon alliterative verse, although his models would likely have been Middle English Arthurian romances or Victorian and modern adaptations. That Tolkien was also thinking about *The Lord of the Rings* and *The Silmarillion* mythology behind his creative works reminds us that none of Tolkien's greatest flawed heroes in the fictional works—for example, Bilbo, Frodo, or Túrin Turambar—have sons or progeny to continue what a leader in Middle-earth has begun in aiding his own people, whether useful or harmful. For a great king to die without an heir, in particular, a son to continue to lead his nation, in medieval terms, poses a disaster for any nation, whether medieval or modern.

In chapter 6, "*Apartheid* in Tolkien: Chaucer and *The Lord of the Rings*, Books 1–3 (1925 to 1943)," Tolkien's repugnance toward *apartheid* (apartness) as defined in his retirement lecture suggests he deeply resented throughout his career being treated as set apart from others because he was a Roman Catholic South African-born medievalist and philologist—a "friendly foreigner"—whose family came from the rustic West Midlands in England. Tolkien's philological studies of Northwestern Middle English dialects relate personally to his own home there, given their origination in the Old English dialect of Wessex. Additionally, his birthplace and home in the west of England while growing up relate to the theme of the Israelites' exile in northern Africa dramatized in the Old English *Exodus*, which he edited and translated, and to his work on philology in Chaucer's commoners' fabliaux of the rustic Reeve and the Miller. These scholarly studies were written simultaneously with the first books of *The Lord of the Rings*. The medieval works introduce prototypes for the queer or "unnatural" in his anti-epic—namely, the Hobbits, Frodo's conception of Farmer

Maggot, and dark Strider, along with many others who appear increasingly strange, the farther away from the "norm" of the rustic Shire in which they happen to live. Intolerance for difference—alterity—threatens community and leads, as Tolkien reveals, to war and devastation.

Chapter 7, "'Usually Slighted': Gudrún, Other Medieval Women, and *The Lord of the Rings*, Book 3 (1925–1943)," argues against the frequently articulated opinion that Tolkien was a misogynist. As a "queer creature" Tolkien was drawn to medieval women similarly abject in his earliest scholarship—specifically other rather than Other in the postmodern essentialized definition of not male. They occupied singular positions in medieval saints' lives and manuals for anchoresses, the latter walled up to separate them from worldly affairs, chief among them the lives of St. Katherine and St. Juliana and the *Ancrene Riwle* (the Anchoress's Rule). In Old Norse and Anglo-Saxon literature, he preferred and adapted the tale of the *Völsunga Saga*'s Gúdrun, and, in relation to *Beowulf*, adaptation and commentary on Grendel's Mother and Freawaru. Similarly, in *The Lord of the Rings*, he creates a few powerful lone female characters—the missing Entwives and the courageous leader Éowyn, the latter so like Arwen in the appendices and her ancestor Lúthien in *The Silmarillion*. These characters begin (like the masculine antiheroes in the trilogy) from an abject and ignoble position in their cultures to finish victoriously, without dependency on men.

In chapter 8, "The Failure of Masculinity: *The Homecoming of Beorhtnoth* (1920), *Sir Gawain* (1925), and *The Lord of the Rings*, Books 3–6 (1943–1948)," I argue that two-thirds of *The Lord of the Rings*, written during World War II and several years thereafter, explores a world dominated by violence in which an arrogant masculinity has failed, leaving it stripped of the female. The failure of might and of masculine heroism logically connects with the similar failure of leadership acknowledged in Tolkien's famous *Beowulf* article; with his alliterative verse-drama, "The Homecoming of Beorhtnoth Beorhthelm's Son," which contains an essay on "Ofermod," or pride, as the chivalric flaw that undercuts leadership by or loyalty to the lord; and with the fourteenth-century Middle English alliterative romance *Sir Gawain and the Green Knight*, in which Gawain queers his own chivalric oaths and vows— the feudal and chivalric practice between men—as homosocial. Tolkien not only coedited this last important work, but translated and lectured on it. Just as the later books of *The Lord of the Rings* mimic these homosocial bonds by means of the Hobbits' own relationships with other Hobbits and Men they serve, chivalry is mocked and upended by the sadistic Orcs whom Frodo and Bilbo literally mimic temporarily, for survival by means of disguise.

The conclusion, "The Ennoblement of the Humble: The History of Middle-earth," sums up Tolkien's concept of the true hero as the most self-effacing of individuals—not only the Hobbit Frodo but Halfelven Arwen and her ancestor Lúthien and the men who love them both. Toward them and the Fourth Age, of Man, the Third Age has been moving all along.

* * *

Tolkien scholars and readers all owe Christopher Tolkien a great debt for his assiduous labors in identifying, collecting, laying out, and editing his father's early and unfinished works so that we could see how this man who never stopped revising always wrote with many, many unfinished works in his mind, one overlapping with the other and intersecting it without boundaries. And to Christina Scull and Wayne Hammond we should all be grateful for their painstaking research into details relating to his life and writings as reflected in the *Chronology* and *Reader's Companion*—everything that might matter in learning whatever and whenever Tolkien read, wrote, published, and revised. Of course, all Tolkien scholars owe gratitude to Peter Jackson as well, for bringing to the entire world greater exposure to the importance of Tolkien's *The Lord of the Rings* by means of his three films.

My debts to other scholars for helping me engender the ideas that resulted in this specific study are manifold. I am especially grateful to those readers of drafts of this book who facilitated what I hope are improvements: Leslie A. Donovan, John Garth, Thomas Honegger, and Tison Pugh, as well as the anonymous readers for the Press. In addition, through generous offers from many others—to speak at their campuses or their conferences or institutes or publish work in their essay collections—my understanding of postmodern Tolkien has developed over the past fifteen years, and certainly since 1992, when *The Lord of the Rings: The Mythology of Power* first appeared in print and touched on the relevance of Michel Foucault for understanding Tolkien. These scholars who created opportunities and provided support for my work or who wrote essays on which I have relied on and been inspired by include: Canon Betty Adam, Douglas A. Anderson, Dorsey Armstrong, Melissa Arul, Harold Bloom, Marjorie Burns, the late Jackson J. Campbell, Julie Couch, Janet Brennan Croft, Deidre Dawson, Leslie A. Donovan, Graham Drake, Michael Drout, the late Kathleen Dubs, George Economou, Lee Edelman, Bradford Lee Eden, Deanna Delmar Evans, Dimitra Fimi, Verlyn Flieger, Judy Ford, Mike Foster, Karl Fugelso, John Garth, Wayne

G. Hammond, John R. Holmes, Shaun Hughes, Kathleen Coyne Kelly, Kristen Larsen, Gergely Nagy, Tison Pugh, John D. Rateliff, Robin Reid, Edward L. Risden, Deborah Sabo, Christina Scull, Alfred Siewers, Jr., Joseph B. Trahern, Jr., Christopher Vaccaro, Richard C. West, Ralph Wood, and many others, namely, those whom I met at conferences, Tolkien at Kalamazoo, and sessions at Western Michigan University's annual medieval conference between 2000 and 2007 (and by means of my editing of the three collections of essays that grew out of those inspiring sessions). My thanks especially go to Bonnie Wheeler, editor of the New Middle Ages Series, who published in her series my earlier coedited collection on Tolkien, *Tolkien's Modern Middle Ages*, and who encouraged the completion of this study, and to former Medieval Institute director Paul Szarmach, who first allowed medievalists to try something new under my own queer rubric "Tolkien at Kalamazoo," borrowed from "Spenser at Kalamazoo" and "Shakespeare at Kalamazoo."

I am also indebted to institutions, institutes, and societies who have hosted my lectures, presentations, and plenary sessions on, or about, Tolkien in which some aspect of this book originally appeared: Baylor University, Bucknell University, California State University-San Marcos, Christchurch Episcopal Cathedral in Houston, the Dallas Consortium of Medievalists, the English Institute of the University of Pécs in Hungary, Houston Baptist University, the International Arthurian Society, Károli Gáspár Protestant University in Budapest, Marquette University, the North American Arthurian Society, the NEH Institute for Teachers on "From Beowulf to Postmodernism: J.R.R. Tolkien's *Lord of the Rings*," the New York City Jung Institute, Pázmány Péter Katolikus Egzetem University in Eger, Hungary, the Rice University Alumni Association, the Rice University Society of Women, St. Hugh's College, Oxford, St. Paul's Episcopal Church in Fayetteville, Arkansas, the Society for the Study of Homosexuality in the Middle Ages, Texas A&M University at Commerce, the Texas Medieval Association, Texas Tech University, the Tolkien Society of Oxford, the University of Bucharest in Romania, the University of New Mexico Institute for Medieval Studies (and its Outreach Seminar for High School Teachers), the University of Vermont English Department, and, most especially, Western Michigan University, not only for my own conference papers but also for allowing me to create Tolkien at Kalamazoo and foster the study of Tolkien as medievalist.

Several chapters originated from conference papers, a plenary roundtable, and a session response. "The Mythology of Magic: Tolkien's *Hobbit* and Andrew Lang's *Red Fairy Book*" was presented in a session on *The Hobbit* organized by Bradford Lee Eden and moderated by Douglas A. Anderson, Forty-Seventh International Congress on the Middle Ages, Western Michigan University, Kalamazoo, MI, on Thursday, 10 May 2012. I served as a respondent to a "Queer Tolkien" session organized by Graham Drake for the Society for the Study of Homosexuality in the Middle Ages at the Forty-Eighth International Congress on the Middle Ages, Western Michigan University, Kalamazoo, MI, Friday, 10 May 2013. I was also tapped to participate in a plenary roundtable on Tolkien and King Arthur sponsored by the North American Arthurian Society at the International Arthurian Society Triennial Conference, University of Bucharest, Romania, on 25 July 2014; and I delivered "Tolkien's Victorian Fairy-Story *Beowulf*" in a session on "Tolkien and Nineteenth-Century Medievalism" at the Fiftieth Annual International Congress on Medieval Studies, Western Michigan University, Kalamazoo, MI, Thursday, on 14 May 2015.

Permission to reprint material from articles published previously in various collections was granted at the time of acceptance and contract by the appropriate editor and/or publisher specifically with an eye to later publication in this future book. However, any previously published material has been for the most altered, expanded, and revised, or adapted for specific use in this book. Material and ideas have come from pages in the following articles or chapter sections, in order of publication: *The Lord of the Rings: The Mythology of Power* (Lexington: University of Kentucky Press, 2001), 26–37; "Tolkien's Women (and Men): The Film and the Book," in *Tolkien on Film: Essays on Peter Jackson's "The Lord of the Rings,"* ed. Janet Brennan Croft, 175–193 (Altadena, CA: The Mythopoeic Press, 2004); "Introduction: Tolkien's Modern Medievalism," and "Tolkien and the Other: Race and Gender in Middle-earth," in *Tolkien's Modern Middle Ages*, ed. Jane Chance and Alfred K. Siewers, 173–188 (New York and London: Palgrave Macmillan, 2005); 'Subversive Fantasist: Tolkien on Class Difference," in *The Lord of the Rings, 1954–2004: Scholarship in Honor of Richard E. Blackwelder*, ed. Wayne Hammond and Cristina Scull, 153–168 (Milwaukee, WI: Marquette University Press, 2006); "'In the Company of Orcs': Peter Jackson's Queer Tolkien," in *Queer Movie Medievalisms*, ed. Katherine Coyne Kelly and Tison Pugh, Queer Interventions Series, 79–96 (Farnham, Surrey, UK, and Burlington, VT: Ashgate Press, 2009); "Tough Love: Teaching the New Medievalisms," *Defining Medievalism(s) II: Some More Perspectives*, ed. Karl Fugelso,

76–98, *Studies in Medievalism* 18 (2010): 76–77, 80–82, 83–91; revised and/or reprinted by permission of Boydell & Brewer Ltd., Cambridge: D.S. Brewer, 2009; and "Tolkien's Hybrid Mythology: *The Hobbit* as Old Norse 'Fairy-Story,'" in *The Hobbit and Tolkien's Mythology: Essays on Revisions and Influences*, ed. Bradford Lee Eden, 78–96 (Jefferson, NC: McFarland, 2014).

The cover image, Giorgio de Chirico's "The Enigma of a Day" (1914), Museum of Modern Art, New York, was selected after virtual dialogue with Tolkienists and medievalists Verlyn Flieger, Karl Fugelso, and Christopher Vaccaro, and with Ryan Jenkins, my ever-helpful editor at Palgrave-Macmillan. This work of art belonging to the *scuola metafisica* most represents melancholy, a sense of the failure of the past, isolation—an image contemporary with the beginning of the "Great War," which so affected Tolkien as well. Palpable is the silence in the scene at daybreak—a customary time for new beginnings—wherein a once-important man, as represented by a statue garbed in outdated clothing, cannot speak, and his community is missing, lost or hidden. Verlyn Flieger suggests that the statue powerfully speaks to her of "the poet isolate between the towers. That's the man you're writing about." She also liked "the stark light and shadow that defines both the landscape and the figure" along with the fact that "the face is turned away from the viewer." I am delighted to have enjoyed my colleagues' help in choosing it.

Abbreviations

Hobbit	*The Hobbit; or There and Back Again.* 3rd edn. London: Allen & Unwin, 1937, 1966; Boston: Houghton Mifflin, 1938, 1967; repr. Boston: Houghton Mifflin, 1997. By page number(s).
Letters	*The Letters of J.R.R. Tolkien.* Ed. Humphrey Carpenter with the assistance of Christopher Tolkien. Boston: Houghton Mifflin, 1981. Identified by addressee, date, and letter and page number(s).
LOTR	*The Lord of the Rings.* 1954–1955, 2nd edn., with Note on the Text by Douglas A. Anderson. Note on the 50th Anniversary Edition by Wayne G. Hammond and Christina Scull. London: HarperCollins; Boston: Houghton Mifflin, 2004. Citations appear within parentheses by book, chapter, and page number(s).
Scull	Christina Scull and Wayne G. Hammond. *The J.R.R. Tolkien Companion & Guide: Chronology*, vol. 1; *Reader's Guide*, vol. 2. London: HarperCollins, 2006. By individual volume title and page number(s).
Silm	*The Silmarillion.* Ed. Christopher Tolkien. 2nd edn. London: HarperCollins, 1999; Boston: Houghton Mifflin, 2001.

Because of the difficulty in working with the many different versions of *The Silmarillion* mythology, although I will point out dates and editions of the various manuscripts and typescripts, generally I will use the edited text supplied by Christopher Tolkien in *The Silmarillion* unless a specific manuscript edited in one of the volumes of *Unfinished Tales* or *The History of Middle-earth* offers a specific insight.

Chronology of Composition and Publication Dates and Significant Events

Dates have been taken from *J.R.R. Tolkien: Life and Legend. An Exhibition to Commemorate the Centenary of the Birth of J.R.R. Tolkien* (1892–1973) (Oxford: Bodleian Library, 1992), Scull and Hammond's *Companion: Chronology* and *Reader's Guide,* Carpenter's *Biography,* and notes by Christopher Tolkien in various publications and editions.

1892
3 January — John Ronald Reuel Tolkien born in Bloemfontein, Orange Free State, South Africa

1895 — His mother, Mabel, and the boys return to England

1896 — His father Arthur Reuel Tolkien (b. 1857) dies on 15 February of rheumatic fever

1903 — Goes with scholarship to King Edward's School, Birmingham, where he begins to read Chaucer in translation and is introduced to Anglo-Saxon grammar

1904 — "What is Home Without a Mother (or a Wife)" (picture completed in Mabel's absence at Aunt Jane Neaves's house)

Father Francis Morgan of the Birmingham Oratory becomes Ronald's guardian after his mother (b. 1870) dies from diabetes complications on 14 November

1910 — Wins an exhibition at Exeter College, Oxford

1911

3 February	Speaks on "Norse Sagas" to the Literary Society, King Edward's School
31 March?	Composes the poetic "The Battle of the Eastern Field," a parody of the *Lay of Lake Regillus* by Thomas Babington Macaulay
September	Composes a poetic parody of Kirby's translation of the *Kalevala* called *The New Lemminkäinen*

1914

22 November	Speaks to the Corpus Christi's Sundial Society about the *Kalevala*
27 November	Reads the poem "The Voyage of Éarendel the Evening Star" (*Éala Éarendel Engla Beorhtast*) to the Exeter Essay Club

1915

27–28 April–3 May	Composes the poem "Goblin Feet" at Oxford at the same time as the poems "You & Me / and the Cottage of Lost Play" and, several days later, the eight-line "Tinfang Warble" and "Kôr: In a City Lost and Dead," followed by "Morning Song"
	Takes a First in English and applies for a commission with the Lancashire Fusiliers before World War I
21–28 November	Composes the poem "Cor Tirion þÆlfwinera þǽra béama on middes," later changed to "Kortirion among the Trees"

1916

22 March	Marries Edith Bratt
28 June	Second Lieutenant Tolkien joins the 11th Battalion of the Lancashire Fusiliers at the front
1 July	Close college friend Rob Gilson is killed but his death remains unreported in the news until 17 July

22 July	Tolkien's King Edward's School friend R.S. Payton is killed in battle
25 October	Tolkien, the battalion signaling officer, begins to fall ill from "trench fever" (transmitted by lice) and three days later enters the officers' hospital at Gézaincourt, an illness that will last off and on until he is released from service on 8 July 1919
3 December	Tolkien's close college friend G.B. Smith dies as a result of battle-wounds

End of 1916–first half of 1917

	Composes *The Fall of Gondolin*
	Composes the prose *The Cottage of Lost Play*, first version of his mythology
16 November	Son John is born in Cheltenham
	First version of "Beren and Lúthien" composed in Yorkshire after birth
1918	Back at Oxford teaching at the English School after recovery
	Begins writing the "Lost Tale" of Túrin Turambar
1919	Begins writing "Turambar and the Foallóke," *Book of Lost Tales*, Part 2
	At work on the *Oxford English Dictionary*
1920	Composes "Ælfwine of England" in "The History of Eriol, or Aelfwine and the End of the Tales"
10 March	Reads a short version of "The Fall of Gondolin" to the Exeter College Essay Club
Trinity Term	Teaches a class on *Sir Gawain and the Green Knight* at Oxford

1 October	Early interest in the *Ancrene Riwle* in the Corpus Christi College Cambridge MS 402 while beginning to teach at University of Leeds as Reader
Christmas	Tolkien writes the first of the Father Christmas letters to son John in response to his query about who he is
1920–1927	*The Hobbit* begins as tales told to his children
1921–Summer 1924	Continues work on *The Children of Húrin*
16 August	C.T. Onions asks Tolkien to work on an edition of *Sir Gawain and the Green Knight*
October	Kenneth Sisam's *Fourteenth Century Verse and Prose* published
1922	George S. Gordon and Tolkien discuss the idea of editing a student's anthology of Geoffrey Chaucer with Oxford University Press
May	Publishes his first book, *A Middle English Vocabulary*, intended for use with Kenneth Sisam's *Fourteenth Century Verse and Prose* (and later published together with it)
22 October	Second son, Michael, is born
December	Publishes a poem indebted to Chaucer about registration at Leeds, "The Clerke's Compleinte," in the Leeds University magazine *The Gryphon*
?End of year	Composes the poem "Iúmonna Gold Galdre Bewunden," from a line in *Beowulf*
1923	
January	Publishes that same poem in *The Gryphon*
26 April	Publishes an unsigned review of Furnivall's *Hali Maidenhed* edition in the *Times Literary Supplement*
Late December	Works on text proofs for the Clarendon Chaucer

1924	
21 November	Son Christopher is born
1925	Elected to Rawlinson and Bosworth Professorship of Anglo-Saxon at Oxford
	Begins editing and translating of "The Old English *Exodus*"
	Writes "Sigelwara Land" article (an article about the Old English *Exodus*)
	Begins *Beowulf* translation and *Sellic Spell*
April	Publishes "Some Contributions to Middle-English Lexicology" in *Review of English Studies*
	Tolkien and E.V. Gordon publish their edition of *Sir Gawain and the Green Knight*
Mid-June	Along with George S. Gordon, finishes reading proofs for the Clarendon Chaucer
July	"The Devil's Coach-Horses" (about a line in Chaucer's *Summoner's Tale*) is published in the *Review of English Studies*
23 August	Begins writing the *Lay of Leithian* (date marked at line 557), the story of Beren and Lúthien
1926	
Early 1926	Constructs first outline of "The Silmarillion" (the earliest version, "Sketch of the Mythology with especial reference to 'The Children of Húrin,'" 28 pages) for his old schoolmaster R.W. Reynolds
Hilary Term	Founds the Kolbítar Reading Group to translate Icelandic sagas
?26 April (?)	Completes translation of *Beowulf* and *Pearl*
Summer	Tolkien may have written the first words of *The Hobbit* while marking School Certificate examination papers

17 November	Delivers a paper on the *Elder Edda* at the Exeter College Essay Club
1926–1927	*The Hobbit* actually composed and written down
1927	
18 February	The Kolbítar Reading Group starts translating the *Völsunga Saga* at Exeter College
26 June	The Kolbítar Reading Group finish translating the *Prose Edda* and the *Völsunga Saga*
27 November	Joins the Arthurian Society, whose president is Eugène Vinaver
1928	Publishes foreword to Walter E. Haigh, *A New Glossary of the Dialect of the Huddersfield District*
1929	Article on linguistic aspects of West Midlands Middle English in "*Ancrene Wisse and Hali Meiðhad*" appears in *Essays and Studies* (possibly originating June 1925)
18 June	Daughter Priscilla is born
1929–1930	Writes a note on the name "Nodens," the name of a god at a Roman temple in Lydney Park, Gloucestershire
Late 1920s	Writes "The New Lay of the Völsungs" and "The New Lay of Gudrún"
1930	Proposes an edition of *Ancrene Riwle* in series of manuscripts to Oxford University Press
28 or 29 January	Attends a Kolbítar meeting with C.S. Lewis and others
Early 1930s	Two lays, "Beowulf and Grendel" and "Beowulf and the Monsters, II," the first, sung to the seven- or eight-year-old Christopher
	Writes much of the long poem *The Fall of Arthur*
1930s–1940s	Edits and lectures on the Old English *Exodus*
1931	Abandons *The Lay of Leithian*

16 May	"Chaucer's Use of Dialects" (later titled "Chaucer as a Philologist" [*The Reeve's Tale*] is read to the Philological Society
?1931–Trinity Term 1933	
	Rhyming draft composed of "The Homecoming of Beorhtnoth Beorhthelm's Son"
1932	Publishes "The Name Nodens" in Appendix I to *Report on the Excavation of the Prehistoric, Roman, and Post-Roman Sites in Lydney Park, Gloucestershire*
December	Publishes "Sigelwara Land," Part I, in *Medium Aevum*
1934	Publishes "Chaucer as a Philologist" (*The Reeve's Tale*) in *Transactions of the Philological Society*
June	Publishes "Sigelwara Land," Part II, in *Medium Aevum*
1935	Agrees to edit the Corpus Christi College Cambridge "Ancrene Riwle" MS for the Early English Text Society
1936	Begins work on *The Lord of the Rings*
	Privately prints "Songs for the Philologists" by Tolkien, E.V. Gordon, and others
25 November	Delivers "Beowulf: The Monsters and the Critics" as the Sir Israel Gollancz Lecture to the British Academy
1937	Publishes "Beowulf: The Monsters and the Critics" in *Proceedings of the British Academy*
21 September	Publishes *The Hobbit; or There And Back Again*
1938 20 February	Letter to the *Observer* about the sources of *The Hobbit* having been derived from epic, fairy-story, and mythology

29 July	Former student and collaborator E.V. Gordon dies
1939	
8 March	Delivers the Andrew Lang lecture at St. Andrews University on "Fairy Stories."
1940	Publishes Preface to John R. Clark Hall prose translation of *Beowulf and the Finnsburg Fragment*
Early 1940s	Completes a comic prose adaptation of the first two-thirds of *Beowulf*, titled *Sellic Spell*
1944	*Sir Orfeo* translation no earlier than this date
January 1945	Publishes "Leaf by Niggle" in the *Dublin Review* Completes alliterative verse-drama, "The Homecoming of Beorhtnoth Beorhthelm's Son"
1946	Elected Merton College Professor of English Language and Literature at Oxford
1947	Supervises B. Litt. thesis of A.J. Bliss, texts of three manuscripts of *Sir Orfeo* With former student Simonne T.R.O. d'Ardenne publishes "'Iþþlen' in Sawles Warde," in *English Studies* Publishes "On Fairy-Stories" in *Essays Presented to Charles Williams*
1948	With former student Simonne T.R.O. d'Ardenne publishes "M.S. Bodley 34: A Re-collation of a Collation" in *Studia Neophilologica*
1949	Publishes *Farmer Giles of Ham*
1950	
6 November	News of the *Sir Gawain and Green Knight* translation reaches Stanley Unwin

1951

8 June — Sends to Oxford University Press all the available working galleys, corrected glossary proofs, and draft notes for most of the pieces (or at least his pieces) in the Clarendon Chaucer

"Middle English 'Losenger'" appears in *Essais de philologie moderne*

1953

15 April — W.P. Ker Memorial Lecture on *Sir Gawain and the Green Knight* at the University of Glasgow

June — E.V. Gordon's posthumous edition of *Pearl* is published, having been revised by Ida Gordon and, in smaller part, by Tolkien

December — Provides foreword titled "A Fourteenth-Century Romance" to his translation of *Sir Gawain and the Green Knight* on the BBC Third Programme

"The Homecoming of Beorhtnoth Beorhthelm's Son" appears in *Essays and Studies*

1954

Receives an Honorary D.Litt. from University College, Dublin, and University of Liège

Writes "The Istari" while compiling an unfinished index for *The Lord of the Rings*; essay published later in *Unfinished Tales*

Former student A.J. Bliss's revised edition of *Sir Orfeo* published

1954–1955 — First volumes of *The Lord of the Rings* appear in print

1955

Former student Mary B. Salu publishes the *Ancrene Wisse* translation with Tolkien's preface dated 29 June 1955

1959

5 June — Delivers his "Valedictory Address to the University of Oxford" during his last term and retires from Merton Professorship

1962

Publishes *Ancrene Wisse* Corpus Christi Cambridge MS 402 edition with Early English Text Society

Believes *Sir Gawain and the Green Knight* and *Pearl* translations nearly finished

Publishes *The Adventures of Tom Bombadil and Other Verses from the Red Book*

Festschrift for Tolkien is published: *English and Medieval Studies Presented to J.R.R. Tolkien on the Occasion of His Seventieth Birthday*

1963

"English and Welsh" is published in *Angles and Britons: O'Donnell Lectures*

1964

Tree and Leaf published

1965

Writes *Smith of Wootton Major* in response to a request for a preface to George MacDonald's "The Golden Key," a work and author he decided he did not like

1966

The original draft of the translation of the Book of Jonah, heavily revised by others, appears in *The Jerusalem Bible*

October — "Tolkien on Tolkien" appears in the *Diplomat*

1967

November — *Smith of Wootton Major* is published

1973

3 September — Tolkien dies

1975

Translation of *Sir Gawain and the Green Knight*, *Pearl*, and *Sir Orfeo* published posthumously

CHAPTER 1

Introduction: "This Queer Creature"

On a scrap of paper Tolkien scribbled an essay he originally titled "A Hobby for the Home" in which he confesses to "A Secret Vice," as he later referred to it in a letter of 1967 and as his son Christopher retitled it.[1] By "Secret Vice," Tolkien meant the invention of secret languages: he relays an anecdote in the essay about an overheard conversation: "I shall never forget a little man—smaller than myself—whose name I have forgotten," he claims. Tolkien and the little man were in a "dirty wet marquee" whose odor was of "stale mutton fat," and on the trestle tables on which they sat they were surrounded by "depressed and wet creatures."[2] Someone was lecturing on army experiences—"map-reading or camp-hygiene" (a few sentences down Tolkien explains that "military arrangements" prevented the two of them from meeting again, so the memory likely stems from an experience he had while in the army during World War I). All of a sudden this little man says, "in a dreamy voice"—and this entire recollection has a dream quality to it—"Yes, I think I shall express the accusative by a prefix!"

Surely this is fiction, or maybe it is Tolkien masquerading as "the little man"—for he loves this "memorable remark." What is magnificent to him is that it reflects a "personal pleasure," like his own for the creation of Sindarin and Quenya, the Elven languages of Middle-earth. He uses other metaphors to note about the little man that "he proved close as an oyster" (not unlike Tolkien himself, who is publicly secretive about his private fears and joys). Tolkien imagines "this queer creature" as inventing languages during wartime, someone who "cheered and comforted himself in the tedium and squalors of 'training under canvas,'" but so that no one

© The Author(s) 2016
Jane Chance, *Tolkien, Self and Other: "This Queer Creature"*,
The New Middle Ages, DOI 10.1057/978-1-137-39896-3_1

else would hear him or study those languages. Tolkien concludes without affect that the little man likely "was blown to bits in the very moment of deciding upon some ravishing method of indicating the subjunctive."[3]

Of course during his entire life Tolkien invented languages, for he describes children, apparently his nieces, making up a language (by using animal names) called Animalic, and also Nevbosh, or the "New Nonsense," a play-language in which he participated. But he never said that he spoke Nevbosh—"I was older in secret vice (secret only because apparently bereft of the hope of communication or criticism), if not in years, than the Nevbosh originator."[4] The next stage in language development, word-form refinement, Tolkien defines as a selfish pleasure, stolen from whatever obligations of family or work one might have, yet, "This must be my excuse for becoming more and more autobiographical—regretfully, and from no arrogance."[5] While communication between two people is the driver behind most languages, he feels in this activity involving pleasure in sound there is a factor more personal: "From here onwards you must forgive pure egotism … My little man, with his interest in the devices for expression of word-relations, its syntactical devices, is too fleeting a glimpse to use."[6] As an adult, Tolkien was apparently alone in his vice, as he was in many of his endeavors during his entire life.

Tolkien's essay, extant in only one manuscript and never published during his lifetime, reveals his desire to create languages as the chief joy in his life, an exemplar of how deeply personal was his commitment to his profession as scholar and to his creation of a fantastic world whose history, peoples, and languages felt like "home" to him. Allegedly, Tolkien wrote the essay, according to Christopher, "a year or more ago" after the Esperanto Congress meeting in Oxford in July 1930. Why Esperanto? This notion of a made-up language intrigued Tolkien, he avers, because it is necessary "for uniting Europe before it is swallowed by non-Europe" and because it was entirely made up by just one man who is "not a philologist." This purpose leads him to his "stealthy subject … nothing less embarrassing than the unveiling in public of a secret vice"—the inventing of languages.[7] Notably, in the alter-ego he calls "this queer creature" he projects himself as abject and set apart from others, without any companion to speak to, while maintaining his persona as a mirror image who can only "speak" by writing to himself.

Why Tolkien regards this confession as embarrassing is unclear, but the lecture is marked throughout by his inimitable humor and personal references to memories of a stranger—a soldier—likely his own persona or a doppelganger. For that stranger, languages "satisfy either the needs of a secret and persecuted society, or the queer instinct for pretending you belong to one"[8]—"queer" and "persecuted," the first adjective, often used throughout his works to describe his characters and himself. A page later he ventures that however inventive languages are, and however individualistic, their inventors need an audience to use them because "they are artists and incomplete without an audience."[9] Certainly he imagines he himself is addicted, like "an opium-smoker."[10] This invention of languages he describes as driven by "The instinct for 'linguistic invention'—the fitting of notion to oral symbol, and his pleasure in contemplating that that new relation is established, is rational, *and not perverted*."[11] What makes it more pleasurable than simply learning a new language is that it is "more personal and fresh."[12]

What Tolkien would like to do is to explain that, at this higher level—which involves the "perfect construction of an art-language"—one must "construct at least in outline a mythology concomitant." This, he himself did, by creating the world in which his several languages are spoken, one with an individual flavor, to be achieved by weaving into it "the threads of an individual mythology, individual while working within the scheme of natural human mythopoeia." This result apparently happens inevitably, for "your language construction will *breed* a mythology."[13] And just before he offers several examples of his word-forms, his language, he reminds us, that because its construction reflects his taste, conditioned by imagination, he will always come back to his own language construction, which is "peculiarly mine," designed by and for him, so may be "too free," "overpretty, to be *phonetically and semantically* sentimental," for which he begs his listener to "be kindly."[14] The examples he provides of different languages (and their English translations) of course come from his Elven tongues. And he defines as the virtue of his language construction as "its intimacy, ... its peculiarly shy individualism," the sharing of which involves the "pain of giving away myself."[15]

What Tolkien says about such projection is key to understanding how he sees himself, and others: that is, as an allegory. In letter 163 to W.H. Auden, written on 7 June 1955, he confesses that "In a larger sense, it is I suppose impossible to write any 'story' that is not allegorical in proportion as it 'comes to Life'; since each of us is an allegory, embodying in a particular tale and clothed in the garments of time and place, universal truth and everlasting life" (212–13). If this was true for Tolkien, why was it true, and how did he allegorize himself—cover up himself in the clothing of fiction? This important statement, grounded in medieval platonic definitions of allegory, nevertheless suggests that every fantasy character invented by Tolkien in some way embodies its own personal moment in its creator's mythos as its creator projects his own self, or story, into it at the time and place in the world in which he lives. Benjamin Saxton has noted in his discussion of authorship in Mikhail Bakhtin and Tolkien that "For Tolkien, the act of narration becomes a metaphor for living in the world."[16] Tolkien's characters in his narratives allow him to do that by means of allowing them dialogic freedom to express their individual difference. They are very often abject—a term associated with Freudian psychology and Kristevan feminist theory.

Certainly Tolkien himself was shy and abject all his life. I believe he viewed himself as Other. Slavoj Žižek, in "Neighbors and Other Monsters," taxonomizes types of the Other.

> First, there is the imaginary other—other people 'like me,' my fellow human beings with whom I am engaged in the mirrorlike relationships of competition, mutual recognition, and so forth. Then, there is the symbolic 'big Other'—the 'substance' of our social existence, the impersonal set of rules that coordinate our coexistence. Finally, there is the Other qua Real, the impossible Thing, the 'inhuman partner,' the Other with whom no symmetrical dialogue, mediated by the symbolic Order, is possible ... The neighbor (*Nebenmensch*) as the Thing means that, beneath the neighbor as my *semblant*, my mirror image, there always lurks the unfathomable abyss of radical Otherness, of a monstrous Thing that cannot be gentrified.[17]

Which must imply that in the neighbor is the monstrous Other, in whom I see myself. In respect to Tolkien, Benjamin Saxton, citing Gary Saul Morson's concept of "sideshadowing," argues that Tolkien illustrates characters' choices by creating a series of "oppositional figures," or foils for one another: Hobbits Frodo and Gollum, wizards Gandalf and Saruman, kings Théoden and Denethor, and the men and brothers Faramir and Boromir: "They also demonstrate that, for Tolkien's characters, 'the other' is always, to some extent, 'me.'" The exemplar Saxton uses is Gandalf the White, who says "I *am* Saruman ... as he should have been."[18]

If this was true for Tolkien, why was it true, and how did he allegorize himself—cover up himself in the clothing of fiction? Tolkien is often most "queer" in his disruption of whatever conventions his world might have expected an Oxford medievalist to follow, which we essentialize as having been the most "Tolkienian," as if his originality as a thinker and fantasy writer did not set him apart from his peers and as if it were always as valued as it is now. The multiplicity of selves may be normative in the modern age (I think of Hermann Hesse's *Steppenwolf* and its image of the individual as a layered onion with many selves—a modernist image, if not exactly a queer one). Tolkien in his own narrative appears more and more postmodern in the fractured self he projects into fantasy through characters such as the everyhobbits Bilbo and Frodo, whom contemporary media pundits perceive as in love, often viewed queerly through a Jacksonian lens.[19] Do we read into him our own postmodern queerness, or is it our own queerly medieval desire as other, to resist and disturb the normative?

Wendy Moffat, who long worked on a queer biography of E.M. Forster, in her 2015 article "The Narrative Case for Queer Biography," reminds readers that "Queer theory began, not just as a totalizing vision—but rather as a totally anti-essentialist one. The goal was to illustrate how *constructed*, how *unnatural* essentialist assumptions about identity were, not merely to observe how power worked on subjects ... the depressingly consistent evidence of homophobia reminds the theorist of the complex and often the limited agency of the queer subject."[20] As a result, Moffat follows Eve Sedgwick in her rejection of teleology for the "unfixed narrative," instead opting for what Moffat calls the "*beside* narrative," meaning "*beside* its subject." Moffat cites Nick Bartlett in believing that fracture, omission, and pastiche mark the genre in the recovery of any queer life and history, in which verification (as she found in studying the life of Forster) comes in "the sliver of text, the piece of ephemera in the archive."[21]

Tolkien similarly resists classification. An outlier, Tolkien queers modernity by means of the medieval. His work is interconnected in terms of his borrowing from medieval literary prototypes and paradigms, his inheritance of Victorian culture and the kind of stereotypes its culture perpetuated, his own scholarship, and his creation of a queer—non-normative—mythology based on a privileging of the marginal. That is, Tolkienian complexity demands that one cannot accurately understand *The Lord of the Rings* without having read carefully his other works, whether scholarly or creative. Consider the exile of Galadriel and Celeborn in the light of his translation of the Anglo-Saxon *Exodus* along with the chapters in *The Silmarillion* on the exile of the Noldor. Similarly, one cannot fully understand his treatment (or erasure) of the female monster in his *Beowulf* article after reading the balanced description of gender in the creation of Middle-earth in the "Ainulindalë" chapter of *The Silmarillion* and some of the out-takes on Galadriel in *The Lord of the Rings* from *The Book of Lost Tales*.

But what is meant by to "queer" and, in terms of Tolkien's medievalism, does it mean anything other than "to subvert"? Does this relate to the queerness of Tolkien's "Queer Creature"? In the broadest sense, Alexander Doty has positioned alterity, or the "queer," in the context of that Derridean *différance* that also marks feminine alienation or otherness in relation to masculine normativity, as defined in recent postmodern and feminist theory.[22] That is, the feminine is always defined as less than and inferior to the masculine norm because not male. Tison Pugh, in the introduction to *Sexuality and Its Queer Discontents in Middle English Literature* (2008), posits the "queer" as encompassing many kinds of alterity, not just the sexual, to include national origin, race, class, and religion. Pugh argues that,

> Because queerness and heterosexuality are constituted within a complex framework of interrelated factors of social identity, they should not stand alone as markers of personal identity. Rather, compulsory queerness relates to the ways in which a person's social class, religion, occupation, personal relationships, and other social factors are linked with sexual identity to construct appropriate ideological normativity; it arises in the chasm between personal identity and social ideal in that the failure to embody the ideal necessarily reveals the falsehoods of gender and the ambivalent power of the queer.[23]

However, Michael O'Rourke, in an essay on "Becoming (Queer) Medieval," taken from a University of Leeds International Congress of the European Middle Ages roundtable on "Queer Methodologies and/or Queers in Medieval Studies: Where are We Now?," questions "queer" as a sign: "Not everyone who works under the sign of queer means the same thing and the term has been used in so many different ways: theoretical, political, and social." He asks, does it refer to the postmodern? The modern homosexual? "Identitarian discourses"? or "[A]ll sorts of non- (hetero-) normative acts, desires, propensities and identities in the period which falls under our view?" In his succinct summary of all the queer methodologies possible, including the otherness of queer studies itself, O'Rourke names the following major medieval approaches, among others: (1) queer gender and sexuality studies as combined with other approaches: disability studies, postcolonial studies, Critical Race theory, or black queer studies; (2) homoaffectional bonds, whether male or female; and (3) queer virginity, particularly among women.[24]

In line with O'Rourke's suggestion of the scholarly and theoretical alterity of queer studies itself, as set apart from the norm, Pugh's taxonomy adds the queerness of medieval study. The medieval *is* queer itself in relation to more significant historical and literary periodicity in university departments, and therefore so also is medievalism, the study of the medieval in any period other than the Middle Ages, its afterlife in reception, making it doubly marginal, the Other Other.[25] Medievalism, as defined by Tom Shippey in his essay "Medievalisms and Why They Matter," is "Any post-medieval attempt to re-imagine the Middle Ages, or some aspect of the Middle Ages, for the modern world, in any of many different media; especially in academic usage, the study of the development and significance of such attempts."[26] According to French medievalist Elizabeth Emery, Shippey's plural—"Medievalisms"—constitutes a necessary emendation because of the multiple forms in which medievalism has appeared over time, that is:

> different scholarly interpretations over periods of time (Jules Michelet's, Joseph Bédier's, and Ernst Curtius'), different artistic representations in varying media (Walter Scott, the Pre-Raphaelites, Richard Wagner, and Ridley Scott), different political or religious claims (Joan of Arc claimed by the Catholic Church, the secular French Republic, the Action Française, and Le Front National), "medieval" analysis of the Middle Ages (François Villon's fifteenth-century ballad "en viel langage françois," written in Old French), and even scholarly studies of the way individuals have been influenced by other uses of the Middle Ages (analysis of Hugo's debt to Sir Walter Scott in imagining the medieval world).

Emery concludes that the term "Middle Ages" is "itself an artificial construct, changing in accordance with the individual or society imagining it."[27]

In terms of popular culture, medievalism in video games and fantasy films can be justified culturally in a way that applies significantly to Tolkienian fantasy. Kim Selling argues that "fantastic literature can in many ways be seen as a reaction against the rationalistic, anti-heroic, materialist and empiricist discourses upon which Western Culture and society are founded."[28] And the medievalist Milton McGatch long ago valorized fantasy's "imaginative adoption of what are conceived to be the ideals of that era" because "Honour, courage, and faithfulness in all things are as necessary to the fantasy hero as to the ideal medieval knight."[29]

The medievalist as Other is an uncomfortable role that medieval scholars over the years have played while attempting to argue to modern literary critics and postmodern theorists the medieval origins of many different kinds of postmodern theory (I am thinking, for example, of Bruce Holsinger's *The Premodern Condition: Medievalism and the Making of*

Theory [2005] and Amy Hollywood's *Sensible Ecstasy: Mysticism, Sexual Difference, and the Demands of History (Religion and Postmodernism)* [2001]). As Pugh brilliantly asks in the conclusion to *Sexuality and Its Queer Discontents*, "what is the gender of a medievalist? ... We can strive for the status of a 'normative' academic identity (although many of us would willingly concede the oxymoronic flavor of that coinage), but in the heady play between self and society, queering perceptions strip us of the full autonomy of self-definition."[30] We might then conclude that medievalists *are* Queer, from a modernist and even postmodernist position, but also from an historical position. If so, medievalists who study the queer in medievalism are Other Other Other.

Recently, in an attempt to formulate what might be called the historical queer, Valerie Traub, in an essay titled "The New Unhistoricism in Queer Studies," notes that contemporary queer studies of French and English early modern literature (mainly by Carla Freccero, Jonathan Goldberg, and Madhavi Menon), in order to advance a "queerer historiography," have critiqued teleological queer perspectives for "promoting a normalizing view of sexuality, history, and time."[31] Certainly teleological queer frameworks in such thinking, according to Traub, imply a presentist hegemony, in that within them the past is always heading toward a necessary present. But, then, is the only means of queer historicism (as Goldberg and Menon suggest in "Queering History" [2005]) to understand the past as other, or Queer?[32] Traub argues that even these critiques show that the "teleological thinking present in queer historicism undergirds a stable edifice of temporal normativity": whereas theorists Goldberg and Menon offer "homohistory" as a means of queer historicism, Traub argues that such a "unitary ontology" promotes a "new essentialism" in the use of "homo."[33] Along the same lines, Traub questions whether teleological thinking about the historical queer implies a presentist hegemony: does it "undergird a stable edifice of temporal normativity"?[34] In other words, is the medieval or early modern sense of the queer "queerer" historiographically because they are both *more* different from the essentialized postmodern queer? Or are we merely lost in the dilemma: past as Other or past as identical to the present?

In Traub's preferred alternative, or "teleoskepticism," which challenges both "heteronormativity" and "straight time," the question must be rephrased. If there is a "queer historicism," can there also exist an "historicized queerness"? *Is* the postmodern essentializing the queer as a common denominator—*and*, in its dehistoricization of the past and its alterity, thereby implying an imperialist Western history? More importantly, are medieval or early modern queernesses "queerer" historiographically because they are *more* different from the essentialized postmodern queer? Or are we merely lost in the dilemma: past as Other or past as identical to the present?

In other words, if "to queer" demands always "disturbing" an identity, as Edelman maintains—which presumably means the "queer" as a category can never be defined, for then it would no longer be queer—Traub concludes that queer historicism might demonstrate how its categories, "however mythic, phantasmic, and incoherent," came to be, whatever the moments and convergences along the way. She notes that "Resisting unwarranted teleologies while accounting for resonances and change will bring us closer to achieving the difficult and delicate balance of apprehending historical sameness and difference, continuism and alterity, that the past, as past, presents to us."[35] Traub is suggesting we remake the queer past into the equivalent of what was known historically as the New Historicism: a detailed look at moment after moment and how a limited space changed over time. She is suggesting that we historicize the taxonomies that categorize our ontology. She wants us to establish an "Images of the Queer" throughout history, although to do so might essentialize queerness in any historical period because difference among the smaller segments of that period would then be elided.

My example of a queer medieval here involves the similar but distinct homosocial bonds evident in the feudalism and/or chivalry of a medieval text whose very overlay reveals its cultural and historical difference as much as the distillation of the idea of a queer medieval. The twelfth-century Anglo-Norman Breton lai *Lanval* by Marie de France critiques and interrogates masculinity and male bonding that occurs through the relationship between vassal and overlord or between knight and king/host. How does queerness become embedded in questions of medievalized feminism and misogyny? How, in short, do we use contemporary theory to retrieve a historicized cultural difference?

Lanval queers both the chivalric and the courtly—the medieval. The beautiful knight, practicing generosity in giving out gifts to his own men, as every knight should, runs out of money, which his feudal lord Arthur fails to replenish; he wanders away from the court, dismounts, and, in a quasi-dream state, is visited by an equally beautiful fairy queen who recognizes his true worth and grants him both her love and her money as long as he does not reveal her existence/name. After he returns to court and renews his gifts to his men, Queen Guinevere becomes infatuated with him one midsummer night, even though he refuses her advances. She then privately accuses him of being gay but publicly charges him—through Arthur—with having made a pass at her, and, therefore, with having committed treason. During his trial in front of the barons, Lanval is rescued by the evidence offered by the Fairy Queen, who then transports him to her own world away from this one. If his foreign overlord Arthur is uncharitable and unsupportive of his vassal, and his liege lady Guinevere is herself disloyal to liege, husband, and king, and, therefore, also treacherous to the king, then feminized Lanval is, perhaps, right to reject the masculine world of chivalric values for the more virtuous, even noble realm of faërie led by a true queen.

Marie de France may have intended her lai as a critique of a masculinized society in which there is no place for sexual difference, whether characterized as queer and embodied in the deviant chevalier Lanval—the knight without a horse—or identified as a male feminized by his beauty (again, Lanval) but signifying the female (that is, as a projection of Marie de France herself).[36] Like Tolkien, Marie may be seen as creating characters as personae for herself, whether they be female or male, the queering of sexual identity is important in constructing a fictional world in which she finds a place, no matter how fantastic. In Lanval she constructs a feminized and powerless male hero—he is alien, from a foreign land—which matches his similar unconventional inability to manage the chivalric and masculine duties of valor and the indoor and courtly virtues of courtesy and feudal homage to a lady. But she also creates the fairy queen—herself as poet?—who understands the knight and rescues him from the primary world in which he is impossibly aberrant.

Similar to Marie de France in her construction of the character Lanval as self-projection, Tolkien creates his own, or focuses on queer medieval characters whose forms of difference are varied: possibly same-sexual, feminist, homosocial, hybrid, postcolonial, and postmedieval, among others. Few scholars have offered a taxonomy of Tolkien's medievalistic poetry and fiction as postmodern,[37] although Tolkien's medievalism has by now been fairly fully documented, given his career as an Anglo-Saxonist who also taught Middle English[38] as well as Old Norse.[39] In a special issue of *Modern Fiction Studies* in 2004, editor Shaun Hughes in his "Introduction: Postmodern Tolkien" prefaces the four sections of the issue, on race, postcolonial theory, the queer, and film in relation to Tolkien's *Lord of the Rings* and Jackson's films with a counter to the negative critical and theoretical reception of the trilogy as both failed novel and as fantasy. Hughes offers Patrick Curry's argument that modern critics do not understand how "*The Lord of the Rings* really is a text whose predominant available meanings powerfully contradict their own [that is, modernist] values."[40] In other words, Hughes suggests that Tolkien's epic queers modernism, a bold subversion unacceptable to aesthetically homophobic modernists. The use of "queers" as a means of suggesting subversion of the conventional is apt; the essays on the queer, by Jes Battis, "Gazing upon Sauron: Hobbits, Elves, and the Queering of the Postcolonial Optic" and Anna Smol, "'Oh … oh … Frodo!' Readings of Male Intimacy in *The Lord of the Rings*," offer two enlightening ways of defining "queer" via postcolonialism and male friendship. I hope to be able to present a more comprehensive understanding of following kinds of difference—queerness—in Tolkien's varied works, as illustrated briefly and somewhat superficially in the summaries of the seven chapters that follow.

Tolkien's composition of fictive and scholarly medieval works (translations, adaptations, literary theory, and criticism) began around 1911 and continued mainly into the thirties, mostly ending by the early fifties. Often he worked on a medieval work simultaneously with a creative one, or on his Silmarillion mythology. Further, his scholarly works in many cases reflect some of the same themes and concerns as his fiction and poetry. To determine how overlays bled into and influenced one another in an interconnected fashion, it is important to keep in mind the dates of composition, of beginning and continuation, often without completion, rather than of publication, which may not have occurred during his lifetime, as detailed records now indicate. Dates of publication, therefore, may be misleading as an indicator of his thought processes at the time of first creation and what he was also reading or researching at the time, then, and during often interminable revisions. By means of this charting, it is possible to see how his work evolved and his thinking developed as a result of a queer medieval uniquely his own, if not as a modernist like James Joyce, T.S. Eliot, or George Orwell, then as a postmodernist and certainly as a postmedievalist.

And what might all this contribute to the newly evident critical interest in Tolkienian queerness? Let us begin to account for resonances by asking more focused questions: if medievalists are queer (other), and Tolkien was a medievalist, was he queer? (And who knows if he was anything but heteronormative in his sexual practices and fantasies?). Echoing Pugh, what was his gender? (Might he have been a Lesbian born in a man's body? A hint of transgender/cis?) If we think of queer "Tolkien" as embodied in the works he inscribed, perhaps it is possible to understand a medievalist who constantly disturbed (or "queered") his *own* identity, from one moment to another, whether as public scholar or as private fantasist. And he queered the medieval by remaking it his own imaginary: for example, in a unique contemporary parodic genre, with peasant "Farmer Giles of Ham" who is no romance knight, finding a space in the antiheroic modern (again, as queered by Tolkien the medievalist). Tolkien also queered his heteronormative marriage and family in his desire to join masculine subgroups like the Inklings (and the more youthful harbingers of those groups) in which he displayed his own more private investment in fantastic and phantasmal fictions. And we cannot forget, what *is* Tolkienian? We have a corpus of works that exist in seemingly infinite variations and revisions, many published by his son Christopher, after all. How can we say, of Tolkien's many moments, of his varied images, which are the most queer, that is, the most medieval? How does Queer Theory enter into the study of Tolkienian medievalism?

In a recent 2013 paper in the "Queer Tolkien" session sponsored by the Society for the Study of Homosexuality in the Middle Ages at Kalamazoo, Steve Yandell, in his use of "Queer," draws implicitly on the theories of Alexander Doty and Lee Edelman, in particular, to examine that which is "other" and invite us to consider in the light of the "Medieval as Queer" three relatively short works by Tolkien, the fairy-stories, "Leaf by Niggle" and "Smith of Wootton Major," and the chivalric romance parody "Farmer Giles of Ham."[41] In his argument, Yandell identifies queerness (and its concomitant marginalization) in genealogical and familial (or class) difference, sexual and gender difference, and literary periodicity and generic difference. Most importantly, he focuses on Tolkienian constructions of creativity and its generation as necessitating the assumption of a "drag" persona in the primary world that depends upon a tension with private (closeted) desire—true also, he suggests, of Tolkien himself in his own life. This brilliant idea of a "drag" persona is one I would like to borrow in looking at Tolkien's often puzzling twin identities, professor and mythologist, a doubling that refracts into many of his own works, themselves extant in so many different versions.

Tolkien remained sensitive throughout much of his writing to issues of the Other—individual, sexual, gender, class, racial, and postcolonial difference—as defined in the contemporary theoretical approaches of Michel Foucault, Julia Kristeva, Gilles Deleuze and Félix Guattari, Homi Bhabha, Alexander Doty, and Lee Edelman, and Emmanuel Levinas, among others. In relation to this study, the problem of individual difference—that which is other, or queer—becomes the hallmark of a "modern" that ranges from the turn of the twentieth century to that of the "postmodern" twenty-first, however concealed by the cloak of fantasy and myth, itself imbued by medieval alterity.

Notes

1. Tolkien, "A Secret Vice," in *The Monsters and the Critics and Other Essays*, ed. Christopher Tolkien, 198–223 (Boston: Houghton Mifflin, 1983), 3. In his foreword to *The Monsters and the Critics*, Christopher acknowledges that Tolkien later revised the line to "almost forty years ago" to prepare it for a second delivery as a lecture twenty years later. The letter in which the new title is mentioned, dated 8 February 1967, is addressed to Charlotte and Denis Plimer (Letter 294, 374). Dimitra Fimi and Andrews Higgens have nearly completed an edition of "A Secret Vice," to be published in London in spring 2016 through HarperCollins.
2. Tolkien, "A Secret Vice," 199.
3. Tolkien, "A Secret Vice," 199–200.
4. Tolkien, "A Secret Vice," 203.
5. Tolkien, "A Secret Vice," 207.
6. Tolkien, "A Secret Vice," 208, 210. "Naffarin" became the next stage in youthful language development, one influenced by Latin and Spanish (209).
7. Tolkien, "A Secret Vice," 198.
8. Tolkien, "A Secret Vice," 201.
9. Tolkien, "A Secret Vice," 202.
10. Tolkien, "A Secret Vice," 206.
11. Tolkien, "A Secret Vice," my emphasis, 206.
12. Tolkien, "A Secret Vice," 206.
13. Tolkien, "A Secret Vice," 210–11.
14. Tolkien, "A Secret Vice," 212, 213.
15. Tolkien, "A Secret Vice," 213.
16. Benjamin Saxton, "Tolkien and Bakhtin on Authorship, Literary Freedom, and Alterity," *Tolkien Studies* 10 (2013): 167.
17. Slavoj Žižek, "Neighbors and Other Monsters," in *The Neighbor: Three Inquiries in Political Theology*, ed. Slavoj Žižek, Eric L. Santner, and Kenneth Reinhard, 143 (Chicago and London: University of Chicago Press, 2005).
18. Saxton, 178; *LOTR* 3:5, 98. See also Gary Saul Morson, *Narrative and Freedom: The Shadows of Time* (New Haven and London: Yale University Press, 1994), 6.

19. See David Lafontaine, "Sex and Subtext in Tolkien's World," *The Gay and Lesbian Review/Worldwide*, November–December 2015, 14–17.
20. See Wendy Moffat, "The Narrative Case for Queer Biography," in *Narrative Theory Unbound: Queer and Feminist Interventions*, ed. Robyn Warhol and Susan S. Lanser, 210–226 (Columbus: Ohio State University Press, 2015), 213.
21. Moffat, 215, 218, 221. See also Eve Kosofsky Sedgwick, *Touching Feeling: Affect, Pedagogy, Performativity* (Durham: Duke University Press, 2003); and Neil Bartlett, *Who Was That Man? A Present for Mr. Oscar Wilde* (London: Serpent's Tail, 1988).
22. Alexander Doty, *Making Things Perfectly Queer: Interpreting Mass Culture* (Minneapolis and London: University of Minnesota Press, 1993), xv.
23. Tison Pugh, *Sexuality and Its Queer Discontents in Middle English Literature* (New York: Palgrave Macmillan, 2008), 15.
24. See Michael O'Rourke, "Becoming (Queer) Medieval: Queer Methodologies in Medieval Studies: Where Are We Now," in "Roundtable: Queer Methodologies and/or Queers in Medieval Studies: Where Are We Now?" *International Congress of the European Middle Ages*, University of Leeds, UK, July 2002, 9–11. The more minor ones in his list, and less appropriate to this volume, include (4) the "history of emotionality"; (5) hybrid or "pack" sexualities (human/nonhuman and human/inanimate objects); and, even, (6) Christ's (or antichrist's) queer body, including the postcolonial queer or the queerly postcolonial. See http://ir.uiowa.edu/cgi/viewcontent.cgi?article=1200&context=mff, accessed 10 November 2015.
25. Queer medievalism (for example, in popular and film culture) is an approach that scholars, including myself, have deployed—see especially Tison Pugh and Kathleen Coyne Kelly, eds., *Queer Movie Medievalisms*, Queer Interventions Series (Farnham, Surrey, UK, and Burlington, VT: Ashgate Press, 2009).
26. Tom Shippey, "Medievalisms and Why They Matter," *Studies in Medievalism* 17 (2009): 64.
27. Elizabeth Emery, "Medievalism and the Middle Ages," *Studies in Medievalism* 17 (2009): 108.
28. Kim Selling, "'Fantastic NeoMedievalism': The Images of the Middle Ages in Popular Fantasy," in *Flashes of the Fantastic: International Conference on the Fantastic in the Arts*, ed. David Ketterer, 211–18 (Westport, CT: Praeger, 2004), 216.
29. Milton McGatch, "The Medievalist and Cultural Literacy," *Speculum* 66 (1991): 597.
30. Pugh, *Sexuality and Its Queer Discontents*, 148.

31. Valerie Traub, "The New Unhistoricism in Queer Studies," *PMLA* 128 (2013): 21–39.
32. Jonathan Goldberg and Madhavi Menon, "Queering History," *PMLA* 120 (2005): 1608–1617.
33. Traub, 22, 33.
34. Traub, 22.
35. Traub, 33, 35, and 36.
36. See Jane Chance, "Marie de France Versus King Arthur: Lanval's Gender Inversion as Breton Subversion," chapter 3 of *The Literary Subversions of Medieval Women* (New York and London: Palgrave Macmillan, 2007), 41–62.
37. Among the few, most significantly theoretical are Robert Giddings's edited collection *This Far Land* in 1983, the Foucauldian portion of my *The Lord of the Rings: The Mythology of Power* (1992; rev. edn. 2001), and Robert Eaglestone's *Reading The Lord of the Rings: New Writings on Tolkien's Classic* in 2005, with Holly Crocker's excellent postcolonial treatment of "Masculinity," 111–23; and, in a rare nonhistorical moment in *Tolkien Studies*, Gergely Nagy's brilliant psychoanalytic treatment of Bilbo and Gollum. See Gergely Nagy, "The 'Lost' Subject of Middle-earth: The Constitution of the Subject in the Figure of Gollum in *The Lord of the Rings*," *Tolkien Studies* 3 (2006): 57–80. But the most important thoroughly postmodern excurses appear in Shaun F.D. Hughes's edition of the *J.R.R. Tolkien Special Issue* for *Modern Fiction Studies* 50(4) (Winter 2004).
38. For Tolkien's reworking of Old and Middle English literature and language, see, in chronological order of publication, Jane Chance, *Tolkien's Art: A "Mythology for England"* (London: Macmillan, 1979; rev. edn. Lexington, KY: University Press of Kentucky, 2001); T[om] A. Shippey, *The Road to Middle-earth* (1982; rev. edn. London: Allen & Unwin, 1992); Jane Chance and David Day, "Medievalism in Tolkien: Two Decades of Criticism in Review," *Medievalism: Inklings and Others* (special issue), ed. Jane Chance, *Studies in Medievalism* 3(3) (1991): 375–88; Tom Shippey, "Tolkien and the Gawain-Poet," in *Proceedings of the J.R.R. Tolkien Centenary Conference*, Keble College, Oxford, 1992, ed. Patricia Reynolds and Glen H. GoodKnight, *Mythlore* 80/*Mallorn* 30 (Winter 1996), 213–20; Bruce Mitchell, "J.R.R. Tolkien and Old English Studies," in *Proceedings*, 206–11; Andy Orchard's "Tolkien, the Monsters, and the Critics: Back to *Beowulf*," in K.J. Battarbee, ed., *Scholarship and Fantasy: Proceedings of the Tolkien Phenomenon*, May 1992, Turku, Finland, Anglicana Turkuensia no. 12 (Turku: University of Turku, 1992), 73–84; Jonathan Evans's "The Dragon-Lore of Middle-earth: Tolkien and Old English and Old Norse Tradition," in *J.R.R. Tolkien and His Literary*

Resonances: Views of Middle-earth, ed. George Clark and Daniel Timmons, 21–38 (Westport, Connecticut, and London: Greenwood Press, 2000); and George Clark, "J.R.R. Tolkien and the True Hero," in *J.R.R. Tolkien and His Literary Resonances*, ed. Clark, 39–52; Miranda Wilcox, "Exilic Imagining in *The Seafarer* and *The Lord of the Rings*," in *Tolkien the Medievalist*, ed. Chance, Routledge Studies in Medieval Culture and Religion, vol. 3, 133–54 (London: Routledge, 2002; New York: Routledge, 2003); Michael D.C. Drout, "A Mythology for Anglo-Saxon England," in *Tolkien and the Invention of Myth*, ed. Jane Chance, 229–47 (Lexington, KY: University Press of Kentucky, 2004); John R. Holmes "Oaths and Oath-Breaking: Analogues of the Old English Comitatus in Tolkien's Myth," in *Tolkien and the Invention of Myth*, ed. Chance, 249–61; Alexandra Bolintineanu, "'On the Borders of Old Stories: Enacting the Past in *Beowulf* and *The Lord of the Rings*," in *Tolkien and the Invention of Myth*, ed. Chance, 263–73; Brian McFadden, "Fear of Difference, Fear of Death: The *Sigelwara*, Tolkien's Swertings, and Racial Difference," in *Tolkien's Modern Middle Ages*, ed. Jane Chance and Alfred Siewers, 155–69 (New York and London: Palgrave Macmillan, 2005); and Jane Chance, "Tolkien and the Other: Race and Gender in Middle-earth," in *Tolkien's Modern Middle Ages*, ed. Chance, 171–86; Richard W. Fehrenbacher, "*Beowulf* as Fairy-story: Enchanting the Elegiac in *The Two Towers*," *Tolkien Studies* 3 (2006), 101–15; Thomas Honegger, "The Homecoming of Beorhtnoth: Philology and the Literary Muse," *Tolkien Studies* 4 (2007): 189–99; and Deborah A. Higgens, *Anglo-Saxon Community in J.R.R. Tolkien's The Lord of the Rings* (N.p.: Oloris Publishing, 2014).

39. Given Tolkien's interest in repurposing Old Norse literature and language in his fiction, see, for the names of the Dwarves derived in part from the *Eddas*, Patrick J. Callahan, "Tolkien's Dwarfs and the Eddas," *Tolkien Journal* 15 (1972): 20; for the antecedents of Gandalf, the Dwarves, the Elves, the Ring, and other elements in Norse mythology, see Mitzi M. Brunsdale, "Norse Mythological Elements in *The Hobbit*," *Mythlore* 9 (1983): 49–50; and Lynn Bryce, "The Influence of Scandinavian Mythology in the Works of J.R.R. Tolkien," *Edda* 7 (1983): 113–19. Tom A. Shippey has focused on Old Norse philology and literature as the core of Tolkien's fiction, in *The Road to Middle-earth*; and also "Tolkien and the Appeal of the Pagan: *Edda* and *Kalevala*," in *Tolkien and the Invention of Myth*, ed. Chance, 145–61; see also Marjorie J. Burns, "Gandalf and Odin," in *Tolkien's 'Legendarium': Essays on The History of Middle-earth*, ed. Verlyn Flieger and Carl F. Hostetter, 219–32 (Westport, CT and London: Greenwood Press, 2000); Marjorie J. Burns, "Norse and Christian Gods: The Integrative Theology of J.R.R. Tolkien," in *Tolkien*

and the Invention of Myth, ed. Chance, 163–78; Marjorie J. Burns, *Perilous Realms: Celtic and Norse in Tolkien's Middle-earth* (Toronto: University of Toronto Press, 2005); Leslie A. Donovan, "The Valkyrie Reflex in J.R.R. Tolkien's *The Lord of the Rings*: Galadriel, Shelob, Éowyn, and Arwen," in *Tolkien the Medievalist*, ed. Chance, 106–32; and Andy Dimond, "The Twilight of the Elves: Ragnarök and the End of the Third Age," in *Tolkien and the Invention of Myth*, ed. Chance, 179–89.

40. Patrick Curry, "Tolkien and His Critics: A Critique," *Root and Branch—Approaches Towards Understanding Tolkien*. Cormarë Series 2, ed. Thomas Honegger, 119 [81–148] (Zürich: Walking Tree, 1999), cited by Shaun F.D. Hughes, "Introduction: Postmodern Tolkien," to *J.R.R. Tolkien Special Issue*, ed. Hughes, *Modern Fiction Studies* 50(4) (Winter 2004): 809 [807–13].

41. I served as a respondent in the "Queer Tolkien" session organized by Graham Drake, Society for the Study of Homosexuality in the Middle Ages, with papers by Stephen Yandell, "Niggle, Smith, and Giles: Medieval as Queer," and Christopher Vaccaro, "To All Elf-Friends and Wizard-Pupils: 'It Gets Better'": Medieval Queer in Modern Categories of Tolkien's *Lord of the Rings*," Forty-Eighth International Congress on the Middle Ages, Western Michigan University, Kalamazoo, MI, Friday, 10 May 2013.

CHAPTER 2

Forlorn and Abject: Tolkien and His Earliest Writing (1914–1924)

"I am got such a big man now because I have got a man's coat and a man's bodice."—Unsent letter by Ronald Tolkien, age four, to his father in South Africa[1]

"Baby does look such a faery when he's *very* much dressed-up in white frills & white shoes ... or even when he's very much undressed I think he looks more of an elf still."—Mabel Tolkien, in a letter to her parents, 4 March 1893[2]

What is meant by "abjection"? According to the *Oxford English Dictionary*, "abject," in its oldest, late medieval, denotation, refers to that which is "cast off, cast out, rejected" (1400–1500), from the Latin, *abjectus*, meaning "thrown down," and derived from *abicere, abjicere*; in more modern senses, "downcast," "brought low," "of low position," "degraded." "Abjection," then, denotes the state of being dejected, or humiliated; abjectness (s.v.).[3] Julia Kristeva, in the first chapter of *Powers of Horror: An Essay on Abjection* (1982), entitled "An Approach to Abjection," characterizes abjection more theoretically and psychologically, drawing from Sigmund Freud and others, to suggest a state of being caused by having been cast off by the mother.[4]

Certainly this definition would seem to apply to young Tolkien. After the death of his mother, Mabel (1870–1904), when, at the age of twelve, he became an orphan, he also became, in both a metaphysical and a literal sense, homeless—and abject. The importance of his mother is magnified in his 1904 sketch titled "Home," created when his dying diabetic mother was in the hospital: it shows him and the man who would become his uncle, in 1905 (Edwin Neave, husband-to-be of his Aunt Jane) seated before the fire, darning socks and mending pants, with a caption reading "What is Home Without a Mother (or a Wife)."[5] Although Mabel came home to Rednal, in Worcestershire, to convalesce, she died on 14 November 1904 at the relatively youthful age of thirty-four. Biographer Humphrey Carpenter acknowledges the effect his mother's death had on him was to make him into a pessimist:

> Or rather, it made him into two people. He was by nature a cheerful and almost irrepressible person with a great zest for life. He loved good talk and physical activity. He had a deep sense of humour and a great capacity for making friends. But from now onwards there was to be a second side, more private but predominant in his diaries and letters. This side of him was capable of bouts of profound despair. More precisely, and more closely related to his mother's death, when he was in this mood he had a deep sense of impending loss. Nothing was safe. Nothing would last.[6]

It is perhaps no accident that Edith Bratt, as the beloved whom he chose as wife, was several years older than he and represented to him a recovery of the kind of safety and comfort of home; it is their relationship that he projects into that of the man Beren and the Half-elf Lúthien in *The Silmarillion* and it is their names that appear on his and Edith's tombstones in Oxford. The importance of "home" and its lack would resonate through much of what he wrote throughout his life.

The best definition of the abject hero in Tolkien's work comes from Melissa Ruth Arul's gendered postcolonial analysis of Elven alterity in *The Silmarillion,* based on Julia Kristeva's theory of the abject. She notes that Noldo Fëanor suffers from a self that is damaged, pitched against the world. She argues that the Elf's sense of inferiority, reinforced by the early loss of his mother Míriel, results in a desire to make himself whole by means of the creation of the Silmarils, or what Arul terms his "fetish." However, because of Fëanor's obsessive desire to recoup their loss to thieving Ainu Melkor, who also killed Fëanor's father, High King Finwë, he and most of his Noldor kin left Eldamar (Elvenhome, that is, Faërie) to follow Melkor to Middle-earth, for which they are exiled for disobeying the Valar and for their Kinslaying at Alqualondë. Arul explains that the "abjection of his kin and the Kinslaying were caused by his failure to integrate into the Symbolic order."[7] In some sense Tolkien's fetish may well have been his continuing interest in founding a world of his own, in what became Middle-earth, a world he could control and call his own. Certainly it was a world infused with medieval constructions and themes, and modeled on many of the medieval works he taught, edited, and translated. There, he felt at home.

Not every reader of Tolkien may realize how abject he was, even at the age of twenty-three, in 1915, after he had finished college with a First and applied for a commission with the Lancashire Fusiliers, given the burgeoning of World War I, and just before marrying Edith Bratt in 1916. Born on 3 January 1892, in Bloemfontein in the Orange Free State, South Africa—where his twenty-one-year-old mother, then Mabel Suffield, had married his banker father, Arthur Reuel Tolkien (b. 1857), on 16 April 1891—the three-year-old Ronald, his younger brother, Hilary, and his mother left Africa for England in 1895 to escape the heat and other irritations of life there.[8] They settled with the Suffield family in Birmingham—but unfortunately never again seeing their father and Mabel's husband, although they were planning to return to South Africa. Four-year-old Ronald's affection for his father is clear from a letter he asked his nurse to write but never sent because that very day Mabel learned her husband had rheumatic fever: "I am so glad I am coming back to see you it is such a long time since we came away from you."[9]

The transition alone from the heat of one country to the cold of the other was traumatic for Ronald—"quite by accident," he is quoted as having observed much later, "I have a very vivid child's view, which was the result of being taken away from one country and put in another hemisphere—the place where I belonged but which was totally novel and strange. After the barren, arid heat a Christmas tree. But no, it was not an unhappy childhood. It was full of tragedies but it didn't tot up to an unhappy childhood."[10] Tolkien's rather puzzling oxymoronic statement—notably, given the journeys of his fictional heroes Eriol, Eärendel, Bilbo, and Frodo from one world to another, one that centers on an abrupt change in climate and circumstances—seems to soften the blow of ill-fortune he and his family had to endure from that point forward, but harsh blow it was.

When Arthur Tolkien died on 15 February 1896, he left Mabel with a meager income primarily from South African mine shares and funds from her brother-in-law.[11] Even though after their return to England Ronald enjoyed a pastoral childhood in nearby Sarehole—immortalized in his creation of the Shire in *The Hobbit* and *The Lord of the Rings*—he only benefited for a short time being taught by his dedicated mother to read and write, especially in calligraphy; to study with her Latin, German, and

French, drawing, and botany; and to learn to play the piano. In letter 54 to son Michael Tolkien, on 18 March 1941, Tolkien writes about the impact of his mother on himself and his life: "Though a Tolkien by name, I am a Suffield by tastes, talents, and upbringing, and any corner of that county [Worcestershire] (howsoever fair or squalid) is in an indefinable way 'home' to me, as no other part of the world is" (44). Once more, it is "home" that he defines for his own son.

Ronald attended the school of his father, King Edward's School, in Birmingham, from 1900 to 1911, with some breaks—for example, in 1902, when for financial reasons he and his brother briefly studied at St. Philip Catholic grammar school at the Birmingham Oratory (and where he met his future guardian, Father Francis Xavier Morgan), followed by summer home-schooling by their mother. Ronald was later able to return to King Edward's School with a Foundation Scholarship that continued for several years. In 1904 when his mother died, leaving both Ronald and Hilary orphans and, because of Mabel's conversion to Catholicism, estranged from the Unitarian Suffields and Baptist Tolkiens, the boys were subsequently shuffled from one relative to another, then to a lodging house. There, sixteen-year-old Ronald in 1908 met nineteen-year-old future wife Edith Mary Bratt (b. 21 January 1889–1971). When Father Morgan discovered the two in love, Ronald was moved in January 1910 to yet another lodging house, where he remained until finally accepted at Oxford, in 1911.

Ronald was not only abject, he was also depressed at that point in his life. Having been told by Father Morgan to break off his relationship with Edith at the end of 1909 and without funding for Oxford—having failed to win an award for a University scholarship for which he had sat in the preceding December 1909—he writes about himself in what has been described as his "earliest surviving diary" on 1 January 1910—just before his eighteenth birthday, on the third—"Depressed and as much in dark as ever. God help me. Feel weak and weary."[12] Later in January when Father Morgan learned that he had seen Edith on her birthday, he was forbidden any further meetings or written contact with her (except to say goodbye) until he turned twenty-one. With virtually no support from anyone close whom he loved or who loved him, he must have felt alone and defenseless. Certainly, for him, a few close friendships, learned societies, and scholarship and writing had always been the means of withstanding isolation and abjection, early on in his education. Both poor and Roman Catholic, he differed from the "wealthy former public schoolboys": he was "potentially the butt of much snobbery."[13] He had also been born in South Africa, which he states openly at the beginning of his Valedictory Address at the end of his career in a tone that even in print manifests his anger over various kinds of prejudice.[14] It is no wonder that as consolation he fell back upon a few close friends and his writing.

This habit began, first, at King Edward's, especially in the Literary Society (where he spoke on "The Modern Languages of Europe—Derivations and Capabilities," in spring term 1910 and on "Norse Sagas" on 17 February 1911); the Debating Society (for which he was secretary in 1910–1911); the rugby team (despite his slight frame, as reflected in photographs at Exeter College), for which he served as secretary and House Football Captain; the social and tea club that he and his friends Christopher Wiseman, Robert (Rob) Quilter Gilson, and Geoffrey Bache Smith named the Tea Club Barrovian Society (TCBS), after the Tea Room at Barrow's Stores in Birmingham. He was also Sub-Librarian, the position at King Edward's that he shared with Christopher and Rob in 1910.

Another interest that Ronald pursued beginning at King Edward's School and continued throughout his life was the love of languages and the meanings and etymologies of words. At King Edward's, he studied Latin and Greek and, in his spare time, Anglo-Saxon (and Gothic, by means of Joseph Wright's *Primer of the Gothic Language* [1892]). Once in Oxford at Exeter College, for which he had won an Open Classical Exhibition at the examinations he retook at the end of 1910, he studied Classics and Comparative Philology (along with Finnish, which he tried to learn on his own).[15]

Of course, close friends and members of the TCBS at King Edward's stayed in touch with him when he went to Oxford in 1911 even though Wiseman and Gilson went to Cambridge and Smith only came to Oxford in 1913.[16] He also threw himself into various positions from the beginning, as prefect of the college; secretary of the debating society, the Stapledon; member of the Dialectical Society and the Essay Club (for which he served as president, in 1914); football (rugby) player; and corporal in the King Edward's Horse, like the Officers Training Corps, but for those born in a colony.[17] Along with other students, he even created his own club for debate and dinner, "The Apolausticks" (which means "those devoted to self-indulgence"), for which he served as first president.

Despite the salving effect of all these memberships and friendships, in one of his earliest poems, Tolkien positions himself as a lonely wanderer.

"Goblin Feet," "You and Me," and "The Cottage of Lost Play" (1915–1917)

In "Goblin Feet," written on 27–28 April 1915 while he was still at Oxford and published two years later, the use of the first-person singular opens up the vision of the twenty-three-year-old as a journeyer. "I am off down the road," reads the first line, the poet venturing forth like so many of his fictional wanderers, whether Bilbo and Frodo, or Eriol/Aelfwine and Eärendel. The speaker is alone—as his wanderers always seem to be—and his destination is faërie, or whatever is "down the "crooked fairy lane" (line 18), a place where "the fairy lanterns glowed" (line 2), and the air is filled with sound of all sorts, the sighing of grass, whirring wings of all sorts, leprechaun (elf?) horns, the padding of gnome feet, described as "little happy feet" (line 15). The poem may have been written solely to charm Edith[18]—indeed, Tolkien himself apparently later disliked it for the silliness of its fairy posturing.

But there are no signs of human presence or any community in which the journeyer might share. The happiness of the fairy community impels the impatient speaker (Tolkien), so different from them in his abjection, to join them: "it's knocking at my heart—Let me go! O! let me start!" (lines 26–27). Magic is twice emphasized (lines 28, 32), connected with the dying light, the warmth, the colors, the sound of their dancing feet. The last line ends, not with his happiness, his embrace of this fairy place, but "the sorrow when it dies"—incompletion, loss, death. In essence, the poem summarizes the cycle beginning with departure from home, crucial to the entry into what Tolkien in his important essay "On Fairy-Stories" will later call the secondary world, the perilous realm, that is, escape to the undying lands of imagination and recovery, and ending with the return to the reality of the primary world. Being cut off from happiness for this near-penniless orphan must have seemed his inevitable fate, given the long separation from Edith and the imminence of joining a war abroad from which he might never return.

Tolkien's feelings of early loss and isolation were in part ameliorated by recollections of having met and fallen in love with Edith, reflected not only in "Goblin Feet" but also in the poem "You and Me and the Cottage of Lost Play," written at the same time (27–28 April 1915), and later revised as "The Little House of Lost Play: *Mar Vanwa Tyaliéva*." The two poems relate to the *prose tale* of "The Cottage of Lost Play" which precedes it in the published edition of *The Book of the Lost Tales, Part One*. The prose tale was written out by Edith on 12 February 1917 in an exercise book containing some of the *Lost Tales*. Two other poems and the tale (the eight-line "Tinfang Warble" and "Kôr: In a City Lost and Dead," followed by "Morning Song," about which we know nothing, written on 3 May) together comprise the springboard for what became *The Book of Lost Tales* (end of 1916–first half of 1917), today extant in two volumes, subtitled *Part One* and *Part Two*, part of *The History of Middle-earth* (1983–1984). The collection contains Tolkien's first efforts at writing a Silmarillion mythology set beyond the western ocean, in Valinor, and in the middle between eastern and western oceans, the so-called "Great Lands," in what eventually became known as "Middle-earth," but only in the 1930s.[19]

In these two early works, the short poem "You and Me and the Cottage of Lost Play" and the longer prose story "The Cottage of Lost Play," Tolkien provides the refuge hinted at by sounds in the night and longed for by the narrator of "Goblin Feet," but one whose discovery in that early poem was frustrated by failure. In the original version of "You and Me and the Cottage of Lost Play" as a short poem, according to Christopher written in Tolkien's undergraduate lodging at 59 St. John's Street, Oxford, also on 27–28 April 1915, but twice revised, both the young lovers Edith and Ronald are characters, "A dark child and a fair" (line 4). They are identified as "You and me" in line 1 and then, "You and Me lost in Sleep," and again, as they gambol over paths "full of shapes,/Of tumbling happy white-clad shapes," they are "with them You and Me" (lines 10, 42–44). They are examples of the children who in sleep meet each other, wander "shyly" hand in hand, eventually entering the Cottage of Lost Play. But despite their debating of "quaint old childish things" (line 56), Tomorrow comes with his "grey hand" (line 59) to guide them back to the real world, never to return—"Where all things are, that ever were—/We know not, You and Me" (lines 64–65). Tolkien's explanation of what they have encountered in this magical dream vision appears in the fantastic story of Eriol (One Who Dreams Alone), in Tolkien's prose tale of "The Cottage of Lost Play."

"The Cottage of Lost Play" deals with the journey of this figurative "son of Eärendel," the Mariner to the Lonely Island (or Tol Eressëa, in "fairy speech")—also called For Faidwen, "the Land of Release," by the Gnomes (the second kindred of the Elves).[20] The fairy-story's basic structure is anticipated here: in the dark, journeyer Eriol arrives at a place of refuge and of homecoming (the Cottage of Lost Play), where Lindo and Vairë and many of their small [elven] folk dwell, including children. The latter are summoned for eating, drinking, and tale-telling to the delightful

Room of the Log Fire by Tombo the Gong. For Eriol, "a new world and very fair was opening to him," a place of merriment and mirth.[21] The heart of the Lonely Island, which Eriol reaches after passing through borders of the Land of Elms (or Place of Flowers), is known as Kortirion, the Citadel of the Island (or the World), a place of wisdom. It is the land where Inwë of the Eldar led the Exiles (the Noldor) before they journeyed to the lands of men. To Eriol, Vairë tells the tale of the fair gardens of Valinor, near a silver sea: a place of joy and light and dance, guarded by the Eldar, to which the earliest children of Men would arrive on the Path of Dreams to find the Cottage of the Children, or of "the Play of Sleep, and not of Lost Play, ... for no play was lost then, and here alas only and now is the Cottage of Lost Play."[22] The Cottage of Lost Play is only part of Tolkien's *faërie*, a realm in which "broken tales and snatches of song" are left to Men via their Poets—from which Lindo and Vairë depart to the Great Lands (east of the Great Sea) to comfort those lonely or weeping children in their beds at night in their dreams and then return with sad tales of what they have found.[23] The tale concludes when Eriol realizes this is the very place about which his father had told him when Eriol was a boy, part of a tradition of beautiful house and gardens visited by his father's fathers, which he as a boy had somehow "seen and heard," one that left him with an eternal sense of restlessness, "as if as longing half-expressed for unknown things dwelt within him."[24]

This conclusion to the prose tale allows Tolkien to appropriate as a base for his mythology the allegorical journey of Eärendel (a shining light or ray, *eorendel*, or *aurora*), the rising sun or the planet Venus at dawn, as John the Baptist, forerunner for Christ. The word *earendel* appears in poem *Crist* I by tenth-century Cynewulf, which Tolkien had read while studying Old English at Oxford,[25] sometime in 1913 or shortly thereafter. The lines, "Eálá earendel! engla beorhtast!/ofer middangeard monnum sended" (O ray! brightest of angels! sent to men over mid-earth), with *middangeard* an Old English loan word from Old Norse for "earth," offer the sun (or Son) as sign of God's love and hope for humankind, a concept that Tolkien will later use to identify his fantasy world as "Middle-earth."[26] The lines serve as the lynchpin upon which rests Tolkien's entire mythology, as a fantasy tracing the trajectory from fall to redemption, like any good fairy-story, according to Tolkien's later essay "On Fairy-Stories"— but one without any explicit Christian context or signification.

Equally important for understanding Middle-earth's kernel mythology is Tolkien's complicated penultimate version of the pseudo-historical and

Anglo-Saxon frame-story of "Ælfwine of England" (1920), featured at the end of *The Book of Lost Tales, Part Two*, which is related to the story of Eriol. Eriol, early on in Tolkien's writings (ca. 1916–1919), comes with his son Heorrenda from Angeln (land of the Angles or English, Anglia)—that is, from the lands to the east of the North Sea—to Tol Eressëa before the fifth-century invaders of Britain, Hengest and Horsa (as suggested by the figure of Hengest in *Beowulf*).[27] Later, Tolkien links Eriol to the invaders in the fairy-story in a little pocket-book titled "Story of Eriol's Life." The mariner, formerly named Eriol, becomes the Anglo-Saxon Ælfwine ("Elf-Friend") and sails west from England to Tol Eressëa, that is, after the invaders had come to England. The Elves relay to Ælfwine the important story of Eärendel the Mariner, who redeemed the Doom of the exiled Noldor. There is, thus, a (pseudo)historical witness to this mythical event, recording (or establishing the civilization of) the link between the Anglo-Saxon Ælfwine and what will eventually be, in the Third Age, in the later twenties and thirties, the mythical Hobbits Bilbo and Frodo of *The Hobbit* and *The Lord of the Rings*.[28]

The creation of a relationship between Tolkien's foundational mythology, British geography, and Old English literature was intentional. In "The Cottage of Lost Play," the city of Kortirion[29] is the fair city of Tol Eressëa, the Lonely Isle of the Elves (or faërie), to which Eriol ("One Who Dreams Alone") journeys "from the lands to the East of the North Sea" (that is, to England), apparently before the Anglo-Saxons had invaded Britain. Of course, it is important to remember that Tolkien changed these relationships between recorded English history and his own mythological history several times during his life. If the Eriol story represents the kernel of Tolkien's mythology, that does not mean its influence is simple, which students often assume. As Christopher Tolkien notes in his "Commentary on *The Cottage of Lost Play*," "The 'Eriol-story' is in fact among the knottiest and most obscure matters in the whole history of Middle-earth and Aman."[30] He also notes that

> in *The Cottage of Lost Play* Eriol comes to Tol Eressëa *in the time after* the Fall of Gondolin and the march of the Elves of Kôr into the Great Lands for the defeat of Melko, when the Elves who had taken part in it had returned over the sea to dwell in Tol Eressëa; but *before the time* of the 'Faring Forth' and the removal of Tol Eressëa to the geographical position of England. This latter element was soon lost in its entirety from the developing mythology.[31]

To understand the geographical location of the city of Kortirion in the mythology of Middle-earth is to realize its ancient legendary location in

Warwickshire (*Kor-* and *War-* being related etymologically by Tolkien)—that is, near Edith, who had lived in Warwickshire until they were married, and then, after their marriage, nearby in Great Haywood in Staffordshire, near Tolkien's camp, before he left (exile-like) for France and after he returned from battle in World War I.[32] For Tolkien, "home" is Edith, "faërie." In his poem dating from 21 to 28 November 1915—also revised much later, in 1937, but written when he was in Warwick on a one-week leave from camp—there is an Anglo-Saxon title provided early on, with a dedication "to Warwick" ("Cor Tirion þǽra béama on midde,"), later changed to "Kortirion among the Trees." In the First Verses of the poem the city is identified as "the Land of Elms,/Alalminórë in the Faery Realms" and the "citadel of the world" (lines 21–22, 33).[33] In the Second Verses the Lonely Companies remain in the "inmost province of the fading isle" (Britain), where "holy fairies" and "immortal elves" dance and sing. The realization of Faery as a real place, "home" to Tolkien, clearly reflects his happiness of having a beloved other.

Other than his relationship with Edith, Tolkien created close friendships in all-male societies, as noted above, maintaining a sense of "home" jeopardized by the loss in World War I of two of his three dearest boyhood friends. After the death of R.Q. Gilson in the Battle of the Somme, he wrote to his close friend G.B. Smith on 12–13 August 1916 about the four members of the TCBS whom he had thought together would "rekindle an old light in the world," but, "So far my chief impression is that something has gone crack. I feel just the same to both of you—nearer if anything and very much in need of you—I am hungry and lonely of course—but I don't feel a member of a little complete body now... Still I feel a mere individual at present—with intense feelings more than ideas but very powerless."[34] The historical context in which Tolkien wrote from 1915 on reveals a world in turmoil and chaos. World War I shattered the perception of European civilization as an oasis from bloodshed—and Tolkien himself participated in that war. Increasingly, he turned back to reading and writing about medieval heroes and antiheroes who provided other models for finding "home" in his burgeoning mythology.

An Early Literary Model: Antihero Kullervo in the Finnish *Kalevala* (1914–1919)

Where did Tolkien find his literary heroes—or antiheroes? Likely his earliest model was the abject Finnish orphan Kullervo. The Oxford medievalist reveals to Christopher Bretherton on 16 July 1964 in letter 257 that "The germ of my attempt to write legends of my own to fit my private languages was the tragic tale of the hapless Kullervo in the Finnish *Kalevala*" (345). Tolkien became interested in the folk antihero and the *Kalevala* while still in Birmingham at King Edward's School in 1911, an interest that continued after he had arrived at Exeter College that fall. At the 1992 Centenary Conference exhibit at King Edward's School, a placard relayed Ronald's interest in "scandalous heroes"—Kullervo, in particular—in a poster of one of his preserved debates from the Debating Society.

The *Kalevala*— the Finnish national epic as it has been called, although not by Tolkien—as compiled by Elias Lönnrot (1802–1884) from traditional oral tales, only loosely connected, from northern Archangel Karelia, between eastern Finland and Russia, was first published in 1835, then issued in an expanded edition in 1849.[35] The Dent Everyman Series published W.F. Kirby's poetic translation in 1907, although Tolkien didn't try his hand at translating it himself till later: in September of 1911 he composed a parody of a small part of Kirby's fifty *runos*, or cantos.[36] In his final year at university, in 1911–1912, he checked out a Finnish grammar from the library—Sir Charles Eliot's *Finnish Grammar*[37]—three times, according to library records, and became interested in creating his own Elvish language of Quenya. Tolkien also composed a prose version of one significant tale, *The Story of Kullervo*, in 1914, in an attempt to contain some of translator W.F. Kirby's prolixity,[38] and he wrote a paper on *The Kalevala, or Land of Heroes*, which he delivered twice to different Oxford college clubs and societies later that year and in 1915.

Tolkien's essay on Kullervo—"On 'The Kalevala' or Land of Heroes" (Kalervonpoika)—exists in two versions, a manuscript and a typescript (together, Bodleian Library MS Tolkien B61), of varying lengths—with the hand-written manuscript including a title page indicating the two dates and two places where he presented them, Corpus Christi College "Sundial" (the Sundial Society), in November 1914, and Exeter College Essay Club, in February 1915. The slightly longer typescript is titled "The Kalevala" and, according to Verlyn Flieger, was written between 11 November 1918 and 1919, but according to Douglas A. Anderson and Christina Scull and Wayne Hammond, as late as 1921 or even 1924 (Scull notes that he typed the longer version in ?1921–1924?, so both dates may be correct).[39] In the manuscript draft—the one cited throughout this chapter because it is earlier—Tolkien describes how he first felt reading the *Kalevala*—"like Columbus on a new Continent or Thorfinn in Vinland the good."[40] Exploring Finland and its body of legends was as if he had "crossed the gulf between the Indo-European-speaking peoples of Europe into this smaller realm of those who cling *in queer corners* to the forgotten tongues and manners of an elder day."[41] What he chiefly admired in the *Kalevala* was a body of forgotten myth.

In the *Kalevala*, the Kullervo cycle occupies cantos 31–36, making an entrance in the epic between the first Väinämöinen cycle (cantos 1–10) and the final Väinämöinen cycle (cantos 39–49).[42] Väinämöinen, or "Calm Waters man," is the chief figure in the epic, sometimes a water-god, shaman, or the first man and founder of the land of Kalevala. In the second Väinämöinen cycle (cantos 16–25), Väinämöinen competes with the smith Ilmarinen (whom he has appointed to forge the mysterious Sampo for the Northland) to win in marriage the Maid of the North, but fails. In the Kullervo cycle, the ignoble hero causes Ilmarinen's wife to die.

A brief synopsis of the complex tale of the Finnish antihero may explain how akin to Kullervo Tolkien must have seemed. What likely fascinated Ronald about the orphan was his utter failure to fit into a world he never understood. Why Kullervo executes so many antisocial acts is due to his brutish birth and captivity as a slave by the unfortunate Untamo, the brother of his father, Kalervo. The rivalry between the two brothers begins with Untamo fishing in Kalervo's grounds and, in revenge, Kalervo sowing oats on Untamo's land, with his dog killing Untamo's ewe for eating the crop. When Untamo's men slaughter all Kalervo's family and burn the house, they also abduct a pregnant woman to serve as maid, who gives birth to Kullervo (called "Warrior" by Untamo). The orphan kicks out his cradle, is put into a barrel and thrown into the sea by Untamo, burned, and hanged, but he survives all perils until Untamo makes him a serf. Even as a serf Kullervo is motivated by the desire to avenge his father: looking after a child, he breaks its hand, gouges its eye, kills it, burns its cradle. When Untamo sets him to clear trees off his land, he ruins the wood. When he must build a fence for his uncle, he leaves out gates and gaps. He threshes rye to chaff and straw to bran. Finally Untamo sells him to Ilmarinen the smith, whose wife assigns him as herdsmen and provides him with a loaf hiding a stone in the middle that breaks his knife—an heirloom from his father. For this malicious act, Kullervo sends all her cows into a swamp for the wolves and bears to kill and then drives those fierce creatures back to kill the wife. Handsome and yellow-haired, but fatherless, the "unloved one considers," and then prays,

> Do not, O good God
> do not ever in this world
> create an unlucky child
> nor one quite unloved
> fatherless under the sky
> motherless—that least of all—
> as you created me, God
> shaped wretched me.[43]

Unloved orphan Kullervo must have seemed an appropriate alter-ego for the similarly orphaned—and, in his own eyes, unloved—Tolkien.

But the story does not end there. When a hag informs Kullervo that he does still have a father and mother alive in Lapland, his mourning mother does not at first recognize him, having lost all her children, including a daughter. Even after he begins living with his parents, his flaw lies in the lack of proper rearing and education: he "did not come to grasp things/ have a man's understanding/for he'd been crookedly reared/stupidly lulled as a child."[44] Ironically, given his desire to find his home, he wrecks his boat when trying to fish, smashes the fish to scum, and in taking taxes in to pay for tithes, he stops the sleigh to offer a maid a ride and then rapes her when she resists (she succumbs to the offer of gold and silver). Of course she turns out to be the missing daughter and sister, who lost her way raspberry-picking. Once they both realize they are sister and brother, she drowns herself, and Kullervo, who does not want to hide away for his crimes, decides to go to war and leave his parents behind. Because he will not stay to help them as they age, only his mother tells him as he leaves that she will cry for him when he is dead (the remainder of his family will not). Yet his father, brother, sister, and mother, one by one, die, and he refuses to attend the burials until he has revenged himself on Untamo, on all his kin and all his holdings—which he then does. When he returns to his empty house, his mother awakens from the grave to tell him Blackie the dog is still there for him to hunt with; with Blackie, at the very spot he raped his sister, his sword (which speaks) when Kullervo asks, elects to kill him. Only Väinämöinen issues a memorial—in echo of Kullervo's words grieving his inability to socialize—as a warning against bringing up a child "crookedly."

In Tolkien's own unfinished prose translation—"The Story of Kullervo," in Bodleian Library MS Tolkien B 64/6—he unifies the original tale by tidying it up. In a letter to W.H. Auden on 7 June 1955, Tolkien declares, "But the beginning of the legendarium, of which the trilogy is part (the conclusion), was in an attempt to reorganize some of the Kalevala, especially the tale of Kullervo the hapless, into a form of my own" (214). Tolkien adapts the tale more than translates it literally, adding details back to the beginning and elsewhere to account for inconsistencies that crop up later in the original Finnish narrative and its English translation, just as a single author would have done in the revision process.[45] Of course this would have been impossible given the many oral contributions over time that went into the initial construction of this entire Kullervo cycle—yet, it almost seems as if Tolkien were that author.

Tolkien rewrites this tale as a fairy-story. It begins, "In the days long ago (when magic was yet new) a swan nurtured her brood of cygnets by the banks of a smooth river"[46]—and he prettifies it or at least moderates some of the original's violence by explaining the protagonist's motivations. In Tolkien's opening, it is the elegant swan, not the humble hen, who is taking care of her brood, and the brood consists of cygnets—unlike the Kirby translation, in which the hen has both chickens and swans whom she separates into two groups, putting the chickens by the hedge and the swans in the river—environments suited to each type of bird—where an eagle, hawk, and a "flying bird" separate them. The eagle bears one—his father as a child, Kalervo—to Karelia; the hawk bears a merchant to Russia; and the third, his father's brother Untamo, the flying bird leaves there in the nest. In both versions, the original and Tolkien's, Untamo grows up to fish in the waters of Karelian Kalervo, even though Kalervo, spying this theft, takes away from Untamo the caught fish, which results in Untamo's vengeful sheep-grazing on Kalervo's pastures, and Kalervo setting his dog on Untamo's sheep—after which Untamo kills all the men and beasts on Kalervo's farm, including Kalervo, leaving only his wife and her twins and two older siblings, in Tolkien's version, to be enslaved (in the original, other brothers and sisters materialize close to the end, rather magically).

Among the many changes and additions by Tolkien, when Kullervo's mother gives birth, it is not only to Kullervo, as in the original, but to twins, Kullervo, or "wrath," and his sister, unnamed originally, who crops up later in the cycle in the original but whose birth is unaccounted for earlier, whom Tolkien calls Wānōna ("Weeping") in emulation of Wenonah, the mother of Hiawatha, in the American poem "The Song of Hiawatha," by Henry Wadsworth Longfellow, according to John Garth.[47] This work had been given a choral interpretation by Samuel Coleridge Taylor at a 1912 summer concert put on by the Music Society at Exeter College.[48] Tolkien also adds a background for Kullervo's sister to explain why she later became lost while berrying: "And a wild lone-faring maiden did Wānōna grow, straying in the grim woods of Untola so soon as she could stand—and early was that, for wondrous were these children and but one generation from the men of magic."[49] And he adds a backstory missing from the original for the mother's gift of the knife to her three-month-old son, a mother who is depicted in Tolkien's version as still grieving the loss of her husband and the slaughter of all else and whom Kullervo sweetly addresses as if a beloved, "O my dearest."

Further, Tolkien provides a just motivation equally missing for Kullervo's behavior while enslaved by his uncle: he swears on his father's "great knife curious wrought ... a blade of marvelous keenness made in his dim days," that, when he is grown, he will avenge the loss of his father and "atone for the tears of my mother who bore me."[50] The deep affection for the mother, so characteristic of Tolkien's own affection for Mabel Tolkien, and the romance-like description of the sword (which diminishes in the original to a kind of rustic handy knife for the shepherd Kullervo) embroiders this fairy story-like version. Tolkien acknowledges in his essay that "The power of mothers is the most arresting characteristic," pointing to Väinämöinen's own turning to his mother when faced with quandary; "this tying to the apron-strings goes on even after death."[51] Interestingly, because Tolkien's fearful Untamo happens to overhear Kullervo's swearing of the oath and imagines Kalervo "reborn in him," his own malicious treatment of the boy becomes more understandable—not merely a reflection on the boy's crooked rearing by no one.

One unusual addition to "The Story of Kullervo" that enhances its fairy-story aspect is the digression concerning Musti the Hound. The dog's role at the end of the original tale is thus accounted for from the beginning, as it was with Kullervo's sister, "these two wild children" who wander in the woods only a month after their father is slain. In Musti's case, he functions in an amazing magical capacity that anticipates that of the hound in *The Silmarillion*'s tale of Beren and Lúthien. From Musti, "the wisest of hounds," and a shape-changer to boot, the twins learn about their father and evil uncle, and "of things even darker and dimmer and farther back even perhaps before their magic days," as if Tolkien is lost in his mythology and not in this specific Finnish tale. Because of Musti's help, in fairy-tale fashion Kullervo is given three magical hairs from the Hound's coat upon which he can call for help from him—"Musti may thy magic aid me now."[52] All the wondrous escapes Kullervo achieves on his own, like those in the original up to and including his hanging, are here attributed to Musti's magic.

Tolkien's organization of the labors of Kullervo from this point on differentiates them carefully by means of a few creative additions. Marking his maturation, Kullervo's great knife Sikki, which belonged to his father and which was given to him by his mother but is unnamed in the original, allows him, in the role of self-designated artist, to carve images of wolves and bears and a great hound on the bark of the tree from which he is hanged to die, after having been sent by Untamo to clear the wood of trees—but, again, failing. In his new role as a bard, Kullervo sings the "Song of Sākehonto," which celebrates his own manliness, nobility, his strength, and valor as epitomized by his axe, his "iron brother" and a symbolic extension of himself as male ("he deemed himself grown to manhood in that now he had an axe in hand, and he sang as he fared him") (13), a confidence bolstered by the magic of Musti "about him."

After Kullervo (now called Sākehonto, perhaps reflective of his changed status as a man) has ruined the forest by slashing trees and making a useless gateless fence, Tolkien changes the names of his characters by addressing them via variations: Untamo becomes Ūlto, and Kullervo, now the son of Kampo (or Kampa), becomes Sāri, or Sārihonto, but the failed labors of the antihero continue (Tolkien never revised the work to make the names consistent throughout). Further, as a now proud man, Kullervo is provided a motivation for what seemed needless anger and antisocial behavior in the original in fulfilling his tasks. Kullervo/Sāri threshes the rye to powder and chaff, irritating Untamo/Ūlto, all the while, in chorus, his mother, two sisters, and brother lament his antagonistic behavior because his uncle threatens to sell him as bond-slave, an event that would leave his mother, especially, and his siblings with no one to help them. Here, Tolkien moves the anxiety and fear of the disregarded mother and the siblings (no father, as there was originally) from the end of his cycle, when Kullervo decides to go to war and leaves his family behind without anyone to care for them. And here it is that Kullervo/Sāri curses his mother and the other brother and sister for their insensitivity toward him: "Let her starve upon a haycock ... Let him perish in the forest."[53] Kullervo/Sāri is apparently angered by the insults of Untamo/Ūlto about his unsuitedness as a laborer and the lack of support from his family, who chide him for that anger, which invariably results in hurt toward them, too, after which he "skulks" in the woodlands. Worse still, when Untamo/Ūlto sends him to set his fishing dragnet, while oaring, Kullervo/Sāri breaks the boat and oarlocks to splinters and ruins the caught fish. Thinking him useless, Untamo/Ūlto then sells him as a bond-slave to the smith, now called

Āsemo (in the Finnish tale, Ilmarinen), whose wife, now Koi, will put him first to work as a servant and then as a herdsman.

But before Kullervo/Sāri departs, upset at having to leave sister Wānōna and the black dog Musti, he must listen to his brother and sister (but not his mother) swear they will not weep if he perishes, so that he answers them in kind. Kullervo/Sāri's mother, unlike his *Kalevala* mother, in a long passage vows she will weep if he dies because he is her "fair one," her "nursling," her "sweet one," and "dearest," again, as if he is her beloved. Strangely, Tolkien makes his hero short and "swart and illfavoured," unlike the blond, comely protagonist Kullervo in the original, whereas his mother identifies herself as "the fair one," "the golden one." But this may be another marking that favors Tolkien's self-projection as the abject hero. Indeed, because Kullervo has to endure thralldom, isolation, and loneliness (except for Musti, who has followed him from afar), he becomes strangely deformed and even uglier: "more ill favoured and crooked, broad and knotty and unrestrained and unsoftened."[54] Of course, despite the charms and prayers of the smith's wife, Kullervo/Sāri breaks his knife, Sikki, in cutting the bread loaf with the stone hidden inside and then in a rage sends in the wolves and bears to kill her cattle and makes a pipe out of the oldest cow's leg. He uses the pipe to make music as he returns to her house and let her know she should milk her "cows," their skins now concealing bears and wolves who devour her, but not before she has cursed him.

Similar to the original in this last episode, except that Kullervo/Sāri, in leaving Koi's homestead on the way to kill Untamo/Ūlto and avenge his father's death, meets the Blue-Robed Lady of the Forest, a character Tolkien invents, who directs him to a place where he sees in the sunlight, but does not recognize, a blond girl, whom he desires as a "comrade." No sled in the snow here, although he offers the girl food and gold; she rejects him for his "ungainliness" and flees, although, of course, he captures her and treats her lovingly (no rape, exactly). Eventually they both confess their backgrounds, and she—Wānōna, of course—realizing that they are both children of Kalervo, drowns herself. Although Tolkien's version ends here, there is an outline in brief that remains indicating there will ensue Kullervo's familiar destruction of everything at the village through the agency of the bears and wolves—including his beloved dog Musti, his brother, sister, and mother—and his invitation to his sword to kill him, as in the original. Youthful Tolkien notes in his essay on *Kalevala* that this is one of the finest examples of animism in the poem, in addition to that of the talking ale in runo 20, 522/546, on the Origin of Beer.[55] As with many of his other translations and adaptations of medieval tales and romances, this is unfinished, as if he wished to avoid the final tragedy. Tolkien's changes to the story result in a much more nuanced explanation of Kullervo's destructive behavior and a more carefully organized unity to the narrative, even as unfinished and incompletely revised as it is.

The Kullervo story influenced other aspects of the Silmarillion mythology, notably his Eärendil writings and the story of Beren and Lúthien.[56] Tolkien began writing the *Lay of Leithian* (originally "Tinúviel," begun in 1917, or the story of Beren and Lúthien) in octosyllabic couplets in August 1925 and continued it until 1931, when he abandoned it.[57] Musti the magical Hound in "The Story of Kullervo" bears a magical resemblance to Huan of Valinor, chief of the wolfhounds in "Of Beren and Lúthien," chapter 19 of *The Silmarillion*.[58] Huan similarly follows the Noldorin Celegorm into exile and finds the fleeing Lúthien, brings her to his master, at which point both he and Huan fall in love with her, and eventually rescues her from imprisonment to sing outside the pits of Sauron where Beren lays. Huan valiantly kills all the wolves sent by Sauron, battling with Sauron himself in the shape of Wolf-Sauron and then serpent until Sauron succumbs to Lúthien and she rescues Beren. When the couple is later assaulted by Celegorm and Curufin, Huan once more saves them by forsaking service to his original lord and terrifying his horse. The hound also protects Lúthien by catching an arrow meant for her and bringing to her an herb that will allow her to heal Beren after having been wounded by another arrow hurled by Curufin.

Loving both of them, Huan also finds a means for Lúthien and Beren to resolve the dilemma that confronts them, she half-Elven and half-Maia, and he human, remaining apart but alive or remaining together but hopeless. Beren, arrayed as the wolf-game of Draugluin, and Lúthien, as the bat-fell of Thuringwethil, together pass through the gate of Angband where she lifts off her disguise and beguiles Morgoth, casting the latter, crowned with the Silmarils, into sleep so that Beren can extricate a Silmaril, as he had sworn to Thingol he would—Carcharoth bites off the hand holding the Silmaril. Once more Huan comes to her aid to attend to the poisoned wound of Beren, and after they have returned to Doriath he hunts and kills the maddened Wolf Carcharoth, but is himself slain. Through his sacrifice the Silmaril is reclaimed from the wolf's belly, although Beren dies but Lúthien, daughter of Melian the Maia and Elwë, the Telerian Elf, does not, until Manwë offers her the choice of life as a mortal, with Beren permitted to live again, and both subject to a second death, which she chooses, to allow the Two Kindreds, the Firstborn, Elder Children of Ilúvatar, and Men, to fuse through them.

Kullervo and Túrin Turambar

Around the same time Tolkien was reworking and typing his paper "'The Kalevala' or Land of Heroes" in ?1921–?1924—which is titled "The Kalevala" in Flieger's edition[59]—he was also writing a long alliterative verse version of *The Children of Húrin*, about his own Kullervo-like hero Túrin Turambar.[60] The "Lost Tale" of Túrin Turambar (1918?) he rewrote throughout his life, as "Turambar and the Foalókë" (Túrin Turambar and the Dragon," in 1919), eventually published posthumously in *The Book of Lost Tales, Part Two*[61]; as an alliterative poem, "The Lay of the Children of Húrin" (1920–1925), published in *The Lays of Beleriand*[62]; and as the prose "Narn i Chîn Húrin: The Tale of the Children of Húrin" [The Tale of Grief] (ca. 1950), published in *Unfinished Tales* and, with a different edit, in *The Children of Húrin* (and also in *The Silmarillion* as chapter twenty-one, "Of Túrin Turambar," the version cited throughout).[63]

Similarities abound between the narratives of each antihero, Kullervo and Túrin, first of all, in the bleak nature of their families. In *The Silmarillion*, about the same time that Beren first saw Lúthien, Túrin, son of Morwen ("Dark-Lady" in Sindarin) and Húrin, lord of Dor-lómin, was born, followed by Lalaith, or Laughter, a sister who died when she was three. She symbolizes the loss of happiness to this family because of the curse on it by Ainu Morgoth. Morgoth cursed Húrin and his family after Húrin's father was captured in a battle and refused to divulge Gondolin's location; Morgoth imprisoned him at Thangorodrim for twenty-eight years. The third child of Morwen and Húrin was Niënor ("Mourning" in Sindarin)—again, symbolic of the family's grief. Because Beren was the kinsman of Morwen's father and Túrin was kinsman of Tuor, Morwen sent Túrin to stay in Doriath for harbor, in fear the Easterlings might take him from her.

Other similarities between Kullervo and Túrin have been listed by editor Flieger in *The Story of Kullervo*, although she believes there are greater differences between the two.[64] I would argue that, like Kullervo, abject Túrin suffered from misfortune and poor choices most of his life because of his pride and anger: he became an outlaw after Thingol's envious foster-son Saeros died as a result of a quarrel; he mistakenly slew Beleg, a Sindarin Elf of Doriath and a great warrior who was Túrin's friend and supporter. After being bound by Orcs, when angry and afraid, he imagined Beleg, coming to rescue him, was an enemy; and most alarming, he married his sister Niënor when, after twenty years, she (in disguise) followed her mother to Doriath to find him, endured a spell of forgetfulness cast upon her by the dragon Glaurung, and in the wild met her brother (called then Turambar). Pregnant, she followed him to hunt Glaurung, where she helped bind his wounds, only to hear the voice of dying Glaurung, which triggered her memory. Understanding she had married her brother, like Kullervo's sister she jumped off a cliff. Like Kullervo in Tolkien's *Kalevala*, Túrin changed his name repeatedly: certainly for protection but also (again, symbolically), as if unhappy with himself, to shift his identity and his bad luck. Among his names were Neithan (The Wronged), Gorthol, Agarwaen, Wildman of the Woods, and Turambar; the Elves of Nargothrond named him Adanedhel for his beauty.

Eventually, in tales that became part of the published *Silmarillion*, Tolkien projects aspects of the antisocial and abject Kullervo into the construction of various flawed heroes: Aulë, Feänor, Thingol, Túrin Turambar, and Eärendil, among others, although it was only in 1926 that Tolkien had finally outlined the whole of "The Silmarillion."[65] Similar to these flawed heroes are those of *The Hobbit* and *The Lord of the Rings*: Gollum and the major Hobbits, including Bilbo, Merry, and Pippin, and of course, especially by the end of the fairy-story, the abject and psychologically wounded Frodo. Smol notes that Frodo's journey into Shelob's lair through dark tunnels to face a female embodiment of primitive appetites which threatens to consume them could also be read in Kristevan terms as a regression into an archaic material space from which the subject has to separate in order to survive.[66] Whatever desire in each of Tolkien's antiheroes threatens to subvert the individual through some weak point, as Gergely Nagy has pointed out about Gollum's desire for the Ring and how it turns "the subject inside out, erasing it," eventually results in a "lost" subject, "the perfect example of Kristeva's abject": "he is the ultimate Lacanian subject whose existence (as it appears) is entirely determined by loss and lack," with the Ring the border between his love and hate of it and himself, according to Gandalf.[67] Indeed, Nagy suggests the Ring itself as the "perfect example of Kristeva's abject."[68]

All Tolkien's flawed protagonists represent some strain of the cosmic failure incarnated in Melkor/Morgoth and bear resemblance to Sigurd, the Old Norse failed hero whose story Tolkien himself retold in verse as

The Legend of Sigurd and Gudrún, and, in more comic form, I will argue in the next chapter, in *The Hobbit*. Further, in many of Tolkien's medievalized works, composed primarily between 1911 and 1950—whether articles on and translations of Old and Middle English works or portions of *The Hobbit* and *The Lord of the Rings*—Tolkien borrows from other abject heroes similar to Kullervo, from Old Norse saga and other medieval texts such as the Anglo-Saxon *The Battle of Maldon* (as will be demonstrated in the following chapters) to create self-projections, as he also does in his verse-drama "The Homecoming of Beorhtnoth Beorhthelm's Son."

Tolkien's very creation of the Hobbits as ordinary and rustic, if smaller than most humans, suggests his own kinship with them: in letter 213 to Deborah Webster he confesses, "I am in fact a *Hobbit*," in that he smokes a pipe, likes gardens and trees and plain food, has a simple sense of humor, and does not travel much (288–89). Tolkien identifies with Hobbits in part because he was himself short—about five feet eight and a half inches tall, "very slightly built," according to letter 294 (addressed to interviewers Charlotte and Denis Plimmer much later in life, on 8 February 1967) (373), as is also evident from his college photos. He was certainly not elf- or fairy-like, as his mother had described him as a baby, except perhaps figuratively, but he himself was conscious of his otherness in various ways throughout his life, understanding that, as he said about himself in one letter, that he was affable but not sociable—not inclined to be around people. As "the little guy," the ignominious exile, in both kinds of his writing, creative and academic, it is clear from Tolkien's own otherness in England as a southern African-born and Roman Catholic orphan—a religious minority in a country wedded to the Church of England, and with family ties to the similarly marginalized and more rustic West Midlands so far from London. An orphan, like Frodo and Kullervo, Tolkien can also be described as if "in exile"—not just at the age of three or four, but for much of his entire life and career. He also identified with the ordinary people of England who survived punishing attacks during World War II and who behaved heroically throughout. Indeed, Tolkien's prime definition of the hero in the twentieth century refers back to the ordinary man living on the small island of Great Britain during World War II: "I've always been impressed ... that we are here, surviving, because of the indomitable courage of quite small people against impossible odds."[69]

While he was teaching and translating those Old and Middle English and Old Norse works of literature, he was similarly concealing himself: as he notes in a letter to W.H. Auden dated 7 June 1955, in relation to his own trilogy, where he describes himself as "the most modest (or at any rate retiring) of men, whose instinct is to cloak such self-knowledge as he has, and such criticisms of life as he knows it, under mythical and legendary dress" (letter 163, 211). We will find him everywhere cloaked in various kind of legendary dress throughout this book, both in the characters he created and those he studied and taught.

Notes

1. Tolkien the child is quoted in Humphrey Carpenter, *Tolkien: A Biography* (London: Allen & Unwin; New York: Houghton Mifflin, 1977), 16; also Scull, *Chronology*, 3.
2. Judith Priestman, ed. *J.R.R. Tolkien: Life and Legend. An Exhibition to Commemorate the Centenary of the Birth of J.R.R. Tolkien (1892–1973)* (Oxford: Bodleian Library, 1992), 10.
3. *Compact Edition of the Oxford English Dictionary, Complete Text Reproduced Micrographically*, 2 vols. (Oxford: University Press, 1971), s.v.
4. Julia Kristeva, *Pouvoirs de l'horreur. Essai sur l'abjection* (Paris: Le Seuil, 1980), translated by Leon S. Roudiez as *Powers of Horror: An Essay on Abjection*, European Perspectives (New York: Columbia University Press, 1982), 1–15.
5. Priestman, *J.R.R. Tolkien: Life and Legend*, 15.
6. Humphrey Carpenter, *J.R.R. Tolkien: A Biography* (London: Allen & Unwin; New York: Houghton Mifflin, 1977), 31.
7. I cite here from Melissa Ruth Arul's unpublished conference paper, "Elvish Identity: A Journey," delivered at the Festival at the Shire Conference, Aberystwyth, Wales, 13 August 2010, and summarize her concept of abjection in relation to *The Silmarillion* in "A Critical Study of the Self and the Other in Selected Texts of Tolkien," her MA thesis completed at the University of Malaya-Kuala Lumpur, 2009, for which I was the External Reader.
8. See Carpenter's chapter on Bloemfontein in *Tolkien: A Biography* 9–16, for the circumstances surrounding Tolkien's parents' emigration to the Republic of the Orange Free State and the family's subsequent departure for Birmingham.
9. Scull, *Chronology*, 3. Also quoted in Carpenter, *Biography*, 16.
10. J.R.R. Tolkien, quoted by Philip Norman, "The Prevalence of Hobbits," *New York Times Magazine*, 15 January 1967, 100.
11. Scull, *Chronology*, 4.
12. Carpenter, *Biography*, 42. Scull designates the diary as earliest, *Chronology*, 17.
13. Priestman, *J.R.R. Tolkien: Life and Legend*, 24 (no. 33, "Exeter College").
14. See the discussion of Tolkien's "Valedictory Address," in chapter 6, 134–35.

15. See Tolkien's letter 163 to W.H. Auden, 213.
16. For these friends and how they fared during World War I, see John Garth, *Tolkien and the Great War: The Threshold of Middle-earth* (London: HarperCollins, 2003).
17. Scull, *Chronology*, 20.
18. See J.R.R. Tolkien, "Goblin Feet," in *Oxford Poetry 1914–1916* (Oxford: B.H. Blackwell, 1917), 120 (of 120–21). For the poem's purpose, see Scull, *Chronology*, 64.
19. For this whole early section on *The Cottage of Lost Play*, see J.R.R. Tolkien, *The Book of Lost Tales, Part 1*, vol. 1 of *The History of Middle-earth*, ed. Christopher Tolkien (London: George Allen & Unwin, 1983; Boston: Houghton Mifflin, 1984; New York: Ballantine, 1992), 1–44. See Peter Gilliver, Jeremy Marshall, and Edmund Weiner, *The Ring of Words: Tolkien and the Oxford English Dictionary* (Oxford: University Press, 2006), 162–64, for Tolkien's history of names for Middle-earth, which originally meant the region in the middle inbetween heaven and hell (162). They explain that,

> In Tolkien's early writings, the lands east of the Great Sea are called the Great Lands, the Hither Lands, or the Outer Lands (though the latter in some writings, confusingly, can mean the lands beyond the Western Sea). Tolkien's earliest poem about Earendel, written in 1914, does refer to 'the mid-world's rim' (HOME II. 268), but the term Middle-earth is never used in *The Book of Lost Tales* (HOME I and II) and does not appear in *The Hobbit*; it seems to have been adopted in the writings of the later 1930s published in HOME V (the Old English *middangeard* is found already in Tolkien's Old English version of the 'Earliest Annals of Valinor'). It then became established as the normal term in *The Lord of the Rings*. In the earlier version of 'The Shadow of the Past' (LR I. ii) 'the middle-world' appears several times, but is once changed to 'the middle-earth'. Perhaps by an oversight, 'the Great Lands' survives from the earlier draft in Faramir's exposition of the history of Gondor (LR IV. V) in one place, but in another is replaced by *Middle-earth*.
>
> (164)

20. Tolkien, *The Book of Lost Tales 1*, 1. Christopher explains that a "son of Eärendel" is "born under his beam," meaning the beam has touched a newborn child, destined to wander (24).
21. Tolkien, *Book of Lost Tales 1*, 4.
22. Tolkien, *Book of Lost Tales 1*, 8.
23. Tolkien, *Book of Lost Tales 1*, 9.
24. Tolkien, *Book of Lost Tales 1*, 20.
25. See Joseph Bosworth and T. Northcote Toller, *An Anglo-Saxon Dictionary* (London: Oxford University Press, 1898, repr. 1976) and T. Northcote Toller, *Supplement* (London: Oxford University Press, 1921, repr. 1966), s.v. *eorendel*, or *earendel*.

26. A connection between the poem and Tolkien's mariner was first noted by Carpenter, *Biography*, 64.
27. See J.R.R. Tolkien, *Finn and Hengest: The Fragment and the Episode*, ed. Alan Bliss (London: George Allen & Unwin, 1982). See also Christopher's discussion, *Book of Lost Tales 1*, 13–14.
28. The best article about these two interrelated figures, Eriol and Ælfwine, is by Michael D.C. Drout, "A Mythology for Anglo-Saxon England," in *Tolkien and the Invention of Myth*, ed. Jane Chance, 229–47 (Lexington, KY: University Press of Kentucky, 2004). Christopher does note that "*the Elvish isle to which Eriol came was England*—that is to say, Tol Eressëa would become England, the land of the English, at the end of the story" (*Book of Lost Tales 1*, 24).
29. Kortirion is also celebrated in a poem titled "Kortirion Among the Trees" [1915] that follows *The Cottage of Lost Play* in Tolkien's *The Book of Lost Tales 1*, 25–37.
30. Christopher Tolkien, *The Book of Lost Tales 1*, 13.
31. Christopher Tolkien, *The Book of Lost Tales 1*, 18.
32. See Christopher Tolkien's notes on the importance of Kortirion in *The Book of Lost Tales 1*, 12–19.
33. Christopher Tolkien, *The Book of Lost Tales 1*, 26.
34. See Scull, *Chronology*, 87.
35. See the summary headnote to the Kullervo excerpts from Kirby's translation in *The Tolkien Fan's Medieval Reader*, ed. Turgon (aka David E. Smith, or Douglas A. Anderson) (Cold Spring Harbor, New York: Cold Spring Press, 2004), 335 (it appears here, in *runos* 31–36, on 337–89). For Tolkien's disclaimer about the *Kalevala* as national epic, see his "On 'The Kalevala' or Land of Heroes," in Tolkien, "'The Story of Kullervo' and Essays on *Kalevala*," ed. Verlyn Flieger, *Tolkien Studies* 7 (2010): 247. He details the history of Lönnrot's compilation in "On 'The Kalevala' or Land of Heroes," 250. Flieger's edition with notes, commentary, and an essay are reprinted in J.R.R. Tolkien, *The Story of Kullervo*, ed. Verlyn Flieger (London: Harper Collins, 2015). Her edition is based on the 1915 version Tolkien delivered to the Essay Club. References, unless otherwise indicated, are to the pagination in the *Tolkien Studies* version.
36. Scull, *Chronology*, 28.
37. See John Garth, *Tolkien at Exeter College: How an Oxford Undergraduate Created Middle-earth* (Oxford: Privately printed by Exeter College, 2014), 21. Garth includes a copy of one library record of Tolkien's borrowing of C.N.E. Eliot's *A Finnish Grammar*, along with Skeat's *Chaucer's Works* II, accompanied by a photo of its copyright page (Oxford at Clarendon, 1890) and a penciled note from Tolkien on one page of the Eliot *Finnish Grammar*.
38. See Tolkien, "'The Story of Kullervo' and Essays on *Kalevala*," ed. Flieger, 211–78.

39. Flieger, "Headnote" to "The Story of Kullervo," 213. The typescript draft appears on 262–76, with notes by Flieger on 276–77.
40. Tolkien, "On 'The Kalevala' or Land of Heroes," 246.
41. Tolkien, "On 'The Kalevala' or Land of Heroes," 247 (my emphasis).
42. The full version of the epic is available in Elias Lönnrot, *The Kalevala*, trans. Keith Bosley (Oxford and New York: Oxford University Press, 1989). It contains an excellent introduction and succinct bibliography.
43. Lönnrot, *Kalevala*, canto 34, 468–69. W.F. Kirby's equivalent lines, translated from Lönnrot's *Kalevala: The Land of Heroes*, 1849, in the 1907 version (London: J.M. Dent) read: "Never, Jumala most gracious,/Never in the course of ages,/Form a child thus mis-created,/Doomed to be forever [sic] friendless,/Fatherless beneath the heavens,/From the first without a mother,/As thou, Jumala, hast made me,/And hast formed me to be wretched." See "The Story of Kullervo," in *The Tolkien Fan's Medieval Reader*, ed. Turgon, 367.
44. Bosley, *Kalevala*, canto 35, 475.
45. See also Verlyn Flieger's essay on the tale, in "Tolkien, *Kalevala*, and 'The Story of Kullervo,'" in Tolkien, *The Story of Kalevala*, 133–63. All references to her essay are from the 2015 publication.
46. Tolkien, "The Story of Kullervo," 214.
47. See John Garth, "'The Road from Adaptation to Invention': How Tolkien Came to the Brink of Middle-earth," *Tolkien Studies* 11 (2014): 28–29.
48. Garth, *Exeter*, 38. Garth notes that the etymologies were neither Finnish nor Longfellow's and entirely Tolkien's invention. The meter of Longfellow's "Hiawatha" is identical to the Finnish octosyllabic line with its four stresses and was also used by Kirby in his translation. Of course it is also used in Old Norse poetry. Tolkien mentions Longfellow's popular "Hiawatha" and its meter in "On 'The Kalevala' or Land of Heroes," 251–52.
49. Tolkien, "The Story of Kullervo," 216.
50. Tolkien, "The Story of Kullervo," 216.
51. Tolkien, "On 'The Kalevala' or Land of Heroes," 255. Tolkien adds the example of the reverence for his mother by reprobate Lemminkäinen, although he feels the tragedy of Kullervo points more to that of brother and sister.
52. Tolkien, "The Story of Kullervo," 217.
53. Tolkien, "The Story of Kullervo," 220.
54. Tolkien, "The Story of Kullervo," 221–22. Cf. Bosley, *Kalevala*, canto 32, 443: the "blue-stockinged gaffer's son" is "yellow-haired, handsome/fair of shoe-upper." Is there a hint of Tom Bombadil in the original? See David Elton Gay, "J.R.R. Tolkien and the *Kalevala*: Some Thoughts on the Finnish Origins of Tom Bombadil and Treebeard," in *Tolkien and the Invention of Myth*, ed. Chance, 295–304.

55. Tolkien, "On 'The Kalevala' or Land of Heroes," 253.
56. For the connection with Eärendel, see Garth, *Exeter*, 38.
57. "The Tale of Tinúviel" (1917), preserved only in later unfinished versions—one a manuscript written over by Tolkien, and one a typescript—was first published in J.R.R. Tolkien, *The Book of Lost Tales, Part Two*, in *The History of Middle-earth*, ed. Christopher Tolkien, vol. 2 (London: Allen & Unwin; Boston: Houghton Mifflin, 1984). The manuscript version appears on 7–41; the revised typescript, typed by Tolkien, very close to the written-over manuscript, with changes noted 41–48, followed by notes, 48–50, changes made to names, 50–51, and commentary by Christopher, 51–70. The unfinished *Lay of Leithian* (1925–1931) was published with extensive commentary and notes in J.R.R. Tolkien, *The Lays of Beleriand*, in *The History of Middle-earth*, ed. Christopher Tolkien, vol. 3 (London: Allen & Unwin, 1985), 150–363.
58. For Flieger's discussion of the two magical hounds, see also "Tolkien, *Kalevala*, and 'The Story of Kullervo,'" 151–52; 160–61.
59. Tolkien, "The Kalevala" (the second, typescript, version), Tolkien, "'The Story of Kullervo' and Essays on Kalevala," ed. Flieger, in *Tolkien Studies* 7 (2010): 262–76.
60. See Scull, *Chronology*, 115.
61. See J.R.R. Tolkien, "Turambar and the Foalókë," in *The Book of Lost Tales, Part Two*, 69–116 (written-over manuscript, followed by notes, 116–18; changes made to names, 118–19; and commentary by Christopher, 119–43).
62. See Tolkien, "The Lay of the Children of Húrin," in *The Lays of Beleriand*, first; early version, 3–94; second; later, version, 94–130.
63. For the incorrectly titled "Narn i Hîn Húrin" (it should be as the text indicates, "Narn i Chîn Húrin," "The Tale of the Children of Húrin"), see J.R.R. Tolkien, *Unfinished Tales of Númenor and Middle-earth*, ed. Christopher Tolkien (London: George Allen & Unwin, 1979; Boston: Houghton Mifflin, 1980), 57–162, with notes, 153–57, and appendix, 158–72. See also J.R.R. Tolkien, *The Children of Húrin*, ed. Christopher Tolkien (London: HarperCollins, 2007). The *Silmarillion* version of the tale (chapter 21), is longer than any other chapter and is based on "'Narn i Chîn Húrin," but represents an interweaving of various texts by Christopher Tolkien: see Scull, *Reader's Guide*, 1061; and Douglas Charles Kane, *Arda Reconsidered: The Creation of the Published Silmarillion* (Bethlehem, PA: Lehigh University Press, 2009), 193–206, and including a table of paragraphs, *Silm* page nos., and primary and secondary source, the primary, mostly from the *Grey Annals*). For a brief comparison of Kullervo and Túrin Turambar, see Richard West, "Setting the Rocket Off in Story: The *Kalevala* as the Germ of Tolkien's *Legendarium*," in *Tolkien and the Invention of Myth*, ed. Chance, 285–94; also Garth, *Exeter*, 38.

64. See Flieger's essay, "Tolkien, *Kalevala*, and The Story of Kullervo." Flieger sees similarities in the early life of each antihero (which I describe as abject) and in Tolkien's life. She also identifies as issues of comparison family (Kullervo has two), incest with a sister, personality, dog, weapons, and the ending, and relates some of these to the Beren and Lúthien story, particularly the use of a magical dog in each.
65. For *The Silmarillion* abject heroes, see, in addition to Arul, cited above, also Jane Chance, "Why Teach *The Silmarillion*? The Mythology of the Abject Hero," *Approaches to Teaching Tolkien's* Lord of the Rings *and Other Works*, ed. Leslie A. Donovan, 56–64 (New York: Modern Language Association, 2015). Tolkien created this sketch of what became the *Silmarillion* for his old fourth-form schoolteacher R.W. (Dickie) Reynolds, who had driven him and L.K. Sands to Oxford in 1911 (see letter 254, to the Reverend Denis Tyndall, on 9 January 1964, 343).
66. See Anna Smol, "Frodo's Body: Liminality and he Experience of War," in *The Body in Tolkien's Legendarium*, ed. Christopher Vaccaro, 39–63 (Jefferson, NC: McFarland, 2013), 60n53.
67. See Gergely Nagy, "The 'Lost' Subject of Middle-earth: The Constitution of the Subject in the Figure of Gollum in *The Lord of the Rings*," *Tolkien Studies* 3 (2006): 57–80; Gandalf's analysis of Gollum appears in *LOTR* 1:2, 54. For the Kristeva discussion on the abject, see *Powers of Horror*, 1–15.
68. Nagy, "'Lost' Subject," 70.
69. These lines from Tolkien's last radio interview, with Denys Gueroult, "Now Read On," BBC Radio 4, 16 December 1970, are available in a rare cassette recording (London: BBC Cassettes, 1980); this interview is discussed in Carpenter, *Biography*, 176.

CHAPTER 3

Bilbo as Sigurd in the Fairy-Story *Hobbit* (1920–1927)

"Nobody can write a new fairy tale; you can only mix up and dress up the old, old stories, and put the characters into new dresses."—Andrew Lang, Introduction to the *Lilac Fairy Book*[1]

"I don't much approve of *The Hobbit* myself, preferring my own mythology (which is just touched on) with its consistent nomenclature ... to this rabble of Eddaic-named dwarves out of *Völuspá*, newfangled hobbits and gollums (invented in an idle hour) and Anglo-Saxon runes."—J.R.R. Tolkien to a friend, quoted by Christopher Tolkien[2]

"The so-called 'children's story' (*The Hobbit*) was a fragment, torn out of an already existing mythology."—Tolkien, in letter 218 to Houghton Mifflin Co., 30 June 1955

It may come as a surprise that Tolkien confesses that a Victorian version of an Old Norse saga was his favorite "fairy-story." The Oxford medievalist declares in the earliest manuscript of his famous essay "On Fairy-Stories"—known as A Proper and written between December 1938 and March 1939[3]—that "The adaptation of the Story of Sigurd (done by Andrew Lang himself from [William] Morris's transl. of *The Volsunga Saga*) was my *favourite without rival*. Even as it stands in the *Red Book* it is no Conte des Fées. It is strong meat for nurseries."[4] Certainly Tolkien had long been attracted to that Old Norse saga as far back as his days at King Edward's School in Birmingham, when he had attempted to read it in the original language; he had also purchased a copy of William Morris's

1870 translation (from which Lang had redacted his own version) while a student at Exeter College, Oxford, with money he had received for the Skeat Prize in English.[5]

So it should be no surprise that in the late twenties Tolkien also composed two Old Norse lays of his own, of Sigurd and Gudrún, after having founded the Kolbítar Reading Group during Hilary Term in 1926 for the purpose of translating Old Norse sagas. He had continued to teach Old Norse from 1926 to 1939 after being designated Rawlinson and Bosworth Professor of Anglo-Saxon at Oxford in 1925. His son Christopher, who edited Tolkien's Old Norse poems for publication, disavows the idea that they were just translations.[6] Yet, Tolkien only told Christopher about them toward the end of his life. And the Professor dismissed his Old Norse adaptations in a 29 March 1967 letter to the English poet W[ystan].H. Auden as "a thing I did many years ago when trying to learn the art of writing alliterative poetry: an attempt to unify the lays about the Völsungs from the Elder Edda, written in the old eight-line fornyrðislag stanza." The term "fornyrðislag," according to Humphrey Carpenter, the editor of Tolkien's *Letters*, refers to the Old Norse term for the stanzaic meter in which the Eddic narrative poems were written, a meter that closely resembled the alliterative meter of Old English poetry.[7] Tolkien titled his long poem of 339 stanzas, "Völsungakviða en nýja" (or "New Lay of the Volsungs"), adding to it 166 stanzas about Gudrún in "Guðrúnarkviða en nýja," the two sagas together published as the *Legend of Sigurd and Gudrún* in 2009. Tolkien notes that the whole *Legend* mainly centers on "material dealing with Sigurd and Gunnar" (Gudrún's brother), according to another letter to Auden, dated 29 January 1968.[8]

Also in the late 1920s, while Tolkien was translating Old Norse sagas such as the *Völsunga Saga* and the *Prose Edda* at Kolbítar meetings and writing his own *Legend of Sigurd* in the vein of Andrew Lang's fairy-tale, he had begun composing *The Hobbit*, continuing with it into the early thirties—all of these works centering on a magical ring. *The Hobbit* was largely composed from stories told to Tolkien's children during the decade of the twenties, especially 1926–1927, according to Christopher Tolkien in his edition of Tolkien's *Beowulf* translation,[9] a date supported by his other children; it has been described recently as an example of Tolkien's favorite genre, the "fairy-story."[10] Tolkien was also continuing work at the same time on early versions of *The Silmarillion*. Lang's and Tolkien's simplified versions of the *Volsünga Saga* provide links to both *The Hobbit* and *The Silmarillion*, especially in terms of their treatment of the supernatural. But Tolkien's cosmic frame for his legends, as we shall see shortly, is borrowed from both Old Norse poetry and, in part, William Morris's translation of the saga.

But how do such seemingly incongruous heroes as the abject Volsung Sigurd and the comic Hobbit, Bilbo, in any way relate to one another? And how can both the legend (or story) of Sigurd and the journey of the unheroic Bilbo in "There and Back Again" be said to share the genre of the fairy-story, as Tolkien defines it? Certainly the adventures of each antihero mirror each other in their concern with a magic ring and a dragon, although each protagonist, for reasons antithetical to the heroic, is cast in Tolkienian terms in two different types of fairy-story. Most importantly, Tolkien queers—subverts—his tragic Sigurd-equivalent protagonist by making him finally humble and unassuming, different from a tragic epic hero, but ultimately heroic, despite his limitations and his own diffidence toward heroism. He makes him comic and ordinary.

While Bilbo's comic role in *The Hobbit* may seem obvious to most readers, how the narrative functions as a fairy-story like Andrew Lang's requires some explanation both in relation to Tolkien's essay "On Fairy-Stories" and in terms of his own adaptation of the Volsunga story in *The Legend of Sigurd*, influenced by William Morris's own story of Sigurd. The cosmic frame of the *Völsunga Saga*, with its emphasis on fate and domination by the gods, differs from that of Middle-earth, as presented in *The Silmarillion*, with its crucial emphasis on the choices made by the individual along the way—on free will, in a theological concept borrowed from Christianity. Once this rather complexly layered context is laid out clearly, the ways in which Tolkien both queers Sigurd as Bilbo and subverts the Old Norse saga narrative, as Lang redacted it, will seem more obviously and uniquely Tolkienian, and imbued by his mythology. And in the narrative that Tolkien creates, as a Hobbit who prefers good food and staying at home to adventure and rescue of lost treasure, Bilbo occupies the prototypical Tolkenian queer role of the hero as other—unlikely, unsuitable in all ways, untrained, and absurd.

THE HOBBIT AND THE LEGEND OF SIGURD AS FAIRY-STORY

Even in the earliest manuscripts of his seminal essay on Faërie, Tolkien contextualized the fairy-story within his general concept of magic, which includes a cosmogonic hierarchy of representation. Only one early manuscript, Manuscript A Proper, served as the forerunner to the Andrew Lang Lecture he was invited to deliver at St. Andrews University on 8 March

1939, which he had begun thinking about a year after he had published *The Hobbit* (1937)—likely between December 1938 and March 1939; another represented a later stage in the evolution of the essay as published in 1947. The earliest version of "On Fairy-Stories," known as Draft A, may be the closest in time to the actual Andrew Lang Lecture (of which no copy remains), and, therefore, indicative of Tolkien's earliest intentions. Details of this lecture did appear a few days later in contemporary reviews in the local newspapers, one of which, an anonymous review that appeared in *The Scotsman* (8 March 1939, 9, col. 2), remarks that Tolkien views fairies as "natural," not supernatural; the fact that they die is "their doom" (that is, their fate, or destiny), according to another review in *The St. Andrews Citizen* (March 1939, 4, cols. 3–5).[11]

"Doom," a word drawn from Old English *dōm*, "judgment," "decree," or "law," according to Bosworth-Toller's *Anglo-Saxon Dictionary*, can also denote "free will" or "choice," as in *Beowulf*, line 894, in reference to "þæt hē beāh-hordes brūcan mōste/selfes *dōme*" (that he might enjoy the ring-hoard by his own *free will*) (my emphasis).[12] Interestingly, this line refers to Sigemund, son of Wæls and uncle (and father) of Fitela, who, in the tale recited by Hrothgar's *scop* in celebration of Beowulf's victory over Grendel, valorously kills a dragon and, thereby, wins his treasure-hoard. In fact, he is the Norse hero Sigmundr (Lang's and Tolkien's Sigurd) who was given a magical sword by a god in the *Völsunga Saga*.[13]

"Doom" is also a word Tolkien uses to describe the final outcome of the Elves' journey in *The Silmarillion*, in particular, the unhappy history of the Noldor and the story of Túrin Turambar. And as "free will," doom is a concept that recurs throughout Tolkien's legendarium, logically connected in Roman Catholicism with the consequence of actions that might result in a judgment, but a surprising one to consider in relation to Tolkien's fairies—or Elves. For Tolkien to use this odd word "doom" for fairies, given its connection with *Beowulf*, suggests the mix of ideas he was working through in the same time period. Natural fairies are, in his mind, the same as Elves: and the fairies of "On Fairy-Stories" are actually the Elves of *The Silmarillion*.

Both fairies and elves are earthly, for one thing: according to another news reporter in *The St. Andrews Citizen* reviewing Tolkien's Lang Lecture in 1939, the professor admitted that "stories about Faerie" are "stories concerning *all that realm* which contains many things besides fauns (great or small), besides elves or fairies, dwarfs, witches, giants, or dragons; it holds the sea, and the sun; the moon, the sky, the earth, and they themselves, when they are enchanted."[14] Various accounts of what Tolkien means here by "Faërie" have been offered by critics, usually paraphrases of his complex text in the final publication of his Lang Lecture as "On Fairy-Stories" (1947), or attempts to analyze his own children's stories (that is, stories in which fairies appear), often approached theologically: notably, *Roverandom*, "Leaf by Niggle," *Farmer Giles of Ham*, and *Smith of Wootton Major*.[15] R.J. Reilly and J.S. Ryan first attempted, separately, to position "On Fairy-Stories" as a Coleridgian explanation of the use of the imagination in constructing the Christianized fantasy of *The Lord of the Rings*, given Tolkien's emphasis in his own essay on the eucatastrophe of the Gospel as the fairy-story's ultimate fantasy, escape, recovery, and consolation.[16]

What Tolkien emphasizes in Manuscript B of "On Fairy-Stories" (written during 1943), as in his published version, is something more complex: the notion that "[e]ver fairy-stories as a whole have three faces: the Mystical towards the Supernatural; *the Magical towards Nature*; and the Mirror of scorn and pity towards Man. The essential face of Faërie is the middle one, *the Magical*."[17] What exactly Tolkien means by these three faces is not entirely clear, either in his theorizing or in its applicability to his own fairy-stories. Helpful in elucidating is a line deleted from the final edited version of "On Fairy-Stories" but which appears in the same passage in Manuscript B: "The mystical may be embodied in the magical and the fairy-tale." This line differentiating the mystical from the magical and the fairy-tale is replaced in the final version of the essay by what Tolkien ascribes to George MacDonald in his fairy-tale *The Golden Key*: "The Magical, the fairy-story, may be used as a *Miroir de l'Omme*; and it may (but not so easily) be made a vehicle of Mystery."[18]

Thus, *The Hobbit* may well be considered a fairy-story because many magical creatures and mythical beings appear in it naturally, in "Nature," including trolls, goblins, giant spiders, Beorn the shape-changer, and most especially, the Elves (or fairies). And, as we have seen, the Tolkienian fairy-story as the mirror of pity and scorn turned toward man relates both to *The Hobbit* and the influential Lang *Red Book* tale, specifically in the misuse of a magical ring and the hero's connection with a dragon. The problem is with the third face: the mystical turned toward the supernatural.

What appears missing in Lang's "Story of Sigurd"—but not in Tolkien's *Legend of Sigurd* and *The Hobbit*—is what makes the latter tales true Tolkienian fairy-stories with all three faces, including the third, namely, the "The Mystical Towards the Supernatural." In *The Legend of Sigurd*

Tolkien begins with cosmic mythology from the Old Norse Poetic (Elder) *Edda* to explain the agency of fate and chance through the gods, namely, Ódin, who sets events in place, and the mischief-maker Loki who walks on his left aside. On a slip paper, one of several about his *Lay of Sigurd* (which is mostly about Sigurd and Brynhild), Tolkien describes its unity through "the way in which a willful deed of Loki, the purposeless slaying of Otr, and his ruthless method of extricating Ódin and himself from the peril into which this deed has brought them sets in motion a curse that at the last brings Sigurd to his death."[19] Ódin attempts to grace his hero with a horse and sword as well as a fair bride, all to punish Fáfnir and Regin for demanding a ransom for Otr, which backfires. The story line is nearly identical to that of Lang.

Tolkien's Cosmic Frame in *The Legend of Sigurd* and the Old Norse *Edda*

As Tolkien indicates in his summaries of its sections, chief responsibility for these events and those that follow from them, comes, neither from the Danish king nor from the vengeful smith Regin, as in Lang, but from Loki himself in the Old Norse cosmic overlay from which he borrows: the first of the Edda's poems, the *Völuspá*, known as "the Prophecy of the Sibyl." Originally Codex Regius, the manuscript of the Poetic or Elder Edda (Copenhagen Royal Collection no. 2365.4), contained twenty-nine poems by various poets on many aspects of Old Norse mythology but missing the legend of Sigurd, found instead in the thirteenth-century *Völsunga Saga*. Tolkien's unification of the two parts results in nine sections of the 121-page *Legend of Sigurd* he titles Upphaf, "Beginning." Like many creation myths Tolkien's starts with emptiness and nothingness— "unwrought was Earth,/unroofed was Heaven—/an abyss yawning,/ and no blade of grass."[20] The work of the Great Gods is the building of the world. Why Tolkien does so takes some explaining, by drawing on a number of his own works.

It is true that at the very beginning of the *Legend of Sigurd*, according to the second stanza of the Upphaf (Beginning), ominous signs exist that the "wondrous world" the Great Gods "well builded" might well be threatened by the old "friends of darkness." Thór's hammer, once welded in the forge, may send them off, but a female seer prophesies the possibility of doom for all three of the chief gods, Ódin, Frey, and Thór (the latter, by means of "the deep Dragon"), except that there shall be one deathless, the serpent-slayer and "seed of Óđin," who will prevent the perishing of earth.[21] Indeed, Tolkien remarks that "[T]he whole is given unity as a study of the way in which a willful deed of Loki, the purposeless slaying of Otr, and his ruthless method of extricating Óđin and himself from the peril into which this deed has brought them sets in motion a curse that at the last brings Sigurd to his death."[22] Óđin, "Lord of Gods and Men," is implicated because of his aid in providing Sigurd with a magical horse, weapon, and bride, Brynhild. And Óđin uses Sigurd to punish the whole Hreidmar family for their greed, the three brothers Fáfnir, Regin, and Otr. But Óđin has his own mission: he wishes to ward off the threat of destruction to their rule by gathering in Valhöll "mighty men" who have lived on earth and died—the only ones who can aid him in the Last Battle—especially his "chosen warriors," the Völsungs, of whom Sigurd is to be "chief of all, their leader in the Last Day." Tolkien explains that "Óđin hopes that by his hand the Serpent shall in the end be slain, and a new world made possible."[23]

Óđin's anointing of Sigurd as his chief hero from the beginning is Tolkien's own invention—it does not come from the original Old Norse legend or from Lang's redaction or from William Morris's translation, which he read early on in his life. Tolkien cautions in his legend that Óđin's desire for a special warrior to aid him is matched by the intentions of sinister Loki, who occupies a Morgoth role in Tolkien's legend: "Evil is not, however, to be found only in the ever-watchful host of the Enemies of Gods and Men. It is found also in Ásgard itself in the person of Loki, by whose deeds, willful, merely mischievous, or wholly mischievous, the counsels and hopes of loathing seem ever turned awry or defeated."[24] Strangely, this walker "at the left hand of Óđin" does not openly undermine his efforts or reject any help he might offer, perhaps because, at the god's right hand,

> [T]here walks another figure, a nameless shadow. It would seem that this poet (seeing that the Northern gods represent but written large the ways of Men in the hostile world) has taken this old legend to symbolize man's wisdom and its ever present accompaniment of folly and malice that defeats it, only to bring forth greater heroism and deeper wisdom; while ever at the right hand walks the shadow that is neither Óđin nor Loki but in some aspect Fate, the real story that must be blended of both. Yet Óđin is master of the Three and the final outcome will resemble rather the hope of Óđin than the malice (shorter sighted) of Loki.[25]

In short, Tolkien, always longing for a happy ending, however blended, emphasizes here the "hope of Ódin."

In Tolkien's rather confusing first lay, "Andvari's Gold," based on the Eddaic fragments in the poem "The Lay of Regin,"[26] the scene is set by the roaming through the world of the three Æsir—Ódin, Loki, and Hœnir—who become trapped by Hreidmar and his sons because of Loki's incidental murder of one of them. Loki kills Otr, shaped as an otter hungering for salmon, with a stone, then stripping him of his pelt, while the falls of Andvari splash and the Dwarf Andvari hunts his prey in the form of a pike. The three Æsir, carrying the pelt, unfortunately reach Hreidmar's house and ask for harbor, where Otr's brother Regin creates "rune-written iron" from the fire while the third brother, the dragon Fáfnir, dreams of gold. When Hreidmar and his two sons recognize the pelt as belonging to the third son, this family demands it be filled with gold as a ransom, which Loki obtains by fetching a net from Rán, queen of Ægir; he then uses it to capture gold in the sea along with the pike Andvari and, in particular, a ring belonging to the Dwarf, which he curses. The gold is described by Ódin as the "seed of evil" in stanza twelve. Even Loki anticipates the gold will result in the unfortunate "doom of kings," "fall of queens," and the "end untimely/of Ódin's hope."[27]

Tolkien in the *Legend of Sigurd* focuses in particular on the treasure—as in *The Hobbit*—that which stirs up the human desire to acquire, an avarice that wants to take and hold. This symbol of treasure recurs throughout other medieval poems, chiefly *Beowulf*, in its focus in what Tolkien calls the second half of the "elegy" in his famous essay, wherein the Last Survivor of a tribe buries treasure where only he can find it, except for the dragon who takes it over. This desire for gold is an important part of *The Hobbit*—the retrieval of the Dwarves' treasure from the dragon Smaug by the Hobbit hero, Bilbo—as is the greed of the Dwarves themselves, particularly, Thorin Oakenshield.

But it is also the raison d'être for much of what occurs in all the Völsunga legends and the *Völuspá* prophecies, with which Tolkien chooses to open his *Legend of Sigurd* in his unifying myth as a symbol. In his "Notes on the Poems, by the Author," Tolkien emphasizes in the first part of his *Legend* that the whole work "Begins with an account of the Hoard" (treasure-hoard) (Niblung treasure, as we learn in William Morris's account in his *Völsunga Saga: The Story of the Volsungs and the Niblungs, with Certain Songs from the Elder Edda* [1870], the full title for the saga)[28] and only then moves to the Völsung family and the history of

Sigmund and his sister-wife, Signy, and, later, old Sigmund's son Sigurd. Tolkien follows the lines of Morris's neatly laid-out narrative account of the story, although Tolkien's offers a different explanation for how the twins Sigmund and Signy come to procreate a son together and how Sigmund in his old age will beget Sigurd with Hjørdis, who will become the wife of King Alf in Morris.

The genealogy of Sigurd as descended from Ódin is very clear in Morris: he opens with a helpful table of characters, devoting a chapter at first to the first son of Ódin, Sigi, who begets Rerir, father of Volsung, leading to the important father of Sigurd, Volsung's son Sigmund. It is Sigmund who extracts the sword from the Branstock brought in by Ódin—in disguise as a huge barefoot one-eyed man—and thereby establishes himself as Ódin's choice. This act angers King Siggeir of Gothland, to whom King Volsung has given Signy in marriage. When King Volsung and his sons visit the couple, despite warnings by Signy that her husband plans to kill them, King Volsung is killed and all her brothers are taken captive and eaten by a mysterious she-wolf said to be Siggeir's mother in disguise—all except Sigmund, whom Signy had covered with honey so he could pull out the tongue of the she-wolf and escape. At this point is when the incest between the twins occurs.

While differing versions of Sigurd's ancestry exist, all—Lang's, Tolkien's, William Morris's—notably stress his lineage from Ódin. Morris, unlike Tolkien, conceals the incest between Sigurd's father, Sigmund, and his father's sister Signy in their own persons. Morris's fable of the exchange of bodies between Signy and the cunning witch-wife means that Signy in disguise meets her brother for the several nights she and Sigmund sleep in one bed and their son Sinfjötli is begotten. Through this son, Sigmund hopes to achieve revenge on King Siggeir, which he does by killing two young children of King Siggeir and Signy. However, the children's gold ring from a toy rolls into a place where Sigmund and Sinfjötli lie hidden and so her brother and their son are discovered. However, King Siggeir buries them alive in a barrow, in which Signy has hidden a sword inside pork they use to cut through the stone and burn alive King Siggeir and his men in the hall, an act in which revenge-minded Signy happily joins. Sinfjötli is later poisoned by a woman whose other suitor is the brother of Borghild (the wife of the king), both of whom he has killed to win her. Sigmund drives her away, and old and childless, marries the daughter of King Eylimi: Hjørdis, "the fairest and wisest of womankind," who has chosen him for her husband.[29] Sigmund is eventually killed in battle by a one-eyed man in a blue cloak and slouched hat—Ódin, once again, who wishes to reclaim his sword—the shards of which are bequeathed by Sigmund to his wife for his unborn son, Sigurd.[30] In disguise as her maid, Hjørdis is nevertheless selected as bride by Alf, the son of Hjalprek, the king of Denmark, because of the incriminating gold ring she speaks of, and in that king's house Sigurd grows up much-loved and educated by Regin, the son of Hreidmar.

Tolkien, however, in his *Legend of Sigurd* openly reveals the ghastly backstory of the incest: Signy demands that the "Dwarvish master,/thy doors open!" and Sigmund replies, "In may enter elvish maiden!" but the knowledge of whom it is each sleeps with is dreadful: "Brother and sister/ in a bed lying,/brief love, bitter,/blent with loathing!"[31] The incest here likely reminded him of Kullervo's incest with his sister, which led to their deaths. Indeed, the second section of this *Legend of Sigurd* centers on Signy, followed by the death of her son Sinfjötli in the third, the birth of her son Sigurd in the fourth, and in the last two sections, only the mentoring and deceit by Regin, and the encounter with Brynhild.

Lang's Sigurd as Tolkien's Antihero

At this point, the part of the *Völsunga Saga* upon which Lang, in particular, focuses in his retelling—as does Tolkien, and which Tolkien used as signal in *The Hobbit*—comes into play. Crucial to what Tolkien means by the "fairy-story" in his major essay on the topic is his preference, "without rival," for Lang's *Red Fairy Book* tale of the dragon-slayer and king's son Sigurd.[32] Notably, Lang's headnote to his redaction indicates that details of this unhappy tale of Sigurd were apparently carved into rock by the Danes who did battle with King Alfred and the Anglo-Saxons in the tenth-century England. This inscription must have appealed to Anglo-Saxon professor Tolkien, who had taught *Beowulf* and other courses in Old and Middle English language and literature at Leeds beginning in 1923 and who had finished his partial translation of *Beowulf* (begun in ?1924–1925) in Oxford at the end of April, 1926, according to a letter to scholar Kenneth Sisam.[33] This translation Tolkien wrote around the same time as he was writing *The Hobbit* and his Norse saga, and long before he presented his groundbreaking essay "Beowulf: The Monsters and the Critics" as the Sir Israel Gollancz Lecture in 1936.[34] Most important in this fact of simultaneity is the emphasis in all these works on the desire for treasure by the principals, in Lang's and Morris's story, and in

Tolkien's *Legend* and *Hobbit*—and by old King Beowulf at the end of what Tolkien calls an elegy. The lure of treasure leads all three, Sigurd, Bilbo, and Beowulf, for different reasons, to confront the Dragon (as Death).

How does Lang's fairy-story relate then to both Tolkien's *Legend of Sigurd* and *The Hobbit*? The key magical device is the ring borne by the hero and the key magical adversary in all three is the stingy and homicidal dragon, Fáfnir in one and Smaug in the other, although, along the way, various avaricious dwarves do figure in all the narratives, including Andvari and Thorin. In Lang's "Story of Sigurd" the principal adversary is Regin the smith, as in Tolkien's *Legend*, his magic turned toward selfish ends. In *The Hobbit* the equivalent magician, in contrast, is good Gandalf, whose role allows Tolkien to connect the natural world of faërie with the mythology of the *Silmarillion*, in the "mystical tending towards the supernatural"—a concept that will be examined later.

In Lang's "Story of Sigurd," the magic ring and the dragon are both connected in the narrative and in the genealogy with Sigurd's tutor, Regin, an agent apparently supplied by the Danish king who had captured Sigurd's mother, a queen in her own right. This smith, sword-maker and magician, helps to arm Sigurd but also plans on betraying him to retrieve his own lost treasure. Regin tells Sigurd to ask the king for a horse—the magical horse, Grani, "swift as the wind"—which the hero in fact obtains from an old man in the forest—likely Ódin, the god of the north—because Grani comes from the breed of Sleipnir, Ódin's horse. After some unsuccessful attempts at crafting a sword on his own for Sigurd, Regin at the hero's request next forges together the broken sword of Sigurd's father for the hero to use in killing the dragon, who guards a gold treasure. Regin explains that the dragon Fáfnir must be killed because this hoard belonged to Regin's own father and that the dragon is actually the smith's metamorphosed brother, who murdered their father for the gold. Another unnamed figure—the killer of the third brother—had provided the gold as legal recompense for having slain Regin's second brother, Otr, for his pelt when he had assumed the shape of an otter to swim and lie in the sun. Unfortunately, because this killer had also wrongfully stolen all this gold from the dwarf Andvari (rather than just a peltfull, to pay the ransom, including one last ring), the dwarf had cursed both the gold and his last ring.

Lang's protagonist Sigurd apparently misses the real point of the magician's tale—the curse of the gold and its role in the story of the downfall of the brothers—for after he defeats the dragon Fáfnir, ill-fortune in magical form dogs him throughout the tale. After he cleverly hides with his sword in a deep pit beneath Fáfnir as he moves to drink and thrusts it into his heart, the dying dragon curses him and anyone else who holds the gold. When Regin tells him to roast Fáfnir's heart so he can taste it and Sigurd accidentally touches it, then licks his finger, he is empowered to understand the speech of woodpeckers, who tell him he should himself taste the heart and become all-wise. They also tell him not to trust Regin, who will betray him; to cut off Regin's head and keep all the gold; and then ride to where a maiden lies sleeping, whom he will awaken. Sigurd accomplishes this by seizing from the dragon's treasure a magical gold helmet, the Helm of Dread, which makes its wearer invisible, and, with his magical horse, leaps over the flames to rescue her: the warrior maid Brynhild. Enchanted for displeasing the god Óðin, Brynhild has vowed to marry a fearless man, who turns out to be Sigurd. Unfortunately, without thinking Sigurd gives her the magic ring cursed by the dwarf.

This paradigm presents a mirror of human weakness in the hero, Sigurd, and other men. It also manifests the supernatural, namely, in the unexplained peril to Sigurd, who is only partly aided by divine mentors. Whether treasure or ring, gold leads to death. And so Brynhild is similarly cursed, for, after Sigurd rides away, he meets and marries Gudrún, a king's daughter who falls in love with him and, with the aid of her mother's magical cup of drugs, induces him to forget Brynhild. Worse, when Gudrún's brother Gunnar magically exchanges shapes with Sigurd to leap over the flames and thereby win Brynhild's hand in marriage, Brynhild, thinking Sigurd has forgotten her, returns to Sigurd the ring of Andvari for his wife, Gudrún. Unfortunately, when Brynhild irritates Gudrún by bragging about the superiority she has gained by means of Gunnar's alleged act of heroism, Gudrún reveals to her the truth about Gunnar's ruse. Mourning the loss of the true hero Sigurd, Brynhild then tells Gunnar she knows the truth about his deceit and feeds Gunnar's younger brother a magical dish that maddens him to the point that he tries to kill Sigurd with a sword—although Sigurd, before he dies, also kills him. In grief, both Sigurd's horse, Grani, and Brynhild die.

Tolkien's version of *The Legend of Sigurd and Gudrún* includes nine parts that follow the Upphaf: on Andvari's Gold, Signy, The Death of Sinfjötli, and Sigurd Born, Regen, Brynhild, Gudrún, Brynhild Betrayed, and Strife. But because this chapter focuses on *The Hobbit*, only the first five apply; the last four parts, on Brynhild and Gudrún in *The Legend of Gudrún*, will be discussed in chapter 7, on women in Tolkien. In his

Legend of Sigurd, he begins with the appropriate backstory in "Andvari's Gold," but then moves to events leading up to Sigurd's birth, namely, the incest between Signy and Sigmund, the death of their son, Sinfjötli, the birth of Sigurd to Sigmund and Sigrlinn, the role of Regin, and then the additional misfortunes that follow on Sigurd and the two women he loves—or who love him—Brynhild, and Gudrún, ending with Brynhild Betrayed, and Strife.

Tolkien's alliterative verse supplies character motivations that help explain the overall narrative, although often details are occluded in the attempt to make short-lined stanzas brief. His version, in its unique humanization, makes Sigurd—alone and abject, like Kullervo—more sympathetic. Once more Tolkien projects himself into this lonely orphan when Fáfnir asks him, "What man begot thee?" (5.30) and Sigurd replies, "As the wolf I walk/wild and lonely,/no father owning/a flame bearing" (5.31). Sigurd's advent and the Völsunga genealogy that comes before, while Morris-like in its attention to family history, bear the mark of Old Norse fate and Loki-interference with the plans of Óđin that Tolkien drew from the *Prose Edda*.

In "Andvari's Gold," an etiological tale about how animals once were gods—Otr the otter hunting salmon, the Dwarf Andvari as a pike, and the dragon Fáfnir transformed by evil deeds, Tolkien makes explicit the original gods' influence on human misfortune, beginning with the first stanza, when Óđin, Loki, and Hœnir walk together at "the world's beginning." The stone that fells Otr in Lang, hurled by "someone," in Tolkien is attributed to Loki "loosing evil" (1.4). These three beg lodging from Hreidmar, but the pelt is recognized by Hreidmar as Regin makes iron marked by runes while Fáfnir sleeps by the fire and he asks for ransom from the "folk of Ásgard." Easy it is for Loki to turn to the sea and obtain a net "noosed with evil" from Rán, queen of Ægir (1.7), which he uses to scoop up Andvari's gold, including the ring, the only gold the Dwarf curses. "Bane it bringeth/to brethren two; /seven princes slays; /sword it kindles—/end untimely/of Óđin's hope" (1.10). Tolkien suggests how Loki always undermines Óđin's plan; he also introduces as sole cause a ring, like the one in *The Hobbit* and in *The Lord of the Rings*, one similarly cursed. Indeed, Óđin reminds Hreidmar that the gold he is granted is "a god's random" but "seed of evil" (1.12) and cursed. The folly of Hreidmar is to ignore the god's pronouncement: Sauron-like he claims, "Redgolden rings/I will rule alone," because he believes they are healing (1.15).

The second and third parts of Tolkien's *Legend of Sigurd*, following William Morris's Old Norse translation rather than Lang's redaction, detail Sigurd's genealogy beginning with Ódin, Rerir's grandfather, followed by Völsung, who marries a Valkyrie and begets the twins Sigmund (Sigurd's father) and foresighted Signy. The latter (Sigurd's aunt) is married unwillingly to King Siggeir of Gautland to knit peace. But Siggeir kills Signy's father and imprisons her ten brothers, all of whom are killed by wolves except Sigmund, who survives by pretending to be a "dwarfish smith" in a cave. Signy's vengeance is to sleep in the form of an "elvish maiden" with her brother and bear a son, Sinfjötli, who resembles her father, Völsung. Tolkien makes clear "Brother and sister/in a bed lying,/ brief love, bitter,/blent with loathing!" (2.31). The sword that Sigmund once drew was taken from Siggeir so the father and son could kill giants. After Sigmund and his son vanquish the Gauts, Sigmund calls Signy, saying they are avenged, but she prefers to die with Siggeir. In the third part, on "The Death of Sinfjötli," father and son kill seven kings, their joy but brief, because a queen whose husband was slain by Sinfjötli and then married to Sigmund poisons his son with beer (3.9–10). As Sigmund bears his body over the way to Valhöllu the boy's grandfather, Völsung, greets them, while awaiting still "the World's chosen"—Sigurd (3.13).

In the fourth and fifth parts, "Sigurd Born" and "Regin," Tolkien combines Morris's *Völsunga Saga* with Lang's emphasis on Regin the smith, returning to "Andvari's Gold" in an end-circle that unifies the *Legend of Sigurd*. Sigurd is born to the aged king Sigmund and the young, blond Sigrlinn, the "bride of Ódin" who apparently wishes to bear "the World's chosen" in Sigmund's bed (4.4). Yet, Sigmund raises his sword Grímnir, it shatters, and he falls in battle, while a strange warrior, "one-eyed, awful," also huge and silent, stays him—fate stepping in once more. Sigrlinn crosses the sea as a bondwoman, bearing a son, and Tolkien, picking up the beginning of Lang's tale in its description of Sigurd's mother married to a Danish king who sends her son to the tutor Regin, returns to the beginning of the saga.

Tolkien's Regin fosters Sigurd (William Morris in his adaptation describes the smith as a "foster-father"),[35] but he also, Loki-like, entices him to kill Fáfnir after telling him about the hoard that the dragon guards: as in Lang, by using Gram the sword and Grani the horse (who is minded by an old "hoar-bearded" man). Because Regin is the dragon's brother and Fáfnir has killed their father, Hreidmar, Regin believes that brothers should share "in brother's ransom" (5.12), even though he has promised it to Sigurd. Sigurd is as heedless and trusting (if not as foolish) as Lang's Sigurd. He dismisses Fáfnir's warning about the curse on the gold, which the dragon declares "gleams with evil," because he attributes the curse of the dragon to the serpent's greed (at the time not knowing Regin and Fáfnir are brothers). When Regin announces to Sigurd that in killing Fáfnir he has killed Regin's brother, and that Regin's smithing of his sword was responsible for Sigurd's success, Sigurd ignores the words of threat from Regin, whom he deems guilt-stricken. Where he learns is from touching his greasy finger to his tongue by accident as he roasts Fáfnir's heart for Regin and suddenly understands birds' speech. The birds offer him pieces of advice different from those Lang list: to eat the entire heart, leaving nothing for the "dwarvish smith" (5.39, 43); to keep all the gold instead of letting his "foe" free and sharing gold with him (5.44); and to cut off his head because "Vengeance he vows for brother" (5.45). So Sigurd kills Regin, who is heading for him with hate in his eyes; he takes the Helm of Horror from the treasure, and he rides to Hindarfell, on the way to which, guided by the birds, he hears about the disobedient Valkyrie Brynhild (who will be discussed in chapter 7).

THE ABJECT HERO: TOLKIEN'S BILBO IN *THE HOBBIT*

The Hobbit splits into two parts Sigurd's adventure involving a cursed ring and treasure: what in one story is cursed and unfortunate in Tolkien's version becomes lucky, magical, and providential. In *The Hobbit*, instead of the Old Norse concept of fate or an eye-for-an-eye tribal code of vengeance that governs events, as it does in the Old Testament and in "The Story of Sigurd," it is luck (or chance), along with Bilbo's own free will, coupled with a lively intelligence and a developing valor as hero, plus a form of Middle-earth providence—universal goodness—that works most benevolently for Bilbo. Whatever luck this Hobbit has—despite his minor flaws as a hero—ultimately aids the diverse and divided communities of Middle-earth.

Certainly from Lang's legend Tolkien borrows the concept of the flawed (or abject) hero for *The Hobbit*, similar to Kullervo in his "Story of Kullervo," and Fëanor and Túrin Turambar in *The Silmarillion*.[36] As heroes, Lang's Sigurd and Bilbo share an ancestry that includes the possibility of nobility, by blood or by heroism, definitely, in Sigurd's case and, less so, in Bilbo's. Sigurd's mother not only descended from kings but she possessed an inner nobility signified by her own magic ring, different from the ring Sigurd obtains from the dragon's hoard. Her magic ring set her apart from her maid, with whom she switched clothing as a disguise before their capture by a king; despite her subterfuge, by means of her ring he identified her as aristocratic. In Bilbo's case, as in his distant cousin Frodo's later on, what "nobility" he has—the nobility of the Fallohide Hobbits—he has inherited from his Took mother. Bilbo's mother and Frodo's grandmother were Took sisters, descended from the Took line that Took of Great Smials had founded, with Isengrim II representing the tenth Thain of the line: Bilbo's mother, Belladonna Took, was the fourth daughter of Gerontius (the "Old") Took (son of the nobly named Fortinbras I and grandson to Ferumbras II, himself the lone brother of the heroic "Bullroarer," or Bandobras, Took). Frodo's mother, Primula Brandybuck, was herself mothered by the youngest daughter of Old Took, who had married a Brandybuck, which makes Bilbo Frodo's cousin.[37] But, of course, both Frodo and Bilbo are Bagginses, their paternal surname reflective of their ancestors' bourgeois (and materialistic) natures.[38] Tolkien, drawing from the original Old Norse idea of Sigurd as ultimately descended from Óðin, creates a genealogy for the Hobbit Bilbo that makes Gandalf's choice of a hero more credible. Gandalf thought of unlikely Bilbo for an adventure because of the wizard's familiarity with and knowledge of the Fallohide branch of the Hobbits and because of his previous experiences with Bilbo's heroic ancestor, "Bullroarer" Took.

Even given this mixed ancestry, at the beginning of *The Hobbit*, Bilbo is neither an established hero nor the burglar for whom the dwarves have been searching. Instead, Bilbo likes to stay at home and smoke tobacco, and he loathes adventures: "Nasty disturbing uncomfortable things!" Bilbo says; "Makes you late for dinner! I can't think what anybody sees in them" (*The Hobbit*, 6). Yet Gandalf correctly suspects that Bilbo will be a good adventurer (contrary to the Hobbit's own low opinion of adventures) because the Hobbit's curiosity about the world outside derives from his grandfather on his mother's side. The "Old Took" was a Hobbit leader, like the other Tooks in this family (their Thainship was hereditary), and adventuresome, unlike most Hobbits. The Tooks, with their Fallohide Hobbit blood, belonged to the smaller strain of Hobbits that originated in the north, in the upper Anduin, lived in trees and loved forests, traveled and had adventures, and were taller, thinner, and more fair and more artistic than the less noble Hobbit strains, the Harfoots and, the least noble of all, the Stoors; the Tooks also associated with the Elves (a typology later described by Tolkien in the prologue to *The Lord of the Rings*).[39] In contrast to the Fallohide Hobbits, the Harfoots, the most common branch of the three and the most typically "Hobbitish," representing a middle strain, were darker and smaller, browner, and friendlier with dwarves; they also liked hills. The least of the Hobbits, the Stoors—Gollum is a Stoor—came from the south, were heavier and often bearded, occasionally wore boots, liked boating and fishing, and were friends with men.

Through his gifted ancestry Bilbo relates to Sigurd, a hero graced with the horse of the Norse god Ódin who reforges the broken sword of his dead father and slays Fáfnir the dragon in an act that, in effect, reaffirms the hero's noble ancestry. How do Bilbo's two major feats—with Gollum and the dragon—despite his lack of a reforged broken sword or horse of Ódin—illustrate Sigurd-like (magical) virtues or powers? Sigurd kills Fáfnir by hiding underneath the dragon and thrusting his father's sword into his vulnerable underbelly. If we focus on the two major monstrous adversaries whom Bilbo confronts during his adventure, Gollum and the dragon (and dwarves), it will be clear how magic works, ultimately, as a force for goodness. Chapter 6, "Riddles in the Dark," is the focal point for Bilbo's meeting with what might be called the "Dark Hobbit"—Gollum—(later described by Tolkien as representative of the Stoor strain of Hobbit-kind), just as chapters 12 and 13, "Inside Information" and "Not at Home," function as the equivalent for Bilbo's signal adventure with the dragon (and dwarves). In each confrontation, a magical ring figures; in each, Bilbo succeeds partly because of his own individual skills and his own Hobbitness and partly because of what appears to be luck; in each, it is some goodness in him and in the universe that is ultimately responsible for the mystical overturning of its opposite.

Further, in each work the "monstrous adversary" may be understood as representing Tolkien's "magical towards Nature." Gollum as a Hobbit has been likened by Bonniejean Christiansen to the oversized manlike Grendel in *Beowulf*, one of the epic poem's two major monsters fought by heroic Beowulf, the other being a dragon—like Smaug.[40] Gollum (as we learn later in *The Lord of the Rings*) killed his cousin Déagol to gain his ring, which works magically through the power that Sauron the Maia (the Necromancer in *The Hobbit*, presumably) invested in it to master the bearer's will and to distort his judgment (Gollum was also tortured while imprisoned by Sauron, which presumably distorted his physical as well as his spiritual being). Bilbo's second major adversary, the dragon Smaug guarding his stolen dwarf treasure at the Lonely Mountain, is not a mythical creature, nor were the dragons in medieval and modern texts with which Tolkien was familiar from boyhood on and about which, as a medievalist, he wrote in his most famous, much reprinted scholarly article, "Beowulf: The Monsters and the Critics," which so influenced their creation in his fiction.[41] Like the avaricious Gollum and the dwarves, and like the dragon of *Beowulf* and Fáfnir of the *Völsunga Saga*, the treasure-hoarding Smaug also represents a natural creation; conquering them, in a more figurative way, symbolizes the quelling of those monstrous equivalents in the hero.

In this respect, even though Bilbo does resemble Sigurd initially in his noble ancestry and determination, courage, and luck, he also mirrors him, at least initially, as an abject (or ignoble and flawed) hero. Heedless Sigurd may be guilty of avarice and pride in continuing on to kill Fáfnir even after Regin warns him of the curse on the dwarf's treasure, but while Bilbo ultimately is not guilty of either, he is also not heroic in any conventionally recognizable way. Initially he keeps Gollum's ring, even though he knows that Gollum has lost just such an object and does not tell him (in Catholic terms, a sin of omission), and later on, he steals the Arkenstone from the dragon's treasure, allegedly to return to the dwarves (a sin of commission). Thematically, in both fairy-stories it is envy, avarice, and wrath (three of the deadly sins) as well as the chief deadly sin, pride, that lead to the downfall of Gollum, or the "Dark Hobbit," the dragon Smaug, and Thorin the dwarf-king.

But one might say these same sins—especially avarice and pride of life—initially seduce Bilbo: in the tunnel the Hobbit does not tell Gollum he has found his ring because he fears for his life. Further, in the confrontation with the dragon, when Smaug questions how he plans to carry a fourteenth of the treasure back to Hobbiton, what works upon Bilbo to convince him to steal the easily portable Arkenstone is a paranoid fear that he is a laughingstock: "Now a nasty suspicion began to grow in his mind—had the dwarves forgotten this important point too, or were they laughing at him all the time?" (*The Hobbit*, 202).

Of course, during that same conversation with Smaug, perceptive Bilbo has enough presence of mind to notice how proud Smaug is, particularly of his strength, which leads him to ask the dragon, timorously, about the legendary soft underbelly dragons are reputed to have (a feature also key to Fáfnir's defeat by Sigurthr in the Edda). While Smaug arrogantly denies having any such underbelly, when he responds to Bilbo's flattery he inadvertently shows off the bare hollow of his left breast exposed to view (*The Hobbit*, 204). Fortunate Bilbo, as a true hero in Tolkien's fairy-story—someone who acts nobly and charitably and is not merely semi-divine or descended from noble ancestors—finds the ring of invisibility that Gollum believes has been "stolen" from him, but which twice saves the Hobbit's life, so that Bilbo retrieves the treasure stolen from the dwarves by the dragon Smaug (and, more figuratively, from Bilbo by the dwarves).

A magic ring that the hero acquires plays a role in *The Hobbit* in two crucial episodes, one by chance, involving Gollum, and one by intention, the latter involving the dragon, Smaug (there is no Gudrún equivalent in *The Hobbit*). The first episode occurs in chapter 5, "Riddles in the Dark," when Bilbo finds a ring—"a turning point in his career, but he did not know it" (*Hobbit*, 64)—and, while he engages in a riddling contest with Gollum whose outcome will determine whether Bilbo will live or die, at a significant juncture it *accidentally* slips upon his finger to render him invisible. Bilbo escapes from Gollum, but not before Gollum happens to ask what has "it got in its pocketses?" And Bilbo also asks himself, "What have I, I *wonder*?," a word perhaps chosen by Tolkien to emphasize the magic involved in the providential answer to the question, for, at the moment that Bilbo puts his hand in his pocket, "The ring felt very cold as it *quietly slipped on* to his groping finger" (*The Hobbit*, 77; my emphases).

The second narrative event that involves a magic ring used against an unusual adversary is split into two related ventures in chapter 12. In the first venture, "Inside Information," Bilbo slips it on to sneak into the dragon's lair at night to conceal himself from the sleeping Smaug and then steals a cup as a proof of his success. In the second venture, in the same chapter, after the ire of Smaug about the theft has become apparent and the dwarves are trapped in the mountain recesses without escape, he puts it on to become invisible and see what Smaug is up to. Ironically, the magic ring is unnecessary on both visits—in the first, because Smaug is gone, and in the second, because visual concealment does not in fact matter to the dragon, whose olfactory sense is exceedingly acute: he smells the Hobbit. Nor does the magic ring matter to Bilbo: it is during this second visit that he cleverly tricks Smaug into revealing the bare spot on his left breast—a "treasure" that will lead to the dragon's later downfall.

In contrast to the "Story of Sigurd," and to underscore the nature of "the Mystical tending towards the Supernatural" in *The Hobbit*, the magic ring does not even matter in Bilbo's third visit to the dragon's lair, in chapter 13, "Not at Home," when, after the desperate dwarves have been locked within for many days and Smaug has blocked the upper door to the tunnel, Bilbo offers to finish his job and "burgle" dwarf treasure stolen by Smaug if they will accompany him to help carry it. However, because the dragon is absent this time, it is initially (and ironically) provident that light instead of invisibility matters because Bilbo's blindness in the dark—literal and figurative—means that he has to depend on the dwarves instead of himself to retrieve a light and then to guide them all out through the palace into the open air at the opposite end from the tunnel. But in the moment, Bilbo's magical invisibility becomes necessary from his perspective as subterfuge for his deceit, to conceal from the dwarves the theft of the precious Arkenstone, part of the treasure he has promised them. The Hobbit, now truly a burglar, knows that "trouble would yet come of it," for this "payment" for his services would far exceed what the dwarves meant to pay him (*The Hobbit*, 213).

Surely Tolkien does not intend for the Arkenstone to be equivalent symbolically to the ring of Sigurd in Lang's fairy-story, even though Sigurd's ring originally stolen from the dwarf Andvari—like the Arkenstone that the dragon wrongfully stole previously from the dwarves—is part of stolen treasure. Representing what Bilbo considers payment for his services as a burglar, it eventually provides a solution to the man–dwarf enmity when he chooses to give it away to Bard, man of Dale, primarily because it signifies the sovereignty that Thorin believes has been stolen from him and, therefore, comes to represent a bargaining chip. The dwarves' apparent avarice poses a problem only for Bard, not, ultimately, for Bilbo, because at the end the Hobbit keeps only two small treasure chests. But at that moment it is Bilbo who seems to resemble the cursed hero Sigurd.

THE FAIRY-STORY AS MYTHMAKING: *THE SILMARILLION* STEPS IN

Apparently Tolkien's "hybrid story" of *The Hobbit*, when it was finally finished, was, as Dimitra Fimi has hinted, also "inseparably linked with Tolkien's mythology."[42] As such, *The Hobbit* constitutes a pivot in the middle between both early and later works, on which his mythology later came to be balanced. Certainly Tolkien himself acknowledged, when he was questioned about *The Hobbit*'s sources, in a letter published in the *Observer* on 20 February 1938, that *The Hobbit* derived from "epic, mythology, and fairy-story."[43] Further, in that same letter even though Tolkien identified as its "most valued" source the Anglo-Saxon epic *Beowulf*—"though it was not consciously present to the mind in the process of writing, in which the episode of the theft arose naturally (almost inevitably) from the circumstances"—he affirmed that "[m]y tale is not consciously based on any other book—save one, and that is unpublished: the 'Silmarillion,' a history of the Elves, to which frequent allusion is made." *The Hobbit*, then, represents both a legendary epic, or what might be termed, in Tolkien's words, the "lesser in contact with the earth," which appears to "draw splendor" from what he labels the "large and cosmogonic," meaning the "romantic fairy-story."[44] The concept is one of a double-genred fiction, one that implies a reading of the work specifically as both Northern epic and romantic fairy-story, and imbued by Tolkien's own mythology.

In the Andrew Lang lecture Tolkien presented at St. Andrews University as "Fairy Stories" on 8 March 1939, he offered his most elaborate theoretical statement about fairy-tales. The lecture followed the publication of his famous *Beowulf* lecture, in 1937, and *The Hobbit*, a year later, in 1937, suggesting that when he penned the lecture, he had already worked through his major ideas about the Old English epic and the so-called children's story, however touched by his work on *Beowulf*, had jelled. Interestingly, Tolkien asserts in his essay "On Fairy-Stories" that much of his own fiction serves primarily as "fairy-stories" and, on that basis, he considers himself as a mythmaker. Certainly fairy-tale scholars such as Jack Zipes have argued for the important social and political role fairy-tales have played since the eighteenth century, as vehicles for ideology and the shaping of manners and mores, despite their later Victorian role as entertainment for children.[45] Scholars have recently begun to explore Tolkien's interest in the late nineteenth-century fairy-tale compilations of Jacob and Wilhelm Grimm and other Victorian storytellers,[46] as well as in the mythmaking of Elias Lönnrot in his epic collection of tales, the *Kalevala*, and in Tolkien's own translation of the Finnish story of Kullervo.[47]

Tolkien's early interest in fairies in children's stories—one that includes the variations to *The Lord of the Rings* and *The Silmarillion* in *The History of Middle-earth*—has been helpfully charted by Fimi in terms of the stages of Tolkien's development as a mythmaker. What she concludes is that "Tolkien's route from fairies to elves shows the evolution of his creative imagination."[48] The problem comes with *The Hobbit*: during his composition of *The Lord of the Rings* much later, the incongruities between the two works—specifically involving the nature and origin of the Ring and the role of Gollum in *The Hobbit* chapter titled "Riddles in the Dark"—necessitated a second edition of *The Hobbit* in 1951.[49]

As a result of this hybridity, "rifts created in Tolkien's ever-evolving legendarium by the publication of *The Hobbit*" emerged, as Fimi also has noted: namely, Tolkien's fairies metamorphosed into Elves, even though, for Tolkien working on *The Hobbit* and *The Lord of the Rings*, "Hobbits became the 'mediators' to Middle-earth."[50] Clearly the Elves themselves, as the mythological heirs to Victorian fairies, remained "still the agents of Tolkien's spiritual concerns" in *The Lord of the Rings* and *The Silmarilliad*, even as they reflect a signal transformation in his mythmaking. Tolkien's first writings on what became cosmogonic (Númenórean) mythology had originated still earlier, in what became the posthumously published *Silmarillion* (and other related material begun after World War I, in 1918, and written and revised throughout Tolkien's life, now available in *The Book of Lost Tales* and *The History of Middle-earth*).[51] By around 1926 Tolkien had worked out "The Earliest 'Silmarillion'" of twenty-eight pages, which he continued revising until 1930.[52]

In *The Hobbit*, Tolkien provides his own mythological analogue through detail drawn from *The Silmarillion* to describe Gandalf as an agent of Manwë. The role of Gandalf as a magician who appears to engineer the adventure for Bilbo in response to righting a moral and legal injustice to the community and the cosmos—the theft of the dwarves' treasure by Smaug—explains specifically how providence works through luck or chance and fate. If Lang's smith Regin metamorphoses in *The Hobbit* into the important figure of Gandalf the magician, Gandalf is, nevertheless, in no way evil or treacherous toward Bilbo. More like Ódin, as Marjorie J. Burns has argued,[53] the wizard represents in many ways the agent of divine forces that Tolkien believes derives from the gods, or God—enabling this fairy-story, not only as a mirror of nature but also as a narrative that delineates the workings of the loftier "Mystical towards the Supernatural." The power that Gandalf exerts to help Bilbo eventually broadens to include all the dwarves and then the forces of good—men, dwarves, Elves—as they fight the Goblins in the Battle of Five Armies, settled by the arrival of the Eagles.

It is true that, from the very beginning, events of *The Hobbit* seem to happen by chance, luck, or accident. Although Gandalf has told the dwarves that they are likely to find a good burglar at the Hobbit-hole of Bilbo Baggins in the Shire, whose door Gandalf has marked with a sign, in fact, Gandalf does not know Bilbo at all and has not visited Hobbiton since the Old Took (Bilbo's grandfather) died (*The Hobbit*, 5). The narrator even tells us that this first meeting between Gandalf and Bilbo occurs "By some curious *chance* one morning long ago in the quiet of the world, when there was less noise and more green, and the Hobbits were still numerous and prosperous" (*The Hobbit*, 5; my emphasis). And yet, the meeting does *not* occur by chance: Gandalf the wizard is instrumental in intervening here at this moment: he confesses that "I am looking for someone to share in an adventure that I am arranging, and it's very difficult to find anyone" (*The Hobbit*, 6). His initial intervention, significantly, happens "in the quiet of the world"—what is described as a "first moment," or point of origin, not like any later time, especially given the fact that Gandalf actually does not reappear in the second half of the story for some time.

From the moment Bilbo meets Gandalf and, thereafter, as Bilbo recalls, Gandalf possesses considerable magical skills—given his nature as a wizard—as exercised in Bilbo's various adventures up to his meeting with Beorn the shape-changer in chapter 7, "Queer Lodgings." Early on Bilbo remembers that Gandalf had given Old Took two "magic diamond studs that fastened themselves and never came undone till ordered," had told "wonderful tales ... about dragons and goblins and giants and the rescue of princesses and the unexpected luck of widows' sons" and devised marvelous pyrotechnics for the Hobbits (*The Hobbit*, 7). Bilbo also recalls that Gandalf had been responsible for "many quiet lads and lasses going off into the Blue for mad adventures" (*The Hobbit*, 7). Not only will Gandalf help awaken the love of the unknown in Bilbo merely by bringing into his life the thirteen song-singing dwarves who knock on his door in response to Gandalf's "queer sign" (*The Hobbit*, 8), Gandalf also uses his authority with the dwarves to convince them that this "excitable little fellow" is "one of the best" in his ferocity—"as fierce as a dragon" (*The Hobbit*, 17).

Further, during the first seven chapters, Gandalf "rescues" Bilbo when his training as a hero is jeopardized by some fearsome magical adversary—for example, in chapter 2, "Roast Mutton," when the Trolls threaten to eat him *and* the dwarves—Gandalf throws his voice to sound like a Troll and divert them into a quarrel until the sun rises and they turn to stone. Gandalf with his sword and wand also rescues them from the Goblins (Orcs) in chapter 4, "Over Hill and Under Hill," and he lights pine-cones in chapter 6, "Out of the Frying-Pan into the Fire," to ward off the Wargs of the Misty Mountains, with the resultant fires catching the notice of the Eagles, who rescue them all from the Goblins joining the Wargs. After the sojourn at Beorn's "queer lodgings," Gandalf departs so that Bilbo can hone his newly acquired valor as a thief until the wizard returns after the Battle of Five Armies, in chapter 18, "The Return Journey."

Gandalf is, in fact, an Istar, a Quenya word for "wizard," according to "The Istari," which Tolkien wrote in 1954 while compiling an unfinished index for *The Lord of the Rings*, published later in *Unfinished Tales*.⁵⁴ Five chiefs of this order with knowledge of the history of the world and its nature functioned as emissaries from the Valar, the Lords of the West, incarnated in men's bodies that aged but did not die. These five included the head wizard, the White Messenger, Curunír (Saruman), or "The Man of Craft," who was skilled in "works of hand" and adept at uncovering secrets; two in sea-blue who went into the East and never returned; one in earth-brown, Radagast, "tender of beasts," who lived among the birds and beasts; and one in gray, the wisest of all but also bearing a staff, Gandalf, or Mithrandír the Gray Pilgrim, Enemy of Sauron. To Gandalf, Círdan, master of the Grey Havens, had entrusted the Third Elven ring, Narya the Red.⁵⁵ A wanderer, Gandalf had neither wealth nor followers and helped all those in need. Known also as "Olórin" to the Valar, this lover of the Eldar was sent to Middle-earth by the Vala Manwë, just as Vala Yavanna, wife of Aulë, had asked Curumo (Saruman) to take Aiwendil (Radagast) there.⁵⁶ Appearing in the Third Age in "shapes weak and humble," the Istari were told to "advise and persuade men and Elves to good, and to seek to unite in love and understanding all those whom Sauron, should he come again, would endeavor to dominate and corrupt."⁵⁷

Each of the chief wizards in "The Istari" corresponds to a Vala or Valar: "Olórin" (Gandalf) to Manwë and his wife Varda; Curumo (Saruman) to Aulë; Aiwendil (Radagast) to Yavanna; and Alatar (a blue wizard) to Oromë, as well as to Pallando (the second blue wizard), but—as Christopher Tolkien acknowledges, this latter "replaces Pallando to Mandos and Nienna."⁵⁸ These wizards, elsewhere in Tolkien's notes in "The Istari," are identified as Maiar, like the godlike Valar in the hierarchy of being on Middle-earth, "persons of the 'angelic' order, though not necessarily of the same rank. The Maiar were 'spirits,' but capable of self-incarnation, and could take 'humane' (especially Elvish) forms ... Now these Maiar were sent by the Valar at a crucial moment in the history of Middle-earth to enhance the resistance of the Elves of the West, greatly outnumbered by those of the East and South."⁵⁹ Tolkien also adds in "The Istari" that many of the "Faithful" in later days believed that Gandalf "was the last appearance of Manwë himself, before his final withdrawal to the watchtower of Taniquetil."⁶⁰

What Tolkien means by the "magical" face of Faërie in his created world, then, results from the supernatural power of the gods—the Valar and the Maiar. This definition of the divine becomes clearer when he distinguishes between magical and scientific operations—the latter, called "mechanisms"—in a passage found in the Manuscript B Miscellaneous Pages of "On Fairy-Stories."[61] Magical power derives from the created world, but its operations differ from scientific operations, despite their often similar appearance: "Magic [sic] does not come from outside the world. Magic is the special use (real, imagined, or pretended) of powers that, though they must derive ultimately from God, are inherent in the created world, exterior to God."[62] An example of this phenomenon occurs in *The Hobbit* when the thrush knocks a snail against the secret stone door barring the entrance to the Lonely Mountain at the exact moment the sun sets and sends a ray of light pinpointing the keyhole, allowing Bilbo to open it magically with the key brought by the Dwarves so they may enter the tunnel (*The Hobbit*, 190). This magical incident forms an exact parallel to the fateful incident in the "Story of Sigurd" when Sigurd accidentally licks the blood of the dragon and magically understands the woodpeckers' prophecy that reveals Regin's perfidious intentions toward him.

In *The Silmarillion* Tolkien fantastically historicizes his discussion of faërie as a "perilous realm" in which magic is natural and derives from God, namely, Eru the One, or Ilúvatar. In the first chapter of Tolkien's *Silmarillion*, "Ainulindäle," a hierarchy of beings derives from the one God, as part of him, a figure whose nature Flieger has described as Neoplatonic.[63] Ilúvatar offers a vision, a new World in which the Music contains each Ainur's being and, as well, Ilúvatar's own: "no theme may be played that hath not its uttermost source in me, nor can any alter the music in my despite. For he that attempteth this shall prove but mine instrument in the devising of things more wonderful, which he himself hath not imagined."[64] As part of the third theme, in extension of himself and all earlier beings as his thoughts, Ilúvatar creates the Children of the World (the Elves and Men) to people his cosmos of Arda, the Earth.[65] To each part of Arda—air, water, earth—Ilúvatar sends the Imperishable Flame, so that the world might exist as Eä, and along with the Flame, any Ainur who wish to go there. Those Ainur who go become the Valar, the Powers of the World, otherwise known as "gods," Tolkien declares.[66]

These gods and their queens, the Valier, are fourteen in number and hierarchize different powers of the Earth and its regions and inhabitants.[67] The four elements of Middle-earth, fire, air, water, and earth, are neatly linked with the hierarchy in this chain of being, beginning with the

Valar and continuing with the two kinds of Elves, the Quendi, with its three races, and the Avari. Highest on earth are the Valar and the Maiar associated with Manwë (the winds and the air) and Varda (the stars), while below are the Valar, Maiar, and other beings—including Sauron—associated with Aulë and the earth from which Aulë harvests gems (the realm of the dwarves and the Noldor).

Like the Ainur, the Elves may choose to make a journey; also like them, they are divided by their choices into groups of greater and lesser being. During the First Age, the Firstborn, or Quendi, initially mean all the Elves, "Those who speak with voices."[68] Later on, the name refers just to the first group of Elves, the Eldar, "The People of the Stars," who accept Manwë's summons to make the Great Journey to Aman and, as a result, benefit by their life there. Those who do not, the second group of Elves, the Avari ("The Unwilling; the Refusers"), refuse the summons in order to stay where they are in Cuiviénen (where the first awakening of the Elves occurred). Once these Elves are slain or die of grief, they retreat to the halls of Mandos (not to return to Middle-earth). Later still there exists a group of the Avari known as the Moriquendi, "Elves of the Darkness," because of their refusal to journey to Aman during the days of the Two Trees. For this reason of never having seen the Light of the Trees, they are known as the "Dark Elves."[69]

Among the first group of the Elves, that is, of the Eldar, a hierarchy of three kindreds exists, depending on how quickly these Elves elect to travel: (1) the Vanyar, first in time on the Great Journey to Aman; (2) the Noldor, next; and (3), after, the Teleri, whose name means "Last." All three kindreds who journey are known later as the Calaquendi, "Elves of the Light," or High Elves. The golden-haired Vanyar are linked with the chief Vala, Manwë (the wind), and love the Light of the Trees; they wander in Valinor and live at Taniquetil. The second group of Eldar, the Noldor, dark-haired and gray-eyed, are identified with the Vala Aulë (earth). Known for their crafts and learning, they are associated with the dwarves because of their craftsmanship and their love of material creation and objects. Because of this earthly link, the Noldor are more easily seduced by the lies of the fallen Vala Melkor, later "Morgoth," who is jealous of their creations. The third group of the Eldar, the Teleri, who love music, are linked with the Vala Ulmo (water). The Teleri lag behind on the great journey, one group, called Nandor, moving south; some stay behind in Falas and are called Sindar (and speak Sindarin). Most of the sea-loving Teleri go west.

Tolkien's Elves paradoxically appear human in hands, face, voice, and language but are neither human nor spirits of the dead, according to Manuscript B of "On Fairy-Stories."[70] Yet the Elves are capable of evil because they have a choice, a free will. Tolkien calls them a "separate creation," "spirits, daemons"; inherent powers of the created world, deriving more directly and 'earlier' (in terrestrial history) from the creating will of God, but nonetheless created, subject to Moral Law, capable of good and evil, and possibly (in this fallen world) actually sometimes evil. "They are in fact non-incarnate minds (or souls) of a stature and even nature more near to that of Man (in some cases possibly less, in many maybe greater) than any other rational creatures, known or guessed by us. They can take form at will, or they could do so: they have or had a choice."[71] The free will of Elves is a concept that Tolkien may have borrowed from Christianity, but in his construction of the Elven history in *The Silmarillion* he is emphatic that it derives from Ilúvatar's act of Thought at the beginning of creation in which Melkor, one of the "offspring of [Eru's] thought," or the Ainur, is free to create his own discordant music, an act that endlessly cycles back into the universe as good by means of Ilúvatar's three musical themes.

Once the essential being of the Elves in *The Silmarillion* is clarified as the Children of God, capable of choice, we may also be able to see their link with the Elves in *The Hobbit*. These Elves transcend the negative connotations of both the smith Regin and the dwarf Andvari in "The Story of Sigurd" through their knowledge and wise counsel and rescue and restoration of others, primarily Bilbo, but also *The Hobbit*'s dwarves, at several key points in their journey. For example, the (Noldor) Elves the company first encounters after the episode with the trolls, in chapter 3, "A Short Rest," sing songs about the dwarves and Hobbit that reveal the Elven understanding of what has happened to them and the Elves provide counsel to them about the happenings of the current day. And when the travelers meet Half-Elven Elrond at the Last Homely House, he teaches them about the High Elven origin of the old swords they have won from the Trolls' lair and about the meaning of their map's rune-letters, particularly a magic spell that will aid Bilbo in opening the door to the Lonely Mountain on the dwarves' New Year, the day on which the "last moon of Autumn and the sun are in the sky together" (*The Hobbit*, 50). Even the (Sindarin) Wood-Elves who capture Bilbo and the dwarves close to the end, in chapter 9, "Barrels out of Bond," although lesser in nature than the other Elves whom the company meets, inadvertently provide the means for their rescue—the wine barrels.

The Hobbit, then, includes a mythological backstory linked to Tolkien's legendarium with its providential network of Maiar and Ainur and the Children of God, Elves, and Dwarves that transcends the fate-driven Old Norse "Story of Sigurd" of Andrew Lang from which Tolkien's fairy-story derives. The key to answering the question posed at the beginning of this section—whether magic has any connection with God, if not with religion—is two framing dialogues between Bilbo and Gandalf at beginning and end of *The Hobbit*. Bilbo initiates the first dialogue by means of his initial "Good morning!" (*The Hobbit*, 5) to Gandalf, to which simple greeting Gandalf responds rather scholastically and literally with an interrogation into the meaning of "good": "What do you mean? ... Do you wish me a good morning, or mean that it is a good morning whether I want it or not; or that you feel good this morning; or that it is a morning to be good on?" (*The Hobbit*, 5). Bilbo's more philosophical and essential reply is important: "All of them at once" (*The Hobbit*, 6). Bilbo means, in truth, that there is goodness in nature (the morning, part of that cosmic good, whether Gandalf wants it or not), goodness in Bilbo the hero-to-be (he feels "good"—well—this morning and he wishes a similarly beneficial, "good," morning to Gandalf), and "goodness" in wizard Gandalf (a morning on which he can do "good", that is, perform his mystical role as a Maia and Istar). All three goodnesses reflect the impact of nature, magic, and mysticism in the end result of this fairy-story.

And at the end, when Bilbo notes that the prophetic old songs of the Elves have been proven to be true, Gandalf sums up the reason that Bilbo has succeeded in his adventure. It is not that the Hobbit did not disprove the prophecies and not that he succeeded because of "mere luck," or "just for [Bilbo's] sole benefit" (*The Hobbit*, 272). Bilbo succeeds because of the combination of his intelligence and valor and lack of pride, along with the aid of wizard Gandalf within a much greater, if providential, universe: "You are a very fine person, Mr. Baggins," says Gandalf, "and I am very fond of you; but you are only quite a little fellow in a wide world after all!" (*The Hobbit*, 272), meaning that he is only one part of a greater whole that providence oversees. Thus, Bilbo can humbly but profoundly reply, "Thank goodness!" with a laugh and a charitable pass of the tobacco jar to the wizard. In his humility unSigurdlike Bilbo recognizes that a larger goodness in him—a universal Good, or God—has facilitated his success, namely, the remedial retrieval of the dwarves' lost treasure from the dragon Smaug by means of a found magical ring and the restoration of peace between the men of Dale and the dwarves by means of the gift of the Arkenstone, for which he is grateful. Bilbo thus subverts Old Norse antihero Sigurd in his total inappropriateness as a hero (but not as a thief), in his ordinariness—in his very nature as a small, hairy-footed Hobbit.

Because of Tolkien's interest in Old Norse saga and prophecy, so bound to mythology of pagan gods, Roman Catholic Tolkien thus emphasizes throughout *The Hobbit*, *The Silmarillion*, and "On Fairy-Stories" that the essential power of Faërie is magical, natural, and derived from the gods, or God. Providence is a paramount force in Middle-earth, meaning, not the specifically Christian concept of Providence, but an analogous force of goodness inherent in the visual materialization of the harmonious music of Tolkien's Ainur that first fills the void and continues throughout the Three Ages and the coming Fourth, of Man, at the end of *The Lord of the Rings*. If Elves and fairies and their magical powers seem to have disappeared in the Fourth Age, of Man, Tolkien reminds that, whatever this diminution of essential being, the goodness of Ilúvatar lives on in it.

Despite its early critical neglect and despite its modern critical interpretation as Jungian or Freudian psychoanalytic narrative,[72] *The Hobbit* is imbued by that mythology that Tolkien would later describe, in the previously mentioned famous letter to his potential new publisher, Milton Waldman of Collins Press, in 1951, as missing in England. It exists, then, not as a muddle of various ideas that impacted negatively on the construction of his later works, or as a simple children's story that we might well ignore, but as the pivot on which his medievalized mythology of magic and his favorite genre, the fairy-story, with its transcendental and even mystical tendencies, is balanced, and by means of which his other works may be interpreted. Epic, fairy-story, and mythology: an understanding of the interrelationship of all three sources—whether Old English and Old Norse epic, Lang's fairy-story of Sigurd, or Tolkien's own mythological "Silmarillion" for the works generated during the same period, *The Hobbit*, and, in particular, the essential critical statement of "On Fairy-Stories"—may provide yet another answer to Tolkien's own professed desire to create a "mythology for England."

NOTES

1. Andrew Lang, *The Lilac Fairy Book* (London: Longmans, Green, 1910; repr. New York: Dover Books, 1968), viii.
2. Christopher Tolkien, "Introduction," in *J.R.R. Tolkien: The Legend of Sigurd and Gudrún*, ed. Christopher Tolkien (Boston: Houghton Mifflin Harcourt, 2009), 4.

3. J.R.R. Tolkien, *Tolkien on Fairy-stories: Expanded Edition, with Commentary and Notes*, ed. Verlyn Flieger and Douglas A. Anderson (London: HarperCollins, 2008), 122; the history of the making of "On Fairy-Stories," an essay unpublished until 1947, is detailed on 122–28. This edition contains all variants from the two major manuscripts of Tolkien's Andrew Lang Lecture (1939), including the final published version as edited by Christopher Tolkien in Tolkien's *The Monsters and the Critics and Other Essays* (1983).
4. Tolkien, *Tolkien on Fairy-stories*, 188–89; my emphasis.
5. See Scull, *Reader's Guide*, 599. Marjorie Burns discusses William Morris's northern influence on Tolkien in *Perilous Realms: Celtic and Norse in Tolkien's Middle-earth* (Toronto: University of Toronto Press, 2005), chapter 4, "Iceland and Middle-earth: Two Who Loved the North," 75–92.
6. See Tolkien, "The Lay of Leithian, in The Lays of Beleriand," in *The History of Middle-Earth*, ed. Christopher Tolkien, vol. 3 (London: HarperCollins, 1985), 159, 304nn, and Christopher's foreword to *The Legend of Sigurd and Gudrún*, 4–5. References to the legends in the latter edition will be indicated by part number and stanza number (e.g., 1.4), often in the text, to keep the narrative straight, although references to any commentary will be indicated by page number(s).
7. Carpenter, *Letters*, 452n3. See also Tom Shippey, "Tolkien's Development as a Writer of Alliterative Poetry in Modern English," in *Tolkien's Poetry*, ed. Julian Eilmonn and Allam Turner, 11–28 (Zurich, Switzerland, and Jena, Germany: Walking Tree Publishers, 2013).
8. Tolkien, letter 295, 379. Tom Shippey, "Tolkien and Iceland: The Philology of Envy," in *Roots and Branches: Selected Papers on Tolkien by Tom Shippey* (Zollikofen, Switzerland: Walking Tree Press, 2007), 187–202, assumed that this poem was intended to fill an eight-page gap in the Sigurðr cycle in the Codex Regius manuscript of the Poetic *Edda*. However, Tolkien's poem is much longer than eight manuscript pages. For the date, see Scull, *Reader's Guide*, 654.
9. *The Hobbit* can be dated as early as 1926–1927, according to Tolkien's oldest son, Father John Tolkien (1917–2003). See the recollections of John, Michael, and Christopher Tolkien in Scull, *Reader's Guide*, 386–87; and John D. Rateliff, *The History of the Hobbit: Part 1, Mr. Baggins*; Part 2: *Return to Bag-End* (London, HarperCollins, 2007–2008): 1:xiv. Father John also voices his dating of the earliest Hobbit stories as being in the mid- to late twenties in the film documentary *Tolkien Remembered*, DVD video (Princeton, NJ: Films for the Humanities and Sciences, 2005).
10. Flieger and Anderson, the editors of the various versions of "On Fairy-Stories," have mused that even Tolkien recognized these flaws in what they describe as "his own fairy-story, *The Hobbit*" in *Tolkien on Fairy-stories*, 16.

11. *The St. Andrews Citizen* (March 1939, 4, cols. 3–5), in *Tolkien on Fairy-stories*, ed. Flieger, 165.
12. Joseph Bosworth, *An Anglo-Saxon Dictionary*, ed. T. Northcote Toller (Oxford: Oxford University Press, 1898; repr. 1976), *s.v.*
13. Fr. Klaeber, ed. *Beowulf and the Fight at Finnsburg*, 3rd edn. (Boston: D.C. Heath, 1950; repr 1968), 162n. A fourth edition exists, with supplemental materials by R.D. Fulk, Robert E. Bjork, and John D. Niles (Toronto: University of Toronto Press, 2008), but this earlier edition is closer in substance to the one that Tolkien would have used.
14. *The St. Andrews Citizen* (March 1939, 4, cols. 3–5), in *Tolkien on Fairy-stories*, 166; my emphasis.
15. Although these stories are termed "shorter works," they are obviously treated as fairy-stories and children's stories: see, for example, Margaret Hiley and Frank Weinreich, eds. *Tolkien's Shorter Works: Essays of the Jena Conference 2007*. Cormarë Series 17 (Zurich, Switzerland, and Jena, Germany: Walking Tree Publishers, 2008).
16. See R.J. Reilly, "Tolkien and the Fairy-Story," in *Tolkien and the Critics: Essays on J.R.R. Tolkien's Lord of the Rings*, ed. Neil D. Isaacs and Rose A. Zimbardo, 128–50 (Notre Dame and London: University of Notre Dame Press, 1968); repr. in *Understanding "The Lord of the Rings": The Best of Tolkien Criticism*, ed. Zimbardo and Isaacs, 93–105 (Boston: Houghton Mifflin, 2004; repr. pb. Mariner Books, 2005), and J.S. Ryan, "Folktale, Fairy-Tale, and the Creation of a Story," in *Tolkien: New Critical Perspectives*, ed. Isaacs, 19–39; repr. in Zimbardo, *Understanding "The Lord of the Rings*," 106–21, which adds a discussion of Tolkien's *Beowulf* essay and G.K. Chesterton on the fairy- and folk-tale.
17. Tolkien, *Tolkien on Fairy-stories*, 226; my emphasis.
18. Tolkien, "On Fairy-Stories," in *Essays Presented to Charles Williams*, ed. C.S. Lewis (London: Oxford University Press, 1947); repr. in *Tree and Leaf, Including the Poem "Mythopoeia*," intro. Christopher Tolkien, 44 (rev. edn. London: Allen & Unwin, 1988; Boston: Houghton Mifflin, 1989).
19. Tolkien, *The Legend of Sigurd*, 51.
20. Tolkien, *Legend of Sigurd*, 59.
21. Tolkien, *Völsungakviða en nýja (The New Lay of the Völsungs)*, in *The Legend of Sigurd and Gudrún*, 59–63.
22. Tolkien, "Notes on the Poems, by the Author," *The Legend of Sigurd*, 52.
23. Tolkien, "Notes on the Poems, by the Author," *The Legend of Sigurd*, 53.
24. Tolkien, "Notes on the Poems, by the Author," *The Legend of Sigurd*, 54.
25. Tolkien, "Notes on the Poems, by the Author," *The Legend of Sigurd*, 54.
26. Christopher Tolkien's commentaries at the end of each of the two legends are extremely helpful in sorting out how his father has amalgamated vari-

ous details from different Norse sources and in relating to them the enigmatic stanzas of the specific part of the lay in question. See, for this first part, 188–92, although the entire commentary for the *Legend of Sigurd* covers 183–249.
27. Tolkien, *Völsungakviða en nýja (The New Lay of the Völsungs)*, in *The Legend of Sigurd*, 70.
28. See *Völsunga Saga: The Story of the Volsungs and the Niblungs, with Certain Songs from the Elder Edda*, trans. Eiríkr Magnússon and William Morris; ed. H. Halliday Sparling (London: Walter Scott, 1870; repr. 1888), 42, from now on, Morris, *Völsunga Saga*.
29. Morris, *Völsunga Saga*, 35–36.
30. Morris, *Völsunga Saga*, 37–39.
31. Tolkien, *Völsungakviða en nýja (The New Lay of the Völsungs)*, in *The Legend of Sigurd*, 82–83.
32. Andrew Lang, "The Story of Sigurd," *The Red Fairy Book* (1890; repr. New York: Dover, 1966), 357–67.
33. See Scull, *Chronology*, 136; and Christopher Tolkien, "Introduction to the Translation," in *Beowulf: A Translation and Commentary, together with Sellic Spell* (Boston and New York: Houghton Mifflin Harcourt, 2014), 2.
34. See J.R.R. Tolkien, "Beowulf: The Monsters and the Critics," *Proceedings of the British Academy* 22 (1937): 245–95, reprinted in Tolkien's *The Monsters and the Critics and Other Essays* (1983) and the Norton critical edition *Beowulf: A Verse Translation*, ed. Daniel Donoghue, 103–29 (New York: W.W. Norton, 2002).
35. Morris, *Völsunga Saga*, 42.
36. See Melissa Ruth Arul, "A Critical Study of the Self and the Other in Selected Texts of Tolkien" (M.A. thesis, University of *Malaya-Kuala Lumpur*, 2009). The incarnate abject hero for Tolkien was Kullervo, the orphan hero of the Finnish epic *Kalevala*, about whom Richard C. West has written in "Setting the Rocket Off in Story: The *Kalevala* as the Germ of Tolkien's *Legendarium*," in *Tolkien and the Invention of Myth: A Reader*, ed. Jane Chance, 285–94 (Lexington, KY: University Press of Kentucky, 2004).
37. Bilbo and Frodo were also linked as distant cousins because their fathers were members of the less noble—in fact, bourgeois—Baggins family, probably to be identified as members of the more conventional, mid-level Hobbit strain, the Harfoots. Bilbo's mother, Belladonna Took, married Bungo Baggins (son of Bungo and brother of Longo), who, in marrying Camellia Sackville, took on her hyphenated name because of its social distinction and fathered the pretentious Otho Sackville-Baggins (who later married the avaricious Lobelia Bracegirdle). Frodo's father was Drogo Baggins, son of Fosco (who was himself first cousin to Bilbo's father,

Bungo). See Tolkien, *The Lord of the Rings*, 22–23 (chap. 1); and the genealogical table of the Bagginns of Hobbiton and the Tooks of Great Smials in Appendix C, "Family Trees," 1074–75.
38. See the chapter "The Bourgeois Burglar," in *The Road to Middle-earth*, ed. Tom Shippey, 51–86 (1982; rev. edn. London: Allen & Unwin, 1992), and especially his comment that Bilbo is "admittedly a *bourgeois*," 66–67.
39. For his discussion of the Hobbit races, see Tolkien, *The Lord of the Rings*, 3–4.
40. See Bonniejean Christiansen, "*Beowulf* and *The Hobbit*: Elegy into Fantasy in J.R.R. Tolkien's Creative Technique" (Ph.D. diss., University of Southern California, 1970); and her article derived from the dissertation, "Tolkien's Creative Technique: *Beowulf* and the *Hobbit*," *Orcrist* 7 (1972–1973): 16–20.
41. See especially Jane Chance, *Tolkien's Art: A "Mythology for England"* (London, Macmillan Press; New York: St. Martin's Press, 1979; repr. Papermac Editions, 1980; rev. edn. Lexington: University of Kentucky Press, 2001), 12–47.
42. Dimitra Fimi, *Tolkien, Race, and Cultural History: From Fairies to Hobbits* (London: Palgrave Macmillan, 2009), 118.
43. Tolkien, letter to the editor, *The Observer*, February 20, 1938, 9.
44. After Tolkien's publisher Allen & Unwin had declined to publish both *The Lord of the Rings* and the much earlier manuscript of *The Silmarillion* (despite their professed desire to publish a "second Hobbit"), Tolkien proclaimed his creative intentions in terms of a larger desire for a national mythology for England in letter 131 to publisher Milton Waldman: "I had in mind to make *a body of more or less connected legend*, ranging from the *large and cosmogonic* to the level of *romantic fairy-story*—the larger founded on the lesser in contact with the earth, the lesser drawing splendour from the vast backcloths—which I could dedicate simply: to England, to my country." See Tolkien, letter 131, 144; my emphasis. See also the mention of this "mythology for England" by Tolkien biographer Humphrey Carpenter, *Tolkien: A Biography* (London: Allen & Unwin; New York: Houghton Mifflin, 1977), 89–90; and by various medievalists who have tried to interpret "mythology for England" in varying ways, including myself, in the earliest edition of *Tolkien's Art* (1978): Carl J. Hostetter and Arden R. Smith, "A Mythology for England," in *Proceedings of the J.R.R. Tolkien Centenary Conference, Keble College, Oxford, 1992*, ed. Patricia Reynolds and Glen H. GoodKnight, *Mythlore* 80/*Mallorn* 30 (Winter, 1996), 281–90; and Anders Stenström, "A Mythology? For England?" in Reynolds, *Proceedings of the J.R.R. Tolkien Centenary*, 310–14.

45. See Jack Zipes, *Fairy Tales and the Art of Subversion: The Classical Genre for Children and the Forces of Civilization* (London: Methuen, 1988; rev. edn., 2011); and Jack Zipes, *Breaking the Magic Spell: Radical Themes of Folk and Fairy Tales* (1979; rev. edn., Lexington: University of Kentucky Press, 2002). See also Verlyn Flieger, "A Mythology for Finland: Tolkien and Lönnrot as Mythmakers," in *Tolkien and the Invention of Myth*, edited by Chance, 277–83. Recently Flieger has edited Tolkien's "'The Story of Kullervo' and Essays on *Kalevala*," *Tolkien Studies* 7 (2010): 211–78.
46. See, for example, T[om]. A. Shippey, ed., *The Shadow-Walkers: Jacob Grimm's Mythology of the Monstrous* (Tempe, AZ: Arizona Center for the Study of Medieval and Renaissance Studies/Brepols, 2005); and Fimi, *Tolkien, Race, and Cultural History*, esp. chaps. 2–5.
47. See T.A. Shippey, "Grimm, Grundtvig, Tolkien: Nationalisms and the Invention of Mythologies," in *The Ways of Creative Mythologies: Imagined Worlds and Their Makers*, ed. Maria Kateeva, 2 vols. (Telford: Tolkien Society Press, 2000), 1: 1–17; repr. in Shippey, *Roots and Branches*, 79–96; and Verlyn Flieger, "'There Would Always Be a Fairy-Tale': J.R.R. Tolkien and the Folklore Controversy," in *Tolkien the Medievalist*, ed. Chance, 26–35; and Verlyn Flieger, "A Mythology for Finland: Tolkien and Lönnrot as Mythmakers," in *Tolkien and the Invention of Myth*, ed. Chance, 277–83.
48. Fimi, *Tolkien, Race, and Cultural History*, 196–97.
49. *The Hobbit*, first published in Great Britain in 1937, appeared in a second edition in 1951, in which the problematic chapter 5, on the riddle game with Gollum, in which Bilbo uses the ring he has found, was revised (this occurred in 1947) to provide a transition to *The Lord of the Rings*. *The Hobbit* was again revised for the third edition, of 1966. See the discussion of how Tolkien revised *The Hobbit* in Bonniejean Christiansen, "Gollum's Character Transformation in *The Hobbit*," in *A Tolkien Compass*, ed. Jared Lobdell, 9–28 (LaSalle, IL: Open Court Press, 1975; repr. New York: Ballantine Books, 1980); and Douglas A. Anderson, ed., *The Annotated Hobbit* (London: HarperCollins, 1988; rev. edn. 2003).
50. Fimi, *Tolkien, Race, and Cultural History*, 197.
51. Tolkien notes circa 1958 that "the cosmogonic myths are Númenórean, blending Elven-lore with human myth and imagination," in J.R.R. Tolkien, *Morgoth's Ring*, ed. Christopher Tolkien, *The History of Middle-earth*, vol. 10 (London: HarperCollins, 1990), 374n2. By which, he means "Mannish," according to J.R.R. Tolkien, *The Peoples of Middle-earth*, ed. Christopher Tolkien, *The History of Middle-earth*, vol. 12 (London: HarperCollins, 1996), 357n17. Basically "The Silmarillion" in its earliest form comprises four lays of the Atani heroes, beginning with the story of Fëanor's making of the Silmarils.

52. See the extant unfinished "Sketch" in J.R.R. Tolkien, "Sketch of the Mythology With Especial Reference to the 'Children of Húrin,'" in *The Shaping of Middle Earth*, ed. Christopher Tolkien, *The History of Middle-earth*, vol. 4 (London: HarperCollins, 1986), 11–75. Scull, *Reader's Guide*, 901–4, provides a helpful but brief summary of the stages in the making of "The Silmarillion."
53. See Marjorie J. Burns, "Gandalf and Ódin," in *Tolkien's 'Legendarium': Essays on The History of Middle-earth*, ed. Verlyn Flieger and Carl F. Hostetter, 219–32 (Westport, Conn. and London: Greenwood Press, 2000).
54. Tolkien, "The Istari," in *Unfinished Tales of Númenor and Middle-earth*, ed. Christopher Tolkien (London: Allen & Unwin, 1979; Boston: Houghton Mifflin, 1980), 388–402; see the brief discussion in Scull, *Reader's Guide*, 432–34
55. Tolkien, "The Istari," in *Unfinished Tales*, 389–90.
56. Tolkien, "The Istari," in *Unfinished Tales*, 90–91, 393.
57. Tolkien, "The Istari," in *Unfinished Tales*, 89.
58. Christopher Tolkien, Notes to "The Istari," in *Unfinished Tales*, 393n.
59. Tolkien, "The Istari," in *Unfinished Tales*, 394.
60. Tolkien, "The Istari," in *Unfinished Tales*, 412.
61. MS 6, Oxford, Bodleian Library, fols. 6–8.
62. Tolkien, *Tolkien on Fairy-stories*, 253–54.
63. See Verlyn Flieger, "Naming the Unnamable: The Neoplatonic 'One' in Tolkien's *Silmarillion*," in *Diakonia: Studies in Honor of Robert T. Meyer*, ed. Thomas Halton and Joseph Williman, 127–33 (Washington, DC: Catholic University of America Press, 1986).
64. Tolkien, *Silm*, 17.
65. Tolkien, *Silm*, 18–19.
66. Tolkien, *Silm*, 20.
67. Tolkien, *Silm*, 25–32.
68. Christopher Tolkien, "Index of Names," in *Silm*, s.v.
69. T[om]. A. Shippey, "Light-elves, Dark-elves, and Others: Tolkien's Elvish Problem," *Tolkien Studies* 1 (2004): 1–15.
70. Tolkien, *Tolkien on Fairy-stories*, 254.
71. Tolkien, *Tolkien on Fairy-stories*, 254–55.
72. See Randel Helms, *Tolkien's World* (Boston: Houghton Mifflin, 1974), 41–55; Dorothy Matthews, "The Psychological Journey of Bilbo Baggins," in *A Tolkien Compass*, ed. Lobdell, 29–42; and Timothy R. O'Neill, *The Individuated Hobbit: Jung, Tolkien, and the Archetypes of Middle-earth* (Boston: Houghton Mifflin, 1979).

CHAPTER 4

Tolkien's Fairy-Story Beowulfs (1926–1940s)

"Beewolf I used to be called when I was at home. Now some call me the Knight of the Golden Hilts."—J.R.R. Tolkien, *Sellic Spell*

Tolkien's high regard for *Beowulf* as a poem endured throughout his life and deeply influenced much of his fictional creation, especially *The Hobbit*, as many scholars have previously argued.[1] In 1937, he published a lecture he had delivered in 1936 as "Beowulf: The Monsters and the Critics," perhaps the most reprinted of all articles on the epic and certainly one that changed the shape of academic study of Old English in the twentieth century by means of its emphasis on the text as literature.[2] Tolkien also translated it for use in his teaching lectures and research (1926), adapted it in poetry and prose several times (between 1925 and the early 1940s), and wrote an essay, "On Translating *Beowulf*," derived from his "Prefatory Remarks" to the translation of *Beowulf* published by John Clark Hall in a revised edition (in 1940).[3]

Tolkien concludes his original "Prefatory Remarks on Prose Translation of *Beowulf*" in its second section, on meter, with a paraphrase of his description of the two parts of the epic from "Beowulf: The Monsters and the Critics," in which he describes the rising and falling moments of the poem as the rise and fall of Beowulf's life, similarly mirrored in the rise and fall of the Anglo-Saxon a literative line, separated as it is by a break. He writes, "*Beowulf* itself is like a line of its own verse written large, a balance of two great blocks, A + B; or like two of its parallel sentences with a single subject but no expressed conjunction. Youth + Age; he rose—fell.

It may not be, at large or in detail, fluid or musical, but it is strong to stand: tough builder's work of true stone."⁴ He might as well be describing the edifice of his own vast publishing career, posthumous or not.

Tolkien considered his famous article to be thematically or topically linked with two of his other works, his now equally famous but less groundbreaking essay "On Fairy-Stories" and his verse-drama "The Homecoming of Beorhtnoth Beorhthelm's Son" (a sequel to the Anglo-Saxon chronicle-like poem *The Battle of Maldon*). In a letter to Anne Barrett on 7 August 1964, Tolkien notes all three "flow together" so well that they might be published as a group. He explains, "The [*Beowulf* essay] deals with the contact of the 'heroic' with fairy-story; [*On Fairy-Stories*] primarily with fairy-story; and [*Beorhtnoth*] with 'heroism and chivalry'" (letter 261, 350). This publication never materialized—instead, "On Fairy-Stories" was published with the fairy-story "Leaf by Niggle" and preceded by "The Homecoming of Beorhtnoth, Beorhthelm's Son," in *The Tolkien Reader* (1966). The idea of cohesion among the original three proposed by Tolkien, however, remains an intriguing idea. Why did Tolkien think of the heroism of *Beowulf* (or what he said about it in his article on Beowulf) as connected with the *fairy-story*?

The answer to that question may lie in his fascination with line 3052 in *Beowulf*, one that he translates into English in a letter to his illustrator Pauline Baynes on 6 December 1961 as "the gold of men of long ago enmeshed in enchantment" (letter 235, 312). "Enchantment" is the key word in the translation, which must have made him think of magic and, of course, fairies and fairy-stories. He does comment on the line at the end of his commentary on his *Beowulf* translation, noting that it is only at the very end of the poem and Beowulf's life that the treasure for which he fought the dragon is buried with him because it is enchanted but also cursed: intended to "draw the invincible Beowulf to his death" (*Commentary*, 352). About this line Tolkien wrote a poem himself, as a young professor teaching *Beowulf* at Leeds University in 1922, using the original Anglo-Saxon to title it: "Iúmonna Gold Galdre Bewunden." Always inspired by medieval poems in both his creative works and his scholarship during his entire career, Tolkien published his poem in the Leeds *Gryphon* in 1923.⁵ This *Beowulf* line also appears in both the A and B manuscript drafts of his famous *Beowulf* lecture, finally delivered in 1936 and published, but of course without this poem, in 1937. He also revised the poem in 1937, publishing it in the *Oxford Magazine* of 4 March and reprinting it finally as "The Hoard" in *The Adventures of Tom Bombadil and Other Verses from the Red Book*,⁶ a collection also reprinted in *The Tolkien Reader*.

The line in *Beowulf* literally denotes gold that is wound about, or enclosed, with or by a spell, or incantation, by men of old, and refers to the Dragon's gold treasure (buried long ago by the Last Survivor) for which the old Dragon and old Beowulf have both just died. And, indeed, a curious fairy-story-like overlay exists in Tolkien's medievalized poem, "Iúmonna Gold Galdre Bewunden," catalyzed by that identical line. As Scull and Hammond note in their commentary on the poem (titled "The Hoard") in their recent edition of *The Adventures of Tom Bombadil*, Tolkien refers to it in a letter to Mrs. Eileen Elgar of 5 March 1964 "as if it were an epitome of the mythology,"[7] that is, of the Silmarillion. In Tolkien's poem "Iúmonna Gold Galdre Bewunden," the gold crafted by the elves appears early in earth's history, before the existence of hell, dwarves, or "dragon's brood," and is stolen by men and then by dwarves—in particular, "an old dwarf in a deep grot/That counted the gold things he had got."[8] Unfortunately, the dwarf doesn't hear the dragon come to steal his gold. And the old dragon, who licks and sniffs his gold while jewels stick to his belly slime, does not hear the "fearless warrior" who summons him to fight.[9]

In this poem, Tolkien replaces the dragon with an old king—as if the warrior Beowulf had aged into this old, unnamed king, apparently, which is exactly what happens to the Geat in the second part of this elegiac epic, as Tolkien describes it in his famous *Beowulf* essay. Except that Tolkien's is an unjust king, as greedy as the dwarf, whose hall is burned and whose gold as part of "an old hoard" is locked behind doors and covered by a grassy mound (and it may be a kind of gloss on the burial mound of the Anglo-Saxon hero). No one can rescue the hoard except the Faery who created it and originally sang songs about it. Of course Tolkien was riveted by the symbol of the gold in *Beowulf*'s Elegy of the Last Survivor, the Last Survivor mourning the loss of his tribe and missing the joy of its fellowship as a result of the tribe's desire for the gold he will now commit to the depths of earth in the hope of preventing further calamity resulting from its possession.

Later on, by 1939, Tolkien may also have been thinking of the sixth- to seventh-century ship burials and treasures like the one at Sutton Hoo in Suffolk[10] (excavated in the same year Tolkien's lecture "Fairy-Stories" was delivered, but occurring after the publication of his *Beowulf* article and *The Hobbit*). However, much earlier excavations in eastern Sweden—as early as 1881–1883—had revealed royal burials (some of them ship burials) dating from the sixth and seventh centuries, which may remind *Beowulf* readers of the poem's opening passage in which a ship burial is provided for a king. For Tolkien's seventieth birthday collection, Norman Davis, who also coedited it,[11] wrote an article about "Man and Monsters at Sutton Hoo," but it was only later that Sutton Hoo was linked to East Anglian ruler Rædwald and *Beowulf*. Using genealogical data, Sam Newton determined that the Wuffing dynasty of Rædwald derived from the Geat (Swedish) house of Wulfing. This house is directly involved in *Beowulf* through Wealhtheow's family and in the poem *Widsith*.[12] The royal progenitor for this family was Woden, whose image appears in a manuscript Tolkien owned and eventually bestowed upon the University of Liège, where his former student Simonne d'Ardenne taught as a professor.[13]

Another Tolkien poem like "Iúmonna Gold Galdre Bewunden" ("The Hoard"), similarly medievalized and fantastic but also modernized in a more juvenile way, anticipates aspects of his humorous prose adaptation of it in *Sellic Spell* (even though the latter more closely resembles another one of his early parodies, of the *Kalevala*, in his *New Lemminkainen*). His earliest published poem, an unfinished parody titled "The Battle of the Eastern Field" published in the *King Edward School Chronicle* in 1911, involves Tolkien's fantasy, one of which he was fond, of an incomplete, discovered manuscript restored and edited. In this respect, consider the fiction of Bilbo and Sam's own *Red Book*, part of which appears as *The Adventures of Tom Bombadil, and Other Verses from the Red Book*—the same collection that offers "Iúmonna Gold Galdre Bewunden" as "The Hoard." So "The Battle of the Eastern Field" was said to have been found by the editor of the *Chronicle* (or by the mysterious G.A.B., aka Tolkien) in the prefects' room at King Edward's School in Birmingham on Friday, 31 March, "a curious fragment in the waste paper basket ... Much of it was so blotted that I could not decipher it. I now publish it with emendations of my own."[14] "G.A.B." continues to insert comments within parentheses throughout the poem, noting that the anonymous author has blotted out portions that G.A.B. is without time to insert.[15] It was later reprinted in 1978 in *Mallorn*, introduced by the modern editor, K.J. Young, as "romantically saved from death in the bin, and restored to posterity," a type of poem that "was all the rage at this particular time."[16]

"The type of poem" Young refers to as "all the rage" was Tolkien's twenty-one-section mock-heroic parody of the classical *Lay of Lake Regillus* by Thomas Babington Macaulay in which fourteen of Macauley's original forty sections have allegedly been blotted out by ink smears (presumably with less for Tolkien to compose).[17] Macaulay's *Lays* were often recited in British public schools, as Winston Churchill himself did at Harrow.[18] And

Macauley's long lay had been published in 1910 in Dent's Everyman's Library, one year before Tolkien composed his own parody.[19] It is clear why Tolkien was drawn to it, given his penchant for noble warriors engaged in defending a special cause. Macaulay's introduction to *Lake Regillus* in his popular anthology of *Lays of Ancient Rome* (1842) acknowledges that this narrative Latin lay is modeled on Homer's epic *Iliad*, more Greek in temper than of his more "purely Roman," very popular and nationalistic *Horatius: A Lay Made About the Year Of The City CCCLX*, published ninety years earlier, to which it represents a kind of sequel.[20]

The Lay of Lake Regillus depicts a battle between the House of Tarquin, mounted on horseback, and the Latines. In support of the commonwealth, the equestrian Twin Gods Castor and Pollux were said to have fought successfully near Lake Regillus in Rome, where a celestial hoof-shaped mark was left in volcanic rock; an ancient temple was thereafter erected to the brothers at the Forum. On the first anniversary of this victorious battle, a ceremonial reenactment—"a grand muster and inspection of the equestrian body"—came to be held annually in Rome, supported both by the censors and Pontiffs, according to Macaulay:

> All the knights, clad in purple and crowned with olive, were to meet at a temple of Mars in the suburbs. Thence they were to ride in state to the Forum, where the temple of the Twins stood. This pageant was, during several centuries, considered as one of the most splendid sights of Rome. In the time of Dionysius the cavalcade sometimes consisted of five thousand horsemen, all persons of fair repute and easy fortune.[21]

It was for this important *commemoratio* that the original *Lay of Lake Regillus* was said to have been composed.

The first two lines of Tolkien's poem "The Battle of the Eastern Fields" invoke both Macaulay's specific poem and also the Roman equestrian ceremonial, to which Ronald's version adds—rather strangely—British Arthurian chivalric focus in the use of the words "knight," "silver grail," and "lords." Certainly there is an imitation of a battle rally in the original: Macaulay's poem begins "Ho, trumpets, sound a war-note!/Ho, lictors, clear the way!" Compare Tolkien's almost identical opening: "Ho, rattles sound your warnote!/Ho, trumpets loudly bray!" However, it does not take long to realize that these "knights" are *students* in red and green who are manning the posts of the knights. "Today the walls and blackboards/Are hung with flaunting script," Tolkien notes in the fifth line of the first section. Despite the fact that the poem appears to deal with a battle on the "Eastern Field" during Lenten Term (the six-weeks "term" before Easter, pointing to the academic term at British schools), brave "knights" garbed in red and green fight over a silver grail and are overseen by "many a haughty Lord"—an early anti-classist view of the aristocracy will persist until the end of Tolkien's life—and, indeed, on a field.[22] The reference to the "Eastern Field" makes clear we are *not* in Rome and *not* actually fighting a war-battle, as reenactment or otherwise. Indeed, this is a rugby game on the Eastern (Road) Field in Birmingham at King Edward's School.

> Full oft a speeding foeman
> Was hurtled to the ground,
> While forward and now backward,
> Did the ball of fortune bound....
> His clients from the battle
> Bare him some little space,
> And gently rubbed his wounded knee,
> And scanned his pallid face. (IV. 14–17; 26–29)

Where Tolkien reveals his joke occurs close to the end, in section XXIII, when "Cupid" (a student apparently known for his love interests) outruns his hosts and "spied the Great Twin Post; /He crossed the line ... (he scored a try? G.A.B.")" (XIII. 9–10), "try" referring in rugby terms to score, and the Great Twin [Goal] Post, the classical mythological Twins, Castor and Pollux. Of course, in section XX the joyful noise then heard is likened more prosaically to the "roar .../When the dinner-hour bull blows" (lines 3–4) and the two teams rock backward and forward until the final call ends the game and a feast follows (section XXI). The sophomoric humor Tolkien provides in GAB's last note exposes the true identity of the battle participants—students: "The Ed. won't let me put any more in. Most of them then went home to bed."[23]

The Arthurian chivalric note is one that Tolkien will employ again, as an overlay in his translations and adaptations of Anglo-Saxon poetry. By 1925–1926, Tolkien was thinking about the poem *Beowulf* and beginning to translate it (a practice he came to adopt whenever he began a new course on Old English, Old Norse, or Middle English), just as he entered on a new phase in his career at Oxford. Christopher Tolkien's recent edition of Tolkien's *Beowulf* translation reveals signs of the fantasized medieval origin of much of his father's later scholarship as well as the epic foundation on which Tolkien constructed his mythology of Middle-earth. And, I might add, similar hints of the Professor's pervasive sense of humor.

Tolkien's *Beowulf* Translations

Tolkien's translation of the Anglo-Saxon poem in *Beowulf: A Translation and Commentary, Together with Sellic Spell* (2014) contains 2665 lines of the 3182 line total in the original text in Friedrich Klaeber, accompanied by Tolkien's annotations of individual lines and passages, his long lecture commentary, and his poetic and prose rewritings and modern comic adaptation of *Beowulf*—the latter, a work more creative than scholarly. The completed *Beowulf* translation itself dates from the end of April, 1926, and was written in Oxford, according to a letter to Anglo-Saxon scholar Kenneth Sisam.[24] However, what we have in Christopher's edition offers three different versions. The first—identified as the B (i) manuscript—is a typescript of the original *Beowulf* up to line 2112 (line 1773 in Tolkien's translation). The second, B (ii), is a manuscript that follows onward from the middle of this last line in B (i) to the last line he translated, 2665. The third version, C, is a typescript made by Christopher around 1940–1942 of the whole translation and incorporates most of the emendations made by Tolkien to B (i) unless he added some later. These emendations mostly involve lines 574–632 of the translation, concerning Grendel's arrival at Heorot and fight with the hero. It is important to note that Christopher's selections of wording in his edited translation are not always based on Tolkien's latest versions. As Christopher explains: "to leave it at that seemed misleading and mistaken. To alter the translation in order to accommodate a later opinion was out of the question."[25] Thus, Christopher's own notes to specific lines indicate which version of the translation he has used and why, as based on Tolkien's marginal comments in the manuscripts and on other material.

In addition to the prose *translation*, Tolkien's creative versions of *Beowulf* include, first, a prose *adaptation* of the first two-thirds of *Beowulf*, titled *Sellic Spell* and completed in the early 1940s.[26] *Sellic Spell* also exists in three versions, A to C, C being the final, plus two other typescripts of C labeled by Christopher as D and E. *Sellic Spell* is accompanied by Tolkien's two versions of his own short, poetic "Lay of Beowulf" in modern English, written in the early thirties and titled "Beowulf and Grendel" and "Beowulf and the Monsters, II."[27] The two parts of the "Lay" narrow the focus to the two monsters' assault on Heorot and Beowulf's fights with Grendel and his mother, along with an ending celebrating the hero's ship-return to the Geats. However, the first Lay, "Beowulf and Grendel," introduces the hero's innovative decapitation of Grendel at Heorot (which is what Tolkien believed occurred in the original epic, based on the Anglo-Saxon denotations), as the Professor explains in a note on his lines 791–92, relative to the Old English phrase *tó lifwraþe* (*Beowulf*, 971*, "to save his life," *Commentary*, 116). The second Lay version adds the second fight, with Grendel's Mother, and her decapitation (rather than her son's) (418, 424). The note in Tolkien's hand on the cover page for the "Lay" reads "Intended to be sung," as if they were happy celebrations of victories, and, indeed, Christopher remembers his father singing to him "Beowulf and Grendel," likely in the early 1930s, when he was only seven or eight (416).

These creative *Beowulf*s differ in nature and style from Tolkien's somber translation of 1926, but all of them share one feature: they omit Beowulf's failure in the battle with the Dragon and his ultimate death, in line with the necessity for a Tolkienian fairy-story (according to "On Fairy-Stories") to end as a eucatastrophe. However, another factor pertains in regard to Tolkien's long commentary on the *Beowulf* translation, which Christopher spliced together from his Oxford lectures on *Beowulf* originally intended for students in an undergraduate course limited basically to lines 1–1650 (out of *Beowulf*'s 3182 lines), along with other notes by his father on the poem. The commentary's shape, then, relative to that of the entire poem, is uneven. Judging from the relatively few carefully selected lines or cruces chosen for analysis closer to the end of the commentary, whether by Tolkien or Christopher, the focus tends to fall on larger issues. It is important to bear in mind also that it is definitely Christopher's edition and his selection of portions of those lectures and annotations for Tolkien's text. He is careful to differentiate his own comments from his father's because of the complexity of the whole: the *Beowulf* translation, an assimilated commentary, and notes. As Christopher acknowledges in his introduction, the versions of the translation, even in Tolkien's hands, had an "intricate history" not always easy to disentangle.[28]

In regard to the ending of the commentary as it relates to the whole poem, Tolkien's annotations, which Christopher gathered from his father's teaching lectures on the first 2207 lines of *Beowulf* and segregated in a separate file, end at the point in the epic at which the third part begins: the theft by the *þeow*, the slave, of the Dragon's cup. Tolkien's final lecture might have ended with line 1650, given the requirement at Oxford

University (where he had been appointed to a professorship in 1925) that all candidates for a BA in English pass a final examination on the medieval by translating passages from the first half of *Beowulf*, one of nine such "papers." To do so, students enrolled in a course or courses in Anglo-Saxon, normally the "general course" in English, in which there was only time enough for intensive translation of about half of the epic, although likely there was some discussion about the remainder of the poem. And the first-half endpoint, at line 1650, involves Beowulf's successful routing of Grendel's Mother and his return from her lair.

The remainder of Tolkien's commentary in Christopher's edition continues to 2207 of the *Beowulf* text, apparently the point at which the *Beowulf* course actually ended, even if the students were responsible only for the first 1650 lines. In addition, for the course Tolkien deleted about 300 lines of *Beowulf* in what he has chosen to both translate and comment upon. In his *Beowulf* article, "Beowulf: The Monsters and the Critics," Tolkien includes a note that points to a second division at line 1887, when young Beowulf and his men enter their boats to leave Denmark, after which the real tragedy, of old Beowulf, follows until the end (3182*).[29] At that point Beowulf and his men return across the sea to the Geats, leaving behind the Danes and his youthful victory over Grendel and Grendel's Mother.

The later adaptation, *Sellic Spell*, was written in the early forties, after Tolkien had published *The Hobbit* (1937), but begun, like the *Beowulf* translation, in 1925, when he came back to Oxford to teach, and mostly written during his first seven years there.[30] Thus it was also written after his Andrew Lang Lecture had been composed, between December 1938 and 8 March 1939 (the latter, the date when the lecture was delivered at St. Andrew's as "Fairy Stories"), although Tolkien only published it as "On Fairy-Stories" after the war, in 1947.[31] In finishing *Sellic Spell* he likely would have had in mind his earlier creative efforts and his definition of the fairy-story. If Tolkien can be considered to have rewritten the harsh "Story of Sigurd" as a fairy-story in *The Hobbit*, as I have recently argued,[32] then I will similarly argue here that Tolkien's translation of *Beowulf*, as interpreted through his notes and commentary on it and his creative adaptations of it, is explicitly marked by his desire to rewrite *Beowulf* as a fairy-story. In this regard, it is important to note how Tolkien ends his course notes and commentary on *Beowulf* and then compare what those comments include with his transformations in his fairy-story *Beowulf* rewritings.

To recreate the Beowulf story as fairy-tale requires the entire omission of the third monster in the original *Beowulf* epic, the Dragon, whose attempted felling by old Beowulf leads tragically and hubristically to his death and to the likely demise of his nation. In line with Tolkien's own definition of the fairy-story in his lecture and essay "On Fairy-Stories," the ultimate fairy-story is the entirely eucatastrophic Gospel story of Christ's Resurrection. Following from this model, Tolkien's creative transformations of an Old Norse saga and an Old English epic also appear to be constructed as eucatastrophe—comedy, with a happy ending—and not as dyscatastrophe, or tragedy (like the original *Beowulf*). But, as Tolkien acknowledges in his equally famous essay, "Beowulf: The Monsters and the Critics" (delivered as a lecture in 1936 and then published), this tragic epic poem will continue to appeal to those who speak a language descended from Old English and live today "in our northern world beneath our northern sky," will continue, that is, "until the dragon comes,"[33] "dragon," a symbol of death that comes to us all. And so Tolkien removes the dragon in rewriting *Beowulf* fairylike. Unlike tragic Geat hero Beowulf, the comic *Sellic Spell* hero, Beewolf, completes his adventures in the land of the Danes, returns home, marries, becomes king, and lives happily ever after. Given *Sellic Spell*'s date of composition in the early forties, so much later than that of the very early *Beowulf* translation in 1926, it is interesting to note that at least two of Tolkien's own fairy-stories were also written (if not published) in the mid-thirties and early forties, "Farmer Giles of Ham" (1936, published in 1949) and "Leaf by Niggle" (?April 1942, published in 1964).[34]

Many of the fairy-story elements in *Sellic Spell* involve the comic character of Beewolf, a figure who seems to derive more from the Beowulf at the opening of *Beowulf* (whom Tolkien calls "Beow"), that is, the son of Danish foundling and progenitor of the Danes, Scyld Scefing, than from his alleged double, the abject tragic Geat Beowulf. About this strange doubleness, Tolkien complains in his commentary that "[T]he unfortunate 'chance' that placed a character in the genealogy of the Scyldings with a name that began with the same letters as the fairy-tale hero, has with the aid of the two scribes both extremely ignorant of and careless with proper names ... produced one of the reddest and highest red herrings that were ever dragged across a literary trail."[35] Because of this snafu, Tolkien seems to want the real Beowulf to be Beow, in that both have an abject nature and history, given the Geat's initial ignoble role as the son of a criminal. Beow, son of an abandoned child set out alone in a ship, grew up to rob "the hosts of foemen"; he "laid fear upon men" (Tolkien, *Beowulf*, 3–5). Like Beow, Beowulf's father Ecgþeow is an exiled homicide whose negative reputation has rubbed off on the young, mostly untried Beowulf, so that Unferth can jeer at him at Hrothgar's court. As Christopher says in the note to Tolkien's line 14, about Beow (18*), "this (and again at 41 (*53)) [sic] is almost the only case in the translation where I have altered a clear reading without any justification in any of the texts, all of which have Beowulf."[36]

Tolkien also discusses this matter of the odd name "Beowulf," given both to the young Danish child and to the Geat hero and wonders if the poet changed it from "Beow." He points to the thematic connection between the two "non-heroic" names, *Scyld Scefing* and *Beow*, Scéaf meaning "sheaf" and "Beow" (the name that also appears in "On Fairy-Stories" in 1947) meaning "barley" (*Commentary*, 145). The Professor concludes that "Beow/Beowulf 'Barley' is the glorification (by genealogists) of a rustic corn-ritual *myth*. Beowulf the bear-man, the giant-killer comes from a different world: *fairy story*" (*Commentary*, 147). He attributes this equivalence to the ignorance of the two different scribes of *Beowulf* (*Commentary*, 148). Interestingly, like both of the figures, Tolkien himself was an orphan, without a father or mother, and poor. The confusion of the two men and the way he characterizes each suggests the origin of his two very different heroes, Beowulf and Beewolf.

So—there is Beowulf, son of Scyld, whom Tolkien calls "Beow," and Beowulf, the Geat hero we know from the dyscatastrophic Anglo-Saxon epic, whom Tolkien also calls Beowulf, and then his very different Beewolf, the mock-hero of the eucatastrophic *Sellic Spell*, with our medievalist connecting the heroes through modal and verbal chiaroscuro, one the inversion of the other. Tolkien achieves this in his *Beowulf* by translating some words in the Anglo-Saxon epic less literally and more figuratively to suit his own definition of the fairy-story, as if the world of the Danes and Geats were a fairy kingdom, and recasting the latter, the *Sellic Spell* version of the northern world of Beewolf, as magical and faërie-like, a comic Victorian fairy-tale more suitable for children. Tolkien seems to be distinguishing the true fairy-story from a story that merely involves fairies (or monsters, who may indeed be human as well as merely human-shaped). In these two respects, he may be imitating Victorian contemporary William Morris, who, along with Eiríkr Magnússon, translated the *Völsunga Saga* involving the Old Norse hero Sigurd into English from the Icelandic, and, as he has done previously, Victorian fairy-story compiler Andrew Lang, whom Tolkien revered even as a child.[37]

In "On Fairy-Stories," Tolkien portrays the tale-teller as creator of a Secondary World in which fantasy suspends disbelief, so that Recovery, Escape, Consolation, and eventually Joy result. But other tales, some with unhappy outcomes, like those favored by Lang, Müller, and Grimm—according to editors Verlyn Flieger and Douglas A. Anderson—"are in the main by-products of the scholarly study of comparative mythology, though they are made as and presented as books for children."[38] For those older scholars, the nineteenth-century's interest in comparative philology and the reconstruction of the history of language as a tree, branching from Sanskrit to Latin and beyond, led to the compilation of oral folk-tales organized around national identities. The interpretation of the folk-tales and their mythologies involved natural or physical meanings (for example, "solar mythology," as proposed by Müller) as an expansion of words in the original languages. Even Andrew Lang preferred anthropology as an explanation: animal worship, animism, and so forth, associated with the dawn of humanity, and therefore appropriate for children before they matured into adults.[39]

What may not be clear is Müller's basis for his philological endorsement of myth on a system of ancient classical mythological exegesis according to natural and etymological explanations. This hermeneutic course was pursued by Plato and later, the Stoics, in a different manner: Apollo as the sun, Phoebe/Diana as the moon, and so forth. Philology per se would not have been condemned by Tolkien; he himself was a philologist, loved words and their original meanings (and created languages of his own based on living languages, Welsh and Finnish, for example, in the Elven tongues). He also taught many early languages, including Gothic, for the several years he taught at Leeds and later at Oxford.[40] Similarly, the anthropological movement that sprang up in the nineteenth and early twentieth centuries—for example, in Sir James Frazer's explorations of ritual in *The Golden Bough*—may have been important in the creation of Tolkien's term "Cauldron of Story." This label referred to the mix of history and legend (myth) that led eventually to the nineteenth-century "fairy-story." About the fairy-story, Jack Zipes, a contemporary scholar of the genre, has revealed its important social and political role in ideology and the education of children as a vehicle, dating from the eighteenth century.[41]

What Tolkien argues for in "On Fairy-Stories" is an aesthetic for the fairy-story that grows out of Christianity, analogous to the fantasy of the Resurrection in its effects on the reader, as I have acknowledged in my chapter in *Tolkien's Art: A Mythology for England*, on the Christian aspects of Tolkien fairy-stories "Smith of Wootton Major" and "Leaf by Niggle."[42] Christianity is the ultimate fantasy for Tolkien, demanding belief based not on reason but on faith. True fairy-stories—again—depend on imagination that leads to sub-creation of fantasy not available in the real world.

In *Sellic Spell* Tolkien shifts from philology (the translation of *Beowulf*) to fantasy—with Beowulf recast as Beewolf, showing that Frazerian, or anthropological, incarnation, as mentioned above, is actually a red herring. For Tolkien doesn't consistently follow Frazer any more than he follows Müller. The fairy-tale compilations of Jacob and Wilhelm Grimm and other Victorian storytellers attracted him[43] in addition to the mythmaking of Elias Lönnrot in his epic collection of tales for Finland, the *Kalevala*.[44] But if he follows any storyteller, it is Andrew Lang, whose eleven fairy-story books in different colors, published almost annually beginning in the late nineteenth century into the early years of the twentieth, center on tales pulled from every country except England. Or else Tolkien is following William Morris, whose translation of the *Völsunga Saga* appears in redacted form in Lang's *Red Book*.[45] However, Andrew Lang makes clear in the introduction to the *Lilac Fairy Book* that

> Nobody ever *wrote* most of the stories. People told them in all parts of the world long before Egyptian hieroglyphics or Cretan signs or Cyprian syllabaries, or alphabets were invented. They are older than reading and writing, and arose like wild flowers before men had any education to quarrel over. The grannies told them to the grandchildren, and when the grandchildren became grannies they repeated the same old tales to the new generation. Homer knew the stories and made up the "Odyssey" out of half a dozen of them. All the tales, all about Theseus and Heracles and Oedipus and Minos and Perseus is a *Cabinet des Fées*, a collection of fairy tales. Shakespeare took them and put bits of them into "King Lear" and other plays; he could not have made them up himself, great as he was ... Nobody can write a new fairy tale; you can only mix up and dress up the old, old stories, and put the characters into new dresses.[46]

In his own fairy-stories, as many scholars by now have noted, Tolkien accordingly incorporated figures from Old and Middle English or in Old Norse literature,[47] given the strong Viking presence in what became England and Scotland.

As noted in the previous chapter, the Oxford medievalist confesses in his essay "On Fairy-Stories" (1936–1938) that a Victorian version of an Old Norse saga was his favorite "fairy-story": "The adaptation of the Story of Sigurd (done by Andrew Lang himself from [William] Morris's transl. of *The Volsunga Saga*) was my *favourite without rival*. Even as it stands in the *Red Book* it is no Conte des Fées. It is strong meat for nurseries."[48] Of course, the *Völsunga Saga* and/or Morris's full translation of it were subjects on which Tolkien was expected to lecture at Oxford, from the late twenties through the forties.[49] But in addition, around 1926 onward, he was at work on, or completing, the unfinished *Fall of Arthur* (1931–1934), to be discussed in the next chapter; "On Fairy-Stories" (1938) (or Tolkien's original 1939 Andrew Lang lecture from which it derived); and his *Hobbit*, published in 1937 but largely written between 1920 and 1927. Most importantly, in that same passage Tolkien also declares that much of his own fiction serves primarily as "fairy-stories" and for that reason he considers himself as a mythmaker. So we return to the fairy-story traces in his prose translation of *Beowulf* and in his more creative adaptations.

Beowulf, The Geat Hero

Remarkably, the fairy-story elements in Tolkien's *Sellic Spell* also crop up more subtly in his prior 1926 *Beowulf* translation. Tolkien's translation is, from what I can tell, largely indebted to the glossary in Klaeber's edition of *Beowulf*, originally published in 1922 (and reprinted in 1928, 1936, 1941, and 1950). It was a standard text for the poem in Tolkien's Old English classes. When Tolkien verges away from Klaeber, by selecting a different denotation, omitting a phrase, or supplementing words in a line, Christopher acknowledges Tolkien's alterations without necessarily attempting to explain why. While I have not checked every Tolkienian translation of a line against Klaeber's glossary as recorded in my own dutifully plotted graduate school translation, what I have found does present some interesting emphases not unlike those found elsewhere in Tolkien's creative fiction, in his articles, and, of course, elsewhere in his excursions into *Beowulf* as also listed in Christopher's edition.

When Tolkien alters a specific denotation in Klaeber's glossary, it is often to heighten the abjection and loneliness of a hero and the monstrosity of his adversaries, to emphasize despair and death, the loss of all hope, or the isolation of a nation. This alternation does not happen often in the last third of the Old English epic, when the Dragon arrives, who stands for Death itself, but in those passages early on which anticipate, or foreshadow, the nihilism of what is to come. At the same time Tolkien imbues his *Beowulf* with fairy-story and romance elements. Conversely, the third part of the *Beowulf* translation—excluded from Tolkien's pedagogical lectures on the poem because of the academic requirements for the BA—includes at least one more positive moderation of the ending, in line with Tolkien's own adaptation of *Beowulf* in *Sellic Spell*.

For example, in Tolkien's introduction of Shield Sheafing of the Spear-Danes for Scyld Scefing—"fēaschaft funden," or "he who first was found forlorn" (7*, 5)—at the opening of the *Beowulf* translation, Klaeber's glossary offers "destitute," "poor," or "wretched" for "fēaschaft," all of which are transcended by Tolkien's use of "forlorn" in the sense of being "left alone," of isolation and abandonment, and lacking in human company, which is less a fact than a sense of how Shield is feeling. And in Tolkien's commentary, following from Klaeber's introduction and the Frazerian anthropological comment, he describes his Shield Sheafing as "the corn-god or the culture-hero his descendant, at the beginning of a people's history, and adding to it a mysterious Arthurian departure *back into the unknown*, enriched by traditions of ship-burials in the not very remote heathen past—to make a magnificent and suggestive *exordium*, and background to his tale" (*Commentary*, 138–39).

Of interest here is Tolkien's acknowledgment of an Arthur-like mystery in the description of Shield Sheafing's funeral rites, echoing the ambiguity of the whereabouts of King Arthur in his unfinished *Fall of Arthur* (written 1931–1934). Tolkien left a scrawled note in which he does suggest Arthur actually dies rather than just falls, as the title of *The Fall of Arthur* stresses, leaving the door open to a "Once and Future King," an eternal Arthur.[50] An Arthurian Shield Sheafing as a Christlike king who never dies, no matter if he falls, because he is continually reborn like the corn-god, seems to fit. In the Arthurian legend, this is important because Arthur has no legitimate or illegitimate heir to succeed to the throne—Mordred himself dying so perversely treacherous to his father and king—and to his nation. That Tolkien likens Shield to an Arthur-figure, eternal, recycling like the corn-god, contrasts him with Beowulf at the end of the Anglo-Saxon epic, who has no apparent heir and whose death will lead to the peril of his nation. The contrast is ameliorated in part in *Beowulf* by the identically named heir of Danish Shield, Beowulf, whose name Christopher changes to Beow, he says, to differentiate the two Beowulfs. However, *Beowulf* students have long accepted "Beowulf" as his name in all the texts—for a reason, perhaps because it is clear the poet is drawing attention to a similarity in abjection for Danish Beowulf and Geatish Beowulf. It is the only case, says Christopher, "where I have altered a clear reading without justification."⁵¹

As *Beowulf* reiterates that Beow was "Scyldes eafera Scedelandum in" (19*), *eafera* meaning "son" or "offspring" also in line 12* as well as 19*—in contrast, in the translation Tolkien emphasizes that Beow was not just Scyld's son but "*the heir of Scyld* in Scedeland" (15–16), also in contrast to the folk-tale hero Beewolf of *Sellic Spell*. Son Beow successfully follows Scyld, the orphan who was clearly wretched at the time he was found as a babe but who ends as a *god cyning* (11*). This distinction is important because "heir" suggests the answer to a king's death, in that his line and nation will be preserved through a descendant, and a recipient of riches, lands, and title—a word Tolkien uses to stress what he knows will be the danger after the fall (or death) of Arthur and the death of hero Beowulf at the end of the poem. Of course the Old English poem forecasts this danger of kinglessness, as does Tolkien in his translation in reference to Beow: "a young child in his courts whom God sent for the comfort of the people: perceiving the dire need which they long while endured aforetime being without a prince" (10–13). And, Tolkien further emphasizes the intimacy and closeness of father and son as an analogue to the relationship between a good king and a loyal people: "Thus doth a young man bring it to pass with good deed and gallant gifts, while he dwells *in his father's bosom*, that after in his age there cleave to him *loyal knights of his table*, and the people stand by him when war comes" (16–20, my emphasis). The Anglo-Saxon *on faeder (bear)rme* (21*) figuratively means, as Tolkien's translation suggests, "in his father's bosom" but, more practically and literally, "while still his son," and, as Tolkien's commentary points out, contextually means Beow is still able to receive gifts in his father's household: "The doctrine that a young man (a prince) should already in his father's lifetime begin the practice of that prime virtue of Northern kings, generosity, by giving gifts to *loyal knights*—gifts which are still technically in his father's *bearm*. It is the gifts and treasures rather than the young man that are in his father's lap!" (*Commentary*, 149; my emphasis).

Note Tolkien's anachronistic use again of "knights" for retainers in the translation, which helps to continue the fairy-story and later medieval delineation of Beowulf's "quest." He also refers to the "Géatmaecgum" (491*) in *Beowulf* as "the Geatish knights" (398). Later on, he refers to Beowulf's men, *Geotena léode* (443*), as "Gothic knights" (357).⁵² And also, in Tolkien's translation, at Hrothgar's court while the warriors race their horses, a *scop*, before telling of Sigemund's deeds, "in his turn began with skill to treat the *quest* of Beowulf and in flowing *verse* to utter his ready *tale*, interweaving words" (707–9, my emphasis). This "tale," in other words, included "in poetry" before "the quest"—an Arthurian romance word that Tolkien added to his original text and that Christopher omitted.[53] The lines in the Anglo-Saxon read, "secg eft ongan/síð Béowulfes snyttrum styrian/ond on wrecan spel geráde,/ wordum wrixlan" (871–74*)—literally, meaning "the warrior began again/Beowulf's undertaking to recite with skill,/and successfully to utter the skillful story,/to vary his words" (my translation; "varying his words," reflecting the Anglo-Saxon poetic practice of incremental repetition in verse that required defined metrical patterns).

Tolkien's fondness in the *Beowulf* translation for a system of reference that privileges fairy-story exaggeration—not just the beginning's emphasis on father–son attachment, suggesting a remediation of the Arthurian happy ending, but most especially a Childe Arthur who will return—is clear from Tolkien's translation of *uncúthne nið* (276*). In Klaeber, the phrase denotes a "strange (or forbidden/awful/uncanny) affliction," referring to what Grendel does in Heorot, but in Tolkien's reworking the word signifies "monstrous malice" (223), identifying the source of whatever is unusual—the malice—as monstrous, and the awfulness as intentional and mean.[54] In Tolkien's own fairy-story adaptation, *Sellic Spell*, Grinder comes to the Golden Hall because he is merely hungry; he doesn't envy the existence of Golden Hall as Grendel does Heorot: "That night [when he meets Beewolf] Grinder was seized with a gnawing hunger"—perfectly natural (*Sellic Spell*, 370). Perfectly natural for a cannibal, even in *Beowulf*: Beowulf does tell Hrothgar, in his initial address in the epic, "I expect that he will, if he is allowed to manage it, eat the Geatish people in the battle hall without hesitation as he often has done" (442–45*, my translation). And in Tolkien's translation, when Grendel abandons his arm in Heorot after Beowulf has twisted it off, the Geat tells Hrothgar, "Nonetheless he hath left behind upon his trail his hand and arm and shoulder"; from "Hwæþere hē his folme forlēt/tō lifwraþe/lāst weardian,/earm ond eaxle" (790–91)/(970–72). Tolkien omits a portion of the original, *tó lífwraþe* ("as life-support" meaning "to guard his tracks," 971*), because he had originally omitted it in his earliest translation (in the commentary, Tolkien notes there was nothing intentional in Grendel's action, even to escape death, tricky as he was, although Beowulf's actual phrasing suggests what he does is intentional, *Commentary*, 297). Grendel here reminds me of Gollum.

As Tolkien moves into the third and most desolate part of the epic, the fight with the Dragon, he pays especial attention to the Elegy of the Last Survivor as he buries the treasure for which all his tribe has forfeited their lives, emphasizing the isolation, the aloneness, that the Last Survivor experiences: "Swá giómormód giohðo mænde/án aefter eallum" (2267–78*). Tolkien translates this as "Even thus in woe of heart he mourned his sorrow, / alone when all had gone" (1909–1910), with Christopher noting that his father has added, as an alternate, apparently, "alone mourning for them all."[55] The lines, according to Klaeber's glossary, read, "Thus sad of mind the joyless one, one after all of them, moaned in sorrow." Nothing there about "alone" in *Beowulf*, "an" meaning "one," which implies singularity—but Tolkien likely wanted to deepen the pathos of being totally alone as the last member of his tribe—echoed in the fearful plight of the Geats after Beowulf's death, and in this case an anticipation of that final scene in the epic.

As Tolkien underscores the malicious intentions of Grendel, he similarly underscores the unwillingness of the "son of Ecgtheow" to leave the earth—the final aloneness. The Old English text "Ne wæs þaet éðe síð,/þæt se mæra maga Ecgðéowes/grundwong þone ofgyfan wolde" (2586–88*), translated via Klaeber, can be rendered as "that was not a pleasant journey (undertaking): that the illustrious son of Ecgtheow was willing to leave the earth." Tolkien translates this first as "No pleasant fare was his that ... the son of Ecgtheow should *witting* leave that field on earth," but then changes it after a strikethrough to "No easy task was his that day (nor such) that the son of Ecgtheow should of his own *will* forsake that field on earth" (2172–74; 2586–88*, my emphases).[56] Tolkien has left out "mæra," meaning "renowned," referring to Beowulf; the appearance of the word "witting" in the first rendition suggests perhaps either Tolkien or Christopher originally wrote but misread "willing," which is what the glossary terms offer. The point is that Beowulf does not intend to do this if he can help it and that he is resistant to death.

At the end, when all is lost, Tolkien makes a change in the text that softens the cruelty of the final scene. For the Old English "swylce giómorgyd *(s)io g(eó)méowle/* (æfter Bíowulfe b)undenheorde/ (song) sorgcearig") (3150–52*, my emphasis), Tolkien offers "a lamentable lay *his lady* aged with braided tresses for Beowulf made" (2644–46, my emphasis). Tolkien changes the mourner in the B (ii) manuscript to "many a Geatish maiden," which also appears in the typed C manuscript, according to Christopher's note.[57] Usually this reference is taken to refer to a single old Geat woman (*sío* is singular), often interpreted by scholars as a reference to Hygd, wife of Hygelac, but possibly to Beowulf's wife, if he had one (for which there is no other possible evidence), or to his mother. Or if not, then it just signifies the generic failure of the iconic image of the peaceweaver, the *frithu-sibb*, pledge for peace[58]—now an *old* woman, no longer able to weave peace through children or marriage—given the coming "days of Evil" filled with slaying and error, ruin and thralldom.[59]

The end scene (which Tolkien includes and comments upon, if briefly) shows the burial mound filled with useless treasure, in echo of the Last Survivor's original (cursed) burial and a backwards ironic gloss on the fugitive slave's finding of the cup hidden in the Dragon's cave. Ironic, too, because the slave hopes the stolen cup will restore him to his master's graces but, as Tolkien notes, nearly stepped on the dragon's head in the dark (2290,* 1929). Tolkien in the long commentary describes this passage as "a very moving treatment of this '*fairy-tale*' situation—remarkable for the 'sympathy' shown by the author for both the wretched fugitive and the dragon" (*Commentary*, 351, my emphasis). From this point on, Tolkien sees this poem as elegy, not as fairy-story—indeed, has always seen it as *dyscatastrophe*. The "interjected 'elegy'" of "ne byð him wihte ðȳ sél" (2277*, 1918), "no whit doth it profit him," for Tolkien, refers to the Dragon: "The whole thing is somber, tragic, sinister, curiously real." It is "sad history": the treasure that might have served as wealth for a marriage to a princess, he concludes, is instead an enchanted gold treasure that enticed Beowulf to his death and thus "rivals the exordium on ship-burial" (32–52*, 25–50; *Commentary*, 352).

Shield Sheafing, Beow(ulf), and Beewolf

In his *Beowulf*-inspired fairy-story, *Sellic Spell*, Tolkien conflates the character known as Beowulf, or Beow—the son of Scyld Scefing, the Spear-Danes founder from the beginning of the epic—with the hero we know as "Bee-Wolf" (or Beewolf) and with Scyld Scefing. Like so many of Tolkien's abject heroes (Bilbo, Frodo, Fëanor, and Túrin Turambar), Beewolf seems anything but a hero when we first meet him and only nominally like abject Geat Beowulf struggling to find a heroic identity for himself. Beewolf more closely resembles the Finnish folk-hero and orphan Kullervo from the epic *Kalevala* who fails again and again and like the gullible hero Sigurd of the *Völsunga Saga*, about whom Tolkien wrote in the *Lay of Sigurd and Gudrún* (1934) (whose magic treasure similarly leads to disaster). Found in a bear's lair at the age of three, Beewolf cannot speak; he grows into a "surly, lumpish boy," who won't work or learn, is held in little account, and "had no place on the benches. He sat often on the floor and said little to any man" (*Sellic Spell*, 360). His only friends, when he arrives at the Golden Hall—which has been plagued by a man-eating ogre named Grinder (Grendel)—are Ashwood, Handshoe, and Unfriend (originally named Unpeace).

Christopher, introducing *Sellic Spell*, which Tolkien had also translated back into Old English (and which also appears in Christopher's edition),[60] acknowledges that it was intended to cut out the "heroic or historical" from the folk-tale, and so its title derives from what Beowulf describes to Hygelac, the Geat king, as the "strange (wondrous) tale" relayed at the feast in Heorot after Grendel's defeat (the tale was probably composed in the "early 1940s").[61] Tolkien's penciled note about this tale warns it is just "*a* story, not *the* story. It is only to a limited extent an attempt to reconstruct the Anglo-Saxon tale that lies behind the folk-tale element in *Beowulf*."[62] Accordingly, the men who accompany Beewolf to the Golden Hall include companions with magical powers: namely, Handshoe (Hondsciōh in *Beowulf*), who literally wears large gloves on his hands that enable him to tear and thrust rocks; next, Ashwood (Æschere), who has a great ash spear that can rout many men; and third, Unfriend, is No Friend (Unferth, or Mar-peace, in *Beowulf*), who regrets to see mighty men in the hall because of his own great self-esteem (*Sellic Spell*, 365). But in this fairy-tale, unlike *Beowulf*, Unfriend is befriended and hugged by Beewolf, which softens him (*Sellic Spell*, 366). Unfortunately, both Ashwood and Handshoe are killed by Grinder; but not, of course, Beewolf, whom Unfriend merely follows to the lair of Grinder's dam and then abandons, returning home after seeing blood that he thinks belongs to Beewolf rather than to Grinder's dam and releasing the rope on which Beewolf needs to ascend after finishing the battle he is still engaged in below. After Beewolf chastises and beats Unfriend, the traitor fashions the sword Gildenhilt as a gift to the hero to assuage his own guilt. When the Scyld-like foundling Beewolf returns home to his own land as a great "knight," he marries the king's daughter and lives on, "long in glory," as king himself. Because the appropriately named Beewolf loves honey as much as he does, it is no accident that we learn, in the final line of the tale, "the mead in his hall was ever of the best" (*Sellic Spell*, 385).

Indeed, Beewolf at the end is described more as a King Arthur than as an Anglo-Saxon lord in an image also used in *Smith of Wootton Major*:

"When the boat came to land, out stepped a great lord, exceedingly tall, clad in shining mail, with a high-crested helm upon his head; and twelve knights were with him" (*Sellic Spell*, 384). Tolkien may have had his own *Fall of Arthur* in mind, for he had begun it at the end of 1931and stopped working on what he had finished thus far in 1934.[63] Tolkien also borrowed from this type of epiphanic moment at the end of *Smith of Wootton Major* (written mid-February 1965),[54] after green-garbed Prentice the apprentice has revealed to the old Cook Nokes that the star is back in the black box, and Nokes accuses him of being tricky and deceitful and admonishes him for his vanity and cunning, when Prentice asks him if he has time for the King of Faery: "To Nokes's dismay he grew taller as he spoke. He threw back his cloak. He was dressed like a Master Cook at a Feast, but his white garments shimmered and glinted, and on his forehead was a great jewel like a radiant star. His face was young but stern."[65]

In addition to this Arthurian flourish, in Manuscript A of *Sellic Spell*, after the battle with Grinder but before Grinder's mother attacks Golden Hall, Tolkien offers a note, later struck, that describes a gift offered to Beewolf by the Queen: a necklace with gems and a ring, that, "If ever hope seems to have departed, turn it on your finger, and your call for help will be answered; for the ring was made by the fair folk of old" (*Sellic Spell*, 395n1). What the line clearly indicates, in the early 1940s, after *The Hobbit* has been published (1937), is that Tolkien is not only thinking of magical rings again but that what is in his head has so intermingled, whether he is writing scholarly articles about Anglo-Saxon history or composing fairy-stories, his Beowulf will always be Beewolf (or Frodo), as his Grendel cannot be other than Grinder.

Reading *Sellic Spell*, one begins to lose sight of the text at hand: is it *The Lord of the Rings*, *The Fall of Arthur*, or *The Legend of Sigurd and Gudrún*? As Tolkien concludes Manuscript A, it is clear that the Professor of Anglo-Saxon at Oxford will always be simultaneously and irrevocably the inventor of Middle-earth. Indeed, in *The Lord of the Rings*, in the whole Rohan episode, Tolkien has refashioned elegiac *Beowulf* as a fairy-story, according to Richard W. Fehrenbacher, which "allows him to rewrite what he saw as the heroic but ultimately doomed pre-Christian world view of *Beowulf* in order to allow for the eucatastrophe, the happy ending denied the Danes but central to Tolkien's project in *The Lord of the Rings*."[66]

Apparently, we, as readers, must never lose sight of how intermingled all these medieval texts and adapted Tolkienian fairy-stories were during the process of invention. It is appropriate to come full circle in this chapter with a gloss on the comic epigraph to *Sellic Spell* that introduces it but also ends the adaptation. A penciled addition about Beewolf's own words in explanation of the antihero's changed name ironically labels him as antihero and unknight, given its emphasis on the *hilts*—all that remain of swords rather than the tools of chivalry, the *swords* themselves. The ironic doubleness of the name and title is applicable to the selves of Tolkien as author and his projections into characters, whether in pedagogical translation or comic fairy-story: "Beewolf I used to be called, when I was at home. Now some call me the knight of the golden hilts; yet I see no reason to change my old name" (*Sellic Spell*, 403).

Notes

1. I have argued this point—that *Beowulf* deeply affected Tolkien's fiction and scholarship, both of which are inextricably blended throughout his career—in my first book on Tolkien, *Tolkien's Art: A "Mythology for England"* (London: Macmillan, 1979; revised edn., Lexington: University Press of Kentucky, 2001). Tolkien's posthumous publications, thanks to Christopher Tolkien and many other new editors, have expanded his corpus so greatly such prior literary criticism is by now outdated without taking it into account, although I have indicated in the Introduction the outlines of previous criticism on Tolkien's use of *Beowulf*, Old English, Old Norse, and Middle English, on 9–10, 15–17.

2. See J.R.R. Tolkien, "Beowulf: The Monsters and the Critics," *Proceedings of the British Academy* 22 (1937): 245–95; the article, of which I have an original offprint, does not italicize the name Beowulf, which might suggest Tolkien intended to refer to the hero—something he would likely do—and not to the work. Of course, the lack of italics in the name could also be a printer's error. The article has been reprinted in the Tolkien anthology *The Monsters and the Critics and Other Essays*, ed. Christopher Tolkien (London: Allen & Unwin, 1983; Boston: Houghton Mifflin, 1984), and most recently in *Beowulf: A Verse Translation*, trans. Seamus Heaney, ed. Daniel Donoghue, 130, Norton Critical Editions (New York: W.W. Norton, 2002). In Wayne G. Hammond and Douglas A. Anderson, *J.R.R. Tolkien: A Descriptive Bibliography* (Winchester, UK: St. Paul's Bibliographies; New Castle, Delaware: Oak Knoll Books, 1993), 3, I count ten separate publications of the article, beginning with the original *Proceedings* article on 30 December 1937; followed by edition reprints published by Oxford University Press; Folcroft Press; Norwood Editions; and Arden Library; continuing with University of Notre Dame Press, in what may have been the first anthology *of Beowulf* criticism; Prentice-Hall, in *The Beowulf Poet:*

A Collection of Critical Essays, Indiana University Press; and with *Interpretations of Beowulf: A Critical Anthology*. I list these to be indicative of the article's importance.
3. For dates, see Scull, *Chronology*, and J.R.R. Tolkien, *Beowulf: A Translation and Commentary, Together with Sellic Spell*, ed. Christopher Tolkien (Boston and New York: Houghton Mifflin Harcourt, 2014). For "On Translating *Beowulf*," see Tolkien, *The Monsters and the Critics*, 71 [49–72]. This latter essay grew out of Tolkien's "Prefatory Remarks On A Prose Translation of *Beowulf*," in *Beowulf and the Finnsburg Fragment*, trans. John R. Clark Hall (1911; repr. rev. edn. London: George Allen & Unwin, 1972), ix–xxvii. Tolkien's comments on meter, "On Metre"—the second part of his "Prefatory Remarks" (xxviii–xliii)—appeared in the first revised edition of Clark Hall, in 1940, but were at that time, according to C.L. Wrenn's later (1949) introduction, part of what had been titled as Tolkien's introduction to Clark Hall's *Beowulf*. In this later edition, the section on meter appears separately in part II along with part I, but remains unchanged, described by Wren "as the most permanently valuable part of the book" ("Introduction," vi).
4. See Tolkien, "Prefatory Remarks," xliii. See also the reprinted version in Tolkien, *The Monsters and the Critics*, 71.
5. J.R.R. Tolkien, "Iúmonna Gold Galdre Bewunden," *Gryphon* 4(4) (January, 1923): 123.
6. See the later revised version of Tolkien's "Iúmonna Gold Galdre Bewunden," reprinted by editor Douglas A. Anderson in a note in his edition of Tolkien's *The Annotated Hobbit* (1966; Boston: Houghton Mifflin, 1988), 288–89. Both the 1923 and 1937 versions were included in Michael D.C. Drout's critical edition of the early manuscript drafts of Tolkien's famed "Beowulf: The Monsters and the Critics" article, in *Beowulf and the Critics*, rev. edn. (2002; Tempe, AZ: Arizona Center for Medieval and Renaissance Studies, 2011), 56–57 and 110–12. In its final form as "The Hoard," it also appears in the critical edition of Tolkien's *The Adventures of Tom Bombadil, and Other Verses from The Red Book*, ed. Christina Scull and Wayne G. Hammond, illustrated by Pauline Baynes (London: HarperCollins. 2014), 98–102; commentary, 240–51, where the various versions are laid out. The new title, "The Hoard," had been added by September, 1946, according to Hammond, *Adventures of Tom Bombadil*, 240, because Tolkien had thought to include it along with the publication of *Farmer Giles of Ham*.
7. The letter is cited in Scull, *Adventures of Tom Bombadil*, 248. The editors discuss how such an epitome as this changes from revision to revision, 248–41.
8. Tolkien, "Iúmonna Gold Galdre Bewunden," *The Annotated Hobbit*, 288.

9. Tolkien, "Iúmonna Gold Galdre Bewunden," *The Annotated Hobbit*, 289.
10. T.D. Kendrick, "The Sutton Hoo Finds. VI. Sutton Hoo and Anglo-Saxon Archaeology," *British Museum Quarterly* 13 (1939): 116–28.
11. Norman Davis, "Man and Monsters at Sutton Hoo," in *English and Medieval Studies Presented to J.R.R. Tolkien on the Occasion of his Seventieth Birthday*, ed. Norman Davis and C.L. Wrenn (London: Allen & Unwin, 1962), 321–29.
12. See Sam Newton, "*Beowulf* and Sutton Hoo," *Saxon: The Newsletter of the Sutton Hoo Society*, 21 (1994): 1–8. See also Newton's *The Origins of Beowulf and the Pre-Viking Kingdom of East Anglia* (Cambridge: D.S. Brewer, 1993); and his "Beowulf and the East Anglian Royal Pedigree," in *The Age of Sutton Hoo: The Seventh Century in Northwestern Europe*, ed. Martin O.H. Carver (Woodbridge, Suffolk: Boydell, 1992): 65–74.
13. Newton, "*Beowulf* and Sutton Hoo," 2. See also 210–11n22 in this study for a discussion of the article on the manuscript with the Woden illustration by Tolkien's former student Simonne Thérèse Rosalie Odile d'Ardenne, "A Neglected Manuscript of British History," in *English and Medieval Studies Presented to J.R.R. Tolkien on the Occasion of His Seventieth Birthday*, ed. Norman Davis and C.L. Wrenn, 84–93 (London: George Allen & Unwin, 1962).
14. J.R.R. Tolkien, aka alleged editor G.A.B., "The Battle of the Eastern Field," *King Edward's School Chronicle* 26(186) (March 1911), 22–26; repr. in *Mallorn*, no. 12 (1978), 24. Subsequent references to the poem will appear parenthetically in the text by section and line number(s), followed by page number(s). Any Tolkien commentary on this poem, whether pseudo-editorial or genuine, will appear in endnotes and not in the chapter text.
15. Tolkien, "The Battle of the Eastern Field," 26.
16. Tolkien, "The Battle of the Eastern Field," 24–28. The editor's comment can be found on 24.
17. See Jessica Yates, "Commentary on 'The Battle of the Eastern Field,'" *Mallorn* 13 (1979): 3–5.
18. Winston Churchill, *My Early Life, 1874–1904* (New York: Scribners, 1996), 15–24.
19. Yates, 3.
20. Thomas Babington Macaulay, *The Lays of Ancient Rome* (London: Longman, 1847), 37 ff.
21. See Macaulay's note to the *Lay of Lake Regillus* in which he adds, "There can be no doubt that the Censors who instituted this august ceremony acted in concert with the Pontiffs to whom, by the constitution of Rome, the superintendence of the public worship belonged; and it is probable

that those high religious functionaries were, as usual, fortunate enough to find in their books or traditions some warrant for the innovation." See http://www.victorianweb.org/authors/macaulay/lays/4.html, accessed 5 July 2015.
22. Tolkien, "The Battle of the Eastern Field," 25.
23. Tolkien, "The Battle of the Eastern Field," 28.
24. Christopher Tolkien, "Introduction to the Translation," in *Beowulf: A Translation and Commentary*, 2. References to individual Tolkien *Beowulf* works in this edition—the *Beowulf* translation, his commentary on it, and his creative adaptations—will appear in my chapter text within parentheses and by short title and either page or line number(s), as appropriate for poetry or prose. To indicate a line number in the Anglo-Saxon *Beowulf*, an asterisk will mark it (following Christopher's practice in the edition), to differentiate that line number from Tolkien's, which is not the same because he has shaped, edited, and shortened the original text to fit his course requirements at Oxford. The notes, headnotes, and introductions written by Christopher are cited in my endnotes rather than in the text to differentiate his editorship from Tolkien's authorship.
25. Christopher Tolkien, "Preface," in *Beowulf: A Translation and Commentary*, viii.
26. See Christopher Tolkien, "Introduction," to *Sellic Spell*, in *Beowulf: A Translation and Commentary*, 359.
27. Christopher Tolkien, headnote to "The Lay of Beowulf," in *Beowulf: A Translation and Commentary*, 415.
28. Christopher Tolkien, "Introduction," 3–11.
29. See Fr[iedrich] Klaeber, Introduction to *Beowulf and the Fight at Finnsburg*, 3rd edn. (Boston: D.C. Heath, 1950), 70. All translations of *Beowulf* (other than Tolkien's) are my own unless otherwise noted and are based on Klaeber's glossary.
30. See Humphrey Carpenter, headnote to letter 9, in *Letters*, 14.
31. See J.R.R. Tolkien, *Tolkien on Fairy-stories: Expanded Edition, with Commentary and Notes*, ed. Verlyn Flieger and Douglas A. Anderson (London: HarperCollins, 2008), 122. The history of the making of "On Fairy-Stories," an essay that was not published until 1947, is detailed on 122–28. This edition contains all variants from the two major manuscripts of Tolkien's Andrew Lang Lecture (1939), including the final published version as edited by Christopher Tolkien in Tolkien's *The Monsters and the Critics and Other Essays* (1983).
32. See Jane Chance, "Tolkien's Hybrid Mythology: *The Hobbit* as Old Norse 'Fairy-Story,'" in *The Hobbit and Tolkien's Mythology: Essays on Revisions and Influences*, ed. Bradford Lee Eden, 79–81 (Jefferson, NC: McFarland, 2014).

33. Tolkien, "Beowulf: The Monsters and the Critics," 34.
34. See Scull, *Chronology*, 188, 253.
35. Tolkien, "Commentary That Accompanies the Translation of Beowulf," 147–48.
36. Christopher Tolkien, "Notes," 107.
37. Eiríkr Magnússon and William Morris, trans. *Völsunga Saga: The Story of the Volsungs and Niblungs, with Certain Songs from the Elder Edda*, ed. H. Halliday Sparling (London: Walter Scott, 1888).
38. Flieger and Anderson, "Introduction," in *Tolkien on Fairy-stories*, 12.
39. Flieger and Anderson, "Introduction," in *Tolkien on Fairy-stories*, 12–13, 6, 20–22.
40. See the very helpful descriptions of medieval lectures and classes Tolkien attended at Oxford, along with texts and subjects for which he was expected to be examined, in Scull, *Chronology*, 32–36, 39–41, 49–52, 59, 63, 66–67. For courses taught at Leeds for which he may have held responsibility, see also 114, 117, 122, 126–27; at Oxford, 130, 133, 136, and so forth, thereafter.
41. See Jack Zipes, *Fairy Tales and the Art of Subversion: The Classical Genre for Children and the Forces of Civilization* (London: Methuen, 1988; rev. edn., 2011); and Jack Zipes, *Breaking the Magic Spell: Radical Themes of Folk and Fairy Tales* (1979; rev. edn., Lexington: University of Kentucky Press, 2002).
42. See Chance, *Tolkien's Art*, chapter 3 (74–110).
43. See, for example, T.A. Shippey, ed., *The Shadow-Walkers: Jacob Grimm's Mythology of the Monstrous* (Tempe, AZ: Arizona Center for the Study of Medieval and Renaissance Studies/Brepols, 2005); and Dimitra Fimi, *Tolkien, Race, and Cultural History: From Fairies to Hobbits* (London: Palgrave Macmillan, 2009), esp. chapters. 2–5.
44. See T.A. Shippey, "Grimm, Grundtvig, Tolkien: Nationalisms and the Invention of Mythologies," *The Ways of Creative Mythologies: Imagined Worlds and Their Makers*, ed. Maria Kateeva, 2 vols (Telford: Tolkien Society Press, 2000), 1: 1–17; repr. in *Roots and Branches: Selected Papers on Tolkien by Tom Shippey* (Zollikofen, Switzerland: Walking Tree Press, 2007), 79–96; and Verlyn Flieger, "'There Would Always Be a Fairy-Tale': J.R.R. Tolkien and the Folklore Controversy," in *Tolkien the Medievalist*, ed. Chance, 26–35; and Verlyn Flieger, "A Mythology for Finland: Tolkien and Lönnrot as Mythmakers," in *Tolkien and the Invention of Myth*, ed. Chance, 277–83.
45. For a discussion of how William Morris and Andrew Lang (and the *Völsunga Saga*) influenced Tolkien in varied ways, especially in relation to *The Hobbit*, see chapter 3 in this volume.

46. Andrew Lang, *The Lilac Fairy Book* (London: Longmans, Green, 1910; repr. New York: Dover Books, 1968), vii–viii.
47. See the discussion of recent scholarship on Tolkien in relation to Old English and Old Norse in the introduction to this study, 9–10, 15–17.
48. Tolkien, *Tolkien on Fairy-stories*, 188–89; my emphasis.
49. See Scull, *Chronology*, 139, 249 (for example, October 1941).
50. See the discussion of the ending of Arthur in J.R.R. Tolkien, *The Fall of Arthur*, ed. Christopher Tolkien (London: Houghton Mifflin Harcourt, 2013), 135, 138–39, and in this study, 119–28.
51. Christopher Tolkien, "Notes," 107.
52. See Tolkien, *Commentary*, 237–42, for the long note he uses to justify this term.
53. Christopher Tolkien, "Notes," 115.
54. See also Tolkien's *Beowulf* translation, 146 (184*), where *sliðne nið* is intentional "fiendish malice," that is, malice by fiends, rather than Klaeber's various glosses as "dangerous/severe/terrible affliction," indicating more passive suffering, in Christopher Tolkien, "Notes," 110n146; also Tolkien, "*Commentary*," 175–76.
55. Christopher Tolkien, "Notes," 122.
56. Christopher Tolkien, "Notes," 125.
57. Christopher Tolkien, "Notes," 129. Christopher points the reader to a version of Tolkien's 1938 lecture on "Anglo-Saxon Verse" included in "The Fall of Arthur" appendix (but not apparently published in *The Fall of Arthur*) in which Tolkien provides an alliterative translation of *Beowulf*'s final lines: "while grieving song Gothland-maiden/with braided hair for Beowulf made," above which lines Tolkien scribbled an alternative translation that reads "while her grievous dirge the grey lady ..." See Christopher Tolkien, "Notes," 129–30.
58. Many scholars have studied the *ides* as peace-pledge: see the summary and listing of previous studies in Chance, *Woman as Hero in Old English Literature* (Syracuse: Syracuse University Press, 1986; repr. Eugene, OR: Wipf and Stock, 2005), 1–11.
59. In regard to *Beowulf*, Tolkien is particularly interested in Danish Freawaru, wed to Heathobard Ingeld, who fails because of a painful past history between the two tribes. See Tolkien's *Commentary*, 336–47. See my discussion in chapter 7, 196–98.
60. See Christopher's acknowledgment of Tolkien's Old English translation of *Sellic Spell* as written after the modern version, in his "*Sellic Spell*: The Old English Text," 406, but also, for the translation itself, which appears in *Sellic Spell*, 407–14.
61. The citation from Tolkien appears in Christopher Tolkien, "Introduction," *Sellic Spell*, 358–59.

62. The citation from Tolkien appears in Christopher Tolkien, "Introduction," *Sellic Spell*, 355.
63. The dates are according to editor Christopher Tolkien, "Foreword," in *The Fall of Arthur*, 11.
64. For the date, see Scull, *Reader's Guide*, 944; the discussion of the fairy-story covers 942–50. See also the introduction to J.R.R. Tolkien, *Smith of Wootton Major*, ed. Verlyn Flieger (London: HarperCollins, 2005).
65. Tolkien, *Smith of Wootton Major* (London: George Allen & Unwin; Boston: Houghton Mifflin, 1967), 56, 58.
66. See Richard W. Fehrenbacher, "Beowulf as Fairy-Story: Enchanting the Elegiac in *The Two Towers*," *Tolkien Studies* 3 (2006): 101–15 (here, 105).

CHAPTER 5

"Queer Endings" After *Beowulf*: *The Fall of Arthur* (1931–1934)

> "Being is in question in *Dasein* {human existence}, and to be in question is, as it were, the *status* of being as a verb, the manner by which its epic is made, its epic or adventure [*sa geste*]. To be in question is essential to essence."—Emmanuel Levinas, in "The Analytic of *Dasein*" (1975), from *God, Death, and Time*

> "Now for Lancelot I long sorely."—King Arthur, in J.R.R. Tolkien, *Fall of Arthur*, canto 1(I.183)

> "The ancient adage designed to dissipate the fear of death—'If you are, it is not; if it is, you are not' [Epicurus, Letter to Menoeceus]—without doubt misunderstands the entire paradox of death, for it effaces our relationship with death, which is a unique relationship with the future. But at least the adage insists on the eternal futurity of death. The fact that it deserts every present is not due to our evasion of death and to an unpardonable diversion at the supreme hour, but to the fact that *death is ungraspable, that it marks the end of the subject's virility and heroism*."—Emmanuel Levinas, *Time and the Other*

In Tolkien's attempt to set down his own medievalized version of the ending of Arthur in alliterative verse, he joins other authors who have dramatized the complexity of Arthur's final moments, although he never actually completed his version—titled *The Fall of Arthur*—and supplied contradictory possibilities for what would have been the ending. Tolkien's models, as cited by editor Christopher Tolkien, include the fourteenth-century *Alliterative Morte Arthure* as well as certain tales from Sir Thomas Malory.[1] But Tolkien might also have had in mind near-contemporary works, such as, Alfred Lord

Tennyson's long poem *Idylls of the King* (published 1858–1885), William Morris's poem "The Defence of Guenevere" (1858), which Tolkien likely read while at Exeter, and T.H. White's *The Once and Future King*, written 1936–1958, parts of which were published seriatim (the first three books in 1938–1940, and the fourth, much later, in 1958).

If, as Christopher argues, Tolkien began *The Fall of Arthur* sometime after abandoning the rhyming couplets of the *Lay of Leithian*—at the end of 1931 and about the time he had finished the alliterative Norse poems known today as *The Legend of Sigurd and Gudrún*—that is, in 1934[2]—then it makes sense that Tolkien may not have finished this Arthurian work because of the intervening event of the completion and publication of *The Hobbit*, in 1937. And, Christopher adds, another interruption: "the emergence of Númenor, the myth of the World Made Round and the Straight Path, and the approach of *The Lord of the Rings*"[3] (to say nothing of the delivery of his monumental Andrew Lang Lecture, "Fairy-Stories," which Tolkien first presented on 9 March 1939). Certainly, as Christopher notes, his father was still thinking about finishing *The Fall of Arthur* as late as 1955.[4]

Although Christopher's introduction does not mention the simultaneity of the early writing of *The Fall of Arthur* with Tolkien's preparation for his famous lecture on *Beowulf*, "Beowulf: The Monsters and the Critics," delivered in late 1936, and its publication shortly thereafter, the Old English epic would certainly have been in Tolkien's thoughts as he worked on *The Fall of Arthur*, if only because of his medieval teaching responsibilities at Leeds, and then at Oxford, beginning in 1925 and continuing on throughout his career. He himself had completed his first translation of *Beowulf* into alliterative verse in 1926, so he knew the poem well.[5] Tolkien desired to write alliterative verse in the manner of Old English and Old Norse poetry, according to a letter written to Tolkien by R.W. Chambers (Professor of English at University College, London) on 9 December 1934. Old English scholar Chambers had read Tolkien's *The Fall of Arthur*, apparently on the train to and from Cambridge, and in his letter about it wrote Tolkien that he "took advantage of an empty compartment to declaim him [Tolkien] as he deserves." Chambers describes *The Fall of Arthur* as "very great indeed ... really heroic, quite apart from its value in showing how the *Beowulf* metre can be used in modern English ... You simply *must* finish it," he tells Tolkien.[6] It is interesting that Chambers references its meter as that of Old English poetry, in particular, that of *Beowulf*, rather than as alliterative Middle English, and in a language one would expect of an Arthurian poem, such as that of the *Alliterative Morte Arthure*. Of course, Tolkien had written other poems in rhyming or alliterative verse: the unfinished *Lay of the Children of Húrin* (1918–1921) and the post-*Battle of Maldon* verse-drama "Homecoming of Beorhtnoth" (1931–1933 to 1945). He also translated into modern English alliterative verse poems from the West Midlands (where he had grown up) that he had taught from the beginning, *Sir Gawain and the Green Knight* (finished 1950), *Sir Orfeo* (no earlier than 1944), and *Pearl* (around 1925–1926).[7] An edition of these three translations was published by Christopher Tolkien in 1975.[8]

This Chambers letter provides an important clue in examining Tolkien's shift from the verse of *The Fall of Arthur* to the "*Beowulf* metre," as Chambers described it. What all three of the original medieval poems and Tolkien's own translations or interpretations involve is the fall or death of a hero or king, in each case, one who has no legitimate heir to take his place and, as king of his nation, no guarantee of a future for his people. That Tolkien was thinking simultaneously about the Silmarillion mythology behind his creative works, as his son and editor Christopher suggests, reminds us that some of Tolkien's greatest heroes (or antiheroes) in the fictional works—for example, Bilbo, Frodo, and Túrin Turambar—lack sons or progeny, whether useful or harmful, to continue what a leader in Middle-earth has begun in aiding his own people. Indeed, like these childless heroes, even Tolkien's Lancelot in *The Fall of Arthur* bears some resemblance to the professor's other abject heroes, according to Christopher.[9] For a great king to die without an heir, a son to continue to lead his nation, in medieval terms, poses a disaster for any nation, whether medieval or modern. And of course Arthur's bastard, Mordred, also dies, leaving the kingdom unmanaged.

How does Tolkien handle the problem of a nation without a legitimate heir to the throne, given the models of heirless kingdoms in medieval works? Such works involve nations seemingly without a future, or a posterity—as when the Geats, in a pagan poem such as *Beowulf*, are likely to be felled by any number of enemies after Beowulf's death, his kinsman Wiglaf notwithstanding; or as with Sigurd's nation in the *Legend of Sigurd and Gudrún*. And does Tolkien handle the problem at all, in a Christian work like *The Fall of Arthur*, and what does his solution to it, if any, tell us about his use of sources, his purposes, and how both relate to his own fictional creations?

Crucial to any answer in regard to *The Fall of Arthur* is its unfinished ending. Does Tolkien intend Arthur to die or does he just sail away to Avalon, in reiteration of his role as "The Once and Future King" in White's later novel of the same? In what is finished of his poem, Tolkien focuses on the *fall* of Arthur and not definitively on his death, as in the "Alliterative Morte," to keep the focus on the elasticity of posterity without children, either on Arthur as the iconic once and future king, or on Arthur as a type of Christ. But what notes remain about Tolkien's intentions in completing it also appear to point to Arthur's actual death—an ambivalence about unhappy endings common to Tolkien in many of his writings.

Arthur and His Men

The Fall of Arthur is slight: it consists only of five cantos, with the fifth left unfinished, for a total of 954 lines (around 220 lines per canto) (the whole, a third the size of *Beowulf*). Each canto emphasizes the king's relationship with another man, often a kinsman: his sister's son Gawain (cantos one and four); or his half-sister's son, traitor Mordred (canto two); or his beloved filial knight—but perhaps more grievous traitor—Lancelot (canto three); and then at the end (canto five), on the consequence of himself as a sonless king, or one without legitimate heirs. This singular focus on central male characters in each canto resembles that of the four books of T.H. White's *The Once and Future King*, which begin with Arthur (Wart) and his coming of age in *The Sword and the Stone* (1938, 1939), followed by the adventures of the young unloved sons of Morgause in *The Witch in the Wood* (1939; later titled *The Queen of Air and Darkness*); then on Lancelot, in *The Ill-Made Knight* (1940); and finally, on Arthur and Mordred's role in his fall, in *The Candle in the Wind*, published together with the earlier three books in 1958.

Just as White begins and ends his book with Arthur, so also does Tolkien his unfinished poem, although many Arthurian narratives (for example, Geoffrey of Monmouth's, Malory's, and Tennyson's) actually trace the life-story of the king from birth to fall. Unlike theirs, Tolkien's more closely resembles the *Stanzaic Morte Arthur* and the *Alliterative Morte Arthure*, which begin *in medias res*, in the first instance, after the Round Table's quest for the Sangrail has ended; or in the second, when Lucius, emperor of Rome, demands fealty at the New Year's feast after Arthur has conquered much of Britain and Europe.[10] More bleakly, Tolkien's poem opens close to the end, when Arthur's signal strategic and final mistake to battle the Saxons to defend the Roman Empire results in his prolonged absence from the kingdom: "so burned his soul/after long glory   for a last assay/of pride and prowess," in a battle of will against fate (I.14–16).

But both Malory's and Tennyson's versions contain the adventures of many other knights that refract back indirectly on the central Arthurian story rather than tightly focusing on the tragedy of Arthur and his relationships with crucial male figures, nephew, son, knight, and friend, and those especial two with their own relationships with Guinevere, wife and lover. And in contrast to White's version, Tolkien's provides a much more loyal and admirable kinsman for Arthur in his half-sister's son, the knight Gawain, who appears along with him at both ends of the whole poem. Tolkien shifts attention in canto two from Morgause's sons, as in the second book of *The Once and Future King* (the brutal Gawain, along with Gaheris, Gareth, and Agravaine), to the principal recreants, the narcissistic queen and wife, Guinever, and Arthur's son, Mordred, who lusts after his stepmother. Tolkien similarly centers on the beloved filial alien and traitor, the knight Lancelot, son of Bors, in canto three; and then on him whom Tolkien perceives as Arthur's true nephew and sister-son, Gawain, in canto four.

In contrast to the enormous series of diverse and seemingly unrelated adventures delineated in Malory's *Morte Darthur*, Tolkien's poem begins in canto one well into the final days in what might have begun in what Christopher Tolkien refers to as the "chronicle tradition," that is, as drawn from Geoffrey of Monmouth's fictionalized *History of the Kings of Britain* and other later versions that borrowed from it.[11] In canto one, Arthur, after having conquered most of Britain, Scandinavia, and Gaul, resists the demand of the Emperor Lucius of Rome to pay tribute by killing him and routing the Romans. Titled "How Arthur and Gawain went to war and rode into the East"—purposing to fight the Saxons and defend the Roman colony from the "heathen"—the canto reveals Arthur foolishly leaving his apparently trustworthy son, Mordred, behind as caretaker of the kingdom. This son of Arthur (and half-sister, Morgause, as in Malory? Tolkien doesn't say who has mothered him) promises that "I will hold unharmed till thy home-coming./Faithful thou has found me."[12] Even Gawain, who wants to go to war, does not suspect Mordred (I.35–38). But it is a dark story from the opening: Arthur realizes when Cradoc arrives and tells him that he has been too long away from his own kingdom that it now lies in jeopardy ("his heart foreboded that his house was doomed"), and that fortune has turned against him (I.151ff; and 177). At this point Arthur calls for Gawain and expresses his need for the absent Lancelot: "Now for Lancelot I long sorely" (I.183), meaning "we miss most now the mighty swords/of Ban's kindred" (I.184–85).

In canto two, "How the Frisian ship brought news, and Mordred gathered his host and went to Camelot seeking the queen," Mordred is described as in thrall to "Guinever the golden with gleaming limbs" (II.27), although it is said "His bed barren; there black phantoms/of desire unsated and savage fury/in his brain had brooded" (II.39–41). Dark-visaged Mordred is described in a very Tennysonian way as purely evil in intention: "the weeping world waking coldly/he leant and laughed, lean and tearless" (II.44–45). Indeed, when Mordred's squire Ivor informs him of the breaking of the Frisian ship and the advent of Arthur, who has learned of Mordred's treachery, Mordred attempts to manipulate Guinever into succumbing to him by denigrating her as "alone lordless in loveless days,/a kingless queen in courts that echo/to no noise of knighthood" (II.126–28). Arthur's dark nephew (II.140) wants to rectify this situation by offering himself to her as husband and king (133–34). Mordred also reminds her that neither Arthur nor Lancelot du Lake, "love remembering/to thy tryst," will return (II.146–47), because the West wanes as the East waxes (II.148–49). As does the crudeness of Mordred's description of Guinever's options: "Thou at my side shall lie, slave or lady,/as thou wilt or wilt not, wife or captive" (II.154–55).

And Tolkien portrays Guinever herself as "cold" in heart (II.159) and "dissembling" (II.161), even with Mordred, for she asks proof of his power, a request he denies cruelly: "What proof of power shall prisoner seek/captive of captor?" (II.171–72). The picture of her stealing away to her own home accompanied by a few faithful followers is equally negative in its self-centeredness and self-pity: she imagines Lancelot feeling sorry for her "woe and wandering by wolf hunted" (II.207) and wonders if he would come to rescue her if she called: "Guinivere [sic] the fair,/not Mordred only, should master chance/and the tides of time turn to her purpose" (II.211–13).

As Christopher notes, his father allows Guinever to have a voice throughout,[13] in this manner much like Tennyson's poignant (or bathetic) version and possibly drawn from a reading of Morris's emotional queen in "The Defence of Guenevere." Tolkien's Guinever is nearly as flawed as Mordred, in echo of Tennyson's flawed characters in *The Idylls of the King*, but in her self-centeredness she also strongly resembles Morris's Guenevere in "The Defence of Guenevere." There, during her trial (for an unnamed crime, but presumably for adultery and treachery), Guenevere delivers a defensive speech to the lords and Gauwaine and accuses Gauwaine of lying while she speaks the truth (rather ironically, on Morris's part, given the adultery of his own wife, Jane). Through her tears she rationalizes her falling in love with Lancelot: "I was half mad with beauty on that day." She also describes the blood in her bed as that of Lancelot wounded in a fight with Mellyagraunce after the latter discovered them together in her bedroom.[14] "Say no rash word/Against me, being so beautiful," she begs, as if innocence and goodness necessarily accompanies beauty. Then, Morris provides a *deux ex machina*: at the final moment, Lancelot arrives on his roan horse, presumably to sweep her away.

In Tolkien's canto three, the most dramatic of the five, "Of Sir Lancelot, who abode in Benwick" in exile, the "noblest knight of Arthur" (III.20) suffers anguish and remorse for having betrayed his lord by yielding to his love for Guinever (III.15), but "love forsaking lord regained not" (line 16). Tolkien initially titled his whole poem "The Legend of Lancelot and Guinevere [sic]," despite the failure of both principals as lovers.[15] Lancelot's dilemma is impossible to resolve: he first admits, "to his lord alone his love giving;/no man nor woman in his mind holding/dearer than Arthur" (III.34–36). Tolkien then uses the same phrasing to describe Lancelot's love for Guinever: "To his lady only was Lancelot's love given;/no man nor woman in his mind held he/than Guinever dearer: glory only,/knighthood's honour, near his lady/ in his heart holding" (III.41–45). Despite this equal pull, even before she falls, Lancelot doubts her and remains "Daily watchful" (III.36–38). Tolkien makes him initially seem more admirable than Guinever—handsome, strong, raven-haired, and splendid. After he has given his love to Guinever only, she takes advantage of him by demanding him whom she "darkly hoarded" solely for herself. In this carefully worded line, Tolkien portrays her differently from any other Arthurian work: she longs for gold and in this greed appears to have replaced *Beowulf's* Dragon and the king who finds the buried gold in Tolkien's *Beowulf*ian poem "Iúmonna Gold Galdre Bewunden."[16] Described in her love for him as "fair as fay-woman" (fairy), "lady ruthless" and "fell-minded" (III.54–55), Guinever, rather strangely, regards Lancelot as treasure, always a temptation in Tolkien:

> But cold silver
> or glowing gold greedy-hearted
> in her fingers taken fairer thought she,
> more lovely deeming what she alone treasured
> darkly hoarded. Dear she loved him
> with love unyielding, ...
> in the world walking for the woe of men.
> Fate sent her forth. Fair she deemed him
> beyond gold and silver to her grasp lying. (III.49–54; 56–58)

Here, Tolkien likely understands her concupiscence as connected both with the god of love, Cupid, and with cupidity, the lust for wealth.

Guinever and Lancelot's desire for one another changes, however, after his slaying of Agravain ("dear to Gawain," III.70), when the lovers are found together in her bedroom (a crucial fact Tolkien does not mention, however) and a melee ensues. Tolkien quickly indicates what follows: the Queen is condemned to death for treachery but then Lancelot kills both Gaheris and Gareth, Gawain's brothers, and rescues her from the fire (compressed into III.68–86). When Lancelot shifts from rage to mourning for his damage to the Round Table and repents his pride and breaking of his loyalty to Arthur (III.87–91), she finds him "strange," and "by a sudden sickness from his self altered" (III.95–96). Disliking her "lonely exile" (III.100) and missing the splendor of what she had before, she uses "searing words" to discover his will (III.102–3). Her "greed thwarted" (III.104), she changes, cooling toward him as he has toward her; Tolkien uses the same wording to describe her change in mood: "Strange he deemed her/from her self altered" (III.106–7). Whereas Guinever is pardoned by Arthur and returns to Camelot as a "great and glorious" queen (III.109–10, 113–14), Arthur refuses to forgive his best knight and banishes him from the kingdom and the Round Table (III.114–20).

The end for both traitors is dark. The anguished Lancelot returns to Benwick accompanied by many of his knights while "Grief knew Arthur/ in his heart's secret" (III.124–25). As in Tennyson, even when Arthur arms for war, he does not summon Lancelot, and Lancelot, half-hoping for a summons, but receiving none, thinks of Guinever in possible danger and hoping for her summons, receives none. The long moving description of Lancelot's rejection and Arthur's secret grief are both necessary for explaining why Lancelot fails later to come to Arthur without summons, as Gawain has said he must (and as Arthur hopes futilely that he will), for Lancelot has been fully and completely denied. Despite this darkness, Lancelot awakens one morning from a dream and sings in greeting to the sun, "lifted shining/in the dome of heaven by death exalted" (III.216–17). Tolkien suggests in the canto's last lines that he dies, or at least accepts this last change, the finality of death: "Death was before him, and his day setting/beyond the tides of time to return never/among waking men, while the world lasted" (III.226–28). Elsewhere, Tolkien debated a later meeting between Lancelot and Arthur, as we shall see.

In canto four, "How Arthur returned at morn and by Sir Gawain's hand won the passage of the sea," Tolkien details the relationship between

Gawain, as the faithful nephew and knight, and Arthur, as his liege lord and kinsman, a more honorable bond between two men that succeeds where Lancelot's fails and that contrasts with Arthur's relationship with the bad nephew (and bastard son) Mordred. Mordred scans the coast for signs of Arthur's returning ships; the "fay-woman," Guinever, has fled, and Ivor's advice is to forget her: "With men deal thou,/woman forsaking and to war turning!" (IV.75), advice Mordred casts away in anger. Interestingly, Mordred recalls "words of witchcraft" that he should not challenge the lord of Benwick (Lancelot's forces who bear the lily) in battle if he wished to avoid ruin (IV.104–7).

Unlike faithless Lancelot, Gawain, who appears at both the beginning and the end of the poem, envelopes the narrative in more than one sense, as a nephew and as a true knight. Appropriately, the men who accompany Arthur in canto one are all Britons: Bediver and Baldwin, Brian of Ireland, mountain-men Marrac and Meneduc, Iwain of Urien's line, currently king in Reged, Errac, Cedivor, "Cador the hasty," kinsman to the queen—but not the Breton Lancelot, Lionel, Bors and Blamore (I.44–51). In canto four, Tolkien stresses implicitly Gawain's role as Arthur's sister-son so that his nephew thus occupies the same role as Wiglaf the Wægmunding in *Beowulf*: the opposite of faithless sister-son Mordred, he will prove supportive of Arthur, although he does so without killing the real monster (Death).

Arthur and Beowulf: "Man on Earth"

Arthur, a gloomy depressive, realizes from the beginning of the poem that he has no future. While Arthur is away from Britain battling, as in the *Alliterative Morte Arthure*, Cradoc informs him that Britain has been attacked by "a hundred chiefs," harbored by his son Mordred who wants his kingdom (I.165–67).

> Now from hope's summit   headlong falling
> His heart foreboded   that his house was doomed,
> The ancient world   to its end falling,
> And the tides of time   turned against him. (I.176–179)

While the story continues to darken further in cantos two to four, Tolkien ends the poem abruptly at the beginning of canto five with a few lines that offer Arthur's realization, as he faces the final battle with Mordred and his pagans, that "Death lay between dark before him/ere the way were won; or the world conquered" (V.46–47). However, as if rethinking this brutal ending, on a separate slip Tolkien wrote sixteen subsequent lines in which Arthur calls Gawain and poses the dilemma of whether to confront the pagans there, or waiting, trusting to "the wind and tide ebbing/to waft us westward," where a better ford might await (V.48–63).

This emphasis on a future that is "No Future" aligns Arthur in *The Fall of Arthur* squarely with *Beowulf* and what Tolkien had to say about the most essential monster—the Dragon—in the epic in his own essay, "Beowulf: The Monsters and the Critics." There, after surveying scholarly approaches to the epic and their flaws, in relation to their orientation and their ignoring of the poem *as* poem, and, in particular, of its Dragon, in its first three-fifths (approximately sixteen pages, 103–19), Tolkien turns at last to its theme in the final two-fifths (eleven pages, 119–30): "man on earth." By this wording, Tolkien means that "each man and all men, and all their works shall die."[17] In this regard, *Beowulf* is a work marked by "the shadow of despair," because the poet, who surveys the past and kings' history and warriors, "sees that all glory (or as we might say 'culture' or 'civilization') ends in night," which makes it not exactly an epic, as it is conventionally taught, but in Tolkien's terms, a "tragedy." This term, according to his essay "On Fairy-Stories," means a *dyscatastrophe*, ending unhappily, as opposed to an *eucatastrophe*, a story that ends happily and provides escape, consolation, and recovery to the reader.[18] The exemplar for the latter is the birth of Christ, "the eucatastrophe of Man's history," just as the "Resurrection is the eucatastrophe of the story of the Incarnation."[19]

In particular, for Tolkien this dyscatastrophe of *Beowulf*, as witnessed in the last chapter, is a "contrasted description of two moments in a great life, rising and setting; an elaboration of the ancient and intensely moving contrast between youth and age, first achievement and final death,"[20] in the first of which the hero battles two major adversaries, Grendel (and his mother) and, at the end, the Dragon. Where there is hope in the first part (lines 1–2199) for the Danes and the Geats who have supported them by means of Beowulf's defeat of Grendel and his mother, the second part (2200–3182), initiated by the slave's theft of the Dragon's cup and ending with old Beowulf's venture in killing the Dragon, is themed by "Defeat," for "Disaster is foreboded. Triumph over the foes of man's precarious fortress is over, and we approach slowly and reluctantly the inevitable victory of death."[21] In fact, Tolkien also describes it as "an heroic-elegiac poem": "in a sense all its first 3,136 lines are the prelude to a dirge: *him þa [ge]giredan Geata leode ad ofer eorðan unwaclicne*" ("The Geats made a funeral pyre, placing the body of their lord in the midst").[22] The adversaries Beowulf faces, inhuman as they are, make this story, according to Tolkien,

> ... larger and more significant than this imaginary poem of a great man's fall. It glimpses the cosmic and moves with the thought of all men concerning the fate of human life and efforts; it stands amid but above the petty wars of princes, and surpasses the dates and limits of historical periods ... the outer darkness and its hostile offspring lie ever in wait for the torches to fail and the voices to cease. Grendel is maddened by the sound of harps.[23]

If Beowulf falls because of an error in judgment, one that misgauges his own ability to quell dragons in old age, his error impacts on the future of the Geats, who will most assuredly be wiped out, given the many enemies Beowulf has made in successfully defeating them in the past to protect his own tribe. Of course he appears never to have married or produced progeny, although it has been noted at his funeral pyre an older woman in braids wails, one who may be his mother or his wife or someone else entirely. The only relative to take up his cause is Wiglaf, Gawain-like in his loyalty to his kinsman. Similarly, Beowulf is not unlike Arthur in his heedlessness over the future of his people. The difference between the two heroes is that King Arthur is Christian but has begotten a bastard son who wishes to kill him and sleep with his fairy wife—and who occupies the role of Beowulf's foil, the Dragon, in attempting to vanquish the king. Surely the poet wants the listeners to make the connection between old and failing Beowulf and the missing husband of Grendel's Mother and father to Grendel (a family whose head is a single mother) and the bachelor Dragon, without a mate or progeny.

What is at stake here? The issue of the heirless king, the nation without a future. Aside from the medieval context that Tolkien borrows from the Arthurian tradition, the medievalist's own anxiety about the headless, futureless, state surely stems from that of his own contemporaries in their Arthurian reworkings. Tennyson, in particular, in *The Idylls of the King*, was similarly concerned about the future of England after the death of Albert, Queen Victoria's consort and father of her children.[24] Like T.H. White, Tolkien wrote many of his works in the thirties during the rise of Hitler and the Nazis; he was also a child in a family without a head. Death and its imminence threatens the nations in almost all his works, in one form or the other, an experience shared with the major Existentialists of the twentieth century—Sartre, Heidegger, Kierkegaard, and others.

To contravene death's importance, he constructs fantasies that attempt to reverse the inevitable through, again, escape, consolation, and recovery. Similarly, Emmanuel Levinas, a post-existentialist philosopher who began writing about death and the future in the thirties and continuing into the seventies—notably, in the collection *God, Death, and Time*—manifests a similar anxiety, having lived through the same horrific period when death took so many.[25] Yet unlike Tolkien, Levinas emphasizes the necessity to maintain a relationship with death: he declares,

> The ancient adage designed to dissipate the fear of death—'If you are, it is not; if it is, you are not' [Epicurus, Letter to Menoeceus]—without doubt misunderstands the entire paradox of death, for it effaces our relationship with death, which is a unique relationship with the future. But at least the adage insists on the eternal futurity of death. The fact that it deserts every present is not due to our evasion of death and to an unpardonable/diversion at the supreme hour, but to the fact that *death is ungraspable, that it marks the end of the subject's virility and heroism.*[26]

A more contemporary theorist who shares Tolkien's existential philosophical concern with death is Lee Edelman, who, like Alexander Doty and others, has developed queer theory within the context of the AIDS plague and its decimation of homosexuals and those they touch in the world. For Edelman in particular, who extends queer theory into a postmodern form of existentialism, there will be "no future" for those who are queer.

QUEER ENDINGS

In his book *No Future: Queer Theory and the Death Drive*, Edelman acknowledges that the conventional image used for political interventions that demand a certain protective action to safeguard the social order is that of the Child. That is, when you want to request a particular action of the state, you say "it's for the children," so that Edelman posits that

> ... *queerness* names the side of those *not 'fighting for the children,'* the side outside the consensus by which all politics confirms the absolute value of reproductive futurism ... queerness, ... figures the place of the social order's death drive: a place, to be sure, of abjection expressed in the stigma, sometimes fatal, that follows from reading that figure literally, and hence a place from which liberal politics strives ... to disassociate the queer.[27]

Is this idea one that might identify Tolkien's own anxieties about a king's (and nation's) posterity in his criticism and fiction as manifestly queer? Perhaps: certainly Tolkien's Arthur has taken no care to beget or nurture children with care, as in the example of Mordred. But in addition note Arthur's own queer desire in Tolkien: when in canto one Arthur realizes that Mordred has rebelled against him and gathered an army, he tells Gawain, "Now for Lancelot I long sorely." This is a desire not only for his first knight's loyalty, support, and friendship but for the literal, physical man himself, Arthur seemingly oblivious to his First Knight's treachery. However, Gawain, still angry over where Lancelot's sorry heart actually lies—with Guinever as much as with Arthur—replies truthfully, if "grave and slowly:/Best meseemeth that Ban's kindred/abide in Benwick and this black treason favour not further." Gawain does leave the door open for Lancelot to repent and prove loyal in purpose by "his pride forgoing,/uncalled coming when his king needeth!" (I.196–97), which Lancelot also fails in doing.

The bond between Lancelot and Arthur on the surface more closely represents the kind of homosocial love typified by king and knight in the most celebrated medieval romances and other works, although here the relationship appears more marked by desire and longing than that between either and the suspect fay Guinever. The coldness between her and Arthur and between her and Lancelot jives with their treatment by Tennyson and White, who portray the lovers as initially loving, or lustful, but later ashamed, or cold; both authors were in fact or were alleged to be homosexual.[28] At the end of *The Fall of Arthur*, Tolkien describes Lancelot and Arthur as if they were separated lovers in this longer description of their falling out and its consequences.

> ... Grace with Arthur
> [Lancelot] sought and fought not. They [the courts] his sword refused
> on that knee no more, knight in fealty
> might he hilt handle, nor his head there lay,
> not Lancelot, love forsaking,
> pardon asking, with pride humbled.
> Loveforsaken, from the land banished,
> from the Round Table's royal order
> and his siege glorious where he sat aforetime
> he went sadly ...
> Grief knew Arthur
> in his heart's secret, and his house him seemed
> in mirth minished, marred in gladness,
> his noblest knight in his need losing. (III.114–23; 124–27)

For both Lancelot and Arthur, then, there is "No Future." Lancelot ends by dreaming, singing, Beowulf-like, forgotten songs that move in his heart, "as a harp-music" (IV.213), while he realizes death is before him. And when Arthur returns to "his lost kingdom" (IV.125), followed by Gawain and his supportive men—which encourages Mordred to move forward with battle along with his Saxon (pagan, Goth) supporters—dark Tolkien describes the turning tide brutally: "Timbers broken,/dead men and drowned, a dark jetsam,/were left to lie on the long beaches;/rocks robed with red rose from water" (IV.227–30). It is a devastatingly dark scene reminiscent not so much of "The Battle of Maldon" as of Tolkien's own alliterative sequel to that poem, "The Homecoming of Beorhtnoth Beorhthelm's Son" (or White's ending to *The Once and Future King*). Indeed, Tolkien might well have named this poem *Arthur's Homecoming*.

In the unfinished sixty-three-line fifth canto titled "Of the setting of the sun at Romeril," Tolkien sounds the same dark note. It begins with "a king of peace" ruling his kingdom in a "holy realm beside Heaven's gateway" (V.10, 11). It ends as do other versions of the fall (and/or death) of Arthur, with the king realizing the extent of the treason and betrayal by his kin and princes, not only of him and his kingdom but Christianity as well: "Princes faithless/on shore their shields shameless marshalled,/ their king betraying, Christ forsaking,/to heathen might their hope returning" (V.14–17). As Arthur surveys the scene, he realizes fully the cruel price he has to pay even at this moment, before conquest of any sort, in the lives of those he loves most, the loss of his friends, the best of his knights, "for faith earning/the death and darkness, doom of mortals" (V.30–31). His sorrow and pity are for his people and his land, "for the low misled and the long-tempted,/the weak that wavered, for the wicked grieving" (V.39–40). Tolkien describes the "righteous" king as fantasizing that he would "pass" in peace by granting pardon and annealing the hurt by means of his guidance (V.43–44), to restore "bliss" to "Britain the blessed" (V.45)—apparently Tolkien draws here from the opening of *Sir Gawain and the Green Knight*. But Tolkien's Arthur realizes (in echo of the end that lies before Lancelot) that "Death lay between dark before him/ere the way were won or the world conquered" (V.46–47), and Death seems to take him.

However, there are sixteen more lines on a paper scrap, according to Christopher, in which Arthur calls for Gawain as he offers two options to his "Liege and kinsman, loyal and noble,/my tower and targe, my true counsel" (V.50–51): first, to attack the walls to kill the "traitor keeper"

(Mordred), which in their position may lead only to death and the loss of hope to chance, or, second, to wait for battle by moving onward to "other landing," allowing the "wind and tide ebbing/to waft us westward" (V.62–63). There, the poem ends, suggesting either a better point for Arthur and Gawain to attack the castle or, given the introduction of the westward destination as a symbol for Tolkien in his own creative fiction as the Other World, that Arthur will pass over to the other side and take up his traditional alternate position as the "Once and Future King."

Tolkien in other extant notes relating to *The Fall of Arthur* alternates between various futures for his principal figures without any certain conclusion. Tolkien created two outlines in August of 1937, the second of which reveals that he intended the Battle of Camlann to be followed by Arthur's slaying of Mordred and his own death, Arthur's transport to Avalon, Lancelot arriving too late, then "[? Rejoins] Queen," and finally "Goes in ship West and is never heard of again."[29] But in Tolkien's notes for the remainder of the canto, after wounded Arthur slays Mordred, what is left is "Arthur dying in the gloom. Robbers search the field,"[30] as in Malory, and as in the ending of "The Homecoming of Beorhtnoth Beorhthelm's Son."[31] In the *Alliterative Morte Arthure* Arthur is buried in Glastonbury.

But also, in other notes, Lancelot sails with Lionel to Romeril,[32] where the queen comes down from Wales to meet him, but she does not know where Arthur is and it is clear that Lancelot no longer loves her. So Lancelot rides west, where a hermit tells him that Arthur has left by the sea, and that is when Lancelot, too, finds a boat to sail west, with a hint of Eärendel's voyage, never to return in this world.[33] Meanwhile, Guinever, in grief, heads for Wales: "grows grey in the grey shadow all things losing who all things grasped."[34] Interestingly, in an early draft of *The Fall of Arthur* that Christopher identifies as *Arthur's Grave*, Tolkien notes that only Gawain has a grave; "there are no burial mounds for Lancelot or Guinivere, and 'no mound hath Arthur in mortal land.'"[35] Yet in a longer penciled passage from *Arthur's Grave* cited earlier by Christopher Tolkien, the emphasis is definitely on a grave for Gawain in Britain by the sea, but the reference to barrows for Guinever and Lancelot is ambiguous: "Britain nor Benwick did barrow keep/of Lancelot and his lady." And, in the same penciled text of alliterative verse, where "No mound hath Arthur in mortal land" appears, the Bay of Avalon is mentioned, which lies "on the borders of the world./up[on] Earth's border in Avalon [sleeping>] biding"—clearly a reference to Arthur's departure to a land beyond "mortal life."[36] But what marginal place did Tolkien have in mind?

Apparently, Tolkien was also attempting to recreate the Arthur legend in comparison to Eärendel's sea voyage to Valinor and that of Sir Lancelot, who likewise made a journey.[37] Christopher reminds us that Gawain's ship Wingelot (Foam-Flower) in *The Fall of Arthur* is the name of Eärendel's ship and that just as Tolkien inscribed the name "Avallon" in a "Silmarillion" context for Tol Eressëa, so also he inscribed "Avallon" for Tol Eressëa in an Arthurian context.[38] What Tolkien might have provided as an alternate to this ending Christopher constructs through the image of Avalon as Tol Eressëa, the Lonely Isle, the "*earthly* Elvish paradise." Christopher Tolkien notes in "The Unwritten Poem," in *The Fall of Arthur*, that

> It seems then that the Arthurian *Avalon*, the Fortunate Isle, *Insula Pomorum*, dominion of Morgan la Fée, had now been in some mysterious sense identified with Tol Eressëa, the Lonely Isle. But the name Avallon entered, as a name of Tol Eressëa, at the time when the Fall of Númenor and the Change of the World entered also (see pp. 151–2) [*sic*], with the conception of the Straight Path out of the round World that still led to Tol Eressëa and Valinor, a road that was denied to mortals, and yet found, in a mystery, by Ælfwine of England.[39]

Around this time, in 1937, Tolkien also wrote that Tol Eressëa was changed to Avallon.[40] In I.189, Gawain responds to King Arthur's desire for Lancelot's return by emphasizing the strength without compare Arthur has already in him and in his loyal legions, "from the Forest's margin/ to the Isle of Avalon"; according to Christopher, this "must mean that Avalon had become a part of Arthur's dominion in the western seas."[41]

Certainly, it is a futureless nation that stands devastated and wasted, deprived of its greatest leaders; felled by the dragon, Death, as Tolkien most feared in his lecture on "Beowulf: The Monsters and the Critics." As a queered ending, it fits Edelman's concept of "No Future": instead of a future that represents a realization of "the fantasy of meaning" for most people, the queer offers only a barrier to any "realization of futurity, the resistance, internal to the social, to every social structure or form."[42] Thus, Tolkien queers the future for both his Arthur and the Elves. For Edelman, because the queer refuses the "substantialization of identity" through oppositionality, it depends upon a sense of history as "linear narrative," or what he calls "the poor man's teleology," in that through time history reveals itself as itself (for the macrocosm of the world as the life does for the microcosm of the individual).[43]

What might Edelman say then about the conjunction of Arthurian narrative with Middle-earth history? He would only conclude that, instead of a future that represents a realization of "the fantasy of meaning" for most people, the queer erects a barrier to any "realization of futurity, the resistance, internal to the social, to every social structure or form."[44] While that seems harsh, he adds, "More radically, though, ... queerness attains its ethical value precisely insofar as it accedes to that place, accepting its figural status as resistance to the viability of the social while insisting on the inextricability of such resistance from every social structure."[45] Postexistentially, Edelman opts for the refusal of hope as affirmation of the future, no matter how perverse, "irresponsible, inhumane," in order to withdraw from the "Ponzi scheme of reproductive futurism" as a good, or an ideal.[46] Such queerness would likely keep us from knowing ourselves or what might be designated as our "good."[47] The queer, then, is linked with the "particularity of the subject" as the "truth" (not necessarily the happiness or the good). Important here to recall that, according to his argument, it is politics, instead, that depends on a future involving the Child and its requisite social order.[48]

What Edelman substitutes for the fantasy of a future (and its concomitant necessary imaginary past) as a means of realization of identity is the present Real: the queer concept of *sinhomo*sexuality that depends on *jouissance*. Edelman's severe form of existentialism demands resistance to any kind of Symbolic as essentialism—by which he means the refusal to "invest" any figurative meaning in oneself as subject by focusing only on the present.[49] The Lacanian word, meaning "symptom," refers to "the singularity of the subject's existence, to the particular way each subject manages to knot together the orders of the Symbolic, the Imaginary, and the Real." Edelman uses a wonderful dress analogy to explain its importance for *sinhomo*sexuality:

> [D]enying the appeal of fantasy, refusing the promise of futurity that mends each tear, however mean, in reality's dress with threads of meaning (attached as they are to the eye-catching lure we might see as the sequins of sequence, which dazzle our vision by producing the constant illusion of *con*sequence)—offers us fantasy turned inside out, the seams of its costume exposing reality's seamlessness as mere seeming, the fraying knots that hold each sequin in place now usurping that place.[50]

By this means whatever homosexuals do with their genitals does not associate them with a "culture of death," given that the queer is linked with morbidity, repetition, and fetishization, but instead the sinthome, a place of meaninglessness they must inhabit and *jouissance* that abhors "sentimental futurism."

What, then, of Avalon? According to J.R.R. Tolkien in a letter written in September 1954, Tol Eressëa is the "*earthly* Elvish paradise" while Valinor is the "land of the *Valar* (the Powers, The Lords of the West)."[51] Of course if Tol Eressëa is to be construed as the equivalent of Avalon, in that imaginary past and symbolic present, Arthur would then remain as both an analogous and eternal savior of Britain and also Christlike in his final moments—a Child who might return would guarantee for his nation a Future and for its citizens a salvation. Yet how like Tolkien that in *The Fall of Arthur* he chose by his lack of a definitive ending—by default—neither the Symbolic nor the Imaginary, despite indicators of Arthur's real death. The ambiguity of no certain future for this king, as both flawed human being and savior of England, in Tolkien's refusal to finish *The Fall of Arthur*, constitutes resistance to the essential through making the present eternal: the joy of maintaining authorial choice, one that might ironically be marked in itself as deathless fantasy and no reality.

Notes

1. Tolkien cited by Christopher Tolkien, "Foreword," in *J.R.R. Tolkien: The Fall of Arthur* (Boston and New York: Houghton Mifflin Harcourt, 2013), 13. Subsequent references to the poem *The Fall of Arthur* will appear in the text within parentheses identifying canto number(s) (in Roman numeral[s], as in Christopher's edition) and line number(s). Any subsequent editorial comment by Christopher Tolkien in the "Foreword," "Notes," "The Poem in Arthurian Tradition," "The Unwritten Poem and its Relation to *The Silmarillion*," "The Evolution of the Poem," or the "Appendix: Old English Verse," with citations from Tolkien poems, will appear in my endnotes to differentiate his editorship from Tolkien's authorship.
2. Christopher Tolkien, "Foreword," in *The Fall of Arthur*, 10–11.
3. Christopher Tolkien, "Foreword," in *The Fall of Arthur*, 11.
4. See Tolkien to Houghton Mifflin, letter 165, 219.
5. See Christopher Tolkien, "Preface," in *J.R.R. Tolkien: Beowulf, Translation and Commentary, Together with Sellic Spell* (Boston and New York: Houghton Mifflin Harcourt, 2014), vii.
6. Letter from Chambers to Tolkien cited in Christopher Tolkien, "Foreword," in *The Fall of Arthur*, 10.

7. See Scull, *Reader's Guide*, 748. A portion of Tolkien's *Pearl* translation was read on London regional radio in August 1936.
8. J.R.R. Tolkien, trans. *Sir Gawain and the Green Knight, Pearl, and Sir Orfeo*, ed. Christopher Tolkien (London: Allen & Unwin, 1975).
9. Christopher Tolkien, "The Poem in Arthurian Tradition," in *The Fall of Arthur*, 106.
10. See Larry D. Benson, ed. *King Arthur's Death: The Middle English "Stanzaic Morte Arthur" and "Alliterative Morte Arthure,"* rev. Edward E. Foster, TEAMS Middle English Texts Series (Kalamazoo, MI: Medieval Institute/Western Michigan University, 1994). Christopher discusses *The Fall of Arthur* in a long discursus on "The Poem in the Arthurian Tradition," in *The Fall of Arthur*, 71–122.
11. See Christopher Tolkien's discussion in "The Poem in Arthurian Tradition," in *The Fall of Arthur*, 73–78.
12. Tolkien, "*The Fall of Arthur*," I.28–29. See Christopher's brief discussion in "The Poem in Arthurian Tradition," in *The Fall of Arthur*, 96–97.
13. Christopher Tolkien, "The Poem in Arthurian Tradition," 106–7.
14. William Morris, "The Defence of Guenevere," in *The Defence of Guenevere and Other Poems*, ed. Robert Steele, 1–15 (London: Alexander Moring/The De la More Press, 1904), 3, 6, 9, 11. Steele notes in his "Introduction" that Morris's poems were influenced by Tennyson's, xli. The poem "Arthur's Tomb" follows "The Defence of Guenevere," in the collection, 19–40.
15. Christopher Tolkien, "Foreword," in *The Fall of Arthur*, 12.
16. See this study, 84–85, for the discussion of "Iúmonna Gold Galdre Bewunden."
17. See J.R.R. Tolkien, "Beowulf: The Monsters and the Critics," *Proceedings of the British Academy* 22 (1937): 245–95; repr. in *The Monsters and the Critics and Other Essays*, ed. Christopher Tolkien, 119 (London: Allen & Unwin, 1983).
18. See Tolkien, "On Fairy-Stories," in *Essays Presented to Charles Williams*, ed. C. S. Lewis, 38–89 (London: Oxford University Press, 1947; Grand Rapids, MI: William B. Eerdmans, 1966). See also this essay with "Leaf by Niggle," reprinted in *The Tolkien Reader* (New York: Ballantine, 1966), 31–99. Most recently, see *Tolkien on Fairy-stories: Expanded Edition, with Commentary and Notes*, ed. Verlyn Flieger and Douglas A. Anderson (London: HarperCollins, 2008).
19. Tolkien, "On Fairy-Stories," in *The Tolkien Reader*, 88–89.
20. Tolkien, "Beowulf: The Monsters and the Critics," 124–25.
21. Tolkien, "Beowulf: The Monsters and the Critics," 127.
22. Tolkien, "Beowulf: The Monsters and the Critics," 126–27. For the *Beowulf* edition used—one that Tolkien had long used himself, but likely in an earlier

edition—see *Beowulf and The Fight at Finnsburg*, ed. Fr[iedrich] Klaeber, 3rd edn. (Boston: D.C. Heath, 1950), lines 3137–38. Subsequent lines from this edition of the original in this chapter will appear within parentheses within the text. The translation is taken from the edition of *Beowulf and the Finnsburg Fragment*, trans. John R. Clark Hall, with prefatory remarks by J.R.R. Tolkien (London: Allen & Unwin, 1911, rev. 1940, 1950), 175–76. (Tolkien's own unfinished translation has been discussed separately in chapter 4).
23. Tolkien, "Beowulf: The Monsters and the Critics," 129.
24. Alfred Lord Tennyson, *Idylls of the King*, ed. J.M. Gray (London: Penguin, 1983).
25. Emmanuel Levinas, in "The Analytic of *Dasein*," (Friday, 5 December 1975), in *God, Death, and Time*, trans. Bertina Bergo (Stanford: Stanford University Press, 2000), 29–30.
26. Emmanuel Levinas, *Time and the Other* [and additional essays], trans. Richard A. Cohen (Pittsburgh, PA: Duquesne University Press, 1987), 70–72 (my emphasis).
27. Lee Edelman, *No Future: Queer Theory and the Death Drive* (Durham and London: Duke University Press, 2004), 3.
28. See Helen Macdonald's recent memoir, *H is for Hawk* (London: Grove, 2015), in which a bereaved daughter consoles herself by caring for a goshawk in imitation of Wart (young King Arthur) in T.H. White's *The Once and Future King* (London: G.P. Putnam's, 1938–1958), and of White himself, who wrote a similar memoir, *Goshawk* (London: Cape, 1939), about the same time as he was writing the first book or two of *The Once and Future King*. Macdonald read the latter as a child; she includes in *H is for Hawk* a long section on White, his family problems, and his homosexuality, the latter whose sadomasochistic cast allegedly plays into his interest in training raptors. Alfred Tennyson's *In Memoriam*, written for Arthur Hallam, is often taken as indication of their homosexual relationship, which would have been illegal and criminal in their day, or of their love for one another. See, for example, Garrett Jones, *Alfred and Arthur: An Historic Friendship* (Hertford, UK: Authors Online, 2001).
29. Christopher Tolkien, "The Unwritten Poem," in *The Fall of Arthur*, 134–36.
30. See Tolkien's brief comments in one of two outlines he composed for *The Fall of Arthur*, in Christopher Tolkien, "The Unwritten Poem," in *The Fall of Arthur*, 135.
31. On the departure of Arthur, see, in particular, Christopher Tolkien, "The Unwritten Poem," in *The Fall of Arthur*, 139–45.
32. See Christopher Tolkien, "The Unwritten Poem," in *The Fall of Arthur*, 136.

33. Tolkien's notes for the remainder of *The Fall of Arthur* include Lancelot's boat-journey into the west, never to return, 136; his voyage into the west is followed by a note that mentions "Eärendel passage," 157.
34. Tolkien's notes on the end of the poem, in Christopher Tolkien, "The Unwritten Poem," in *The Fall of Arthur*, 137.
35. See Christopher Tolkien, "The Unwritten Poem," 161.
36. For this longer passage from *Arthur's Grave*, see Christopher Tolkien, "The Unwritten Poem," in *The Fall of Arthur*, 138–39.
37. Christopher Tolkien, "The Unwritten Poem," in *The Fall of Arthur*, 160.
38. Christopher Tolkien, "The Unwritten Poem," in *The Fall of Arthur*, 160n and 161.
39. Christopher Tolkien, "The Unwritten Poem," in *The Fall of Arthur*, 162–63.
40. Christopher Tolkien, "The Unwritten Poem," in *The Fall of Arthur*, 156.
41. Christopher Tolkien, "The Unwritten Poem," in *The Fall of Arthur*, 145.
42. Edelman, *No Future: Queer Theory and the Death Drive*, 4.
43. Edelman, *No Future: Queer Theory and the Death Drive*, 4.
44. Edelman, *No Future: Queer Theory and the Death Drive*, 4.
45. Edelman, *No Future: Queer Theory and the Death Drive*, 3.
46. Edelman, *No Future: Queer Theory and the Death Drive*, 4.
47. Edelman, *No Future: Queer Theory and the Death Drive*, 5.
48. Edelman, *No Future: Queer Theory and the Death Drive*, 6.
49. Edelman, *No Future: Queer Theory and the Death Drive*, 18.
50. Edelman, *No Future: Queer Theory and the Death Drive*, 35.
51. Christopher Tolkien, "The Unwritten Poem," in *The Fall of Arthur*, 156.

CHAPTER 6

Apartheid in Tolkien: Chaucer and *The Lord of the Rings*, Books 1–3 (1925–1943)

"I do not claim to be the most learned of those who have come hither from the far end of the Dark Continent. But I have the hatred of apartheid in my bones; and most of all I detest the segregation or separation of Language and Literature. I do not care which of them you think Whiter."—J.R.R. Tolkien, "Valedictory Address"

"You should never have gone mixing yourself up with Hobbiton Folk, Mr. Frodo. Folk are *queer* up there."—Farmer Maggot, *LOTR* (1:4, 9 my italics)

Was Tolkien a racist or an anti-Semite? The Professor has come in for charges of anti-Semitism ever since he noted in a 1964 BBC radio interview conducted by Denys Gueroult that the Dwarves were intended to represent the Jews: "The Dwarves of course are quite obviously—wouldn't you say that in many ways they remind you of the Jews? Their words are Semitics obviously, constructed to be Semitic."[1] At the same time, Tolkien wrote in letter 176 to Naomi Mitchison on 8 December 1953 that "I do think of the 'Dwarves' like Jews: at once native and alien in their habitations, speaking the languages of the country, but with an accent due to their own private tongue" (229), referring here to the settlement of the Jews in countries where their tongue is not native to them.[2] Additionally, in a letter allegedly written to W.R. Matthews in 1964, but which I cannot locate in the *Letters*, Tolkien indicated that "The language of the Dwarves … is Semitic in cast, leaning phonetically to Hebrew (as suits the Dwarvish

© The Author(s) 2016
Jane Chance, *Tolkien, Self and Other: "This Queer Creature"*,
The New Middle Ages, DOI 10.1057/978-1-137-39896-3_6

character)."[3] However, Magnus Åberg notes in "An Analysis of Dwarvish" —a twenty-three-page single-spaced article dated 27 September 2011— that "Khuzdul is, as said above, in many ways similar to primary world Semitic languages, and where I have lacked examples it has been easy to fill out my analysis on the analogy of Hebrew and its relatives."[4]

Tolkien was very careful overall to differentiate the nature of his languages in reflection of the culture of the peoples who spoke them and in line with their histories. Aside from the philological aspects of Dwarvish—the Dwarves' own language invented by Aulë at the time of their creation, which occurred in darkness, because he wanted so much to pass on to the forthcoming Children his knowledge that he did not wait for Ilúvatar's approval and hid this from him (*Silm* 43). As a result, the Dwarves were condemned by Ilúvatar to sleep in darkness under stone until the Firstborn had been created. Appropriately, the consort of disobedient Aulë, Yavanna, governs growing things, such as trees and plants, in her attractiveness to the Firstborn, to balance philosophically Aulë's association with material things of the earth, such as stones and jewels.[5] John Rateliff also acknowledges that the Dwarves first surfaced during the *Lost Tales* period (1917–1920), characterized as evil, associated with goblins, "mercenaries of Mordor," and in nature, avaricious.[6] In this early respect, they descend from their Old Norse heritage as similar to the greedy Dwarf Andvari in the *Völsunga Saga*. Further, in letter 30 to German publishers Rütten & Loenig Verlag drafted on 25 July 1938, Tolkien indignantly replied that, "if I am to understand that you are inquiring whether I am of *Jewish* origin, I can only reply that I regret that I appear to have *no* ancestors of that gifted people" (37).

At his retirement ceremony as Merton Professor of English Language and Literature, Tolkien in his "Valedictory Address to the University of Oxford" on 5 June 1959 made a bold statement that summed up his long career: he acknowledged his own South African birth and the kind of national, linguistic, and personal difference that can segregate, and therefore alienate an individual or groups of individuals from acceptance within various kinds of community. He declares, "I do not claim to be the most learned of those who have come hither from the far end of the Dark Continent. But I have the hatred of apartheid in my bones; and most of all I detest the segregation or separation of Language and Literature. I do not care which of them you think Whiter."[7] *Apartheid*, or "aparthood," in Afrikaans, according to the *Webster's New Universal Unabridged Dictionary*, denotes "(in the Republic of South Africa) a rigid policy of segregation of the non-white population" or "any system or practice that separates people according to race, caste, etc."[8] Tolkien means apartheid both literally and figuratively.

From a personal and academic stance, Tolkien is implicating the political divisions in English Departments in Great Britain caused by the hegemonic position of literature, which tended to diminish the role of languages and those who taught them. During much of the early twentieth century, the study of language (for example, the early vernacular languages of Old and Middle English) had been separated from the study of literature (modern literature after Chaucer to 1900). Feeling isolated in the academic community over his long career because of his professed field of Language (Old and Middle English), Tolkien also felt called upon to do battle with critical adversaries—his colleagues in Literature—or to seek means to connect both in the English Department curriculum. It is no accident that Tolkien quotes from "The Wanderer" in Old English on the page following his discussion of his hatred of apartheid in his "Valedictory Address."[9] Identifying himself with the isolated speaker in the Old English dramatic monologue, Tolkien uses the famous *ubi sunt* passage from this poem—"Hwær cwóm mearh, hwær cwóm mago?" (Where is the horse gone, where the young rider?)—to point out his own apparent role as a lone exponent of Language, with new generations of scholars failing to understand its importance because of their inability to read Anglo-Saxon. He then follows the passage from "The Wanderer" in the address with an example of another language—his invented Elvish—to be understood, apparently, as another beleaguered and marginalized type of language. Because his fiction writing grew out of his love of philology, he saw literature and philology as inextricably mixed.[10] And he had long felt that his colleagues at Oxford unfairly denigrated his fantastic fiction.[11]

What is especially bold about this formal leave-taking of academia is the deliberate use of a politicized word like *apartheid*, drawn from the class and race issues of the day, for a country in which differentiation between those black and those white has caused so much suffering and turmoil, to describe what he had himself perceived and experienced as a medievalist. The previous academic and cultural separation of the medieval from the modern, of language from literature, reminds us today of how queer the study of the medieval is and has been for more than a century, as Tison Pugh previously reminded us at the beginning of this study. Pugh and Angela Jane Weisl have more recently taxonomized the often pejorative associations of the word in *Medievalisms: Making the*

Past in the Present, based on the definition of "medieval" in the *Oxford English Dictionary*:

> Etymologically drawn from the Latin *medium aevum*, "medieval" in its current form may be constructed on analogy with "primeval," an unwitting suggestion of many of the assumptions of primitivism so often assigned to the period ... As the meanings proceed, these cultural productions become associated with a series not of facts but of stereotypes as further definitions expand from the objective to the subjective ... from which we might assume that someone "medieval" is someone imbricated in irrational, primitive, and destructive behaviors.[12]

From these definitions and assumptions, one might surmise that the modern study of the medieval, as opposed to the study of the renaissance (a word Pugh and Weisl define in contrast to the medieval because of its renascent senses), equally involves not only the necessity of acquiring the knowledge of various languages to read the literature but also superfluous negative characterizations of those who perform that study.

Even though Tolkien's interest in the Middle Ages clearly shaped his scholarly writing, it is not always as clear that this interest equally colored his fiction, although scholarship over the past thirty-five years has advanced many examples of how that works. That most general readers fail to see this medievalness is not so strange: our assumptions about fantasy, like Tolkien's in "On Fairy-Stories," depend upon its usefulness as an escape from reality. There is, therefore, no necessary correlation between fantasy and the historical medieval. Further, many readers look for entertainment instead of meaning in fantasy, especially Tolkien's. Yet, as John Clute and John Grant aptly note, in *The Encyclopedia of Fantasy* (1997), fantasy should be subversive: "It could be argued that, if fantasy (and debatably the literature of the fantastic as a whole) has a purpose other than to entertain, it is to show readers how to perceive: an extension of the argument is that fantasy may try to alter readers' perception of reality ... Most full fantasy texts have at their core the urge to change the reader; that is, full fantasy is by definition a subversive literary form."[13]

Tolkien, for whatever the reason, may have appeared to focus solely on his medieval study in his public professional practice and in scholarship. However, it is possible to discern the personal Tolkien even in the most scholarly of his articles—and along with that, his desire to break down barriers between himself and others. That *The Lord of the Rings* offers to his readers the means of subverting or changing how they feel about serious issues becomes much clearer when we trace out what medieval works Tolkien himself was translating, reading, and continuing to teach while he was beginning to think about a sequel to *The Hobbit*, as early as the 1930s, if not before. In some of those medieval works, issues of race or class were being raised that would begin to be played out in the Germany that Adolf Hitler would make over into a playing field for the extermination of those who differed from the so-called Aryan ideal of the fair-haired: not only the Jews, but gypsies, homosexuals, and the disabled. This issue of racial and class difference must not have been unfamiliar to Tolkien as a South African-born professor who returned to Oxford to teach in 1925, but whose colleagues, even if similarly trained at Oxford or Cambridge, were for the most part born in England (certainly not Ireland or Scotland), and likely raised in upper-class families whose wealth accompanied their privilege. Certainly Tolkien's closest friends were not necessarily upper class—he partnered with his working-class student E.V. Gordon, for example, in working on the *Pearl* and *Sir Gawain and the Green Knight*. Tolkien had been sensitive to his own status as an orphan, alien-born, and comparatively poor relative to others at King Edward's School and at Exeter College. That sensitivity made its way inevitably into what he researched and wrote about in his scholarship.

Did Tolkien make explicit this hatred of apartheid earlier in his career? And if not, why did he wait so very late to admit it openly? Arguing to the contrary, previous literary critics of Tolkien have observed a conservative monarchism, Roman Catholicism, and even racism. Brian Rosebury acknowledges in his *Tolkien: A Cultural Phenomenon* that "commentators in Tolkien, sensing his non-subscription to the secular-left consensus, and indifferent to his declared purposes, have found construing his work is a coded right-wing polemic even more helpful."[14] Fred Inglis, arguing that the Shire is an aristocracy, states categorically that Tolkien is "ineffably English, with England's old and grim snobbery and stupidity, and England's excellent idealism and high-mindedness ... Tolkien is no Fascist, but his great myth may be said, as Wagner's was, to prefigure the genuine ideals and nobilities of which Fascism is the dark negation."[15] In the same collection, Nick Otty, in a witty essay titled "The Structuralist's Guide to Middle-earth," determines that "the politics of Middle-earth are openly paternalistic (in so far as it is possible to be 'open' about paternalism ... So at the Council of Elrond, Aragorn reveals his paternal and selfless concern for all the lesser folk of Middle-earth (like a Tory cabinet minister, or a Platonic Guardian, or a mole-hunter in a John le Carré novel)."[16] Further, says Otty, the Orcs are "swart" and "slant-eyed," that is, "both black and oriental."[17] And in relation to class, "the Shire, for example, is an unreal agricultural community of gentle work-shy landowners with plenty of time to smoke and dream in their burrows. How the plenty of food in which they take such delight is grown, harvested, marketed, transported, etc. is never even hinted at. Almost the only workers mentioned are gardeners."[18]

If the Hobbits are "gentlemen" and the Orcs, "working class" (as they have been designated, inaccurately, by John Carey in *J.R.R. Tolkien: An Audio Portrait*), what, then, is Tolkien?[19] Not a paternalistic, right-wing, classist, racist, monarchist-Fascist, but an author who has created a fictional world in which there exist individual, class, racial, and national differences that he personally found abhorrent. Rosebury counters Otty's and Carey's observations by suggesting that Tolkien's attitude toward work is "close to John Ruskin's; and not too remote from Marx's. All the benign peoples in Tolkien have a distinctive kind of productive work. The Hobbits are essentially farmers; the fact that Bilbo and Frodo have no occupation—except 'burglary' and writing books, neither of which ties them to one place—is a narrative convenience, like their being bachelors."[20] Of course it is a simplification even to say that the Hobbits are farmers—what of Merry and Pippin, who come from gentry? Whatever may seem innocent and provincial about the Hobbits in the first chapters of *The Lord of the Rings*, however, eventually darkens, as World War II must have darkened every human activity leading up to its conclusion and aftermath.

Of interest in this study in relation to the writing of *The Lord of the Rings* is the fact that while Tolkien was editing Middle English poems he was thinking, as early as the thirties, about what would become the continuation of *The Hobbit*, as he notes in letter 199 to Caroline Everett on 24 June 1957. He declares, "The general idea of the *Lord of the Rings* was certainly in my mind from an early stage: that is from the first draft of Book 1 chapter 2 [The Shadow of the Past], written in the 1930s" (258). If *The Hobbit* originated from stories told to his children and been composed in the twenties, as his older children have attested (in chapter 3 of this study), actually becoming the final *Hobbit* in the early thirties, nevertheless, this book was not in fact published until 21 September 1937. Given the pressure to produce a "Second Hobbit" by Allen & Unwin, Tolkien wrote portions of *The Silmarillion* and the remainder of the trilogy between 1936 and 1948, as he notes in his letter to W.H. Auden, on 7 June 1955 (letter 163, 216). He tells Caroline Everett in letter 199 (259) that he reached the last words of book 3 in 1942–1943. And, in the same letter to Auden, Tolkien acknowledges that World War II, at least in part, held up his progress toward the epic's completion: "I was stuck for ages at the end of Book Three. Book Four was written as a serial and sent out to my son [Christopher] serving in Africa in 1944. The last two books were written between 1944 and 1948. That of course does not mean that main idea of the story was a war-product. That was arrived at in one of the earliest chapters still surviving (Book I, 2)."

In short, the actual writing of *The Lord of the Rings* can be divided chronologically into major segments: the first, leading up to the end of book 3, starting in the thirties and written concurrently with various Chaucer projects, especially those dealing with the fabliaux and the Commons, along with the long-unfinished Clarendon Chaucer anthology, and philological articles related to the Midlands dialects he associated with "home." But there is then a second segment, from books 4–6, far darker, in many respects, written during the war and its post-war consequences, and coinciding with his work on other Middle English poems, especially *Sir Gawain and the Green Knight*. The two very different kinds of works, I will argue in this chapter and the next, blended. Or rather, Chaucer and his rustics must have had an effect on the creation of the Hobbit society of the Shire—a stratified hierarchy of more and less noble individuals and families—just as the wartime letters to his own son in 1944 must have fed his own anxiety into the various journeys of the Fellowship members that form the subjects of the end of the Third Age in Middle-earth (*LOTR*, bks. 4–6) and the darker world England and her allies were experiencing.

In particular, the Chaucer articles, especially "Chaucer the Philologist," aside from Tolkien's interest in the use of dialects in the comic tale of the Reeve and in their emphasis on issues of class and social hierarchy, were likely catalyzed by the abjection Tolkien experienced while growing up. As a slightly built, poor, Roman Catholic orphan—born in distant South Africa, the "Dark Continent," and affiliated with West Midlander families, he was educated among an elite group of young men—and rugby players—at King Edward's School and Exeter College Oxford. At the same time, the horrors of World War I that he and his friends suffered through and died from must have sealed his abhorrence toward any kind of violence and war. Simultaneously, these experiences must also have reified the comfort and safety of membership in youthful clubs and societies, bonding with his friends, and, at least initially, in being a Lancashire Fusilier in the army with soldiers from his region, and then, upon his return from the Battle of the Somme, living without those friends who died in the war. No surprise that, during his adult life, he was drawn to all-male reading groups, a long friendship with fellow scholar and fantasy and science fiction author C.S. Lewis, and companionship with his own grown children and graduate students, some of whom were women.

What is emphasized in the last three books of *The Lord of the Rings* is indeed the monstrosity of the antagonists faced by Frodo and Sam, in particular, and a vast battlefield of ongoing war and death, where these anti-heroes, small and ineffectual as they may be, continually bested those who queer all that is civilized and human. And yet, from the very beginning of *The Lord of the Rings*, the issue of social and cultural difference marks the speech and behavior of the Hobbits in their home environment, creating a miniature war among its inhabitants. The trilogy in its six books as the narrative progresses provides darker and darker inversions of the norm. Hobbits from the Shire and Hobbiton meet others markedly different in character and trustworthiness, just as more dangerous Others, such as the trolls, goblins, Barrow-wights, and Dark Riders give way to the Orcs (as mutant Elves), and the fallen Maiar, like the dark wizard Saruman and, of course, monstrously disembodied Sauron in the second half, who differ from the Elves and the good Maiar who help protect and save the company of the Fellowship and civilization.

In this chapter, primarily devoted to the first few books of *The Lord of the Rings*, it is the concept of "Apartness" and difference that marks both Tolkien's scholarship and his fiction—barriers between individuals and peoples that keep them separated, such as language and geography that create cultural differences. Here he locates the seeds of those dark blooms that will grow into racism, neocolonialism, and war in the last half of his anti-epic.

APARTHEID/APARTNESS IN PHILOLOGICAL SCHOLARSHIP (1925–1930)

Tolkien was consistently interested in the area of England where he grew up and where his mother's family was from—Gloucestershire—and the language and dialects that originated in and dominated that region, particularly the Southwest Midlands and other areas not far from Wales. His appendix on "Nodens" appears in a report of the Society of Antiquaries published in 1932 on first-century BC excavations of a fort (or hill-town) dug in 1928–1929 in Lydney Park, Gloucestershire, on the west bank of the Severn River and not far from Cheltenham, where Tolkien's son John was born, and close to the Forest of Dean. The park is named for the River

Lyd, which flows into the Severn and through the town. In his article, Tolkien creates an asterisk philology—to use Thomas Shippey's term for how a word can be plumbed to open up a world—by analyzing the origins of the name "Nodens" and identifying it with a god important to Celtic myth for whom the Romans built a temple on the old fort's site.[21] Nodens also has a statue in the park at Lydney. Tolkien discovers (as he has in the exploration of other words, like "losenge," which is a hybrid blend of Latin, German, and French) that as cultures evolve they vary the meanings of similar words in expression of their different usage.

Typical of Tolkien's love of philology and appreciation for others who delve into the study of dialects to enhance our understanding of how language has developed is his foreword to *A New Glossary of the Dialect of the Huddersfield District*, by Walter E. Haigh, published by Oxford University Press in 1928. This glossary introduces a particular South Yorkshire dialect that was still spoken in an isolated area near the Pennines, which, for that reason, retains many archaic characteristics of an older language influenced by the north. How such words were used and pronounced therefore appeared necessary to both Haigh and Tolkien. Because so many of these words are obsolete or, given their use by the elderly, soon to be obsolete, preservation seemed optimal. Haigh admits a second purpose: "to show that the dialect (like others) is not, in either words or speech, the haphazard invention of ignorant country folk in the past, as is often supposed, but is of ancient origin through several generations of regular development, and of as worthy lineage therefore as standard English itself."[22] England, of course, given its history of invasions by peoples from Scandinavia, Germany, and Norman France, is a jigsaw of dialects differentiated by geography. As in Italy, where Italian as its artificial national language derived from Tuscan dialect—and historically less a unified nation than a grouping of different city-states—so the native tongues in almost every region are dialects and not Italian. So Tolkien adds his support in a foreword that stresses the "humour" and "raciness" of the illustrations used, so that the dialect words in colloquial instances spring to life, however dead they may be in isolation. To understand such dialect words means communication is advanced and community therefore fostered.

Why Tolkien supported this project in particular reveals his own history and circumstances: the Huddersfield District is bordered by the North and Western Midland, where he grew up, so that it features aspects derived from the Scandinavian invasions of East and West, meaning Yorkshire and Lincolnshire and Lancashire, where he was from. As a "friendly foreigner" to this district, he searches still for family likeness: "Many centuries have gone by since men could distinguish the English, Danish, and Norwegian inhabitants of these parts. The words introduced by the invaders, too, have been shaped, like the people, by a later history shared with the older elements, to a common family likeness."[23] And of course the Northwest Midlands in the fourteenth century served as the focus of the Alliterative Revival, of Anglo-Saxon verse and accentual meter: *Sir Gawain and the Green Knight, Pearl*, the *Wars of Alexander*. However, Tolkien cautions against allowing assumptions to color such study with disdain: "The homely survivals in dialect are often of ancient lineage, and not the chance mutilations of literary English by the unlettered."[24] Such a caution also goes for the sounds of a dialect that are regarded as "merely uncouth and illiterate."[25] Ever protective of the possible loss of a language or dialect, Tolkien advises others to take note of how this "friendly foreigner"—himself—ends his remarks "by congratulating Huddersfield on the possession at once of an enthusiast such as the author of book."[26] Perhaps the Professor is also inviting others to congratulate Tolkien, as the compiler of so many Middle English glossaries, a friendly foreigner anxious to bond with groups of his own, through whatever means possible.

"Sigelwara Land" and the Old English "Exodus"

Another example, not of an entire language or dialect so much as a focus on two specific Anglo-Saxon words, demonstrates Tolkien's interest in race and the Dark Continent, both coincidental with the fact of his early life experience in South Africa, appears in an article published in 1925. The long, two-part philological note, titled "Sigelwara Land," isolates for discussion these same two words in the passage about the Ethiopians in the Old English *Exodus* (lines 69–72).[27] The text itself, the Old English version of the biblical book of Exodus, from the unique manuscript Oxford Bodleian Junius 11, he began editing and translating into prose in 1925 when he moved back to Oxford as the Rawlinson Professor of Old English, but never published in his lifetime, although his unfinished edition he used as the basis for lectures in an advanced class he offered at Oxford in the thirties and forties. The Old English *Exodus*, like its original, dramatizes the flight of the exiled Israelites from Egypt and their passage through the Red Sea. The very subject, although biblical and Old Testament, is *apartheid*—as understood through class (the protagonists are slaves), nation (they are Israelites in exile), and religion (their faith is

Hebraic). Figuratively, their flight, according to the introduction to the translation in the commentary, signifies more allegorically the exile of the soul from God's grace: Tolkien describes it as "at once an historical poem about events of extreme importance, an account of the preservation of the chosen people and the fulfilment of the promises made to Abraham; and it is an allegory of the soul, or of the Church of militant souls, marching under the hand of God, pursued by the powers of darkness, until it attains to the promised land of Heaven."[28] The final product was not published until much later, in 1981, and then pulled together from his notes and manuscripts by former student and later Somerset College Honorary Research Fellow Joan Turville-Petre.[29]

The Anglo-Saxon lines Tolkien focused on in his article read "Sigelwarena land,/Forbærned beorh-leoðu, brune leode,/hatum heofoncolum"; in his translation, Tolkien renders this in both edition and article as "the Sundwellers' land, hill-slopes scorched and folk grown swart under the hot furnace of the skies."[30] Tolkien's comments in the article especially are laced with humor. The phrase "Sigelwara land" functions as an Anglo-Saxon appositive for the Ethiopians, whom Tolkien defines as classically graced initially because the Olympian gods had visited them. But in Old English, according to Tolkien, Ethiopia is usually referred to as "Sigelwara land" because of the color of its inhabitants' skin and its implied infernal landscape, that is, a fiery one that burned sinners black. "Their country," Tolkien notes, "was too like hell to escape the comparison, and the blackness of the inhabitants became more than skin deep. A diabolic folk, yet worthy perhaps of a note, if not a visit."[31]

For this etiological explanation of the color of their skin—black, like those consigned to hell, itself said to be a very hot site—the Old English compound *Sigelwara* usually appears in geographical descriptions or in descriptions of hell. Tolkien notes that "Ethiopia was hot and its people black. That Hell was similar in both respects would occur to many."[32] The compound also appears in homilies (used like the "Weder Geats" of a people) to refer to the Ethiopians as "devils, worshipped rather than worshippers."[33] Specifically, the word "Sigel" in *Sigelwara* can mean "sun" or "jewel," most likely the sun, scholarly Tolkien cautions, "Yet it cannot be ignored that Ethiopia was also a land of gems."[34] Thus "Sigelhearwa," Tolkien concludes, "would be made black by the sun."[35] For *hearwa*, in the *Sigelwara* compound (Sigel + hearwa), Tolkien finds Old Norse words for "dusky" that apply to the wolf, the eagle, the raven (the topos for the beasts of battle) and also to a name for one of the twelve sons of Praell and Pi'r, "who were with their twelve sisters the ancestors of all slaves."[36]

Margaret Sinex, in discussing the classical and medieval sources for Tolkien's imaginary Haradrim in *The Lord of the Rings* (3:6.5, 247) as "monsterized Saracens," observes more generally that he "mirrors the Western Europeans' methods of constructing their imaginary Saracen," in three ways: first, in terms of a binary of light and dark, Scythian and Ethiopian, saved and damned; second, in terms of the role of climate and geography in "racial theorizing"; and third, in the use of color to "guide audience response."[37] Dimitra Fimi has also traced the source lines of Tolkien's racial theorizing in his time from nineteenth- and twentieth-century anthropology and social Darwinism in her chapter on "A Hierarchical World" in *Tolkien, Race, and Cultural History: From Fairies to Hobbits*, although Tolkien was always very clear that he understood peoples to be differentiated on the basis of their languages rather than their races, as he made explicit in his article "English and Welsh."[38]

What appeals to Tolkien here, as in the piece on the Huddersfield dialect, is the capture of two cultures in transition, blended—the Ethiopian peoples and the Israelite slaves in a translation from Latin into Anglo-Saxon likely written by Christian monks. In the introduction to his edition commentary, he notes that similarities in the language exist in both *Exodus* and *Beowulf*, as they do in both *Andreas* and *Beowulf*, mixing the heroic and religious, although again he warns that borrowing phrases was a common practice.[39] In the article, Tolkien senses that "[g]limpses are caught, if dim and confused, of the background of English and northern tradition and imagination, which has colored the verse treatment of Scripture, and determined the diction of poems."[40] He also likes words whose origins mirror their diverse cultures: "*Sigel* may be taken as a symbol of the intricate blending of the Latin and Northern which makes the study of Old English peculiarly interesting and controversial; *hearwa* of that large part of ancient English language and lore which has now vanished beyond recall, *swa hit no wære.*"[41]

Tolkien's *Exodus* is imbued with heroic diction drawn from the Anglo-Saxon in order to valorize his protagonists, Moses and the Jews, the exiled peoples: the "chieftain" Moses, to whom God gives the "lives of his kinsmen," is "prince of his people, a leader of the host, sage and wise of heart, valiant captain of his folk." The "enemies of God," Pharaoh's race, receives plagues and the "fall of their princes," so that "mirth was hushed in the halls bereft of treasure."[42] A poem thus reminiscent of *Beowulf* during the deadly visitation of the hall Heorot by the monster Grendel, *Exodus* describes how "far and wide the Slayer ranged grievously afflicting the people" (*Exodus*, 21). For the chieftain Moses, "high the heart of him who led the kindred" (*Exodus*, 21); the war scene, with the "gallant men" led by him, is elaborated with Germanic martial imagery and description of the brightness of the host and the flashing of the shields (*Exodus*, 22). Abraham, son of Noah, who follows as tenth in generations after Moses, is also described in the poem as in Germanic-like exile (*Exodus*, 28). And when Moses leads the Israelites in flight, they, too, represent "Exiles from home, in mourning they possess this hall of passing guests, lamenting in their hearts" (*Exodus*, 31).

These scholarly examples of *apartheid* and "apartness" are set in ancient Africa. While Tolkien the medievalist identified racial difference as an expression of geographical and national difference and its concomitant marginalization in English, Northern, and Hebraic traditions, he focused, in addition, on class differences—exiled peoples forced to live in foreign lands as wretched slaves. Tolkien was also fascinated by the figure of the Old English *wraecca*, the word from which modern "wretch" derives but which refers literally to the exile in Old English. Given the comitatus nature of Old English society—one predicated upon the bond between the retainer and a gold-lord, the retainer providing service and valor in battle when necessary, the gold-lord providing food, a hall, and reward for valor in mead ceremonies—the man without a gold-lord, in exile, was truly a man alone. The Old English elegy *The Wanderer* dramatizes the situation of a man who may be a *wraecca* because he has lost not only his gold-lord but also his comitatus to some kind of calamity; it is clear he is a wanderer in exile left to treasure only memories of his fellow warriors and his gold-lord.

Tolkien cites a passage from the Old English "Wanderer" at the end of the "Valedictory Address" in which he has expressed his loathing of apartheid, meaning his own sense of "apartness." He specifically refers to it after his bitterly ironic comment that at last a scholar born in the Southern Hemisphere (like him), but from Australia and New Zealand, is to be awarded an Oxford chair of English.[43] "Not quite the condemned criminal," Tolkien admits; as he "steps off," he repeats the famous *ubi sunt* passage from the elegy in his Anglo-Saxon exclamation beginning "Hwǣr cwóm mearh" (Where is the horse gone?) (which he terms "Language") followed by his own "Nonsense," referring to his own elegiac Elven passage, "Ai! Laurië lantar lassi súrinen!" (Alas! As gold fall the leaves in the wind!).[44] Northern versus southern, English versus South African, Old

English versus Elven—he ends here with an analogy between the university and his own comitatus (*duguð*) in Elvish and the glad certainty that it has "not yet fallen by the wall," because so many of those he has taught have attained what he has not—truly, a *dréam* "not yet silenced."[45] In his note he explains the sound as merrymaking and music of the men's voices in the king's hall to which he refers.

The very marriage and interweaving of Latin with the northern and Anglo-Saxon is not just a matter of aesthetic appreciation for Tolkien: it anticipates many other forms of more explicit reconciliation he will celebrate in his writings. Tolkien was also anti*apartheid* in a more cosmic and multicultural sense: throughout his mythology he promotes the intermarriage of races—Maia, Elf, and Man—and the fellowship of species—Elf, Man, Dwarf, and Hobbit—in order to blend their strengths in governance and parliamentary representation. He even sees the three types of Hobbits—Harfoot, Fallohide, and Stoor—as separated unnecessarily by geography, so that much of *The Lord of the Rings* maps out the gradual toleration of an obnoxious Stoor—Gollum—by a merciful and tolerant Harfoot, the Fallohide Frodo. Throughout Tolkien's scholarship he was drawn to medieval texts that present encounters and oppositions between characters from different regions of England and, perhaps, the earthly and the magical or demonic.

During much of the twenties and thirties, when Tolkien was still teaching at Leeds and then especially after his move to Oxford in 1925, when he was working on the Old English *Exodus*, his courses expanded to include other medieval languages, as much on Middle English poetry as on Old English. His most significant projects included, chiefly, his edition of *Sir Gawain and the Green Knight* with his former student E[ric].V[alentine]. Gordon (1896–1938), for which he was preparing a glossary for the difficult northern dialect, and of Geoffrey Chaucer's *Canterbury Tales*, with George S. Gordon (1881–1942), Merton Professor of English at Oxford and eventually Vice Chancellor of the University. *Sir Gawain and the Green Knight* finally appeared under an Oxford Clarendon Press imprint in 1925, reprinted with corrections in 1930 and, after continuing to be reprinted eight times, in a second edition, revised by Norman Davis, in 1968.

The other Middle English project was a Clarendon Chaucer student's anthology on which he and George S. Gordon were collaborating, beginning in 1925, with Tolkien reading proofs in June for some of its text pages and constructing a glossary. The Clarendon Chaucer would never be published—Tolkien returned what he had completed of his galley proofs, corrected glossary proofs, and draft notes nearly two and a half decades later, in June of 1951. In explanation, Tolkien wrote to D.M. Davin on 8 June 1951 that "I deeply regret the whole affair. The material contains much that is fresh and a prodigious amount of labour—sp. in the construction, reduction, and revision of the glossary. But I was given the very sticky end of the stick, and need say no more."[46] Apparently there was more to this story, but whatever that involved must wait until some future time to be revealed, because neither he nor others did, at least publicly.[47]

Chaucer's Rustics and Other "Dubious Characters"

In a spin-off from the Chaucer anthology glossary preparation, Tolkien also delved into an examination of the dialects of the two northern clerks in Chaucer's fabliau of the *Reeve's Tale*, reading a draft of "Chaucer as a Philologist" to the Philological Society on 16 May 1925, which eventually made its way into the *Transactions of the Philological Society* in 1934 as a seventy-page article titled "Chaucer as a Philologist: *The Reeve's Tale.*"[48] Another article from the same time period, an explanation of the phrase "the Devil's coach horses" from the fourteenth-century poet's fabliau of the *Shipman's Tale*, was published before the long first article, in the *Review of English Studies* in July of 1925. In these two articles on the meaning and importance of certain Middle English words and dialects in Chaucer's fabliaux, for which the editing (at least in part) was to be Tolkien's responsibility, we can glean some sense of the Professor's interest in and concern for dismantling class differences through a focus on etymologies and denotations. The tales both involve tale-tellers who are both rogues and members of the Commons—Chaucer's Shipman and the Reeve.

In "The Devil's Coach-horses," Tolkien argues somewhat tongue-in-cheek that the word *aver* (West Midland *eaver*, from Old English *afor* and *eafor*) in Chaucer's description of the Shipman's horse in the *General Prologue* also appears in the twelfth-century *Hali Meiðhad*, a treatise on female virginity, but the word in Chaucer does not refer (as it seems to) to a rotting boar, which the devil appears to be riding, but instead, and almost equally irregularly, to a large cart horse.[49] Tolkien relates his philological analysis back to Chaucer's Shipman in his conclusion: "The devil appears to have ridden his coach-horses like a postilion, but he was in worse case than Chaucer's shipman who 'rood upon a rouncy as he couthe,' his steeds seem indeed to have been heavy old dobbins that needed all his spurring."⁵⁰ Tolkien a few years later, in 1929, published an essay on this work and on *Ancrene Wisse* (also known as the *Ancrene Riwle*, or *The Anchoress's Rule*), in "*Ancrene Wisse* and *Hali Meiðhad*," in *Essays and Studies by Members of the English Association*.⁵¹

In the second article, the substantial seventy-page "Chaucer as a Philologist: *The Reeve's Tale*," published in *Transactions of the Philological Society* in 1934, Tolkien explores the dialectical features of the speech patterns of Chaucer's two northern English clerks who come to mill corn at a very southern mill owned by a proud miller. The dialectical differences between the language of the post-plague country bumpkins from the rural north and that of the miller and his wife and daughter in the more settled and preferred southern region enhance the triumph of the clerks' *quiting* (getting even with) the miller—who steals their corn after the miller tells his wife to unleash their stallion to run after the miller's mares. By later furtively sleeping with both the miller's daughter and wife—Aleyn, literally, in the bed next to Malyne's parents, or in the case of the wife, after switching the baby's cradle to the end of John's own bed while the miller snores—the clerks enjoy a much richer and more satisfying revenge on the ignorant southerner. The latter believes that his wife—in fact, the bastard child of the parson—holds an enviable social stature in the community because of the parson's perceived "high" birth. Like Chaucer, Tolkien clearly sides with the country bumpkins from the north and not with the deceitful and proud southern miller (a type similarly negative in the Shire of *The Lord of the Rings*).

In both these cases, Tolkien selects as subjects those Chaucerian figures whose very comic realism stems from their background as commoners. In the *General Prologue* portrait, the Shipman is duped into buying a *rouncy* (a nag) because—while he knows about ships and the seas—he does not know about horses one rides on dry land. The northern clerks who are similarly tricked by the crafty southern miller (by pressing his thumb on the scale and having his wife unloose their stallion), on the other hand, use the miller's regional stereotyping (classifying individuals by their speech patterns, as if speech represented the educational level or literacy of the man) strategically. The clerks accept the miller's hospitality but, in fact, use the subterfuge of their apparent simplicity to *swive* the miller's wife and daughter.

Just as Chaucer satirizes the pride of the "highborn" wife and daughter of the miller in the *Reeve's Tale*, who are swived by both the crude clerics, first one, then the other, while her husband snores, Tolkien also similarly inverts the implied value system of the social hierarchy of the three medieval estates (aristocracy, clergy, commons). Superior social class, place of birth, or inherited wealth in Tolkien may or may not accompany true gentility, or *gentilesse*, as Chaucer describes literal and figurative courtesy in the *Wife of Bath's Tale* in the speech of the Loathly Lady to her ignorant and boorish husband, the young knight, and in Chaucer's short poem "Gentilesse." In both Tolkien's scholarly articles on Chaucer's language and his reworking of Chaucerian class satires in his own fantasy, he expresses sensitivity to class and racial or regional differences that arise in literary contexts. As Chaucer does in the *General Prologue* to the *Canterbury Tales*, wherein certain members of the Commons, like the ideal humble Parson and his brother the Plowman, exemplify Christian ideals—in contrast to the hypocritical monk and friar and the manipulative summoner and pardoner—Tolkien also subverts classist presumptions and stereotypes and promotes virtue and charity.

Even in Tolkien's article on the Middle English word "losenger," published in 1953, but likely prompted by a draft article on the word by his former Belgian B.Litt. student Simonne Rosalie Thérèse Odile d'Ardenne and delivered in the second conference he attended at her university, the University of Liège, in September 1951, he plays with the origins of a word. As usual, Tolkien the storyteller's head in this article is full of mythological conceits: he notes that the word's history is complex, for "few [words] spring direct like Athene from the head of Zeus; far more have, like the Norse god Heimdallr, nine mothers."[52] A blend word in related languages, a hybrid: like so many other philological studies by Tolkien, this one examines the result of the "contact (and in various degrees: the blending) of alien languages in northwest Europe," namely, the "Germanic invasions of Northern Gaul."[53] But for this large important matter Tolkien chooses just one word—"losenger," which is Middle English but derived from Middle French and with Latinate origins.

There are apparently two *losenge* words in French—and here Tolkien ratchets up his audience's interest in "words of a sound-pattern at once unusual and identical, that cannot be connected at all, except by such fantasies." *Fantasies*: he is once more constructing stories. Even though *losenge* is his word, there exists a second *losenge* as a "rhombus, a diamond-shaped figure (especially in heraldry), a small cake or tablet, a pane of glass," in French. He found the first *losenge*, our storyteller continues, "where I first met the *losengeour*, in pursuit of another nefarious character, the *totelere*," that is, in Chaucer. *Losenger* in French and meant "to slander," found in Chaucer's *Legend of Good Women* when Alceste speaks to the God of Love to say there "is many a losengeour" in his court, meaning a flatterer, slanderer, backbiter, or liar.[54] Our storyteller Tolkien makes his article into a detective narrative about the "dubious character the *losengeour*." For, he tells us, forty-five years ago a schoolmaster told him that "He [the losengeour] was a flattering liar, and he was so called because he used the kind of language found on *lozenges*," referring to panes of glass in church windows on which the wealthy paid to have their virtues recorded. When the panes' style was imitated in cheaper ways, it was termed *losenger*[55]—that is, fakes, repeated, but with less authenticity and value.

Tolkien's interest in hybrid Old and Middle English words drawn from a variety of languages again conceals a subtext: an interesting secret, a truth about a lowlife, even in the court of Love (or perhaps especially there), or in the material history of chivalry and aristocracy. Tolkien often debunks the pretensions of nobility and the mistruths of the ignorant, as is clear in his most famous fictional work. His ultimate goal in *The Lord of the Rings* is of course to fantasize a world in which differences among individuals and peoples have become so dangerous that they must be controlled and erased, without respect for their right to exist. The hierarchy of control and power recorded in the hidden message on the One Ring suggests the necessary hierarchy, from the nine mortal men who hold rings (Black Riders) to the seven (Dwarf lords) to the three (Elven kings) to the one (Sauron), allowing only that One the right to make decisions and to flourish in the world:

> Three Rings for the Elven-kings under the sky,
>   Seven for the Dwarf-lords in their halls of stone,
> Nine for Mortal Men doomed to die,
>   One for the Dark Lord on his dark throne
> In the Land of Mordor where the Shadows lie.
>   One Ring to rule them all, One Ring to find them,
>   One Ring to bring them all and in the darkness bind them
> In the Land of Mordor where the Shadows lie. (*LOTR*, 1:2, 50)

Although how Tolkien fully creates the darkened world in which world war must take place between the Free Peoples and those of Mordor is so complex it can only be suggested by example of the darkening process it has taken to arrive there, which, in the six books of *The Lord of the Rings*, follows the sequence seriatim, from the Fellowship's experience initially with the nine, then with the seven as represented by the Mines of Moria, then with the three—the Elves whom they meet—and last, with the one, in Mordor.

The Lord of the Rings: The Homely and the Alien

Tolkien's narrative in the first three books of *The Lord of the Rings* moves his central characters gradually, in the first book from the Shire and Hobbiton outward to Bucklebury, Buckland, the Old Forest, Tom Bombadil's house, the Barrow-downs, Bree, and Weathertop; in the second book, to Rivendell, Moria, Lothlórien, and the Great River, when the company of the Fellowship splits; and in the third book to Fangorn, Rohan, Helm's Deep, and Isengard. From what seems the safety and familiarity of home and homeliness, or at least, Tolkien's home—Hobbiton is on the same latitude as Oxford on a map of Middle-earth recently found in a copy of *The Lord of the Rings* owned by Pauline Baynes and annotated by Tolkien—the constant change of setting gradually becomes darker and more ominous, alternating between places of danger and threat of violence and places of rescue and harbor, as I have previously argued.[56] Through differences in landscape Tolkien creates narrative patterns throughout the trilogy to dramatize by means of mirroring from book to book how their journeys successfully introduce the Hobbits to stranger and ever more alien beings and peoples, beginning with Old Man Willow, the Black Riders, and the Barrow-wights. Readers and viewers of Peter Jackson's films may have become inured to the gradually widening gyre of different beings, nations, tribes and species, Hobbit, Dwarf, human, and Elf, to whom the members of the Company are initially introduced, and then many other differentiations among these, the Noldorin, Teleri, and Sindarin Elves, with even more exotic species and types such as Maia, Balrog, Ent, and Orc, whom the parts of the divided Company encounter while apart. If the last three books focus on the end-journey to Mordor via the Marshes, Cirith Ungol, Minas Tirith, Gondor, the Pelennor Fields, the Houses of Healing, Mount Doom, the field of Cormallen, and only at last a return to the Shire, they center on the dead, ruin and destruction, the lost past, monstrosity, domination and persecution, terror, war, and the constant presence of imminent death and danger. The Free Peoples are eventually united against the Dark Lord and all the minions and species and nations under his control, whether living dead, mutant, or monster, their aberrations a symbol of the unnatural and perverse means used to reduce others to nothingness.

To draw on Emmanuel Levinas and Slavoj Žižek is helpful in understanding what Tolkien attempts to do as his travelers increasingly encounter not just the other, that is, the neighbor who is difficult to empathize with because of his differences from us, but as Žižek describes it, "radical Otherness, of a monstrous Thing that cannot be gentrified," in his essay "Neighbors and Other Monsters."[57] Tolkien sets up a grid of interlocking class and regional (place of origin) differences in the first book of *The Lord of the Rings* to show how stereotyping originates and why. At a low level such suspicion and intolerance are necessary for self-defense of the individual and the group: the community recoils from anything that is too different to protect it from change and accommodation, which might be dangerous. But later on, when each of the Hobbits has had an adventure as a stranger in a strange land, it becomes clearer that Tolkien is extending the boundaries of class and regional difference into those of racial and national difference. Being a Hobbit in a land of Men by nature leads to racial stereotyping and sometimes discrimination. Only in the most enlightened countries and cultures of Middle-earth are the inhabitants able to recognize nobility as cutting across race and national origin: the Elves of Lórien immediately recognize the nobility of the Fellowship and reward its members with appropriately chivalrous gifts. If enlightenment and civilization are predicated upon education, diversity of opinion, and acceptance of those who are other, the opposite is also true: darkness and inhumanity couple in an atmosphere of fear, prejudice, intolerance, and ignorance.

As Tolkien's masterwork is a fantasy, by subversion in *The Lord of the Rings* we should understand "queer," in the sense of the adjective that describes those individuals who differ from others of their kind and in the sense of the verb "to queer," when actions disturb the harmony of the community or the stability of an institution or proceeding. Where class difference creates impassable barriers to communication, there is prejudice, intolerance, and ignorance, all of which lead to isolation, segregation, and ultimately the workings of evil, that is, displacement and discord. I would argue that Tolkien is neither a snob nor a Fascist in his own fantasies but, indeed, a subverter of those very class differences that so often characterize Old English snobbery. Peace and harmony among members of different classes represent the utopian vision in which Tolkien most delights in three of his own fantasies: the fairy-stories of *Farmer Giles of Ham* (1949) and *Smith of Wootton Major* (1967)[58] and the epic of *The Lord of the Rings* (1954–1955).

In *Farmer Giles of Ham*, it is the rustic protagonist who occupies the role of the romance genre's knight-errant and reveals his aristocratic nature, in contrast to the foppish, do-nothing knights of the king's court. And in *Smith of Wootton Major*, it is the humble rustic, the smith named Smith, who knightlike learns how to navigate the threshold into the perilous realm of fäerie to fulfill a quest. In the third and most important work, the xenophobia and classist stereotypes of some of the old, narrow-minded, and provincial farmer Hobbits provide the seeds of suspicion, disapproval, and dislike that will blossom into the dark and fascist domination of the town later on by the miller Sandyman and his cohorts Sharkey (the wizard Saruman) and Worm, close to the end of *The Lord of the Rings*, in "The Scouring of the Shire."

In this work, Tolkien's longest fairy-story, it is through the farmers and commoners who behave heroically that he also subverts class difference. One purpose in the latter, especially, is to alert us to the dangers of stereotyping in class prejudice, which usually stems from a xenophobia based on fear and ignorance. Those who appear alien or different from us, in appearance or behavior, are perceived initially as not trustworthy. Cognitive science and theory have shown us fear of otherness that results in stereotyping is likely rooted in the need to survive, dating from our Pleistocene forebears, according to Lisa Zunshine.[59] Patrick Colm Hogan explains that facial similarities activate the medial prefrontal cortex, making us believe these are trustworthy likely because of similar national (racial, ethnic, or tribal) identity.[60] A like prejudice against others who differ in Middle-earth generally stems from classism, racism, or sexism. What begins as disparagement of those from a different class, whether lower or higher, can serve also as the foundation of fascism and domination by the powerful. Throughout his fantasy writings Tolkien consciously promotes an understanding of the individual by acknowledging the classist and racist boundaries erected by the ignorant and ill-motived who feel threatened by differences in the other.

The Shire offers initially what seems a pastoral innocence that belies a tendency that could eventually lead to its destruction. Gandalf, for example, worries that the "charming, absurd, helpless hobbits" there might become enslaved by Sauron, yet even Gandalf identifies them as the "kind, jolly, stupid Bolgers, Hornblowers, Boffins, Bracegirdles ... not to mention the ridiculous Bagginses" (*LOTR*, 1:2, 49). They are protected because Sauron has "more useful" servants, but the Dark Lord is always a threat because of his "malice and revenge." And yet the difference between the isolated, safe, jolly Shire and the distant, evil Dark Power is not as marked as it might seem, for power struggles exist among the different Hobbit families in the Shire region, absurd in some cases and significant in others. Indeed, sensitivity to this politics of difference in the Shire, a faculty born of nurture and nature, marks the special ability of Bilbo and Frodo—their power—that will facilitate Frodo's mission and attract followers.

The political problems in the Shire grow out of its deceptively "safe" isolation from the rest of Middle-earth. Its inhabitants distrust those who come from outside because they differ from them in ways they do not understand. A stranger such as a Brandybuck arouses mistrust, and the inhabitants band closer together; later and more ominously a Dark Rider will arouse that same mistrust. Sandyman the Miller, through his suspicious notice of the queerness of the visitors to Bag End (among whom are the strange Dwarves and the magical Gandalf), from the beginning creates a problem for Frodo. This queerness therefore extends also to Bag End itself and ultimately, by association, to its owners, Bilbo and then Frodo (*LOTR*, 1:1, 23, 24). Sameness, in contrast, implies the familiar and secure, and sameness means Hobbitlike. The Hobbits relish what is natural for them, which involves physical activities, living close to nature—dwelling in holes, eating, smoking tobacco. To do otherwise is un-Hobbitlike. "Hobbits," Tolkien once acknowledged, "have what you might call universal morals. I should say they are examples of natural philosophy and natural religion."[61] Marks of distinction—wealth, education, even leadership—can set a Hobbit apart, make him seem different. The major political problem for any potential leader, then, is to maintain the trust of those led—to make leadership seem "natural" and to diminish his own "queerness."

Bilbo and Frodo and the Shire

Bilbo and Frodo, unfortunately, both appear queer, or different, to the inhabitants of the Shire. Bilbo is allegedly very rich but also "very peculiar" because of his seemingly perpetual youth: "It isn't natural, and trouble will come of it!" claim the villagers of Hobbiton (1:1, 21). Part of this "trouble" results from social inequities that his wealth and good physical fortune exacerbate. In addition, however, Bilbo seems strange to the other inhabitants of the Shire because he has been changed by his travels—his knowledge of the world—and by his possession of the Ring, which has stretched him thin. In other words, as the reader soon learns,

Bilbo's awareness of moral issues—his knowledge of good and evil—has been expanded by his having carried the Ring for so long, while that very awareness has debilitated him. The tug between the desire of the self for the Ring (for the "Precious," or for what the individual wishes to incorporate into the self) and the Hobbit's desire to think of others beyond himself (to protect the Shire and the world by keeping the Ring hidden from Sauron's eye) has made him thin. It is no accident that the natural wearing of the Ring on the finger renders its wearer invisible, for when the Ring masters its wearer, it also begins to erase the *identity* of the wearer, which is predicated on the ability to make choices, and he becomes self-less without being selfless. Unfortunately, Bilbo never connects any change in himself with the Ring itself, instead taking "credit for that to himself, and he was very proud of it. Though he was getting restless and uneasy. *Thin and stretched* he said. A sign that the ring was getting control" (1:1, 32). Ironically, the Ring appeals to the desires of the self for gold, power, and love as a means of mastering that individual.

The anticipated "trouble" is, however, averted in part by Baggins's generosity. He shares his money with his friends and relatives: "He had many devoted admirers among the hobbits of poor and unimportant families" (1:1, 21). Again, generously sharing his fortune allays the fears of difference among the less fortunate Hobbits. He is considered "well-spoken," polite, and gentle, largely because, as well-off as he is, he treats his servant the Gaffer (Sam Gamgee's father) with great deference for his knowledge—reversing the usual master–servant relationship: "Bilbo was very polite to him, calling him 'Master Hamfast,' and consulting him constantly upon the growing of vegetables—in the matter of 'roots,' especially potatoes, the Gaffer was recognized as the leading authority by all in the neighbourhood (including himself)" (1:1, 22). Bilbo has also taught the gardener's son Sam to read (1:1, 24)—a Middle-earth reflection of the Victorian ideal of educating the poor. The mutual respect of the Hobbit aristocrat and the gardening servant-authority underscores Bilbo's gifts as an astute politician.

Two major social problems engage the political skills of Bilbo. First is the arrival of Frodo, an orphan (not unlike Tolkien in this respect) and his heir, which causes the Sackville-Bagginses (Bilbo's other close heirs) consternation because their expected inheritance will presumably be reduced. Second is the necessary inheritance of Bag End (and its "treasure") by Frodo, predicated on the disappearance of Bilbo at the advanced age of 111 after a magnificent (and long-expected, according to the chapter title) birthday party. Because of the continued enmity of the detested Sackville-Bagginses after the disappearance, Frodo will inherit similar familial problems requiring his political skills.

The birthday party, in the Shire, represents a symbolic paradigm for the ideal relationship between master and servant, wealthy aristocrat and members of the populace. As a site for potential self-aggrandizement and indulgence—which would not have been tolerated by the inhabitants within had they been either not invited or invited but expected to bring gifts—its signification for the political Hobbit Bilbo is to mark the abundance of self-confidence, largess of the self, by giving gifts to all who attend and by offering them the splendor of fireworks, songs, dances, music, games, and fine and abundant food. It is, then, the perfect symbolic and political moment for Bilbo to disappear—that is, his largess signifies the disappearance of selfishness and masks his literal individual disappearance. At this party no one is not invited, and every guest is given presents, in the Hobbit fashion. Indeed, the liberality of Bilbo in inviting everyone to his birthday party is, as the Gaffer reminds the suspicious and manipulative Sandyman, another, more positive aspect of Bilbo's "queerness." The party thus also symbolizes Bilbo's enduring political concern for others—he is noble, a true gentleman, because he thinks only of others. And Hobbits, who have the custom of giving presents to others on their own birthdays, are in general the least acquisitive of beings. The Sackville-Bagginses—Otho and his wife, Lobelia—attended even though they "disliked Bilbo and detested Frodo" (1:1, 28), largely because of the magnificence of the invitation.

Politic Bilbo in his speech to the Hobbits expresses his fondness for them all and praises them as "excellent and admirable" (1:1, 30). This speech is important, for the occasion also honors his heir-nephew's birthday, which means Frodo will come of age and therefore Bilbo must make his disappearance. But even generous Bilbo, as a natural aristocrat, has difficulty in ridding himself entirely of the Ring: Hobbit that he is, he is still related to the Sackville-Bagginses and thus shares in their excessive (even for Hobbits) greed. Desire is a part of what the Ring represents.

The Ring of course works its power—illustrating the nature of the novel as a work about power—because more than anything it wishes to return to its maker-master and therefore wants to be put on (to make the wearer naturally invisible but supernaturally visible to the Eye of Sauron). In relation to the individual, then, possessing the Ring means that the individual eventually loses any sense of who he is and what he truly wants.

The specialness of the Ring—and therefore the specialness it confers on its owner—enhances the self, fills the individual with the illusion of power. And perhaps that specialness is what has made him "queer" to others. Bilbo initially has difficulty giving up the Ring to Gandalf—he wants to keep it, or the Ring wants him to—and he loses sight of that faculty of the Ring, which makes him mistrust others as different and therefore (as with Sandyman) not with-me, not for-me: "'Now it comes to it, I don't like parting with it at all, I may say. And I don't really see why I should. Why do you want me to?' he asked, and a curious change came over his voice. It was sharp with suspicion and annoyance. 'You are always badgering me about my ring: but you have never bothered me about the other things that I got on my journey'" (1:1, 33). Bilbo protests that he wants to keep the Ring because it is his—he found it: "It is my own. I found it. It came to me." It is the last gift, the one he most has to give away—first to Gandalf and then to his heir Frodo. As with Frodo on Mount Doom, however, fighting first with himself and then with Gollum, Bilbo resists Gandalf as an adversary, using the same language as Gollum: "It is mine, I tell you. My own. My precious. Yes, my precious" (1:1, 33).

To free himself Bilbo has to let it go—which he finds difficult. Gandalf's demand for the Ring (as it lies on the mantel) arouses Bilbo's suspicions that the wizard is a thief. Gandalf wins him over by saying, "I am not trying to rob you, but to help you. I wish you would trust me as you used," to which Bilbo responds with an admission that "I felt so *queer* ... And I don't seem able to make up my mind" (1:1, 34). What does the queerness represent, if not Bilbo's power in the Shire, which he regrets giving up—his power as "lord"? His specialness as an individual, the reason he is young perpetually, wealthy, generous? Although difficult for Bilbo to give up the Ring, yet death—which Bilbo's "disappearance" ultimately signifies—is what all humans must pass through. Renunciation is the final gift: to allow the self to grow and mature, the individual must learn to be selfless. Thus, the "presents" given to Bilbo's relatives are all "corrective," intended to change menial sins in the relatives (for example, a pen and ink bottle to a relative who never answers letters). Despite this admonitory and educational function of the gifts, "The poorer hobbits, and especially those of Bagshot Row, did very well" (1:1, 38).

The gift that Bilbo gives to his nephew Frodo is similar in function—the Ring. With this possession comes the necessity for the quest—no "gift" at all but an unequaled opportunity for individual and even heroic maturation. Frodo at age fifty (when Gandalf pronounces the need for the quest to return the Ring) indeed "comes of age," becomes himself, an individual. But in this narrative, unlike the normal bildungsroman (novel of education or maturation) on which this work is modeled, Frodo must *return* his "gift" to its maker, Mount Doom. With such a "return" of the gift to its maker—to its "mother" source rather than its "father" creator, Sauron—the Ring is the ultimate Hobbit birthday gift. Instead of going on a quest to obtain some significant knowledge or item of value, Frodo goes to divest himself (and the world) of this power. In life, if maturity means the loss of the child to adulthood, then this quest reverses that idea: the adult Frodo must attempt to recuperate the child, as the Ring returns to its origin.

True, that political Hobbit Bilbo "rules" his Shire through self-abnegation and generosity; however, the rule implied by the dominating Ring is entirely different. As the inscription testifies, it allows for differences—among Elves, Dwarves, Men—but only because there is "One Ring" intended to align their differences and bind them in Mordor (1:2, 50). Returning the Ring to its origin means resistance to domination by the One—that is, to sameness, homogeneity—and therefore acceptance of difference and diversity. Frodo, even more different from other Hobbits than his unnatural cousin Bilbo, is better suited to this quest.

The Bag End, Hobbiton, and Brandybuck Hobbits

Within a context of multicultural and multiracial difference in *The Lord of the Rings*, which takes all six books to develop, Tolkien describes all four of the Hobbit heroes as different from other Hobbits, yet, nevertheless, as Hobbits, still marginal beings, ordinary and even antiheroic. According to the Miller, "Bag End's a queer place, and its folk are queerer," apparently because of "the outlandish folk that visit [Bilbo]: dwarves coming at night, and that old wandering conjuror, Gandalf," *outlandish* meaning "queer and different," but also meaning "out of land" (*LOTR*, 1.1, 24), alien, foreign. The term is used of various individuals and families considered strange by Shire rustics (*LOTR*, 1:1, 22).

Frodo, different from Bilbo because of his Brandybuck mother's dark familial roots in Buckland, "where folks are so queer," says Old Noakes (1:1, 22), may be marginally acceptable to the Shire only because of his cousin Bilbo's wealth and favor, which the villagers have also regarded as queer. This Brandybuck "queerness" is caused by living on the wrong side of the Brandywine River, according to Daddy Twofoot "right agin the Old Forest ... a dark bad place" (*LOTR*, 1:1, 22), and also by the fact that they use boats on the big river, which "isn't natural," says the Gaffer, at least for Hobbits (1:1:23). Indeed, Frodo's father, Drogo Baggins, was a "decent respectable hobbit" until he drowned in an uncustomary river outing after marrying Miss Primula Brandybuck (Bilbo's first cousin on his mother's side), on taking out a boat one night after a grand dinner at the home of his father-in-law, Old Gorbadoc. Apparently either Drogo's weight sank the boat or Primula pushed him in (1:1, 23), but the incident orphaned Frodo, who was adopted by Bilbo as his heir. Like Bilbo, whose perpetual youth from having borne the Ring makes him seem queer, Frodo also seems "queer," largely because at the age of fifty he hardly seems older than someone "out of his tweens" (1:2, 43). Interestingly, Tolkien himself was fifty in 1942, around the time he was working on the last three to four books. And just as Frodo Baggins begins his fictive life as an orphan specifically from "across the river," so also does orphan and South African-born Tolkien (from across the river, so to speak) take up the quest narrative.

The tension between the "normal" and the "queer" Hobbit will blossom in later chapters and books into the larger ontological complexity of *The Lord of the Rings*. The question Tolkien addresses is this: How can individuals (and nations) so different from one another coexist in harmony? After Bilbo's disappearance—that is, upon his successful self-renunciation when it comes to spurning the Ring—Frodo's first test as Lord of the Manor comes of course from the Sackville-Bagginses, who offer him low prices for other things in Bilbo's house not given away and who spread rumors that Gandalf and Frodo conspired to get Bilbo's wealth. That Frodo can tolerate his own difference is symbolically clear to the reader (if not to Lobelia Sackville-Baggins) because he is accompanied by his cousin Merry Brandybuck, who, like Frodo's mother, hails from Buckland near the Old Forest. But Frodo mistakenly assumes at first that Bag End is his "inheritance"—his for keeping. As time passes, Frodo perpetuates Bilbo's reputation for "oddity" (1:2, 42) by continuing to give birthday parties for his absent cousin. His closest friends are Merry Brandybuck (one of the "queer" Brandybucks), Peregrin Took, and other younger Hobbits who descend from the Old Took and were fond of Bilbo, whose mother was Belladonna Took.

Difference, for Tolkien, leads to recklessness (youthful parentless Frodo, stealing mushrooms and venturing into others' lands), adventure (Bilbo and Frodo going off on their respective journeys), and ultimately wisdom and understanding. Difference can also be social—the difference between a Baggins and a Gamgee, which is artificial and serves no valid purpose if used as a means to separate the two. The validity of lower-class occupations involving manual labor (for example, gardening, domestic service) is ultimately certified by Sam's heroism in literally carrying Frodo up Mount Doom, just as Gollum's moral deficiency is validated by his final contribution to civilization and cosmic good when he disobeys his "Master," Frodo, and steals the Ring—but in fact saves Middle-earth. The servant—Sam or Gollum—ultimately contributes as much or more to Middle-earth than Master Frodo. For Tolkien it is the generosity of the Master but also his obverse chief weaknesses—pride and avarice—that depend on and demand the unflagging support and dedicated valor of the humble servant, whose chief strength *is* his humility but whose chief weakness *is* his lack of self-assertion. Tolkien's point is that each serves the other; where the difference of one ends, the complementary difference of the other begins.

The Ivy Bush and the Green Dragon in Hobbiton

The descendants of the Gaffer and Sandyman, Sam and Ted, share a conversation similar to that of their rustic fathers at the inn, the *Green Dragon*, when it nears the time for fifty-year-old Frodo to depart on his journey. Both Sam and Ted speak in a near-illiterate way, Sam using "ain't" occasionally and Ted, dialect ("No thank'ee" [*LOTR*, 1:2, 44]). It is these inhabitants whom Frodo describes as "too stupid and dull for words," imagining darkly that "an earthquake or an invasion of dragons might be good for them" (*LOTR*, 1:2, 62). This patronizing snobbery, while it does not last long in Frodo, is matched by a kind of lower-class Hobbit "blackface" exaggeration on the part of Sam when he is discovered eavesdropping by Gandalf: "Lor bless you, Mr. Gandalf, sir!" he cries, explaining he was doing nothing. "Leastways I was just trimming the grass-border under the window" (*LOTR*, 1:2, 63). And he then begs Frodo in terror (and mirroring the rustic Hobbits' xenophobic and class-conscious culture) not to let Gandalf hurt him: "Don't let him turn me into anything unnatural!" (*LOTR*, 1:2, 63).

Sméagol/Gollum

In contrast to Gollum, who speaks in sentence fragments and in baby-talk, Sméagol tends to speak in complete sentences, using the first-person pronoun, and to reflect an upwardly mobile and socially aspiring Hobbit self who wishes to bond feudally with his master and "lord," Frodo. It is not just that Sméagol has pledged himself as *villein* or serf to a manorial lord manqué and obligates himself almost chivalrously to his overlord—"a mighty lord"—when he swears upon the Ring of his master in a feudal parody of homage: "'We promises, yes, I promise!' said Gollum. 'I will serve the master of the Precious. Good master, good Sméagol'" (*LOTR*, 4:1, 618). The oath in itself is a means to Sméagol's reclamation of humanity (or Hobbitness)—his return to civilization and to urbanity and literacy as a mark of normalcy, the norm reflected in his use of whole and complete sentences with subject, verb, and object. Sméagol swears by the Precious not to return it to Sauron in Mordor, and it is this bond of honor in an oral contract that keeps him sane and whole: "From that moment a change, which lasted for some time, came over him. He spoke with less hissing and whining, and he spoke to his companions direct, not to his precious self ... [H]e was friendly, and indeed pitifully anxious to please. He would cackle with laughter and caper, if any jest was made, or even if Frodo spoke kindly to him, and weep if Frodo rebuked him" (*LOTR*, 4:1, 618–19).

The Brandybucks and Tooks of Buckland

Just as the farmer Hobbits and the servile Gollum speak ungrammatically and childishly (suggesting the seeming insignificance of their class), Tolkien also initially equates both Merry and Pippin with a literal Hobbit aristocracy. Meriadoc Brandybuck comes from Buckland, like Frodo's mother Primula Brandybuck, and he inhabits Brandybuck Hall, as have others of his Hobbit line for some time. Peregrin Took bears the family name of General "Bullroarer" Took (Bandobras, in the *Red Book*). This "son of Isengrim the Second" can ride a horse and mirrors the gentry in carrying genes of upper-class superiority (emended to "son of Isumbras the Third" in the 2004 edition, in Tolkien's "Prologue Concerning Hobbits and Other Matters," *LOTR*, 2). When the Gaffer and Old Noakes view with suspicion the Brandybucks and Tooks of Buckland, it is only in part because these Fallohide Hobbits are different and "unnatural" in their affinities for traveling by water and for exploration and adventure. It is also because their difference resides in their upper-middle-class and actual aristocratic stature within the community, which the rustics fear as otherness and potential arrogance and domination.

MERRY AND PIPPIN OF BUCKLAND, NEAR THE OLD FOREST

Furthermore, Frodo's fellow Hobbits Merry and Pippin and his servant Sam have "conspired" (Tolkien's word) behind Frodo's back to accompany him on his journey. This "conspiracy" grows despite Frodo's protective attempts to keep the purpose of his mission (and the existence of the Ring) from them. Frodo's misguided attempts to shield them from danger seriously underestimate their own "queerness" (for Brandybucks and Tooks live beyond the river next to the Old Forest) and thus undermine their own potential for heroism and adventure (to say nothing of their common Hobbit desire to serve, epitomized by the gardener Sam Gamgee, the most modest, socially and personally, of the Hobbits). In *The Lord of the Rings* difference is fueled by the power of words, polarizing the forces of good and evil, social class, and political group.

Interestingly, just as Bilbo and Frodo seem queer to the Commons in the Shire because of their wealth, the aristocratic Bucklanders also seem queer and alien to them. The adventures Frodo has with Hobbits outside of the Shire involve both his and his Bucklander companions' upper-class status and encounters with others' perceptions of them, not so much worthy of respect as suspicious, unusual, or alien. Immediately following this adventure Merry takes them past Brandy Hall to an "old-fashioned countrified house" that Frodo has picked because it is out of the way and resembles a Hobbit-hole more than a dignified hall. This more humble dwelling is not in fact Brandy Hall, which was built by Gorhendad Oldbuck, who then changed his name to Brandybuck. As a measure of the Brandybucks' importance, as Gorhendad's family grew, so did Brandy Hall, until it came to have a hundred windows and to suggest a small country. Hence the country acquired the name "Buckland," although "most of the folk of the old Shire regarded the Bucklanders as peculiar, half foreigners as they were" (*LOTR*, 1:5, 98–99). But then the Hobbits of the Shire also view the Hobbits of Bree, farther on, as "Outsiders" of little interest, "dull and uncouth" (*LOTR*, 1:9, 150). Is it class (or just cultural or regional difference of any sort) that invokes these narrow stereotypes?

What Tolkien appears to be doing is marking the conventional boundaries separating the social classes—as well as laying the ground work for the hero, of course, to emerge from our boorish Hobbits in his epic-romance. If we return to the exaggerated class differences at the very beginning of *The Lord of the Rings*, we mark an initial level of ignorance in both Frodo and Sam: the arrogance of the gentry and the upper middle class in Frodo and the self-effacing belittlement of the underclasses in Sam. Interestingly, neither really speaks that unnatural way again in *The Lord of the Rings*, as if they were here being used to stage the boundaries of class separation Tolkien will unravel by the end of his narrative. What is natural to Sam, despite his exaggerated common dialect in some places, is his love of tales of Elves: "Lor bless me, sir, but I do love tales of that sort," he cries, so that when Gandalf promises him a punishment that involves going away with his master, Sam is described as "springing up like a dog invited for a walk" (*LOTR*, 1:2, 63–64). It seems a dehumanizing and exaggerated image for the Hobbit who will end up as a mayor. If the first rustic scene provided the commons' view of the "queer" upper classes, at least of Bilbo and Frodo, Gandalf's reaction to Sam mirrors the general medieval (aristocratic) view of the commons as thieving, lying, and dishonest.

Farmer Maggot, Good Friend to the Brandybucks

One of Frodo's first educational experiences on his journey is an encounter with another member of the Commons, who teaches him that class differences do not signal moral inferiority. For example, it is not clear to Frodo whether Farmer Maggot is friend or foe (1:7, 132); certainly his name suggests a disgusting creature associated with the eggs of flies and decaying organic matter, death, the earth. And to adult Frodo, whose youthful memories recall the anger of Maggot and his dogs over the theft of mushrooms, Farmer Maggot looms as an adversary. Other rustic Hobbits speak equally ignorantly or childishly. Frodo, caught trespassing several times when he was a boy at Brandy Hall, fears Maggot because Maggot beat him and threatened to let his dogs eat him if it happened again. The privilege of upper class may have permitted Frodo's trespassing, but the abusive behavior of Maggot toward the young Hobbit confirms Gandalf's image of the peasant as *villein*, villain and serf at the same time. Yet in Maggot's view, it was Frodo himself whom he recalls as "reckless," one of the "worst young rascals" (1:7, 136).

If Farmer Maggot, a churl (freeman), is viewed as "trouble" by Frodo, he is nevertheless described as "a good friend to all the Brandybucks" by Pippin (*LOTR*, 1:4, 91). Indeed, on the Hobbits' journey, Farmer and Mrs. Maggot now kindly offer food and protection to the Fellowship (and along the way reverse the Shire image of the Bucklanders and their odd habits as "queer" and "unnatural"). Farmer Maggot, viewing with suspicion both the "outlandish folk" of Hobbiton and the Black Riders he met who were looking for Frodo (*LOTR*, 1:4, 95), anguishes that "You should never have gone mixing yourself up with Hobbiton folk, Mr. Frodo" (*LOTR*, 1:4, 94). Farmer Maggot's wife is even more protective of him: she warns, "You be careful of yourself, Maggot! ... Don't go arguing with any foreigners" (*LOTR*, 1:4, 96). Those outside the home boundaries surely are "foreigners," aliens, "outlanders," the other—and therefore dangerous.

But whether these aliens are different because of their origin of place, their dialect, their class, or their race and family makes no difference either to the bourgeois orphan Frodo or to the uneducated underclass commoners, the Maggots. And that is Tolkien's point: Frodo has found a friend where he initially harbored fear of an adversary and the friend is a rural commoner, not an aristocratic Brandybuck or Took. Frodo will (pointedly) later call Mrs. Maggot (not without irony on Tolkien's part) a "*queen* among farmers' wives" (*LOTR*, 1:5, 102, my emphasis). In truth, a protective Maggot has shielded the Hobbits from the inquiries of a hooded Black Rider and the recklessness of youthful Frodo foreshadows what will evolve into his heroic obligation to return the Ring to Mount Doom in Mordor. Nevertheless, Farmer Maggot remains a Hobbit whose final advice to Frodo reverts finally to the typical suspiciousness of the Shire: "Folk are *queer* up there" (1:4, 94; my italics).

The Gatekeeper at Bree

At a time when dark forces are gathering, this apparent class prejudice is not unusual behavior. At the West-gate of Bree, the gatekeeper finds it suspicious that Hobbits from the Shire are traveling at night—although he inquires politely about their business and their names—and he is met with resistance by Frodo, who, not liking his tone, brusquely informs him it is their business and not his (*LOTR*, 1:9, 151). When the gatekeeper reminds him that asking questions at night *is* his business, what silences him is a patrician response from Bucklander Merry: "We are hobbits from Buckland, and we have a fancy to travel and to stay at the inn here ... I am Mr. Brandybuck. Is that enough for you? The Bree-folk used to be fair-spoken to travelers, or so I had heard" (*LOTR*, 1:9, 151). Merry assumes that the Bree gatekeeper has heard of the Brandybucks of Brandy Hall, and he further challenges the gatekeeper's own Bree sense of courtesy, as if reminding him of appropriate etiquette under the normal circumstances. Yet even Butterbur at the Prancing Pony calls them "Outsiders," travelers from the Shire (each region apparently marking those who are different from them in various ways). Where these differences are greatest outside the first two books and the ending chapters occurs in Rohan and then in Gondor, in the respective cases of Merry and Pippin, in books 3 and 5. In one latter instance of cultural and racial difference, the Men of Rohan, as epitomized by Hama's cold eye, in book 3 witness the arriving Fellowship splinter group of Gandalf, Aragorn, Legolas, and Gimli skeptically; and in book 4, another example of the same, Faramir of Gondor and his company protecting the Window to the West on the border of Gondor view the splinter Fellowship group of Frodo and Sam equally suspiciously. What Tolkien decries is condemnation of any sort of alterity as queer and "unnatural." In *The Lord of the Rings*, Tolkien's disapproval of xenophobia gets played out through the Shire rustics' fear of outsiders and the suspicion and fear with which Dwarves view the Elves; Elves, the Dwarves; and Men, other Men and strange creatures of all sorts, especially Hobbits.

The Hobbit Taxonomy: Families, Tribes, Peoples

Tolkien's solution to the problem of alterity in class, place of origin, or race is to create a hybrid hero who mingles tribal differences ontologically. The Bagginses mix Fallohide with Harfoot—a kind of Everyman Hobbit that Tolkien begins by constructing a genealogy for Bilbo and Frodo that mixes bourgeois Hobbitness—from the Shire Baggins—with chivalrous Tookishness (in Bilbo), and (in Frodo) unnatural explorer-like risk-taking in the outlander/outlandish Brandybucks from Buckland. That this combination will lead to heroism—or at least antiheroism—allows us to assume this as an ideal. It is not from the Shire Hobbits but from the "queer" and "unnatural" Brandybucks and Tooks, as the ancestors of Bilbo and Frodo from outside Hobbiton, that the Hobbit heroes have inherited their sense of adventure and epic mission. Bilbo's adopted heir Frodo, also his cousin, shares his birthday of 22 September and his last name, Baggins, as well as his Took ancestry on his mother's side. Specifically, Primula Brandybuck was Frodo's mother and Bilbo's first cousin (that is, Primula's mother was Old Took's youngest daughter, just as Bilbo's mother was Belladonna Took, the oldest of Took's daughters); Drogo Baggins, Frodo's father, was Bilbo's second cousin. Not only are Bilbo and Frodo linked by ancestry and then by law, but the orphan Frodo was also brought up in Brandy Hall, where he presumably played with Merry (and perhaps Pippin) (*LOTR*, 1:1, 23). Frodo seems as queer as Bilbo, as longing for adventure, and as close to Bilbo's Took relatives through his "closest friends," Merry and Pippin (*LOTR*, 1:2, 42), who will prove to be the most heroic of all three branches because of the blending of differences.

The Hobbits, with their three branches distinguished by regional differences and affiliations with other races—Harfoots, Stoors, and Fallohides—incarnate three medieval-like estates as well, although Tolkien's heroes tend to come, at least in part, from the Fallohides, the loftiest of the branches. The stocky large-footed Stoors of the south associated with the Great River Anduin and "highlands and hillsides"—from which Gollum springs—are also "less shy of Men" ("Prologue," *LOTR*, 3), and, therefore, associated with them in their middling position in the hierarchy of being. The small brown beardless Harfoots live in the mountains of the west and like holes and tunnels, much like Dwarves, the species they most resemble; many of the Bagginses, as well as other members of the Shire, are Harfoots (the less attractive and more materialistic sides of Bilbo and Frodo). The Fallohides, the equivalent of Elves, come from the north; they are, like medieval aristocrats, skilled in song craft and hunting, and love trees and forests. In delineating the heroic aristocracy of the Fallohides, Tolkien cautions that these Hobbits were never explicitly warlike, although Bullroarer Took had participated in defeating the Orcs in the Battle of Greenfields, in S.R. 1147 ("Prologue," *LOTR*, 5). In the Shire only the richest and the poorest continued to live in holes, the poor Hobbits having "mere holes," but the "well-to-do," more luxurious digs, and the noble Tooks of Great Smials and the Brandybucks of Brandy Hall both lived in peace in "one ancestral and many-tunnelled mansion" for many generations ("Prologue," *LOTR*, 7).

Note Tolkien's medievalized and aristocratic description in the "Prologue Concerning Hobbits and Other Matters" of the Fallohides, from whom especially Merry and Pippin and, to a lesser extent, Bilbo and Frodo, derive: "Being somewhat bolder and more adventurous, they were often found as leaders or chieftains among clans of Harfoots or Stoors. Even in Bilbo's time the strong Fallohidish strain could still be noted among the greater families, such as the Tooks and the Masters of Buckland" ("Prologue," *LOTR*, 3). The Tooks, so Tolkien tells us, had "long been pre-eminent; for the office of Thain had passed to them (from the Oldbucks) some centuries before, and the chief Took had borne that title ever since" ("Prologue," *LOTR*, 9). The Thain functions as master of the Shire-moot and as captain in times of muster and call-to-arms. Tolkien reminds us: "The Took family was still, indeed, accorded a special respect, for it remained both numerous and exceedingly wealthy, and was liable to produce in every generation strong characters of peculiar habits, and even adventurous temperament. The latter qualities, however, were now rather tolerated (in the rich) than generally approved" ("Prologue," *LOTR*, 9). But "The Took" is the title still given to the paterfamilias, just as a number might be added to a name of a descendant of an ancestor when necessary (for example, Isengrim the Second).

In acknowledgment of another, Elven and creative, Fallohide trait reflective of thoughtfulness and reverence for the past—that is, songcraft and artistry—all the Hobbit heroes from *The Lord of the Rings* and *The Hobbit* either write books or collect manuscripts. Bilbo's diary, the *Red Book of Westmarch*, provided the source for the War of the Ring and was housed at Undertowers. Copies of the *Red Book* were made for the "descendants of Master Samwise's children" ("Prologue," *LOTR*, 14). A very important copy was written in Gondor for the great-grandson of Peregrin Took, although kept in Great Smials. Further, Tolkien notes, "Since Meriadoc and Peregrin became the heads of their great families, and at the same time kept up their connexions with Rohan and Gondor, the libraries at Bucklebury and Tuckborough contained much that did not appear in the Red Book" ("Prologue," *LOTR*, 14). Meriadoc, in particular, is singled out as an author of books about Rohan and Eriador (although he had help from the Elves of Rivendell); he is particularly interested in the relationship of Shire words with those of Rohan ("Prologue," *LOTR*, 15). In each case—Merry with Rohan and Pippin with Gondor—the heroism of the aristocratic Hobbit is preserved in heroic tales and learned treatises about the respective *region* with which each has been associated. Although Peregrin is not an author, he collects manuscripts by Gondor scribes.

It is axiomatic that Bilbo and his second cousin Frodo belong to the bourgeoisie of the Shire, the very wealth of Bilbo that was acquired through adventure at the Lonely Mountain the subject of endless gossip and scheming by his relatives, the Sackville-Bagginses. Yet Bilbo's paternalism as a typical Victorian head of the household also expresses itself in his unconventional education of his gardener's son, Sam Gamgee.

Sam

And the very humble and insignificant gardener's son Sam himself aids Frodo in the fulfillment of his quest, selflessly spurns the Ring, and carries his master (when Frodo can no longer walk) up Mount Doom. Tolkien describes *The Lord of the Rings* in letter 131 to Michael Waldman as "anthropocentric," because of the "acts of will and deeds of virtue of the apparently small, ungreat, forgotten in the places of the Wise and Great," as seen through Hobbits (a type of Man), in particular, the "chief hero," rustic Sam (160, 161). According to Tolkien in letter 246 to Eileen Elgar, Sam is "a more representative hobbit than any others," by which he means that he is vulgar, smug, cocksure, and ready to assess on the basis of limited data drawn from "traditional 'wisdom'" (329). But his very conceit has been tempered by his love for Frodo: "He did not think of himself as heroic or even brave, or in any way admirable—except in his service and loyalty to his master" (329). We are reminded of Beorhtwold, the old warrior in "The Battle of Maldon" who generously gives his life in support of his proud chief, Beorhtnoth, even though in this case it is the master, Frodo, and not the servant, who sacrifices his life in the Shire.

That Tolkien in his works intends a level playing field for aristocrat, bourgeois, and commoner—whatever their social status or wealth—is clear from the interrelationships the Hobbit heroes all seemed to have maintained throughout their own lives (and, in the Prologue, those of their descendants). Tolkien takes care to pinpoint the initial aristocratic and manorial associations of Merry and Pippin while distinguishing from them the commoner Master Samwise Gamgee (and the bourgeois bachelor knights Bilbo and Frodo Baggins). Ordinary folk stay within their class, Tolkien suggests—unlike the extraordinary hero-Hobbits of *The Lord of the Rings* and the upwardly mobile miller Sandyman.

For Sam represents the Horatio Alger of fantasydom, although Tolkien both identified with him and regarded him as "vulgar." By means of Bilbo's education of him (and in particular through tales of the Elves), Bilbo may have simultaneously whetted Sam's appetite to travel, to accompany his master Frodo, to behave at least as heroically as his master, en route to Mount Doom, to understand the Elven languages and speak some of them, and ultimately to lead the Shire as mayor upon his return. Through Sam's rise from barely literate gardener he progresses, first, to comrade and companion of the Ringbearer and, then, to Ringbearer-bearer as Frodo inches up Mount Doom. The metaphor of a leader as gardener is apt: Sam prunes the garden of the Shire as much as he fertilizes it with the magic of *elanor* he brings back from Lórien. As mayor of the Shire he leads the community, long after, in the narrative as it is continued in the appendices.

Sam's father reveals a potential similar to Sam's (although it remains undeveloped), in the latter's moral and intellectual progress, as do his two daughters, who transcend Sam's own bourgeois position as mayor. In the conversation among the rustics that introduces the book, gardener Ham Gamgee (Sam's father) defends Frodo and Bilbo to the miller, Sandyman (whom he does not like), chiefly because Bilbo has been kind to him, consults him as an authority on growing vegetables, addresses him politely as "Master Hamfast," and has taught his son Sam to read and write (*LOTR*, 1:1, 22, 24). But the Gaffer reflects his own class background and culture in his resistance to Bilbo's classlessness and egalitarianism when he warns Sam not to fraternize with the upper class: "'*Elves and Dragons!* I says to him. *Cabbages and potatoes are better for me and you. Don't go getting mixed up in the business of your betters, or you'll land in trouble too big for you*, I says to him. And I might say it to others,' he added with a look at the stranger [from Michel Delving] and the miller" (*LOTR*, 1:1, 24). Sam's two daughters also attain a loftier status in the community, one, by serving Arwen, the other, Lady Took, as a handmaiden; one takes up the pen to continue the writing of annals begun by Bilbo and Frodo and carried on by Sam.[61]

Merry and Pippin

And yet Merry's course leads upward to aristocratic heroism that will be long celebrated, whereas Pippin's leads downward, in an indenture that marks the servant who must toil to repay the sum for which he has sold his freedom, his life. By giving the two more minor Hobbits the full aristocratic names of Peregrin Took and Meriadoc Brandybuck, Tolkien plays with their figurative aristocratic status as Hobbit heroes. *Peregrin*, the name for a type of falcon, suggests the laws of chivalry and the code of the hunt that a nobleman must learn. *Meriadoc*—a name modeled on *Gorbadoc*, the figure central to the sixteenth-century aristocratic tragedy and the name of Old Master Gorbadoc, the father-in-law of Drogo Baggins (Frodo's father)—reminds the astute reader of the social and political strata of an earlier time (*LOTR*, 1:1, 23). The Brandybuck and Took representatives—Merry and Pippin—also reflect inversions of each other, and as foils dramatize change in class: Merry serves as a heroic thane to his lord, part of a *comitatus* ethic characteristic of Old English works of literature like the elegy "The Wanderer" or the epic *Beowulf* or the heroic chronicle entry "The Battle of Brunanburh." But Pippin functions merely as a servant to a servant—Denethor, steward to the king of Gondor—and wears the livery of a noble household and who saves the family by acting as a messenger to fetch Gandalf at the moment the crazed Denethor places his unconscious son Faramir on his funeral pyre to burn with him.

Tolkien emphasizes the drama of class mobility by repeating the same symbolic feudal ritual for all the Hobbits incrementally. When Merry pledges as a "kingsman" to King Théoden of Rohan and when Pippin, in a mirror image of that same scene, indentures himself as servant to the steward to kings, Denethor, we see replayed similar first estate/third estate feudal symbolism as between Gollum and Frodo in their contracts with each. But it is a feudal contract—no matter how it varies—that involves a superior and inferior member. Merry is inspired to heroism by Théoden's regal demeanor and heroic behavior on the battlefield—and most especially by Éowyn-as-Dernhelm's solitary resistance to the Lord of the Nazgûl, as displayed by her attack on him. Pippin, in contrast, is motivated by guilt and pride to serve the steward, in recompense for the loss in book 3 of Denethor's beloved son on his and Merry's behalf. Certainly the motivation of both Hobbits comes from noble impulses, genes, and histories in their own families, whether of General Took, who was said to have married a fairy wife, or of the Brandybucks, named after the Brandywine River near the Old Forest and wealthy in the oldest sense of old money.

Yet in each case the Hobbit disobeys his lord and steps out of his class and rank. That Tolkien applauds the inner nobility of Merry and merely approves of the dutiful debt-repayment service of Pippin is clear from the limitations placed on each Hobbit. Merry dons armor and joins the similarly disobedient Dernhelm on the battlefield. Pippin, wearing livery, disobeys Denethor's order to stay there with him and instead runs away to Gandalf the wizard for help, as if to signify a lack of trust in his own ability to rescue Faramir on his own (as indeed Denethor has belittled him into feeling he should not).

In the first case Merry's disobedience (like Éowyn's) has been foreseen in a prophecy that memorializes racial and gender difference—that no *man* (as, indeed, neither woman—nor Hobbit—is) can fell the lord of the Nazgûl. Ironically, Gandalf first introduces Pippin to Denethor as a Man, Peregrin Took, while Pippin decries this untruthful term of opprobrium, at least to him, and insists he is a Hobbit, a Halfling: "Man! Indeed not! I am a hobbit and no more valiant than I am a man, save perhaps now and again by necessity" (*LOTR*, 5:1, 749). Or does Pippin mean that, as a Halfling, he is, in fact, a half-man? As if to be a man was the norm and a Hobbit is literally and metaphorically "half"—less than—any man. One Hobbit—the heroic Merry who kills the Lord of the Nazgûl—is, indeed, essentially Not Man, or Noman, like Ulysses who deceives the Cyclops Polyphemus in the cave. The other Hobbit—the guilt-bound Pippin—is essentially not a Man, but a Halfling, a servant to a servant, Denethor, who imagines he should be king and, therefore, as a servant to a servant, No One, Nothing.

Both trajectories, of course, are adumbrated by the epic (or false-epic) journeys of Sam and Frodo, who exchange places with one another in a reciprocal symbolic and symbiotic relationship of lord and servant (who leads whom on the path up Mount Doom?). Ultimately, at the end of the anti-quest, it is Frodo as its servant who bears the Ring back to its origin. Frodo is, of course, simultaneously the hero and lord commanding both his valet and gardener Sam and Sméagol his *villein*. Is Frodo an aristocratic lord when Sam carries him like a sleepy weary child at the end?—or a sack of potatoes? Is Sam not still a laborer who labors and serves? Just so is Gollum the reptilelike Stoor, who creeps along sniffing and snuffling and who masters—lords it over—the civilized Sméagol who serves both him and Frodo, and who seeks to educate him into civilized behavior and understanding. These are ironic impostures in each case.

Where all four Hobbits resume the aristocratic romance behaviors they ape at the beginning is at the end, when they return to the Shire and find that the Shire is no longer a pastoral retreat for nobility and that their servants form but an industrialized community of entrepreneurial and middle-class horror. Saruman has degenerated to Sharkey (reminiscent of the fish-eating Gollum and the ignominious Worm). Both of them are affiliated with the factory-owned mill of Sandyman. Sad to say, it is the true bourgeoisie who dominate the community, the true nobility having abandoned the community. The burgher and the businessman join hands in the crassest land development one might imagine.

Gollum

We think of other antiheroes in *The Lord of the Rings*—Gollum, scarcely more than a shadow of a living thing, bites off the Ring still on Frodo's finger and incidentally also saves Middle-earth. Of all these queer and unnatural Hobbits, Gollum is the most disgusting and least sympathetic. Both Sam and Frodo regard Gollum as queer and unnatural. For Frodo, Gollum is the Shire equivalent of a Brandybuck living across the river, so that the Ringbearer initially reacts to Gollum's strangeness—his "queerness"—as Sandyman did to him—with suspicion and indignation. Frodo himself wishes Gandalf had killed Gollum when he had had the chance. Yet it is because of Gollum that the quest is completed. Despite seeming initially different, Gollum remains a much diminished Hobbit. Descended from the wandering, matriarchal Stoor branch of the Gladden Fields, he is not a typical Harfoot Hobbit from the Shire or Bree or a fair, adventuresome Fallohide from the upper Anduin or Eriador (the branch of the Hobbits from which leaders often come, and the line from which the Tooks, Brandybucks, and Bolgars descended). In this sense Gollum represents a Hobbit alter-ego for Bilbo–Frodo, both of the Bagginses so queer and different from others in the Shire because of their Fallohide–Harfoot mixed ancestry.

The Free Peoples' understanding of Sauron's intolerance for other viewpoints works to their advantage when the Dark Lord imagines the Free Peoples' motivations are identical to his: Sauron never realizes that they do not want war, that they do not have a new lord in mind to replace him, and that they wish to destroy the Ring. Which brings us to the rest of *The Lord of the Rings*.

Notes

1. J.R.R. Tolkien, Interview with Denys Gueroult, "Now Read on," *BBC Radio 4*, 16 December 1964. Transcript was printed in "J.R.R. Tolkien, An Interview," *News From Bree*, 19 November 1974, 3–5. There is also a cassette: London: BBC Cassettes: 1980.
2. See John Rateliff, *The History of The Hobbit, Part 1: Mr. Baggins* (London: HarperCollins, 2007), 76–80.
3. Cited in Renée Vink, "'Jewish' Dwarves: Tolkien and Anti-Semitic Stereotyping," *Tolkien Studies* 10 (2013): 123 [123–46]. Vink is responding to an article by Rebecca Brackmann, "Dwarves are not Heroes: Antisemitism and the Dwarves in J.R.R. Tolkien's Writing," *Mythlore* 109/110 28(3–4) (2010): 85–106.
4. A website to which Vink refers in the note above compares Khuzdul and Semitic languages (Hebrew and Arabic): see http://www.forodrim.org/daeron/md_kuzdul.pdf, accessed 23 August 2015). However, the website is devoted to the pdf by Åberg, "An Analysis of Dwarvish" (2).
5. Douglas Charles Kane points out that chapter 2 of *The Silmarillion*, "Of Aulë and Yvanna," was entirely compiled by Christopher Tolkien from Tolkien's writings, the first part coming from a manuscript titled "Of Aulë and the Dwarves" in a folder labeled "Amended Legend of Origin of the

Dwarves" and bears a relation to chapter 13 in the "later *Quenta*," "Concerning the Dwarves." See his *Arda Reconstructed: The Creation of the Published Silmarillion* (Bethlehem, PA: Lehigh University Press, 2011), 54. Noting that Christopher "does push the limits of editorial intervention," he adds that Christopher thought the origin of the Dwarves belonged earlier in the history than where his father had placed it (55).
6. Rateliff, *Mr. Baggins*, 76, referring to the *Gnomish Lexicon*, in which *nauglafel* means "dwarf-natured, i.e., mean, avaricious" (*Book of Lost Tales* 1:261; *Parma Eldalamberon* 11:59).
7. J.R.R. Tolkien, "Valedictory Address to the University of Oxford, 5 June 1959," in *The Monsters and the Critics and Other Essays*, ed. Christopher Tolkien, 224–40 (London: Allen & Unwin, 1983; Boston, MA: Houghton Mifflin, 1984), 238; but also see Mary Salu and Robert Farrell, eds. *J.R.R. Tolkien: Scholar and Storyteller: Essays in Memoriam* (Ithaca: Cornell University Press, 1979), 15–32.
8. *Webster's New Universal Unabridged Dictionary* (New York: Barnes & Noble, 1996), 97.
9. Tolkien, "Valedictory Address," 239.
10. See Thomas A. Shippey, *The Road to Middle Earth* (London: Allen & Unwin, 1982; Boston, MA: Houghton Mifflin, 1983; rev. edn. London: HarperCollins, Grafton, 1992; Boston MA: Houghton Mifflin, 2003), which documents Tolkien's love of philology as the foundation of his fiction and his mythology.
11. See Humphrey Carpenter's comments in his interview in the film *Tolkien Remembered* (Princeton, NJ: Films for the Humanities and Sciences, 1993).
12. Tison Pugh and Angela Jane Weisl, *Medievalisms: Making the Past in the Present* (London and New York: Routledge, 2012), 5.
13. John Clute and John Grant, eds., *The Encyclopedia of Fantasy* (London: Orbit, 1997), s.v. "Perception" and "Fantasy," quotations which have been combined in this single citation.
14. Brian Rosebury, *Tolkien: A Cultural Phenomenon* (Houndmills, Basingstoke, Hampshire: Palgrave Macmillan, 2003), 160.
15. Fred Inglis, "Gentility and Powerlessness: Tolkien and the New Class," in *J.R.R. Tolkien: This Far Land*, ed. Robert Giddings, 25–41 (London: Vision Press; Totowa, NJ: Barnes & Noble Books, 1983), 39.
16. Nick Otty, "The Structuralist's Guide to Middle-earth," in *J.R.R. Tolkien: This Far Land*, ed. Giddings, 154–178, here, 172.
17. Otty, 173.
18. Otty, 166.
19. John Carey, interviewed in *J.R.R. Tolkien: An Audio Portrait*, presented by Brian Sibley (London: BBC, 2001).

20. Rosebury, *Tolkien: A Cultural Phenomenon*, 161.
21. J.R.R. Tolkien, "The Name 'Nodens,'" Appendix I, in R.E.M. Wheeler and T.V. Wheeler, *Report on the Excavation of the Prehistoric, Roman, and Post-Roman Site in Lydney Park, Gloucestershire*, Reports of the Research Committee of the Society of Antiquaries of London, no. 9 (London: Oxford University Press, 1932), 132–37; repr. *Tolkien Studies* 4 (2007): 177–83.
22. J.R.R. Tolkien, Foreword, to Walter E. Haigh, *A New Glossary of the Dialect of the Huddersfield District* (London: Oxford University Press, 1928), viii.
23. Tolkien, Foreword, *A New Glossary of the Dialect of the Huddersfield District*, xv.
24. Tolkien, Foreword, *A New Glossary of the Dialect of the Huddersfield District*, xvii.
25. Tolkien, Foreword, *A New Glossary of the Dialect of the Huddersfield District*, xviii.
26. Tolkien, Foreword, *A New Glossary of the Dialect of the Huddersfield District*, xviii. For a brief biography of Haigh, see Janet Brennan Croft, "Walter E. Haigh, Author of *A New Glossary of the Huddersfield Dialect*," *Tolkien Studies* 4 (2007):184–88.
27. J.R.R. Tolkien, "Sigelwara Land," pts. 1 and 2, *Medium Aevum* 1 (1932): 183–196; and 3 (1934): 1–70, here, lines 69–71.
28. J.R.R. Tolkien, *The Old English Exodus: Text, Translation, and Commentary by J.R.R. Tolkien*, editorial apparatus by Joan Turville-Petre (Oxford: Oxford University Press, 1981), 33.
29. Tolkien, *Exodus*, 21; my emphasis.
30. Tolkien's note to the published edition, *Exodus*, 3, line 69, acknowledges that the original manuscript lists "Sigelwara," expanded by Tolkien to "Sigelwarena." The word *beorhhleoðu* was expanded from *burh* in the manuscript by Thorpe. The translation appears on 21.
31. Tolkien, "Sigelwara Land," pt. 1, 183.
32. Tolkien, "Sigelwara Land," pt. 1, 192.
33. Tolkien, "Sigelwara Land," pt. 2, 108.
34. Tolkien, "Sigelwara Land," pt. 2, 106.
35. Tolkien, "Sigelwara Land," pt. 2, 109.
36. Tolkien, "Sigelwara Land," pt. 2, 110.
37. Margaret Sinex, "'Monsterized Saracens,' Tolkien's Haradrim, and Other Medieval 'Fantasy Products,'" *Tolkien Studies* 7 (2010): 175–76 [175–96]. See also Brian McFadden on racial difference in relation to the Ethiopians and Tolkien's Swertings (another name for them) in "Fear of Difference, Fear of Death: The Sigelwara, Tolkien's Swertings, and Racial Difference,"

in *Tolkien's Modern Middle Ages*, ed. Jane Chance and Alfred Siewers, Jr., 155–169 (New York: Palgrave Macmillan, 2005).
38. Dimitra Fimi, *Tolkien, Race, and Cultural History: From Fairies to Hobbits* (London: Palgrave Macmillan, 2009), 131–59; see also J.R.R. Tolkien, "English and Welsh," in *The Monsters and the Critics and Other Essays*, ed. Christopher Tolkien, 162–97 (London: George Allen & Unwin, 1983).
39. Tolkien, *Exodus*, 34–35.
40. Tolkien, "Sigelwara Land," pt. 2, 111.
41. Tolkien, "Sigelwara Land," pt. 2, 111.
42. Tolkien, *Exodus*, 20.
43. Tolkien, "Valedictory Address," 238.
44. Tolkien, "Valedictory Address," 239.
45. Tolkien, "Valedictory Address," 240.
46. In the Oxford University Press Archives and included in Scull, *Chronology*, 375–76.
47. John Bowers is at work on a study of this Clarendon Chaucer anthology.
48. J.R.R. Tolkien, "Chaucer as a Philologist: *The Reeve's Tale*," *Transactions of the Philological Society* (1934): 1–70.
49. See J.R.R. Tolkien, "The Devil's Coach-horses," *Review of English Studies* 1 (1925): 331–36.
50. Tolkien, "The Devil's Coach-horses," 336.
51. J.R.R. Tolkien, "*Ancrene Wisse* and *Hali Meiðhad*," *Essays and Studies by Members of the English Association* 14 (1929): 104–26. Much later Tolkien composed a preface for the translation of *The Ancrene Riwle* by his former student M(ary). B. Salu and later edited the same text for the Early English Text Society. See J.R.R. Tolkien, preface to *The Ancrene Riwle*, trans. M.B. Salu (London: Burns & Oates, 1955; Notre Dame, IN: University of Notre Dame Press, 1956); and J.R.R. Tolkien, ed., *The English Text of the Ancrene Riwle: Ancrene Wisse*, Early English Text Society 249 (London: Oxford University Press, 1962).
52. J.R.R. Tolkien, "Middle English 'Losenger': Sketch of an Etymological and Semantic Enquiry," *Essais de philologie moderne* 129 (1951): 63.
53. Tolkien, "Middle English 'Losenger,'" 63.
54. Tolkien, "Middle English 'Losenger,'" 64–65.
55. Tolkien, "Middle English 'Losenger,'" 64.
56. This discovery of the annotated map listing Tolkien's notations on the latitudes between Oxford and Hobbiton and Mirkwood and Ravenna was reported in the *Guardian* on 23 October 2015 in a copy of *The Lord of the Rings* sold at Thornton's Book Store in Oxford, previously owned by Pauline Baynes, Tolkien's primary illustrator, and now for sale by Blackwells for 60,000 GBP: see http://www.theguardian.com/books/2015/oct/23/jrr-tolkien-middle-earth-annotated-map-blackwells-lord-of-the-

rings and circulated by Sarah Laskow on public media (*Atlas Obscura*, Facebook) at http://www.atlasobscura.com/articles/found-a-map-of-middle-earth-annotated-by-tolkien-himself?utm_source=facebook.com&utm_medium=atlas-page, accessed 23 October 2015. Additionally, for the pattern of contrast throughout the epic, home versus threat, see the chapter on "Heroic Narrative and the Power of Structure," in Jane Chance, *The Lord of the Rings: The Mythology of Power*, Twayne Masterwork Studies, 99 (New York: Twayne/ Maxwell Macmillan, 1992), 109–16; rev. edn. (Lexington, KY: University Press of Kentucky, 2001), 128–38.
57. Slavoj Žižek, "Neighbors and Other Monsters," in *The Neighbor: Three Inquiries in Political Theology*, eds. Slavoj Žižek, Eric L. Santner, and Kenneth Reinhard (Chicago and London: University of Chicago Press, 2005), 143. The passage is discussed in the introduction on 4–5.
58. See J.R.R. Tolkien, *Farmer Giles of Ham* (London: George Allen & Unwin, 1949; Boston: Houghton Mifflin, 1950); repr. in *The Tolkien Reader* (New York: Ballantine Books, 1966) and elsewhere; and J.R.R. Tolkien, *Smith of Wootton Major* (London: George Allen & Unwin; Boston: Houghton Mifflin, 1967), repr. in *Redbook*, December 1967: 58–61, 101, 103–7; also ed. Verlyn Flieger (London: HarperCollins, 2005).
59. See Lisa Zunshine, *Strange Concepts and the Stories They Make Possible: Cognition, Culture, Narrative* (Baltimore, MD: Johns Hopkins University Press, 2008), 12.
60. Patrick Colm Hogan, *Understanding Nationalism: On Narrative, Neuroscience, and Identity* (Columbus, OH: Ohio State University, 2009), 30; cited in Jane Chance, "Introduction: Cognitive Alterities: From Cultural Studies to Neuroscience and Back Again," in *Cognitive Alterities/Neuromedievalism*, ed. Jane Chance and Antony D. Passaro, *Postmedieval: A Journal of Medieval Cultural Studies* 3(3) (Fall 2012): 247–61.
61. Philip Norman, "The Prevalence of Hobbits," *New York Times Magazine*, 15 January 1967, 100.

CHAPTER 7

"Usually Slighted": Gudrún, Other Medieval Women, and *The Lord of the Rings*, Book 3 (1925–1943)

"Invisibility thus cuts in different directions, offering some ultimate power while denying others basic presence. Invisibility's inherent dualism, I submit, is directly relevant to gender constructions, particularly the ways that dominant masculinity establishes its quiet claims to power over others, especially women. Aligning itself with an expansive invisibility that subjects others to its machinations and designs, masculinity asserts its comprehensive dominance by passing unnoticed."—Holly Crocker, *Chaucer's Visions of Manhood*, 3[1]

Much criticism has been expended on the issue of Tolkien's alleged misogyny, or at least, his creation of fictions in which few females occupy key roles, except as supernal figures who govern a realm soon to disappear (Galadriel—indeed, an Elf, or Míriel, mother of Fëanor), or monsters like the giant spider Shelob and a mother like Grendel's in *Beowulf*, who wishes to eat the prey she has captured. Other female characters in *The Lord of the Rings* are lesser daughters left behind, old women nurses, or bar maids soon to be pregnant with children. In his own life and career, his mother loomed large as his tutor, as did his wife, Edith Bratt, the pianist mother of his four children (and originally, his soul-mate, as indicated by his name for her as the female Halfelven hero Lúthien). There were also his students, some of them female, who achieved success as medievalists, precisely as scholars or writers guided by him. And, of course, his lone daughter, Priscilla, took over the Tolkien Society as its permanent president. Where,

© The Author(s) 2016
Jane Chance, *Tolkien, Self and Other: "This Queer Creature"*,
The New Middle Ages, DOI 10.1057/978-1-137-39896-3_7

then, does this strangely conventional polarity of the "dark and the light" originate?

Tolkien's representation of women has been criticized for decades as either nonexistent or hopelessly conventional and traditional, given the era in which he lived.[2] Laura Michel, in "Politically Incorrect: Tolkien, Women, and Feminism" (2006), notes aptly that, "For years, Tolkien has been criticized, attacked, explained, forgiven, and mainly misunderstood when it comes to the matter of women."[3] A recent collection, *Perilous and Fair: Women in the Works and Life of J.R.R. Tolkien* (2015), edited by Janet Brennan Croft and Leslie A. Donovan, includes essays on women in Tolkien in relation to historical perspectives, the power of gender, specific characters, earlier literary contexts, and women readers, with its specific purpose defined as refuting "simplistic claims that Tolkien has nothing useful, relevant, or modern to say about women. We also intend to confirm that critics have engaged fruitfully with issues surrounding the feminine and female power since the early days of Tolkien scholarship and that they continue to do so."[4] A significant collection for its topic, it is by no means complete, however—one important issue continues to dominate most of these articles and their approaches to women: they center primarily on characters in *The Lord of the Rings* and *The Silmarillion* without any buttressing from Tolkien's scholarship (his letters, excepted), or non-fantasy translations and adaptations.

Why should Tolkien's medieval scholarship be worth considering in this regard? Note, for example, his important comment in the introduction to his lectures at Oxford on the Eddaic poem *Guðrúnarkviða en forna*, the Old Lay of Gudrún, in which, according to Christopher, he remarks that, "'curiously enough' he was more interested in Gudrún, 'who is usually slighted and considered as of secondary interest', than in Brynhild." For Tolkien, Brynhild is an "irruption" that does not last long. In contrast, Gudrún endures a "long agony ... and her passion and death remain only in the background of the tale, a brief and terrible storm beginning in fire and ending in it."[5] Gudrún's role as the antagonist would seem to cast her in a pejorative role, but, instead, rather surprisingly, endears her to Tolkien. His remark casts a new light on what he values in women (or at least in female literary characters) and suggests that readers have in part misunderstood his treatment of them during his life and in some of his creative writing. For Tolkien, Gudrún's love for Sigurd positions her as exceptional and worthy, despite her later madness and violence. Tolkien queers that female stereotype as he does so many other norms. Indeed, the charm she holds for Tolkien provides a clue to his reconstruction of women as often alone in the tribulations they endure, without support, and yet both entitled and determined to achieve what they perceive as necessary for the society or community in which they live. For this reason, it is nearly always a mistake to divorce his academic production from his creative and fantastic output, as the two are almost always hybrid, in the sense that they blend into one another.

As is usual with Tolkien, he often holds a double perspective, or he attempts to create one: a conventional perspective in his relationship with family and friends, but in his work as a professor—in his teaching (lectures and notes) and his scholarly and literary writings—rather different and unique. The reason for this double perspective stems from his early life and culture, dominated as it was by male peer groups at school, church, university, and in the army, however briefly, during World War I. But the medieval literature in Old Norse and Old and Middle English on which he spent much of his early career between 1925 and 1934, in teaching, translating or editing, and, later on, writing about, often centered on female figures with whom he sympathized. Three examples I will explore in greater detail include the medieval anchoress (or saint); Gudrún, drawn from the *Völsunga Saga*; and, surprisingly, Grendel's Mother in *Beowulf*.

In every case, there is usually some personal similarity between the female figure and himself. The medieval anchoress in the *Ancrene Riwle* (the Anchoress's Rule) who walled herself off from the world in order to pray and meditate is provided a rule for her reclusive life by a cleric from Tolkien's own native (often culturally denigrated) West Midlands, writing in a similarly unfashionable northern-flavored dialect of Middle English. For a woman today to seal herself permanently inside an anchorhold would be considered odd, or queer, behavior. Yet as seen throughout this study, Tolkien often identifies with characters considered abject and abandoned, as alone—like the other odd, lone, or antisocial male characters with whom he identified, such as Kullervo, Sigurd, and Beowulf. And he does project into even his most scholarly of articles this general empathy for alterity of all types, which would, of course, include women.

Certainly, readers only of *The Lord of the Rings* may find some of what I will argue surprising, but understanding his approach to these figures and the works in which they appear may also illuminate the alleged but mistaken explanation for the absence of women in *The Lord of the Rings*. As he wrote in letter 165, to the Houghton Mifflin Co., on 30 June 1955 (220), "The only criticism [about *The Lord of the Rings*] that annoyed me was one that it 'contained no religion' and 'no Women,' but that does not matter, and is not true anyway." While there is not space for an exhaustive treatment of these figures, or even a more superficial survey of all, these three suggest a significant pattern. First, however, a few reminders about how subversive Tolkien can be in his support and regard for both medieval and modern women, given his conventional background and culture.

Conventional Tolkien

In so many ways, Tolkien grew up a man of his generation, conservative in his estimation of women's place in society and their biological difference from men, largely because the society he inhabited was almost wholly male. His early life at King Edward's School, Exeter College, and in the Lancashire Fusiliers during World War I depended upon mentoring by male teachers, professors, and tutors and male friendships.[6] The literature he was required to read involved male heroes and their battles. Oxford and the Anglo-Catholic Exeter College were all male at the time Tolkien began, first, to study Classics (meaning authors of Greece and Rome), under tutors Lewis R. Farnell (*Cults of the Greek States*) and E.A. Barber, and then (as his special subject), Comparative Philology, for which he studied under philologist Joseph Wright (*English Dialect Grammar* and *Primer of the Gothic Language*).[7] When Tolkien switched to the new Honors School (faculty) of English in 1913, he concentrated on the history of the English language and related Germanic languages and studied Old and Middle English under tutor Kenneth Sisam and Old Norse (the *Gylfaginning* and the *Völsunga Saga*) under William Craigie.[8] At the Essay Club in Trinity term of 1913 he declaimed on Norse sagas and then, when he won the English prize, bought William Morris's *Story of the Volsungs, House of the Wolfings*, and *Life and Death of Jason* (along with J. Morris Jones, *A Welsh Grammar*). His role models in 1914, Morris and Edward Burne-Jones, had entered Exeter College in 1852, creative forces behind both the Pre-Raphaelites and the Arts and Crafts movement.[9]

As noted previously, Tolkien also belonged to all-male social and literary clubs—the TCBS, at King Edward's School, and at Oxford, the Exeter College Essay Club, the literary Apolausticks, a society that he founded (the name, what Garth calls a "spoonerism for *apostolic*"),[10] the Stapledon Society (a student union), the philosophical Dialectical Society, and later, the Inklings.[11] He also played rugby (*rugger*) as a winger in the Rugby Club, despite his slightness, and belonged to the Boat Club.[12] When, on 28 June 1914, Archduke Franz Ferdinand was assassinated in Sarajevo, and on 4 August war was declared by Britain on Germany, Tolkien continued to live at Oxford with other young men, even while delaying enlistment (except for joining the Officer Training Corps, where he was Class II rather than Class I). After wedding Edith on 22 March 1916—who may have been pregnant at the time with their first child, John, given his birth on 16 November of the same year—Tolkien left for France in June 1916 and, ultimately, for the Battle of the Somme. He returned in November of the same year with trench fever (apparently caused by lice, although it has also been regarded as a form of post-traumatic stress syndrome brought on by the violence and death of war). Most importantly, as John Garth notes—having tracked Tolkien's relationships with many of these young men from King Edward's School and then Exeter—that "The war killed 23 of the 57 who had matriculated with him in 1911."[13] Later on, even after Tolkien had begun teaching at Leeds and then at Oxford, this homosocial pattern of participating in all-male reading and discussion groups continued, as, for example, in the Kolbítars and the Inklings.[14]

What were Tolkien's views on women? Details from his early life may elucidate the opinions on women he expressed in his letters, medieval scholarship, and literary works. Note Tolkien's sage advice on marriage and relations between the sexes in letter 43 (48) to his son Michael, the night before the latter's wedding, on 6–8 March 1941: "In this fallen world the 'friendship' that should be possible between all human beings, is virtually impossible between man and woman...Later in life when sex cools down, it may be possible. It may happen between saints...But a young man does not really (as a rule) want 'friendship', even if he says he does." This realistic assessment of gender difference in the earlier twentieth century and, in particular, an admission of the more sexual relationship desired by young men, is coupled with a negative view of romantic (courtly) love, given its artificiality, selfishness, and unsuitability for those heading toward matrimony, as expressed later in the same letter:

> It idealizes "love"—and as far as it goes can be very good, since it takes in far more than physical pleasure, and enjoins if not purity, at least fidelity, and so self-denial, "service", courtesy, honour, and courage. Its weakness is, of course, that it began as an artificial courtly game, a way of enjoying love for its own sake without reference to (and indeed contrary to) matrimony. Its centre was not God, but imaginary Deities, Love and the Lady. It still tends to make the Lady a kind of guiding star or divinity... This is, of course, false and at best make-believe. The woman is another fallen human-being with a

soul in peril. But combined and harmonized with religion (as long ago it was, producing much of that beautiful devotion to Our Lady that has been God's way of refining so much of our gross manly natures and emotions. [48–49]

Interestingly, Tolkien perceives women, even intelligent women, as different from men in a love relationship: more practical, less selfish and romantic, and also, curiously, needing to be male-centered and led, even "fertilized":

> Women really have not much part in all this. Though they may use the language of romantic love, since it is so entwined in all our idioms. The sexual impulse makes women (naturally when unspoiled more unselfish) very sympathetic and understanding ... the servient, helpmeet instinct, generously warmed by desire and young blood ... Every teacher knows that. How quickly an intelligent woman can be taught, grasp his ideas, see his point—and how (with rare exceptions) they can go no further, when they leave his hand, or when they cease to take a *personal* interest in *him*. [49]

For this reason, Tolkien continues, falling in love actually indicates—whether a young woman realizes it or not—that what she wants is to become the mother of the young man's children (50).

Tolkien's most startling advice about women and men in this same letter refers to the greater sexual needs of men, the more monogamous nature of women, and the danger of not using contraception if terrible mistakes are to be prevented. Women "have, of course, still to be more careful in sexual relations, for all the contraceptives. But they are instinctively, when uncorrupt, monogamous. *Men are not* ... No good pretending. Men just ain't, not by their animal nature ... Brigham Young (I believe) was a healthy and happy man. It is a fallen world, and there is no consonance between our bodies, minds, and souls" (51). No fantasy here. Finally, when he states in letter 44, also to Michael, on 18 March 1941, that "Nearly all marriages, even happy ones, are mistakes" because with more time "more suitable mates" could have been found, does he hint here at some kind of mismatch with his own wife? By this date, when he was forty-nine and Edith was fifty-two, they had been married for twenty-five years and had conceived four children. There is no other evidence that they were unhappily married and, of course, he immortalized Edith as Beren's beloved Lúthien on their tombstones.

Yet, given Tolkien's prodigious creative and scholarly output and his need to share what he had written with others in small groups of friends like the Inklings and clubs like the TCBS—as he had done with Edith when they were younger, when she transcribed many of his efforts—it is odd that there are few mentions of what Edith thought about his writing, especially later in life. His relationships with his Aunt Jane Suffield Neave, who became a teacher, with Elizabeth Mary Wright, former pupil, scholar, and wife of his professor Joseph Wright, and those learned women students whom he taught and tutored over a long period, either at Leeds or Oxford, suggest that some of them might have been better suited to him as a companion than Edith. Among those, his most distinguished, according to the list in John D. Rateliff's excellent article, "The Missing Women: J.R.R. Tolkien's Lifelong Support for Women's Higher Education," were Mary Challans (Mary Renault), Barbara Pym, Simonne d'Ardenne, Ursula Dronke, and others.[15] That his mentoring of so many women students was unusual in his day is attested by Rateliff in his comparison of Lewis and Tolkien: "Lewis had a distaste for female research students that led him to denigrate them both in public and in private. By contrast, Tolkien was deeply supportive of his female research students and did all he could to further their researches and subsequent careers."[16]

In line with Tolkien's intense friendships with only a few college friends and students and his frequent retreat to the safety of words, languages, and his created mythology when the world became too threatening, he himself turned to the comfort and warmth of family life. His Belgian B.Litt. student and later professorial colleague, collaborator, and close friend, Simonne Thérèse Rosalie Odile d'Ardenne (1899–1986), remarks on their forty-year relationship—she even lived with the Tolkiens for a year—and the paternal quality of the role he played with her as father and teacher, in addition to other roles as her friend, a Christian, an artist, and a humanist. It was Tolkien as paterfamilias that she chose to elaborate on as most characteristic of his humanity:

> All his letters, extending over about forty years, tell of his concern about his children's health, their comfort, their future: how best he could help them to succeed in life, and how to make their lives as perfect as possible. He started by giving them a most pleasant childhood, creating for them the deep sense of home, which had been denied to him, as he lost his father when he was a young child, and his splendid mother a few years later. And to

provide all this Tolkien accepted the heavy and tedious burden of examining in several English universities, which, of course, took up much time that he might have devoted to his research. But, however busy he was, he always found time to rush home and kiss his younger children goodnight.[17]

Simonne's statement, along with the long list of scholarly articles and editions that Tolkien published during his lifetime and left unfinished for his son Christopher and others to edit and publish—aside from his creative writing—would seem to undermine any negative assumptions by his colleagues that he had not written much at all.[18] Of even greater interest is his close friendships with Simonne and other women students, given his rather conventional attitudes toward women as expressed in his letters.

TOLKIEN'S WOMEN: STUDENTS, SAINTS, AND HOLY WOMEN

Tolkien supported the research for and writing of the editions of two medieval lives of women saints, *St. Julienne* and *Seinte Katerine*, both taken up as edition projects by Simonne T.R.O. d'Ardenne, and essays about and an edition and translation of the *Ancrene Wisse/Riwle* (the *Anchoress's Rule*) by his younger student Mary B. Salu. She had written about the *Ancrene Wisse/Riwle* during the period between 1941 and 1949 in her B.Litt. thesis on the manual's Middle English grammar and assisted him in his own work on the text. Simonne, so close to Tolkien's family that she lived with the Tolkiens for a year in 1932–1933 and completed her thesis with him on the Middle English "Liflade ant te Passiun of Seinte Iulienne" in 1936,[19] had hoped Tolkien, who had worked together with her on an edition of *Seinte Katerine*, would collaborate with her on the Early English Text Society (EETS) editions of both *Seinte Katerine* and *Sawles Warde* (both extant in Oxford Bodley 34). The former edition, however, when published in 1981, listed E.J. Dobson as coeditor, and the latter edition was never published.[20] The pair did publish two jointly written articles, "'Iþþlen' in *Sawles Warde*," in 1947, and "MS. Bodley 34: A Re-Collation of a Collation," in 1947–1948.[21] Simonne's regard for him—she was only seven years younger than he—is evidenced by her published notes about him and their work together in a festschrift for his retirement and in Mary Salu's coedited memorial volume of essays.[22]

The Ancrene Wisse (Riwle): The Anchoress's Rule

In addition to the mythology of *The Silmarillion*, which Tolkien spent much of his life writing and never finished, the medieval text he also read, transcribed, edited, glossed, indexed, translated, and published in book form between 1920 and 1962—even after he retired—was, surprisingly, the early thirteenth-century (second quarter) *Ancrene Wisse* (also known as the *Ancrene Riwle*). While *The Lord of the Rings* is often said (inaccurately) not to involve females as central characters and to attract only male readers, the *Ancrene Wisse*, as its author titles it, or *The Anchoresses' Guide*, was originally addressed to three "well-born" women taking up the life of an anchoress,[23] but written by a man—likely their ecclesiastical confessor—who cared deeply about them. The author was apparently from the West Midlands, familiar with early forms of Northern and West Midlands dialect, and deeply spiritual—not unlike Tolkien himself. Tolkien acknowledges that the manuscript he used eventually in his edition—the Corpus Christi College Cambridge MS [CCCC] 402: *A Rule for Nunnes or Recluses*—according to an inscription at the foot of folio 1 was a gift of John Purcel, from a South Shropshire family, to a house of Augustinian canons at St. Wigmore in Herefordshire. Later, in the fourteenth century, it belonged to St. James Abbey, also at Wigmore.[24]

As early as 1920, Tolkien, then at the University of Leeds, became interested in the Corpus Christi manuscript of the *Ancrene Wisse* held at Cambridge.[25] He commented on it in two linguistic or philological articles, one published in 1925 in the *Review of English Studies* ("Some Contributions to Middle-English Lexicography") and the other in 1929 in *Essays and Studies* ("*Ancrene Wisse* and *Hali Meiðhad*"). He also proposed to Kenneth Sisam a simple text and glossary edition in 1930 for Oxford University Press he would begin after he finished the Clarendon Chaucer (which he did not in fact finish, although he handed in what he had done to the Press in the fifties).[26] It was instead his Oxford B.Litt. "candidate" M.E[laine]. Griffiths who attempted a partial transcription, near full glossary, and index, even though he kept a photographic facsimile of the Corpus MS at home to study.[27] He finally committed to an edition—one of a series of different manuscript versions of the *Ancrene Riwle*—for the EETS in late 1935.[28] Apparently the edition was delayed because of an argument between Tolkien and the EETS about whether the text should be line by line, as his own transcription read, with references to it in glossary and index, or to the typescript book. Although the EETS eventually agreed with Tolkien, the edition for various reasons (and obstacles) was not published until 1962.

About the obstacles: first, *The Hobbit* was published in 1937, then the War interrupted; Griffiths left the projects and in her place Mary B. Salu then came on board, finishing the index along with her thesis on grammar and phonology, and in 1955, having advanced to lecturer at the University of Reading, her own translation with Tolkien's preface.[29] As Merton Professor of English Language and Literature (meaning, responsible for Middle English and not just Anglo-Saxon) Tolkien had lectured on the work, but he only handed over the final manuscript to the EETS in September 1958, before he retired, after which ensued a new round of arguments about line-lengths and how they should be handled. Again production was stymied, this time by dental problems, appendicitis, his wife's health, a printers' strike, and—*The Lord of the Rings*.[30] To Rayner Unwin he said in letter 223 of 31 July 1960 (301–2),

> I am in fact utterly stuck—lost in a bottomless bog … The crimes of omission that I committed in order to complete the [*Lord of the Rings*] are being avenged. The chief is the *Ancrene Riwle*. My edition of the prime [manuscript] should have been completed many years ago! … The proofs actually arrived at the beginning of this June, when I was in full tide of composition for the *Silmarillion*, and had lost the threads of the M[iddle] E[nglish] work.

The work, in Tolkien's eyes, still required a "supplementary introduction," which diminished into a preface, and then, corrected proofs. It was finally delivered in 23 January 1962 and published later in the same year.[31]

In his preface to Salu's translation, written in 29 June 1955, Tolkien describes it as the *Ancrene Wisse*, or the "Guide of Anchoresses" (one of the oldest copies of the work, but not the original). It is the equivalent of the Rule of St. Benedict for nuns and more than nuns, anchoresses, who enclosed themselves in small rooms or houses often adjacent to churches. Salu explains in her translator's note that the title *Ancrene Riwle* refers to the genitive plural, a correction of Sir Thomas Morton's title in the singular, *Ancren Riwle*, in his 1853 edition of the Cotton Nero British Library MS A.14. Tolkien's preface helps to explain the difference in the two titles, *Ancrene Wisse* (*Anchoresses' Guide*) being the author's title in Corpus Christi College Cambridge 402 (likely written around 1230, but after 1225, according to Salu).[32] Tolkien notes that its "language now appears archaic, almost 'semi-saxon' as the term once was, after nearly seven and a half centuries; and it is also 'dialectical' to us whose language is based mainly on the speech of the other side of England, whereas the soil in which it grew was that of the West Midlands and the Marches of Wales. But it was in its day and to its users a natural, easy, and cultivated speech. Familiar with the courtesy of letters, able to combine colloquial liveliness with a reverence for the already long tradition of English writing."[33] According to d'Ardenne, who published her thesis as *An Edition of Þe Liflade ant te Passiun of Seinte Iuliene* in Liège in 1936, the *Riwle* author wrote in the tradition of religious writing associated with Ælfric: rhythmic alliterative prose that also appears in women's saints lives (St. Juliana, St. Margaret, St. Katharine), *Sawles Warde* (homilies, actually a translation freely done of Hugh of St. Victor's *De anima*), and *Hali Meiðhad* (Holy Virginity), contained in the same manuscript, Bodley 34.[34]

Tolkien, himself, in his prior 1929 article, "*Ancrene Wisse* and *Hali Meidhad*," had similarly described the prose of *Ancrene Wisse* as characteristic of that Middle English writing found in women's saints lives and other religious works, which suggests that his students well understood what their professor had taught them in his lectures.[35] That together they three were advancing an argument for a medieval women's literary and religious tradition obviously occurred to the two women professors. Tolkien, however, was interested in these works for a slightly different reason, both philological and literary. True, its eight parts emphasize, first, many kinds of prayers, vocal, such as the Office of Our Lady, the Office of the Dead, psalms, Litany, Hours of the Holy Ghost, Paternosters, and so forth. In addition, this first part is followed by seven other parts, stressing regulation of the senses, feelings, temptations, confession, penance, love, and external rules. But throughout it manifests a hybrid form of dialect like those other works cited above, at a time when Old English had not fully emerged as Middle English—which delighted Tolkien.

According to Tolkien, the thirteenth century in the west of England offered an "alive" English, one "more traditional and organized as a written form, than anywhere else," because it was not yet "West Midlands."[36] What he means by this cryptic statement is that the English of the *Ancrene Wisse* in the Corpus Christi MS is "older," "less queer" (his words) than that of the *Ormulum*, and that it has "preserved something of its earlier cultivation."[37] So it is not yet conscious of its inferior status as a dialect from the humble west, as if the language had taken on an anthropomorphized character as a rustic: "It is not a language long relegated to the 'uplands' struggling once more for expression in apologetic emulation of its betters or out of compassion for the lewd, but rather one that has never fallen back into 'lewdness', and has contrived in troublous times to maintain the air of a gentleman, if a country gentleman."[38] Thus what we have is an "accidental" form of language in a single text that cannot be explained by geography.

Because of the "relative isolation and more or less definite natural boundaries" at the time it was written, the "A" MS of *Ancrene Wisse* (or CCCC 402) is "at once self-consistent and markedly individual," meaning, descended from an Old English form that had not been trammeled by mixing because the scribe spoke the same language as that of Bodley 34 (the "B" MS, or the legends of the so-called Katherine Group, for which Tolkien prefers the name *Hali Meiðhad* group).[39] Given that the A and B manuscripts are so similar in language, Tolkien believes that they derive from one ancestor, AB, linked with Dorset, Lichfield, even the "Northern border of the (East) Midlands," but not separated. Likely this copying would have taken place at a center where the "native tradition was not wholly confused or broken" and "native language was not unfamiliar with the pen."[40] Tolkien surmises it was Herefordshire, with its school of philology and study of "genuine Norse," because of its links with both A and B, but also because of its "'relative isolation,' which endures to this day, between Wye and Severn." "[I]ndividual linguistic development" could progress there "undisturbed" (yet bear some relation to the English of La3amon). He praises these "scholarly Westerners" as "the most efficient dialect translators in M.E.," because they "transform alien Norse words from their natural eastern shape into precisely the form they should have had if they were ancestral in the West."[41]

Tolkien's high regard for the originality of a dialect that seems to provide the missing link between West Saxon Old English and West Midlands Middle English is matched by the *Ancrene Wisse*'s personalization of its religious text and its human comedy, not unlike Tolkien's own, whether in his fiction or his scholarship. Its "intimate style," as Dom Gerard Sitwell terms it in his introduction to the translation, makes it seem modern, such as descriptions of the anchoresses and other sisters in other houses and of the types of the flatterer and backbiter later called "characters" in the seventeenth century. The *Ancrene Wisse* observes that "It is said of anchoresses that almost every one of them has some old woman to feed her ears, a gossip who purveys to her all the talk of the countryside, a magpie as it were, that chatters to her about all she has seen and heard, so that there is now a saying: 'From mill and from market, from smithy and from anchor-house one hears the news.' Christ knows, this is a grievous saying; that an anchor-house, which ought to be the most solitary place of all, should be spoken of together with those three places in which there is most gossip."[42] Sitwell also notes the ability of the author to create a scene by means of specific detail, like any fiction writer: "He will illustrate his remarks by references to contemporary customs and incidents of daily life, the knight's shield hung in the church, the impertinence of Slurry, the cook's boy, washing dishes in the kitchen, the dogs sneaking round the table of the medieval hall."[43] Finally, his humor: about an anchoress eating with guests outside her dwelling, in "External Rules," part eight, Sitwell warns "this is carrying friendship too far, for it is very much against the nature of any order, most of all against the 'Order' of an anchoress, who is completely dead as far as concerns the world. One has often heard of the dead speaking with the living but I have never found that they ate with the living."[44]

After spending some thirty-seven years working on the *Ancrene Wisse*—in terms of his lectures to students, the edition, the articles, the tasks of transcription and translation he gave to his students and his mentoring of them, the oversight of Ker's introduction, and the complex proofs, Tolkien surely identified with this Herefordshire author. Hereford lies on the River Wye in the Cotswolds, close to Gloucestershire, the Malvern Hills, and Birmingham—the West Midlands from which Tolkien himself originated. No less important to him was this text also devoted to women and, in this respect, not unlike *Beowulf* and the *Völsunga Saga*, both of which involve women.

From the Females in *Beowulf* to Brynhild and Gudrún

That Tolkien perceived *Beowulf* as a fairy-story, which I argued in chapter 4, is clear also from the way he fashions the unhappy history of its scholarly treatment in the opening pages of "Beowulf: The Monsters and the Critics": as a dark fairy-story.[45] He imagines the poem as a child christened as Poesis, or "Poeseos Anglo-Saxonicae egregium exemplum," by the first cataloger of Anglo-Saxon manuscripts to mention it, [Humphrey] Wanley (1672–1726), in the role of the priest who christens it in his catalog of Anglo-Saxon manuscripts, the *Thesaurus*, edited by George Hickes and published in 1705 in Oxford.[46] Its fairy godmother in charge of its guidance is Historia, aided by her ladies Philologia, Mythologia, Archaeologia, and Laographia. Unfortunately, the poem itself is in its rearing forgotten as a poem. This omission makes Tolkien indignant, especially because scholars have regarded it as valuable as a source for history, pagan, primitive, allegorical, or epical, and as an heroic lay, or manual—as anything but what it is, a poem (as is clear from its name).

Tolkien then creates another story after the first, simpler, more important, about repurposing old and broken materials from something once grander: a man inherits a field in which old stone from a hall lays broken, although he has reused some stone in building a house for him to live. When friends ignore the stones to look for useful material goods such as coal, engravings, building materials, and so forth, they disparage him for rebuilding an old tower. "But from the top of the tower the man had been able to look out upon the sea," Tolkien notes.[47] This tale about perspective Tolkien seeks to prove as truthful, for he has little respect for the scholars and others who so misunderstand the poem qua poem and ignore the importance of its words in its interpretation.

What's interesting about these two stories (fairy-story and exemplum) in this article is that the various branches of knowledge in the first are personified as female. Traditionally, the medieval cleric gendered personifications of abstractions, particularly in Latin, as female and the various mythological deities seemed to morph into them in time. But the tension between male and female here—the poem (Poesis) as lone and abject male hero, and later, isolated, even estranged, male poet and tower-builder (or perhaps the latter is the reader of the poem)—and the tools used by the scholar (history, philology, mythology, archaeology, and folklore), as female and critical or threatening, anticipate the later battle that lone hero Beowulf will have with the three monsters—most particularly, the female, Grendel's Mother, when the hero finds himself lacking a sword.

Although one might also interpret the two opening narratives as reflective of the sexes in another way, more theoretically but still gendered, as Clare A. Lees reminds us in her article on "Men in *Beowulf*":

> Only in relation to the first allegory can the second be interpreted as symbolically masculine. Tolkien works through the feminine—the older school of philology—in order to erect his own interpretation. That interpretation, which is allied with the poet's own vision by the figure of the tower (the poem, the masculine, the Phallus), looks out upon the sea (the Other, the feminine, the past). Historical criticism, in Tolkien's eyes, fails at least in part for reasons associated with gender: both the "feminine" and "masculine" allegory have the potential to destroy, or rather deconstruct, the poem. At the same time, and in both allegories, Tolkien casts the poem's "true" defenders as male (Wanley, the poet, and the critic). The second allegory offers Tolkien a means of reconstructing the poem's aesthetics, replacing philological criticism with the New Critical universality of the transcendental gaze. The masculinism of this second allegory, in other words, offers a beginning for literary criticism.[48]

Interestingly, in her interpretation, Lees herself almost completely elides the female.

Yet still another interpretation might construe both narratives more personally and autobiographically as about Poesis, the name of the newborn and the Latin word for poetic art, in reference to the neglected and mistreated poem *Beowulf*, with whom Tolkien strongly identifies because he sees it as an elegiac epic about the inevitability of death—life continuing only "until the dragon comes," the last line of his article reminds us. As an abject child and poem, in other words. When Tolkien entered Exeter as a first-year student, he intended to study Latin and Greek, but then switched to the modern languages, Old Norse, Gothic, Old and Middle English, perceived at the time as inferior and ignoble in comparison with the classical. And he wished to study literature—poetry—and to write it. So, like *Beowulf*, a great poem qua poem previously neglected by readers interested only in how it might be excavated for history, anthropology, mythology, philology, and so forth, Tolkien felt unsupported and alone in his desire to create a monumental work that might offer insight and illumination by utilizing old materials from the past: neglected medieval literature he loved and came to teach and transform into a mythology of his own. His desire to use New Criticism to interpret *Beowulf* in this very article would indeed treat the poem as a poem and thereby render him as a defender of it and, at the same time, bolster his own more creative medievalistic mission.

In *Beowulf* other women characters do appear—Wealhtheow, Danish Hrothgar's queen and cup-passer, and Hygd, Geat Hygelac's queen. Others are referred to in allusions and digressions, such as Freawaru, Ingeld's queen, whose marriage as a peaceweaver will unfortunately provoke old enmities between enemy tribes. There is also the wailing woman at the end of *Beowulf*, who may be his mother, his wife, or just a woman grieving his loss. The Anglo-Saxon social roles these women occupy in the literature and their origins in Old Norse saga have been fully analyzed, long after Tolkien died.[49] But their roles do not fully embody Tolkien's realizations of women. Nor are they really at the center of the poem for Tolkien, not even Grendel's Mother, whose introduction occurs in medias res and in the very middle of the poem, but for Tolkien so subsumed under the larger humanoid figure of her monstrous son that he seems to ignore her.

Beowulf's dragon most attracts Tolkien in his article—not just the Encircler of the world, Miðgarðsormr, "the doom of the great gods and no matter for heroes," but the literal Dragon whom Beowulf battles unsuccessfully, modeled on Fáfnir, the dragon of the *Völsunga Saga*.[50] Both dragons appear in the poem, Tolkien reminds us in his famous essay, one indirectly, within a minstrel's eulogy for Beowulf, and one as a monster battled by our hero, the latter compared to the "dragon-slaying Wælsing" who stars in the *Völsunga Saga*.[51] The difference between the northern hero Sigurd and the Anglo-Saxon hero Beowulf is that the latter does not actually kill the Dragon without help from Wiglaf. Sigurd's slaying of Fáfnir, Tolkien notes, is the reason it is recognized as the greatest act of the "greatest of heroes—*he wæs wreccena widest maerost*" (he was most famous of wretches, or exiles) (*Beowulf*, lines 898–99).[52] That Sigurd was a *wrecca*, like Beowulf and his father, and succeeded where the ignominious son of *wrecca* Ecþeow could not, creates circles of abjection. Tolkien himself, as an orphan, and abject, clearly identifies most especially with Beowulf the failure: "*He is a man, and that for him and many is sufficient tragedy.*"[53] What he means by this is rephrased a few pages later: "Its author is still concerned primarily with *man on earth*, rehandling in a new perspective an ancient theme: that man, each man and all men, and all their works, shall die."[54] It is not just an Anglo-Saxon theme, but also a Christian one. But the Dragon does not care about souls.

For Tolkien in his article, there are basically just two monsters, Grendel and the Dragon. He declares that the two adversaries create "an opposition between two halves of roughly equivalent weight, and significant content," not unlike the balance of the two half-lines in any single line of Anglo-Saxon verse.[55] Those two halves provide an opposition of ends and beginnings.

> In its simplest terms it is a contrasted description of two moments in a great life, rising and setting; an elaboration of the ancient and intensely moving contrast between youth and age, first achievement and final death. It is divided in consequence into two opposed portions, different in matter, manner, and length: A from 1 to 2199 (including an exordium of 52 lines); B from 2200 to 3182 (the end).[56]

For Tolkien's purposes Grendel's Mother and Grendel share the same marred humankind, derived from Cain's progeny. This is important to Tolkien, for the balance between the two moments, two ages, and the two battles occurs at the point at which "new Scripture and old tradition touched and ignited."[57] Because Tolkien views Beowulf's battle with Grendel's Mother as overlapping that of her son, creating a first "half" that occupies two-thirds of the whole poem would appear to disrupt any real symmetry between the two parts. To allocate equal significance to the hero's battle with Grendel's Mother would likely mar Tolkien's argument concerning the careful symmetry of opposition between the first half, when old Hrothgar, king of the Danes, is saved from Grendel's assaults on Heorot by young Beowulf, and old Beowulf, king of the Geats, who dies despite the young Wiglaf's aid in the fight with the Dragon. It means, too, that "Man, alien in a hostile world, engaged in a struggle which he cannot win while the world lasts, is assured that his foes are the foes also of Dryhten, that his courage noble in itself is also the highest loyalty: so said thyle and clerk."[58] According to Tolkien, he observes about this "heroic-elegiac poem" that "in a sense all its first 3,136 lines are the prelude to a dirge: *him þa gegiredan Geata leode/ad ofer eorðan unwaclicne*, one of the most moving ever written," the Anglo-Saxon lines that reference the Geats' construction of a sturdy pyre for their dead king.[59]

Does Tolkien mention Grendel's Mother in any of the earlier variants for his published article? Hardly at all. There exist two drafts, A and B, held at the Bodleian, from which Tolkien crafted and expanded his "Beowulf" lecture. In the A manuscript he does relay Sir Archibald Strong's summary of the poem, which includes Grendel's Mother's vengeful attack and Beowulf's slaying of her.[60] In the B manuscript Tolkien initially retains Strong's quoted summary (but later omits it): "Grendel's Mother, seeking vengeance for the death of her son, renews the attacks. Beowulf tracks her to her lair, a cave at the bottom of a deep mere, and slays her." Yet Tolkien remains critical of Strong's summary, likening reading such a summary to estimating a great man by his skeleton.[61]

Key to Tolkien's interpretation of the two monsters in the article is their descent from the *wræcca* Cain, both exile and wretch, who killed his own kind, like Beowulf's father, Ecgþeow, and Grendel and Grendel's Mother. This is important to Tolkien, for the balance between the two moments, two ages, and the two battles occurs at the point at which "new Scripture and old tradition touched and ignited."[62]

Tolkien's "Beowulf" Teaching Translation

In Tolkien's own *Beowulf* translation, he also glosses the ancestry of Grendel from *Cáines cynne* (107*), the race of Cain, who slayed his brother, Abel (Genesis 4:1–16, the only biblical reference in the poem, which he acknowledges), for which Cain was cursed and punished by God.[63] The Tolkien translation describes Grendel as a "a fiend of hell," an "unhappy one," who "inhabited long while the troll-kind's home; for the Maker had proscribed him with the race of Cain. That bloodshed, for that Cain slew Abel, the Eternal Lord avenged: no joy had he of that violent deed, but God drove him for that crime far from mankind. Of him all evil broods were born, ogres and goblins and haunting shapes of hell, and the giants too, that long time warred with God" (lines 85–91). The *Beowulf* text merely specifies the other creatures "of the race of monsters" (*fīfelcynnes*, 194b*) as the more conventional "giants and elves and evil spirits,/likewise giants" ("eotenas ond ylfe ond orcneas,/swylce gīgantes") (112–13*), but Tolkien apparently did not wish to translate "ylfe" as elves, similarly cursed, beings over whom he may have felt proprietorial given his Silmarillion mythology.

Tolkien's translation does also include Grendel's Mother, whose introduction in lines 1042–49 (1255–63b*) reminds us that she lives in great misery: "Plain was it made and published abroad among men that an avenger to succeed their foe lived yet long while after that woeful strife—Grendel's mother, ogress, fierce destroyer in the form of woman. Misery was in her heart, she who must abide in the dreadful waters and the cold streams, since Cain with the sword became the slayer of his only brother, his kinsman by his father's blood."[64] In other words, the curse of Cain, "an outlaw branded with murder"—Tolkien adds "outlaw" here for "hē þāfāg gewāt/morþre gemearcod" ("he then departed guilty/marked by murder," 1263b–64a*) and also for Grendel—continues on through the figure of a woman who acts by necessity like a warrior in exacting revenge through death, her punishment. If misery is in her heart, it suggests her humanity in the pain of the loss of her (apparently) sole son during an exile outside of any other contact. And because she is of the race of Cain, so also is her son Grendel "doomed of old" and similarly "outlawed by hate as is the deadly wolf" (lines 1051–52, 1052–53; 1266–67*). Tolkien adds "as is the deadly wolf," as well as "outlaw" for him, the *heorowearh* (accursed foe, 1207a*, in Klaeber).

Of course the duty of Grendel's Mother is clear: Lone Survivor of her tribe, it is up to her, female or no, "grimhearted, ravenous...minded to go upon a journey full of woe to avenge the slaying of her son" (lines 1061–63).[65] The vengeful task of Grendel's Mother Tolkien describes in his translation in a way that accentuates her womanliness: she "crept" into the hall while the Ring-Danes sleep, but making "haste" as she goes, apparently intent on avoiding any opposition. One reason for this precaution here as in the original Anglo-Saxon is her lesser power and skill: "Less indeed was the terror, even by so much as is the might of women, the terror of a woman in battle compared with armed man" (lines 1065, 1067–69). No man has time to grab his helm or corselet because she is so hasty and intent on saving her life, female that she is. So, "Swift and close had she clutched one of those noble knights as she departed to the fen"—it just happens to be Hrothgar's dearest "knight," a term Tolkien uses to designate Æschere and others as warriors (1077–80).[66] And then she grabs her beloved son's severed arm as she flees. This would be a poor showing for any warrior interested in obtaining treasure, and hardly any true battle, to seize a man in sleep and "rent" him in his bed.

In the battle with Beowulf beneath the "surging sea," this "creature that with cruel lust, ravenous and grim, had a hundred seasons held the watery realm" (1247, 1249–50), puts her claws on him like a woman who does not know how to fight: "She clutched then at him, seized in her dire claws the warrior bold" (1252–53). She cannot pierce his ring-mail with her "cruel fingers" (1255) but nevertheless bears him off to her "abode," her "abysmal hall." Tolkien describes her as a "monstrous woman" and, as he has for Grendel, as "she-wolvish outlaw of the deep" (1268–69).[67] Although Beowulf hits her head so that his sword "sang out its lusting song of war" (1271–72), it fails the prince—the first time ever "its glory fell" (1277).[68] Finally he seizes her (of course) "by her locks" (1286), bowing her down, while she "clutched at him" (1289). She, at last "bestride the invader of her hall"—another odd image, either comic or, as I have previously argued, sexualized, intended "to avenge her son and only child" (1292, 1293–94).[69] But the ring-mail protects Beowulf, so that when he sees a monstrous old sword, he grabs it and cuts through the "bony joints" of her neck, then, in a kind of violent hate killing, "Through and through the sword pierced her body" (1311–12). Oddly, Tolkien offers no notes or lecture commentary for the passage in his translation about the battles with Grendel's Mother, which begin in Tolkien's lines 817–818 [1002–3*], after a description of the damage to Heorot wrought by Grendel as he tried to escape Beowulf and his doom, and ends at 1393 [1663*] with Beowulf describing to Hrothgar the mighty sword he saw on the wall that he used to slay Grendel's Mother.

Later, Hrothgar reads this very story about the monstrous race of Giants descended from Cain but destroyed by the flood (1416–19) in an inscription on the gold sword hilt made by "trolls of old," to use Tolkien's inventive phrase (1406–7; from *enta ærgeweorc*, 1679,* "ancient work of giants"), and brought back from the cave of Grendel's Mother by Beowulf.[70] Similarly, in reference to Wiglaf's *ealdsweord eotonisc* (2616*), "old sword made by giants," given to him when grown by his father Weohstan after taking it from Swedish Onela's nephew Eanmund, whom he had slain: a reminder that after Beowulf dies, the Swedes will renew their feud with the Waegmundings, Wiglaf's tribe. This treasure made by the progeny of Cain, from whom Grendel and his mother descend, symbolizes the long history of feud—kinslaying—initiated by Cain in murdering his brother.

Tolkien's Teaching Commentary: Grendel's Mother and Freawaru

In his commentary, Tolkien emphasizes the link between these descendants from the race of Cain and the Healfdanes. The inscription on the sword hilt of the story of the race of Cain as progenitor is analogous to the opening of *Beowulf*, with the descent of a "Beow" or "Beowulf I" from the Danish line initiated by their orphaned progenitor, Scyld Scefing, and also serves as a warning to the Danes against homicide and kin-murder. Tolkien reminds us that Healfdene ancestry is "blended with the heraldic military eponym Scyld, the corn hero *Sceaf*, and Beowulf I, certainly an alteration (or corruption) of Beow 'barley.'"[71]

For this reason, rather than including any additional interpretations of Grendel's Mother, Tolkien expatiates at length in his commentary about the danger posed to and by the love between Freawaru and Ingeld, in lines 1697–1739 [2020–69*],[72] an allusive passage that indirectly glosses the whole middle section of *Beowulf* involving Grendel's Mother. This passage, fifth of the episodes, concerns the Heathobards' long-held feud with the Healfdenes. Freawaru, Hrothgar's daughter, is affianced to Ingeld, son of Fróda of the Heathobards, to be married at Heorot.[73] However, in line 1715 [2041*], it is clear to Tolkien that this marriage will fail: when Freawaru departs with Ingeld for the hall, she brings Danes with her who wear treasure won from old battles with the Heathobards. After one old Heathobard warrior spots a Dane wearing such an heirloom, he "eggs a young man, until he kills one of the Danes who wears his father's trappings."[74] So the feud is rekindled because of the desire for treasure and revenge, a prevalent theme in Tolkien's works. Ingeld's problem is to choose between love of his wife and support for the feud's rekindling. According to Tolkien, Ingeld takes up the feud, attacks Hrothgar and the Danes, and Heorot is burned, but the Heathobards are defeated and Ingeld dies.[75]

This unfortunate allusion to Ingeld leads Tolkien to think about Alcuin (ca. 797) and his rhetorical question to Speratus, Bishop of Lindisfarne, "What has Ingeld to do with Christ? Quid Hinieldus cum Christo?" Of special interest to Tolkien is the Heathobard link with peace through the name of Ingeld's father, "Fróda," from the Norse Fródi, *frið* (peace)—a name highly suggestive of Froco the Hobbit, who is himself largely committed to peace. There may be an older historical "Fróda," one whom Tolkien calls mythical, "of the Great Peace."[76] Freawaru, of course, is named after "Frey," the lord. What Tolkien sees, ultimately, is a love story that exists both in Norse and in English:

> In Norse the love of Ingeld becomes, in the fierce and brutalized Viking atmosphere, degraded, a sign of softness and wantonness; no man should ever have given way to it and been forgetful of the duty of murder. Not so in English. The love is a good motive, and the strife between it and the call of revenge for a slain father is held to be a genuine tragic conflict—otherwise Ingeld's story would not be heroic at all, and certainly not one that any minstrel would have sold for a single dragon (let alone a Shylockian wilderness). But the love referred to is passionate love, not the mere reverence for queen and consort and the mother of the royal children. The general suggestion of the tale in (Norse and English) is that the tragedy occurred soon after the marriage.[77]

So, given the political nature of marriages in uniting feuding tribes, how does love enter?

Tolkien the romantic suggests perhaps the prince came in disguise to the enemy's "stronghold" or perhaps on an embassy and "the beautiful princess captivated Ingeld's heart, as *eorlum on ende ealuwǣge bær*" (she bore the ale cup to the nobles) (2021*[1698–99]).[78] Ironically, the ale cup was passed by the peace-pledge, the *friðusibb* (used of Wealhtheow in 2017*), as a means of weaving peace among the men of the tribe, the word *freoðuwebbe* ("peaceweaver," used in 1942* antithetically and ironically of Mōdþrýðo), referring to the Anglo-Saxon woman's other major social role. Tolkien adds that both the lovers' names, *Fréawaru* and *Ingeld*, have a "Frey-element," *Frea* and *Ing*; further, the god Frey fell in love with Gerðr, also a daughter of his enemy, Gymir the giant.

There are allusions to Freawaru and Ingeld and their unhappy end in Heorot in each of the two *Beowulf* lays Tolkien composed, "Beowulf and Grendel I," and "Beowulf and the Monsters," primarily because of Beowulf's desire for trophies.

Tolkien's Lays, "Beowulf and Grendel I" and "Beowulf and the Monsters"

Tolkien once more connects the monsters with curses against the hero that will result in death and the end of community, specifically, the burning of Heorot by the Heathobards. Each monster, whether son or mother, threatens Beowulf with an unexplained curse should the monster's severed head be used as a mounted trophy on the walls of Heorot. In the first lay, Beowulf will be doomed to a "hard and stony" death-bed; in addition, Grendel promises "a red fate fall on Heorot" (presumably, burning), which curse Beowulf ignores, hanging Grendel's head (but not his arm) in Heorot.[79] True, Grendel has always hated the sound of the music emanating from Heorot—signifying both the joy of community shared by the comitatus, or *duguth*—in contrast to the misery and isolation of the recreant, the *wrœcca*, the exile and demon, descended as he is from Cain as a murderer. But the end of the first lay shows the "demon's head" hanging in the hall as hall-songs ring out, until "flames leapt forth and red swords rang,/and hushed were the harps of Heorot."[80] These lines are obviously connected to the ruinous attack by the Heathobards on the Danes predicted in Tolkien's discussion of the young lovers Freawaru and Ingeld. Also Tolkien imagines a hoary-headed Beowulf on that "hard and stony bed" burned by dragon venom and bleeding as he ironically, too late, recalls "the light of Heorot."

In the second lay, "Beowulf and the Monsters," Grendel is envisioned as coming to Heorot and hearing laughter and song, interrupted by his carnage; in this lay Beowulf rips off Grendel's arm and claw as a trophy for Heorot. Grendel's Mother is a "fiend" whose mission, as an angry mother, is "to avenge the death her son did die/and his blood there spilled by Beowulf."[81] This "mother of trolls" is once more minimized as a warrior: "shrieking," this female monster "fled" the hall of Heorot. A strange line describes her: "she fled, but none could keep her *tryst*/ since her son found death in Heorot" (my emphasis). The use of the word "tryst"—often for a rendezvous—suggests a love interest. Is this meant to be ironic? Or a reminder that she has no one of her own kind to love, neither husband nor son? The *OED* lists six related denotations for tryst, "generalized from 'an appointed station in hunting,'" but always an appointment, agreement, covenant, at a specific time and place, or at a time, or a gathering to buy or sell.[82] Obviously no warrior would wish to meet her at any time or place, given her own vengeful homicide. Only Beowulf—a mock-lover in his battle with her in the original poem, as I have argued elsewhere previously, given the suggestive symbolism and diction—journeys to where "the demons dark did dwell."[83]

Beowulf's battle with her atop the skulls of men that the monsters have killed and eaten is similar to that in Tolkien's *Beowulf* translation except that here she begs him, "O! Ecgtheow's son" (and note the rhetorical appeal of this mother to Beowulf as a son) not to cut off her head, or, she threatens, "hard and stony be thy death's bed/and a red fate fall on Denmark!"[84] But Beowulf the Geat claims his fate and takes her head back to Heorot anyway. As in the first lay, Beowulf drinks in the hall and gazes at her head while "the light in the eyes of the demon shone."[85] And the last stanza of the second is identical to that in the first lay: the "demon's head" hangs while minstrels sing, "till flames leapt forth and red swords rang" so the music in Heorot ends, in an allusion to the tale of Freawaru and Ingeld. And Beowulf dies the same kind of hard death, while the Dragon's "venom burned him, and he bled,"[86] as was threatened by the curse of Grendel's Mother.

Grendel's Mother and Freawaru both seem to be caught as in a web, the result of an inescapable fate caused by the greed and desire for vengeance on or by the men with whom they are tied, whether by birth, marriage, or ancestry. Their fates are not so different from those of Brynhild and Gudrún, whose stories Tolkien composes in the *Legends of Sigurd and Gudrún*.

Brynhild and Gudrún

The Valkyrie Brynhild, the bride chosen for the orphan Sigurd by Óðin, and the Burgundian Gudrún, daughter of King Gjúki, who falls in love with Sigurd, appear in Tolkien's adaptations of the *Völsunga Saga* beginning in sections 6 (Brynhild) and 7 (Gudrún) of *The Legend of Sigurd*. However, Brynhild kills herself after Sigurd is murdered and only Gudrún continues on in her own sequel, *The Legend of Gudrún*. That Tolkien prefers Gudrún to Brynhild may surprise most readers. As he notes in his introduction to lectures he gave at Oxford on the Eddaic poem, the "Old Lay of Gudrún," or *Guðrúnarkviða en nýja*, "curiously enough" he found

Gudrún, "who is usually slighted, and considered as of secondary interest," of greater interest, perhaps because of her absolute loyalty to the man she loves and her desire for vengeance against those who have harmed him and her. Christopher notes, "By implication, [my father] contrasted the long agony of Gudrún with the irruption of Brynhild, who soon departs, 'and her passion and death remain only in the back ground of the tale, a brief and terrible storm beginning in fire and ending in it.'"[87] According to Tolkien,

> Gudrún is a simple maiden, incapable of any great plans for profit or vengeance. She falls in love with Sigurd, and for herself she has no further motive. A sensitive but weak character, she is capable of disastrous speech or action under provocation. The occasions of this that are described are her fatal retort to the taunting of Brynhild, which more than anything is the immediate cause of Sigurd's murder, and in the sequel, the Slaying of the Niflungs, her terrible deeds at the end when driven to madness and despair.[88]

This explanation alone hardly seems adequate to convince anyone of Gudrún's superiority.

Brynhild is by far the more notable woman and warrior, as a Valkyrie handpicked by Óðin to bring Sigurd to Valhöll as his companion in the Last Battle: the leader who will slay the Serpent with his own hand. Sigurd initially hears from the prophetic raven (in the section on Regin in *The Legend of Sigurd, Regin,* 5.52) about this sleeping "sun-maiden" in the hall on the mountain Hindarfell in the realm by the Rhine governed by the Gjúkings, or Burgundians, Gunnar and Högni.[89] In the Brynhild section, Sigurd spots what he thinks is a sleeping knight surrounded by a "fence of lightning," over whom his horse Grani leaps; it is Brynhild, who awakens, noting that Óðin has indicated it is time for her to marry "the World's chosen"—Sigurd, son of Sigmund (*Brynhild*, 6.3-4, 7-10). At that moment they plight their unyielding troth by drinking together from a cup. Unfortunately, Brynhild believes she can only marry a king, so she urges Sigurd "thy lordship win" (6.22) and returns to her land while Sigurd travels on to Gjúki's house.

Equally unfortunately, when Sigurd later arrives in Niflung land, Gudrún's mother, Grímhild, awaits, "guileful in counsel,/ grimhearted queen/grey with wisdom,/ with lore of leechcraft,/ lore of poison,/with chill enchantment/and with changing spells" (*Gudrún*, 7.9). Sigurd sings in the Burgundian court of his adventures defeating the dragon Fáfnir, winning the gold hoard, and then awakening Brynhild, a point at which he abruptly ends his song (7.18). After he joins Gunnar and Högni in defeating many foes, Sigurd returns to his own country, is anointed king by a mysterious one-eyed man with flowing beard (Óðin) and told to marry his bride. Sigurd recalls Brynhild saying she will wed a king, which he has now become; however, Grímhild dreams of marrying her daughter to this lord, which she achieves by offering Sigurd a potion that compels him to fall in love with the first woman he sees—that is, Gudrún (7.37–39). Gudrún requires no magic potion: having dreamt she catches a golden hart with towering horns (7.2), from his first appearance riding alone on his horse Grani she has gazed on him in wonder (7.7). And so they marry, which interferes both with Brynhild's plan and, behind her, Óðin's.

Meantime, Grímhild urges her weak-willed son Gunnar to woo and marry the queen Brynhild, accompanied by Sigurd. As they approach the flames surrounding the wall enclosing Brynhild, Gunnar convinces Sigurd to exchange horses with him because his horse Goti no longer will bear him. Sigurd, having accepted his mother-in-law's counsel, rides on Grani in the shape of Gunnar and introduces himself to Brynhild as Gunnar, offering her a great brideprice (*Brynhild Betrayed*, 8.28–29). After sleeping together with his sword Gram lying between them, in the morning Sigurd places Andvari's magic ring on her hand as token of their bond (8.33). When they return to the Rhine, Brynhild sees an unsmiling Sigurd seated next to Gudrún and turns cold, remembering the oath they swore (*Strife*, 9.3–4). While Sigurd hunts the hart, the two women down at the river vie with one another over who is more queenly: Gudrún, with the better king, who slew Fáfner; or Brynhild, with Andvari's ring given her allegedly by "Gunnar" (9.10). Brynhild accuses Gunnar of cowardice and secret treason, which has made her an oath-breaker (9.19). In her hatred for Gunnar and his brother and her grief over the loss of Sigurd, Brynhild reveals to Sigurd the truth of Gunnar's deception toward them both. In anguish Sigurd confronts Gudrún, who worries about Brynhild's sickness and baleful purpose toward them, and Gunnar offers gold to Brynhild as a remedium (9.36–38).

When Gunnar learns that Sigurd slept next to Brynhild that first night, he feels betrayed by his blood-brother, Sigurd, and tells his sister and brother of his shame and betrayal, and hers, too (9.42–46). Like Sigurd, Högni laments "Woe worth the words/by women spoken" (9.50), but Gunnar, wishing to slay Sigurd, turns to wolfish Gotthorm, plying him with promises of gold and lordship, enchanted wine and wolf-meat (9.52). Dying Sigurd, stabbed in his bed by Gotthorm, awakens Gudrún, "to her bliss drowning/in blood flowing" (9.61) and Sigurd, to acknowledging Brynhild as responsible for loving him best (9.63). Brynhild curses the Niflungs with ill-fortune for being "cruel forswearers./Oaths swore Sigurd,/all fulfilled them" (9.67), and then, garbing herself in her war gear, falls on her sword (9.72). Sigurd is, however, welcomed to Valhöllu as "seed of Óðin" who will stand deathless in the day of Doom (9.80). *The Legend of Sigurd* ends with the "woe of Gudrún" that will unfortunately last to the end of days (9.82).

In *The Legend of Gudrún*, she walks through the woods hating life, "witless wandering" (2).[90] Tolkien creates her so lovingly that it becomes clear why he finds her so interesting. True, her fate is dark: Atli the Hun, Budli's son, is trampling the Goths and despoiling the land and, having heard of the hoard of gold obtained by Sigurd and of the beauty of Gudrún, seems certain to appropriate both. (Interestingly, Tolkien places Atli in Mirkwood [6]). The strategy devised by their mother, Grímhild, is, of course, to wed Atli to their sister: "let us bind him in bonds/as brother wedded" (9). What distinguishes Gudrún in her grief is her artistry in weaving a tapestry to tell her story of love for Sigurd, surely attractive to Tolkien who himself grieved much of his early life and who cared so deeply about love that endures, projecting into his craft a similar artistry. She includes in it the initial origin of the ring, the hoard, and the birth of the seed of Völsung, Sigurd himself, all engineered by Óðin in his blue mantle and by flame-haired Loki (11–18). Her chief enemy is her mother, who wants for her a queen's power, "over all women else/on earth upraised" (20), whereas Gudrún dreams only of her golden days as a maid before Sigurd came (21). Threatened by her mother if she does not comply—Grímhild's eyes are "deep and dreadful/dire with purpose" (28)—and a lustful, greedy Hun king, Gudrún remains ominously cold and silent, hating her brothers for what they have done to her and Sigurd, even after she joins Atli as queen in Hunland (32).

When the two men are summoned to a feast by Atli's herald Vingi and, in encouragement, Högni receives "a ring only" from their sister," wolf's hair woven around it—wolves awaiting the end, he notes (44)—and Gunnar receives "runes of healing" on wood (45), they ignore all signs of peril. It is a ring of doom, Andvari's ring, as the runes are themselves "stained and darkened," as their mother recognizes, "writ with cunning" (48). Vingi jeers at them that at Gjúki's courts "no kings are left" if they are ruled by a woman who judges a lord's "weighty words" (50); then he tempts them with the possibility of taking over the throne because of Atli's age and decrepitude

(51–52). While Högni is reluctant to trust his mother's counsel (57), having been misdirected in the past, and with Vingi's "venom-tongued" oath to rest in hell if the runes lie, they arrive in Hunland to face the gallows and the beasts of battle—but first the brothers hang the liar, Vingi. In place of death to them, Atli demands ransom—Gudrún's gold won by Sigurd—but they refuse, for, as Atli accuses them, they are "feud-forgetful" and guilty of "friend-murder" (75).

Gudrún, "at heart weary," does not care about *weregild* but is torn by how the battle with this "troll-people" (82) rends her little-loved brothers (80) and she calls the Goths to arm (83). After Atli has captured both brothers to avenge the death of Sigurd for her (115), he tramples Gunnar at her feet as she calls the Hun lord evil and begs him not to kill them—she swears by her children with him, Erp and Eitill (116). The dilemma she faces, whether to side with a foreign husband she was forced to marry, but hates, or to support loathed brethren who have undermined all she loves, is like that experienced by Danish Freawaru. Married to Heathobard Ingeld—whom Tolkien imagines she loves—she suffers for her people when he is spurred into battle with them by the necessity of feud and mourns, we assume, when he is killed. At least for Gudrún there exists the possibility of avoiding further death and destruction through wergild—at least, the half that belongs to Gunnar (118–19)—if she is willing to grant Gunnar the torn-out heart of Högni. This treacherous act eventually occurs but only after the heart of a thrall is offered instead and then Högni himself freely agrees to give it up. Gunnar, however, reveals to Atli that they have thrown all their gold into the Rhine. The "gold-tormented" Atli hurls him, naked, into a snake-pit, while his sister, consumed by darkness, hatred, and wrath, waits. Gunnar, stung by a huge adder—an appropriate symbol of the greed represented by the dragon Fáfnir, the brothers, venomous Vingi, and Atli—dies. At the funeral feast, Gudrún reveals to Atli that she has killed their children Erp and Eitill, mixed their hearts with honey in bowls made of their silver-bound skulls, and offered their bones to the dogs (147). After Atli collapses in a faint, Gudrún, dressed in dark clothes, later comes in to awaken him and stabs him. Despite his curse, she burns the house and all, sickens with hate, and again remains "witless wandering in the woods alone" until she casts herself into the sea (157–58). Her last words, mostly about her five sorrows, are to Sigurd, to whom she pledged her love as he did to her (164).

Tolkien's final stanza appeals to "lords and maidens" to "Lift up your hearts," despite this sad old tale and its instance of the loss of glory and gold (166). Its significance grows out of vow-breaking: of mother to daughter, brothers, to sister, lover to lover and husband to wife (although not intentional, in Sigurd's case), wife to husband, kin to kin, and nation to nation (155). In relation to the latter violation, it is important to recall that the Burgundians initially killed the brother of Budli, Atli's father, as reparation (*The Legend of Sigurd*, 7.15). Thus, underlying the whole saga of both Sigurd and Gudrún is a larger feud left entirely unresolved by marriage or any other means of reparation.

Like Grendel's Mother, Gudrún kills Attila's sons just as the former kills Hrothgar's favorite retainer, Æschere, in recompense for Beowulf's killing of her son. Gudrún also encourages her traitorous brothers, who lured Sigurd into marrying her and then killed him to be led into battle and certain death at the hands of the husband she was forced to marry. This Gúdrun is drawn from the Elder Edda, filled with the poison of bitterness over her loss, to represent a type of Old Norse Medea who will kill her own sons as revenge for her husband's adultery. Or like Ovid's Philomela who with her sister Procne feeds Procne's husband Tereus his own son Itys as a meal after Tereus has raped her and cut off her tongue (Gúdrun's tapestry resembles the one Philomela wove to reveal the truth about Tereus's crime). If Grendel's Mother is an "aglæcwíf," a monstrous or battle-woman (line 1259), so also is this dark bride, Gúdrun.

In the context of Gudrún's bitterness, most interesting is Tolkien's discussion of Beowulf's description of Unferth's excessive beer drinking, in *Beowulf*, line 531, by using a phrase that seems to mean the opposite, *beore druncen*, as in "he had drunk a little beer." This litotes (or understatement) Tolkien also uses ironically to describe Gudrún's unhappiness in "The Lay of Atli" (*Atlakviða*): "[I]t is said, as she greets her brothers riding to their doom in Attila's hall, "bjóri vas [hón] lítt drukkin," which literally means "small beer had she drunk." Tolkien understands this about Grendel's Mother more figuratively in the B draft of "Beowulf: The Monsters and the Critics" to mean that "none of the joy of the alien folk and hall in which she was perforce queen was hers."[91] Drinking beer in the hall, where so many important ceremonial occasions were held to celebrate a victory and the cup passed from warrior to warrior as a sign of community, fellowship, and safety, usually signified joy and peace. A similar use of litotes for terror occurs in *Beowulf*, line 769, when Grendel attacks Heorot and dispenses *ealuscerwen*, a bitter drink, to the Danish nobles inside.

Thus, to return to Tolkien's apparent ignoring of Grendel's Mother as central in "Beowulf: The Monsters and the Critics": only at first glance does this omission appear strange, given the fact that three monsters, not just the two male monsters, plague the hero in the Anglo-Saxon poem (as I have argued elsewhere in response to this essay), representing antitypes of the social roles of the retainer, the peaceweaver, and the gold-lord.[92] In addition, Tolkien's emphasis on the life of Beowulf (another abject hero favored by him) explains his interest in perceiving the epic as two-part—the first part, devoted to the young Beowulf who has to expiate the taint of his father's crime by heroism; the second part, devoted to the hero as an old king who misjudges his own prowess in the face of the threat posed to his tribe by the Dragon.

Nevertheless, on the basis of this apparent erasure of Grendel's Mother alone, Tolkien can hardly be considered a misogynist, even in *The Lord of the Rings*, which in the epic itself features very few women in major roles. Two major episodes pertain to this examination of women in *The Lord of the Rings*: one is the meeting of Merry and Pippin with Treebeard, where the Hobbits learn that the Entwives have disappeared, and why; the other, when the Hobbits arrive at Rohan and Eowyn the Shield-maiden is intentionally left behind by her uncle, Théoden, and the rest of the Fellowship. If this seems a very small number of women, it may not be Tolkien's misogyny that is responsible.

THE FLIGHT OF THE FEMALE IN *THE LORD OF THE RING*, BOOK 3

Tolkien himself objected to the idea that *The Lord of the Rings* has no women (or religion), because it was not true, as he notes in a letter to Houghton Mifflin on 30 June 1955 (letter 165, 220). Yet the apparent absence of women in Middle-earth—in particular, the third and fourth books as the split Fellowship journeys on, and the reasons for that absence—is central to understanding Tolkien's narrative. One pivotal episode involving gender and racial difference concerns the Ent Treebeard and his meeting with the Hobbits Merry and Pippin in *Two Towers*. Within the larger epic, it dramatizes in miniature the ways that prejudice and intolerance develop and how the rejection of alterity—when stereotyped as pejorative—can be halted. Indeed, stereotyping and the refusal to accommodate difference has dominated the epic from the beginning of volume 1. The Ents, the tree shepherds, introduce a species estranged both from other species (like the Hobbits) but equally and irremediably, perhaps, from their own gendered counterparts, the Entwives.

While the Ents, as the leaders of trees, have been taught to speak by the Elves (*LOTR* 3:4, 468) and are graced with movement—in fact, they cut off Saruman's escape from Isengard—the trees of the Old Forest are rooted and envious of those creatures that can move. In addition, the Ent Treebeard explains to the Hobbits Merry and Pippin a gender difference within the Ent species that has nearly led to their extinction—the Ents have lost the Entwives because they are so self-absorbed. The Ents differ radically from the Entwives: Ents enjoy travel and seeking out new trees, whereas Entwives like cultivating their gardens in one place (*LOTR* 3:4, 475–76). Whereas Ents love the trees, woods, and slopes, Entwives like lesser trees, meads, sloe, wild apples (fruit), and herbs. When the Hobbits meet him, Treebeard sings a song of dialogue between an Ent and an Entwife, but because of the Entwives' flight, he therefore has to play both their parts. Interestingly, the difference between them has been memorialized in this elegiac song: the Ent wants the Entwife to say his land is fair, but she wants a different kind of land; each wants the one to come to the other—but the Ent says he will come only in winter, which is fine with her, although the Ents do not come (*LOTR* 3:4, 477).

Yet, despite Treebeard's insensitivity, he is no tyrant. Treebeard at first proclaims his lack of interest in anyone else's perspective or cause, although his self-centeredness has not resulted in totalitarian domination over or manipulation of others: "I am not altogether on anybody's 'side,' because nobody is altogether on my 'side,' if you understand me: nobody cares for the woods as I care for them, not even Elves nowadays" (*LOTR* 3:4, 472). Treebeard's isolationism, however, has allowed the more aggressive Saruman to cut up the trees and leave them to rot. Treebeard confesses that "I have been idle. I have let things slip. It must stop!" (*LOTR* 3:4, 474). So preoccupied with his own point of view, Treebeard has to learn how to understand others—including younger members of his own species and even the insignificant Hobbits—in order to rectify the situation. From Treebeard's point of view, for example, because Ents move so slowly, being hasty, a trait of Hobbits, in his eyes, is considered bad (*LOTR* 3:4, 465). Further, Treebeard has forgotten that, unlike the Ents, the Halflings do not stand to sleep (his forgetfulness once more demonstrates an insensitivity to the other) (*LOTR* 3:4, 478). Treebeard thinks he is talking to Entings, not to Merry and Pippin, who are not baby Orcs but a species new to him (*LOTR* 3:4, 464).

The danger, then, of self-absorption is a lack of sensitivity to and respect for the differences of others that can develop into prejudice and intolerance. But Treebeard corrects his mistakes. Manifesting a new sensitivity to the Other, he introduces the Hobbits to a very appropriate Halfling companion, the Ent Bregalad, also known as Quickbeam for his hastiness, and therefore Treebeard is certain that they will "get along together." It is perhaps noteworthy that the un-Entlike Quickbeam might know of a tree that would please Entwives (although birds have torn off the fruit and the Orcs have cut the trees, which makes them silent and dead) (*LOTR* 3:4, 483).

Éowyn, sister-daughter (niece) of the king of Rohan, in "The King of the Golden Hall" epitomizes the female stereotype of caretaker for the children and the aged in the kingdom and also the object of desire for Gríma (*LOTR* 3:6, 520), known outside the kingdom as Wormtongue. She is perceived as "fair and cold" when Aragorn first sees her, assisting her uncle, King Théoden, at the meeting with Gandalf and the company, and, though "stern as steel" and the "daughter of kings," appears to Aragorn incomplete, or at least immature—"like a morning of pale spring that is not yet come to womanhood" (*LOTR* 3:6, 515). Éowyn's role will be fuller and more balanced in terms of her social and political expertise as shield-maiden, leader, and future ruler. Like the Old English queen Wealhtheow in *Beowulf*, wife of Danish king Hrothgar, and the new bride, Freawaru, daughter of Hrothgar, Éowyn in Tolkien's text passes the cup at a hall ceremony to knit up peace after feasting in a joyful gift-giving—specifically, the shining mail and round shields bestowed upon Aragorn and Legolas and the cap of iron and leather chosen by Gimli from the king's hoard. In Tolkien's text, "The king now rose, and at once Éowyn came forward bearing wine. '*Ferthu Théoden hál!*' she said. 'Receive now this cup and drink in happy hour. Health be with thee at thy going and coming!'" (*LOTR* 3:6, 522). The Rohirrim (modeled on Old English) means "Fare well [hale] Théoden!"[93] In the text she also passes the cup to Aragorn (but trembles as she does so, which reveals her infatuation).

Although in the text of *Two Towers* Théoden names Éomer, his sister-son, as his heir, at the suggestion of Háma, the hall-guardian (who has released Éomer from prison), it is to Éowyn that Théoden entrusts his people—no mean responsibility—when he and the Company depart for battle. Théoden is not thinking of Éowyn when he asks Háma for someone in whom "my people trust." For Théoden, Éomer is he whom he is unable to spare or leave behind, "the last of that House" (of Eorl). His more perceptive hall-guardian, Háma, corrects him: "I said not Éomer ... And he is not the last. There is Éowyn, daughter of Éomund, his sister. She is fearless and high-hearted. All love her. Let her be as lord to the Eorlingas, while we are gone" (3:6, 523). In Théoden's absence, *as lord*, she will lead the folk of the Golden Hall. Thus, in the text, as the splinter Fellowship departs, Éowyn stands dressed in mail and lays her hands upon the hilt of a sword. We will not see her again until the third volume, where she fully occupies the role of a shield-maiden, very much like a Valkyrie, except also as a savior of Middle-earth, or at least part of it, and not unlike the queer Hobbits Frodo and Gollum, "usually slighted."[94]

In *The Lord of the Rings* and *The Silmarillion*, culturally marginalized women such as Éowyn or Lúthien serve heroically and epically, reflective of the balanced cosmos imagined by Tolkien in the fantasies "Anulindalë" and the "Valaquenta" and the cosmos's empowerment by principles of rule gendered as both male and female. His letter of advice on marriage to his son Michael notwithstanding, Tolkien models his heroic women, as various scholars such as Leslie A. Donovan have observed, on both Anglo-Saxon and Old Norse models. In that letter and elsewhere Tolkien reveals an understanding of the limited gender roles demanded by different societies for women, modern and medieval, real and fantastic. He aptly anticipates and understands female difference as the result of a culture in which men play a dominant role biologically, socially, and philosophically, but in his fantasies—his "fairy-stories"—that difference offers another form of enforced abjection that his female heroes overcome.

The ultimate kind of love, for Tolkien, is divine and not human, although humankind retains a trace of the divine in its composition and regains some of that on this earth through love for another. In letter 44 to his son Michael on 18 March 1941 he writes,

> Out of the darkness of my life, so much frustrated, I put before you the one great thing to love on earth: the Blessed Sacrament... There you will find romance, glory, honour, fidelity, and the true way of all your loves on earth, and more than that: Death, by the divine paradox, that which ends life, and demands the surrender of all, and yet by the taste (or foretaste) of which alone can what you seek in your earthly relationships (love, faithfulness, joy) be maintained, or take on that complexion of reality, of eternal endurance, which every man's heart desires.(54)

But in all the cases of love between two very different types or person or people, it is invariably the female whom he depicts as more noble and often more heroic and generous.

Notes

1. Holly A. Crocker, *Chaucer's Visions of Manhood* (New York and Houndmills, Basingstoke, and Hampshire, UK: Palgrave, 2007), 3.
2. See the careful delineation of the different types of responses to Tolkien's women (or lack of them) in criticism of the past twenty-five years, with a close analysis of how Tolkien's women in *The Lord of the Rings* reflect aspects of the Old Norse mythological Valkyries, in Leslie A. Donovan, "The Valkyrie Reflex in J.R.R. Tolkien's *The Lord of the Rings*: Galadriel, Shelob, Éowyn, and Arwen," in *Tolkien the Medievalist*, ed. Chance, 106–32.
3. Laura Michel, "Politically Incorrect: Tolkien, Women, and Feminism," in *Tolkien and Modernity*, vol. 1, ed. Frank Weinreich and Thomas Honegger, 55–76 (Bochum and Jena, Germany: Walking Tree, 2006), 56.
4. Janet Brennan Croft and Leslie A. Donovan, "Introduction," in *Perilous and Fair: Women in the Works and Life of J.R.R. Tolkien* (Altadena, CA: Mythographic Press, 2015), 7. In this collection, seven articles have been reprinted from sources ranging from 1984 to 2007, along with a new article on "The History of Scholarship on Female Characters in J.R.R. Tolkien's Legendarium: A Feminist Bibliographic Essay," by Robin Anne Reid, 13–40.
5. J.R.R. Tolkien, "Notes to the Poems, by the Author," in *The Legend of Sigurd and Gudrún*, ed. Christopher Tolkien (London: HarperCollins, 2009), 55.
6. See John Garth's study of these male friendships and their role in Tolkien's life during his schooling at Exeter, in the war, and afterward, in *Tolkien at Exeter College: How an Oxford Undergraduate Created Middle-earth* (Oxford: Privately Printed by Exeter College, 2014), and in *Tolkien and the Great War: The Threshold of Middle-earth* (London: HarperCollins, 2003).
7. Garth, *Tolkien at Exeter College*, 8.
8. Garth, *Tolkien at Exeter College*, 25.
9. Garth, *Tolkien at Exeter College*, 4.
10. Garth, *Tolkien at Exeter College*, 12.
11. Garth, *Tolkien at Exeter College*, 13.
12. See the photo of the group in 1914, in Garth, *Tolkien at Exeter College*, 17, and playing rugby, 62–63.
13. Garth, *Tolkien at Exeter College*, 47.
14. There are many studies of the Inklings: see the foundational study by Humphrey Carpenter, *The Inklings: C.S. Lewis, J.R.R. Tolkien, Charles Williams, and Their Friends* (London: George Allen & Unwin, 1978). A very recent study by Philip and Carol Zaleski examines the religious and

spiritual affiliations and interests of the group in *The Fellowship: The Literary Lives of the Inklings, J.R.R. Tolkien, C.S. Lewis, Owen Barfield, and Charles Williams* (New York: Farrar, Straus and Giroux, 2015).
15. John Rateliff, "The Missing Women: J.R.R. Tolkien's Lifelong Support for Women's Higher Education," in *Perilous and Fair*, ed. Croft, 41–69.
16. Rateliff, "The Missing Women," 67.
17. S.T.R.O. d'Ardenne, "The Man and the Scholar," in *J.R.R. Tolkien: Scholar and Storyteller: Essays in Memoriam*, ed. Mary Salu and Robert T. Farrell, 33–34 (Ithaca and London: Cornell University Press, 1979).
18. Tom Shippey defends Tolkien from these charges of laziness in the film *Tolkien Remembered* (Princeton, NJ: Films for the Humanities and Sciences, 2005), DVD video (38 minutes), by suggesting in fact that he was writing reams of fantasy and mythology rather than his research, which of course he was also doing in addition to his teaching, administration, and attention to the myriad details involved in academia. But Tolkien was also editing many medieval texts and constructing glossaries for them as well as mentoring various students and helping to raise four children.
19. See Scull, *Reader's Guide*, 202–7.
20. d'Ardenne declares, in Tolkien and d'Ardenne's article, "MS. Bodley 34: A Re-Collation of a Collation," *Studia Neophilologica* 20 (1947–1948), 65–72 (in a passage quoted by Scull, *Reader's Guide*, 203), "This edition begun long ago was interrupted in 1938–1945, when we were otherwise engaged. It is now, however, nearly completed on the basis of a careful review of the manuscript itself, and will, we hope, shortly be in print." In her coedition of *Seinte Katerine*, with E.J. Dobson, EETS no. 7 (Oxford: University Press, 1981), Simonne also notes that the war in 1939–1945 halted progress on the jointly edited work (vii).
21. The references are to d'Ardenne and Tolkien, "'Iþþlen' in *Sawles Warde*," *English Studies* 28 (1947): 68–70; and "MS. Bodley 34: A Re-Collation of a Collation," 65–72. See the discussion of their collaboration in Scull, *Reader's Guide*, 202–4.
22. d'Ardenne wrote an article for Tolkien's festschrift: "A Neglected Manuscript of British History," in *English and Medieval Studies Presented to J.R.R. Tolkien on the Occasion of His Seventieth Birthday*, eds. Norman Davis and C.L. Wrenn, 84–93 (London: George Allen & Unwin, 1962). The "neglected manuscript" refers to MS Liège University Library 369 C, which boasted an illustration of Woden; Tolkien had donated the manuscript to Simonne's university, the University of Liège, in echo of his words in his *Losenger* article about the word *losenge*—that it was "the first gift, perhaps, of *perfidia anglosaxonico*" (84). See J.R.R. Tolkien, "Middle-English 'Losenger': Sketch of an Etymological and Semantic Enquiry,"

Essais de philologie moderne 129 (1951): 63–76. But see also d'Ardenne's note about his humanism in "The Man and the Scholar," 33.
23. For their identity, see *The Ampleforth Journal* (Spring 1931), 153, as noted by Dom Gerard Sitwell, "Introduction," in *Ancrene Riwle*, ed. Salu, ix.
24. See J.R.R. Tolkien, ed., *The Ancrene Riwle: the English Text of the Ancrene Wisse*, EETS 249 (London: Oxford University Press, 1962), xvii–viii, xxiv.
25. See Scull, *Reader's Guide*, 44.
26. John Bowers is working on an edition of the Clarendon Chaucer as it exists in the unfinished draft manuscript held by Oxford University Press.
27. Scull, *Reader's Guide*, 44–45.
28. Scull, *Reader's Guide*, 45.
29. *The Ancrene Riwle (The Corpus MS: Ancrene Wisse)*, translated into English by M[ary].B. Salu, with an introduction by Dom/Father Gerard Sitwell and a preface by J.R.R. Tolkien (London: Burns & Oates, 1955).
30. Scull, *Reader's Guide*, 46–47.
31. Scull, *Reader's Guide*, 47, 48.
32. Salu, *Ancrene Riwle*, xxiv.
33. Tolkien, "Preface," in *Ancrene Riwle*, ed. Salu, v.
34. S.T.R.O. d'Ardenne, Introduction to *An edition of Þe liflade ant te passiun of seinte Iuliene*, Bibliothèque de la Faculté de philosophie et lettres de l'Université de Liège, fasc. 61 (Liège: Faculté de philosophie et lettres; Paris: E. Droz, 1936), xlii–vii, cited in Salu, "Translator's Note," *Ancrene Riwle*, xxv.
35. J.R.R. Tolkien, "*Ancrene Wisse* and *Hali Meiðhad*," in *Essays and Studies by Members of the English Association* 14 (1929): 104–26, here, 107.
36. Tolkien, "*Ancrene Wisse* and *Hali Meiðhad*," 105.
37. Tolkien, "*Ancrene Wisse* and *Hali Meiðhad*," 106.
38. Tolkien, "*Ancrene Wisse* and *Hali Meiðhad*," 106.
39. Tolkien, "*Ancrene Wisse* and *Hali Meiðhad*," 106–7.
40. Tolkien, "*Ancrene Wisse* and *Hali Meiðhad*," 111–12. See also Arne Zettersten, "The AB Language Lives," in *The Lord of the Rings, 1954–2004, Scholarship in Honor of Richard E. Blackwelder*, ed. Wayne G. Hammond and Christina Scull, 13–24 (Milwaukee: Marquette University Press, 2006), 15–16, which includes a detailed list of the *Ancrene Wisse* manuscripts on 18–19.
41. Tolkien, "*Ancrene Wisse* and *Hali Meiðhad*," 114–15.
42. "The Custody of the Senses," in *Ancrene Riwle*, ed. Salu, 39.
43. Dom Gerard Sitwell, "Introduction," in *Ancrene Riwle*, ed. Salu, viii.
44. Salu, *Ancrene Riwle*, 183.
45. Tolkien, "Beowulf: The Monsters and the Critics," *Proceedings of the British Academy* 22 (1937): 245–295; repr. in *The Monsters and the Critics*

and *Other Essays*, ed. Christopher Tolkien, 5–48 (London: Allen & Unwin, 1983; Boston: Houghton Mifflin, 1984), 104.
46. J.R.R. Tolkien, *Beowulf and the Critics*, ed. Michael D.C. Drout, Medieval and Renaissance Texts and Studies, vol. 248 (Tempe, AZ: Arizona Center for Medieval and Renaissance Studies, 2002), 165–66.
47. Tolkien, "Beowulf: The Monsters and the Critics," 106.
48. Clare A. Lees, "Men and *Beowulf*," in *Medieval Masculinities: Regarding Men in the Middle Ages*, Medieval Cultures 7, ed. Clare A. Lees, 129–48 (Minnesota: University of Minnesota Press, 1994), 133; she discusses both narratives on 130–34.
49. See Jane Chance, *Woman as Hero in Old English Literature* (Syracuse, NY: Syracuse University Press, 1986; repr. Eugene, OR: Wipf and Stock, 2005); and Helen Damico, *Beowulf's Wealhtheow and the Valkyrie Tradition* (Madison: University of Wisconsin Press, 1984).
50. Tolkien, "Beowulf: The Monsters and the Critics," 109, and again, 113.
51. Tolkien, "Beowulf: The Monsters and the Critics," 109.
52. Tolkien, "Beowulf: The Monsters and the Critics," 113.
53. Tolkien, "Beowulf: The Monsters and the Critics," 115.
54. Tolkien, "Beowulf: The Monsters and the Critics," 119.
55. Tolkien, "Beowulf: The Monsters and the Critics," 30, 126.
56. Tolkien, "Beowulf: The Monsters and the Critics," 28.
57. Tolkien, "Beowulf: The Monsters and the Critics," 122.
58. Tolkien, "Beowulf: The Monsters and the Critics," 122–23.
59. Tolkien, "Beowulf: The Monsters and the Critics," 127–28, in reference to lines 3137–38 of *Beowulf*.
60. Tolkien, *Beowulf and the Critics*, 34; Andrew Strong, *Beowulf, translated into Modern English Rhyming Verse* (London: Constable, 1925).
61. Tolkien, *Beowulf and the Critics*, 83.
62. Tolkien, "Beowulf: The Monsters and the Critics," 122.
63. See the extended excursus on the sword hilt, its provenance in the "ancient work of giants," the relation between Christian and pagan, and then Hrothgar's sermon, in J.R.R. Tolkien, "Commentary," in *Beowulf: A Translation and Commentary, Together with Sellic Spell*, ed. Christopher Tolkien (Boston and New York: Houghton Mifflin Harcourt, 2014), 304–12; on Cain alone as progenitor of such races, see Tolkien, *Beowulf and the Critics*, 158n33.
64. Tolkien, *Beowulf: Translation and Commentary*, 49. Because Tolkien's line numbering in his translation differs from the original *Beowulf* (given his omissions), his line numbers will generally appear first within a parenthetical citation, followed by the equivalent lines in Klaeber's *Beowulf*, starred. See Fr[iedrich] Klaeber, ed. *Beowulf and the Fight at Finnsburg*, 3rd edn. (Boston: D.C. Heath, 1950).

65. Tolkien, *Beowulf: A Translation and Commentary*, 50.
66. Tolkien, *Beowulf: A Translation and Commentary*, 50.
67. Tolkien, *Beowulf: A Translation and Commentary*, 56.
68. Tolkien, *Beowulf: A Translation and Commentary*, 57.
69. Tolkien, *Beowulf: A Translation and Commentary*, 58.
70. Similarly, in reference to Wiglaf's *ealdsweord eotonisc* (2616*), "old sword made by giants," given to him when grown by his father Weohstan after taking it from Swedish Onela's nephew Eanmund, whom he had slain.
71. Tolkien, *Beowulf: A Translation and Commentary*, 332.
72. Tolkien, *Beowulf: A Translation and Commentary*, 324–43.
73. Tolkien, *Beowulf: A Translation and Commentary*, 326.
74. Tolkien, *Beowulf: A Translation and Commentary*, 327.
75. Tolkien, *Beowulf: A Translation and Commentary*, 327–28.
76. Tolkien, *Beowulf: A Translation and Commentary*, 330–31.
77. Tolkien, *Beowulf: A Translation and Commentary*, 337.
78. Tolkien, *Beowulf: A Translation and Commentary*, 338.
79. Tolkien, *Beowulf: A Translation and Commentary*, 418.
80. Tolkien, *Beowulf: A Translation and Commentary*, 419.
81. Tolkien, *Beowulf: A Translation and Commentary*, 421.
82. *The Compact Edition of the Oxford English Dictionary, Complete Text Reproduced Micrographically*, 2 vols. (Oxford: University Press, 1971), 2: 439b–40a.
83. Tolkien, *Beowulf: A Translation and Commentary*, 422.
84. Tolkien, *Beowulf: A Translation and Commentary*, 424.
85. Tolkien, *Beowulf: A Translation and Commentary*, 424.
86. Tolkien, *Beowulf: A Translation and Commentary*, 425.
87. Tolkien, "Notes on the Poems, by the Author," in *The Legend of Sigurd and Gudrún*, ed. Christopher Tolkien (London: HarperCollins, 2009), 55.
88. Tolkien, "Notes on the Poems, by the Author," in *The Legend of Sigurd and Gudrún*, 52.
89. Tolkien, *The Legend of Sigurd and Gudrún*, 118–19.
90. *The Legend of Gudrún*, 253–308, lacks sections, like *The Legend of Sigurd*; references are to stanzas, of which there are 166.
91. In the B manuscript, in Tolkien, *Beowulf*, 94–95. The full passage states: "Systir fann þeira/Snemst at [þeir] í sal kómu/Bræðer hennar báðir,/Bjori vas [hon] litt drukkin" [Their sister first saw them as the seats they neared,/ both her dear brothers—little beer had she drunk]. See Finnur Jónsson, *Atlakviða* (Copenhagen: Thieles Bogtrykkeri, 1912), 102; and Lee M. Hollander, ed. *The Poetic Edda* (Austin: University of Texas Press, 1962), 285–86. *Beowulf*, line 531, in reference to *beore drunken*, "having drunk beer," is discussed by Tolkien, in note 125 to "'Beowulf' and the Critics, A" in Tolkien, *Beowulf*, 189.

92. Jane Chance [Nitzsche], "The Structural Unity of *Beowulf*: The Problem of Grendel's Mother," *Texas Studies in Literature and Language* 22 (Fall 1980): 287–303. This article has been reprinted in six different venues.
93. See T. Northcote Toller, *An Anglo-Saxon Dictionary Based on the Manuscript Collections of the Late Joseph Bosworth, Supplement* (London: Oxford University Press, 1921, repr. 1966), *s.v.*
94. For the Valkyrie-influenced Éowyn in *The Lord of the Rings*—the only fully human female character in the epic, aside from Farmer Maggot's wife, Rosie Cotton, and Lobelia Sackville-Baggins, Galadriel being an Elf, Shelob, a giant spider, and Arwen, Halfelven—see Donovan, "The Valkyrie Reflex," 106–32, esp. 122–27.

CHAPTER 8

The Failure of Masculinity: *The Homecoming of Beorhtnoth* (1920), *Sir Gawain* (1925), and *The Lord of the Rings*, Books 3–6 (1943–1948)

"Yet this element of pride, in the form of the desire for honor and glory, in life and after death, tends to grow, to become a chief motive, driving a man beyond the bleak heroic necessity to excess—to chivalry."—Tolkien, "Ofermod," in *The Homecoming of Beorhtnoth, Beorhthelm's Son*

"The Other who dominates me in his transcendence is thus the stranger, the widow, and the orphan, to whom I am obligated."—Emmanuel Levinas, *Totality and Infinity*[1]

In the world that Tolkien creates in *The Lord of the Rings*, especially the second half, it has been stripped of women: that is its failure. Female Ents have abandoned the male Ents because of their self-centeredness, so there is no fertility, no blooming, and no Entlings. The men of Rohan have left behind their women—particularly Éowyn, the shield-maiden, and—as an all-male phalanx (so they think, not realizing she is masked as the warrior Dernhelm)—have moved forward for battle, thus underestimating the female. Her uncle-king, Théoden, is old and blind to his own limitations, much like Hrothgar at the beginning and then old Beowulf at the end of the Old English epic. Théoden cannot see that Wormtongue has the deceptive tongue of a serpent. Nor can he see how powerful his own warrior daughter might be, if allowed. In the world Denethor, Steward of Gondor, inhabits, one male-dominated and of postcolonial appetite, subordinates are made for subjugation, including his sons. After the Orthanc world of Saruman and as far away as the dark fires of Mordor, there exists nothing feminine except

Sauron's cat, Shelob, a caricature of the dehumanized female, a brooding breeder of young and ravenous monster to all.

This male-dominated world Tolkien paints is one in which masculinity is failing, a code for which, in medieval terms, is usually expressed through knighthood and chivalry, in romance, and (for Tolkien) in heroic epic. As Tison Pugh remarks in the introduction to his book *Queer Chivalry: Medievalism and the Myth of White Masculinity in Southern Literature*,

> the tropes of medieval romance define knightly masculinity, and the standard plots of these narratives feature the quest of a single knight seeking valiantly to win his lady's love … Medieval romances stress the ideals of courage, courtesy, loyalty, honor, etiquette, and mercy and, in so doing, glorify chivalric masculinity as a gendered panacea to a range of narrative obstacles and cultural traumas.[2]

However, Tolkien's Dark Riders offer queer parodies of knights so bent in will to obedience to an overlord in their pursuit of violence and death that they lack all personality and any subjective or personal singleness. The Orcs suggest an even more surreal type of masculinity run rampant, degenerating into sadism and brute overthrow of anything gentle.

Holly A. Crocker, in "Masculinity," implies masculinity has failed in *The Lord of the Rings* because, in postcolonial terms, it functions as the dominant register, so invisible a universal it exists without a binary (which would normally include femininity) and without bounds. She declares,

> By positing kind as a racializing geography that exceeds the human, Tolkien's trilogy calls attention to the status of masculinity as 'the apparatus of cultural difference,' as Homi K. Bhabha puts it (1995:58). In a final sense, then, to speak of masculinity in J.R.R. Tolkien's *The Lord of the Rings* is not ridiculous, since this trilogy reveals that masculinity's privileged invisibility is staked on the production of difference as a strategy of rule.[3]

Its very exaggeration in the course of the anti-epic, through the powerful characters who seem to dominate but fail—Sauron, Saruman, the Miller, Wormtongue, the Orcs, Denethor, and so forth—suggest this obstacle is one Tolkien's less masculine heroes can overcome because of their very lack or deficiency of masculinity—their own very invisibility, or smallness and unimportance within the dominion of power. As Tison Pugh notes about the Hobbits, as small dwarflike creatures who have hairy feet (but not hairy chests), they suggest feminized men. Bachelors Bilbo and Frodo both make tea and serve meals to (uninvited) male guests as would women and servants. Merry and Pippin, in particular, and sometimes Sam, in his role as spy and eavesdropper, often behave like children, especially at the beginning of the fairy-story.

Tolkien's approach is one that valorizes the least heroic characters in the epic-romance and by this means subverts convention through fantasy. This approach also deconstructs—unhinges—the medieval literary and heroic idealization of the epic-romance. Not only in *The Lord of the Rings*, but in addition, as I argue here, throughout his other fiction and his scholarly writing, Tolkien registers his abhorrence to prejudice, segregation of the other, and isolation of those who are different, whether by race, nationality, culture, class, age, or gender. Even in Tolkien's scholarship he is supremely conscious of precisely those individuals or groups or races who might be considered marginal within a system of exclusion, that is, who exist on the peripheries of society, often in exile, or as outcasts.

Masculinity and Medieval Errantry

The failure of might and masculine heroism in *The Lord of the Rings* logically connects with the similar failure acknowledged in the earlier discussion of Tolkien's *Beowulf* article. In this chapter, such failure is exposed more explicitly in two additional works: first, in his own early alliterative verse-drama, *The Homecoming of Beorhtnoth Beorhthelm's Son*, a continuation of the Old English chronicle entry for the year 991 that was expanded into the poem *The Battle of Maldon*, which Tolkien's former student and colleague E.V. Gordon edited in a student's edition in 1937.[4] Second, his interest had been piqued early on by the difficult Northwest Midlands Middle English dialect of the fourteenth-century alliterative romance *Sir Gawain and the Green Knight*, associated with a region of Britain not far from where he grew up in the West Midlands, about which he was always protective. This romance Tolkien coedited with E.V. Gordon in an edition first published in 1925, primarily by compiling its impressive glossary. He also lectured and wrote about it and translated it into modern English.

Tolkien's teaching lectures on the Old English fragmentary poem *The Battle of Maldon*, "Brunanburh," and poetry from the *Anglo-Saxon Chronicles* are mentioned in the *Oxford University Gazette*, as early as 1928.[5] In addition, *The Homecoming of Beorhtnoth* was initially written as a rhyming draft around ?1931–1933 (Trinity term), according to Scull's *Reader's Guide*, and "in existence" by 1945, states Humphrey Carpenter.[6] Tolkien had also written a short essay to follow it titled "Ofermod," which critiques both the lord Beorhthelm for his *ofermod*, or excessive pride, a flaw that results in the loss of the battle and his men. In the essay, Tolkien then links the much later

Sir Gawain to Beorhthelm for his equally despicable chivalry, similarly sparked by the knight's pride in his exploits. A closer examination of both figures, also including Tolkien's headnote on Beorhtnoth prefacing the drama, suggests a basis for what Tolkien will ascribe to the failure of masculinity.

The Battle of Maldon *and* The Homecoming of Beorhtnoth

In this Anglo-Saxon poem *The Battle of Maldon*, the Essex ealdorman Byrhtnoth, likely sixty-five years old, foolishly allows the invader Vikings (actually, the Norwegians) the opportunity to cross the Pante River (Blackwater) in southeastern England at low tide so as to allow them to fight the outnumbered English fairly and thereby loses the battle and his life. The account ends with the routing of the English and the death of Byrhtnoth (whose headless body is later recovered and buried at Ely Abbey). What is most moving in this poem is the homosocial loyalty of Byrhtnoth's old retainer Byrhtwold—close to the end of the chronicle entry—who promises never to yield even until death. Byrhtwold urges the remaining English force not to flee, despite the body of their lord lying hewed down in the dirt, with these passionate words: "Hige sceal þe heardra, heorte þe cenre,/mod sceal þe mare, þe ure mægen lytlað" (Temper must be the more resolute, courage the keener,/spirit must be the greater, the weaker our might).[7] Byrhtwold insists he means to die "by the man so dear" to him, "be swa leofan men" (line 319).

Tolkien borrows the old retainer's words in several of his works. In *The Homecoming of Beorhtnoth Beorhthelm's Son* he uses them ironically for young Torhthelm. Torhthelm imagines that he hears the soon-to-die retainers in the hall voicing their heroic ideals (actually, monks chanting in the abbey) as he aids the old cynical peasant Tídwald in retrieving what is left of the ravaged and headless body of Beorhtnoth to carry back to the monks of Ely: "Will shall be the sterner, heart the bolder, spirit the greater, as our strength lessens."[8] Tolkien also echoes these lines in the chapter "The Choices of Master Samwise" in *The Lord of the Rings*, after Sam has killed Shelob, when he realizes the Orcs have taken what he imagines is the dead body of his master, Frodo, at whose side he should still be. Overcome by near-exhaustion and the burden of the Ring he now bears, Sam forces himself to go back and enter the dark tunnel to follow the Orcs: "His weariness was growing but his will hardened all the more" (*LOTR* 4:10, 736).[9] There are other echoes from *The Battle of Maldon* in this same chapter, such as the identical situation of a servant having to step up in support of a dying or dead master at a time of impossible choices, when only willpower is left (in Sam's case, after his appeal in Elvish to Elbereth Gilthoniel and the witnessing of the light from the phial of Galadriel Frodo has been holding in his hand).

Tolkien's verse-drama sequel, preceded by a headnote titled "Beorhtnoth's Death" and followed by an essay titled "Ofermod," was published in 1953 in *Essays and Studies by Members of the English Association* and reprinted in *The Tolkien Reader* (1966). That is, it was written while Tolkien was in the process of publishing *The Lord of the Rings*. According to an unpublished Tolkien letter to Rayner Unwin, Tolkien himself recognized a connection between *The Homecoming of Beorhtnoth* and *The Lord of the Rings*. Christina Scull notes, "When in 1966 Ballantine Books ... proposed to publish a 'Tolkien Reader' with a selection of his shorter works, Tolkien recommended in particular the inclusion of *Beorhtnoth*, which, 'with the accompanying essay on 'Heroism' ["Ofermod"] ... is very germane to the general division of sympathy exhibited in *The Lord of the Rings*."[10]

The history of the composition and origins of *The Homecoming of Beorhtnoth* has been reconstructed by Scull and Hammond, via Christopher Tolkien, who notes that a portion of the verse-drama appears in the first known manuscript of his father's poem "Errantry," about a mariner's journey, the initial version of which was published in *Oxford Magazine* in 1933 and later in *The Adventures of Tom Bombadil and Other Verses From the Red Book* (1962).[11] In his preface to *The Adventures of Tom Bombadil*, Tolkien proclaims that Bilbo composed "Errantry," and that, in the 1940s, it became the song that Bilbo sang at Rivendell, "Eärendil was a mariner," in *The Lord of the Rings* (2.1).[12] Further, Tolkien describes the poem as originally a nonsense rhyme, but one applied "incongruously" by Bilbo, out of pride, after his return, to the High-elvish legends of Eärendil.[13] "Incongruously," because Eärendil in *The Lord of the Rings* is not only the mariner Earendel at the end of *The Silmarillion* but also the wanderer Éarendel in Tolkien's latest version of the poem "Éalá Éarendel Engla Beorhtast," in *The Book of Lost Tales, Part Two* (1984), as well as in the original, "The Voyage of Éarendel the Evening Star," also in *The Book of Lost Tales, Part Two*.[14] And in the Old English poem *Crist*, in the *Exeter Book*, Éarendel is the planet Venus described as a mariner crossing the sky in the evening "on an endless quest," in "Éala Éarendel engla beorhtast/ofer middangeard monnumn sended" ("Hail Earendel, brightest of angels, above earth [Middle-earth] sent to men"), referring to the morning or the evening star as a sign of hope (and, given its context, to the Resurrection of Christ)—the very origin of the Silmarillion mythology.

Tolkien's earliest version of the poem "Errantry" is dated before 1914, according to his letter to Mr. Rang in August 1967—likely 24 September 1914 when he stayed with the Brooks-Smith family—a version that he also read to the Exeter College Essay Club on 27 November 1914.[15] According to the *OED*, the word "errantry" derives from the Old French *errant*, originally two words, which became confused along the way: one meaning is travel or journey, another, to stray or wander. In relation to knights' errantry, the word refers to the knight's journey abroad for adventures and demonstration of prowess. So these multiple meanings for errantry and for the wanderers Earendel and Bilbo also suggest how so much of Tolkien's fictional work replays the "knights errantry" of those protagonists whom he envisions as heroic and who provide, if not redemption, then redemptive actions for the communities they inhabit.

Like them, Byrhtwold, the loyal but aged retainer of Byrhtnoth who sacrifices his life out of love for his lord in *The Battle of Maldon* (and whose words are repeated in *The Homecoming of Beorhtnoth*), provides a note of hope and inspiration in his own knight errantry. It is the subordinate warrior code that cements the bond between lord and warrior, no matter how flawed the lord. In *The Battle of Maldon*, the poet explains the reason for the loss of the battle (and with it, the disintegration of this comitatus): "ða se eorl ongan for his *ofermode*/alyfan landes to fela laþere ðeode," or, in Tolkien's translation of these lines in "Ofermod," "then the earl in his overmastering *pride*/actually yielded ground to the enemy,/as he should not have done."[16] Beorhtnoth gave the Danes an opportunity to fight on equal ground by crossing in low tide (cut off previously as they were by rising waters), but therefore lost the battle. The reason for Beorhtnoth's pride—according to Tolkien in his essay, "Ofermod"—lies in the lamentable advent of chivalry: "Yet this element of pride, in the form of the desire for honor and glory, in life and after death, tends to grow, to become a chief motive, driving a man beyond the bleak heroic necessity to excess—to chivalry." This occurs when a chief considers his men as a means to the end of self-glorification, hardly heroic. Not only does Beorhtnoth die in the *Battle of Maldon* as a result of his pride, but it is also left to retainer Beorhtwold and others like him to defend his lost lord in what has become a hopeless skirmish. Appropriately, Tolkien's critique of Beorhtnoth in *The Homecoming of Beorhtnoth* is rendered via the old farmer Tídwald's education of the foolish young minstrel-dreamer, Torhthelm: the wise old man denigrates Beorhtnoth's abuse of his aged warrior Beorhtwold (and his other men) in his claim that, "When the poor are robbed/and lose the land they loved and toiled on,/they must die and dung it. No dirge for them, and their wives and children work in serfdom."[17]

In this respect, the poem *Beowulf* recently has been treated as undermining the heroic way of life, a failure in the masculine code that depends upon homosocial bonds between retainer and lord and the earning and giving of treasure as reward for heroism and loyalty. David Clark notes, in his chapter "Heroic Desire: Male Relations in *Beowulf, The Battle of Maldon*, and *The Dream of the Rood*" in *Between Medieval Men* (2009), the homosocial bonds between Hrothgar and Beowulf, Beowulf and Hygelac, and Beowulf's retainers and Beowulf. Hrothgar, who felt "æfter deorum men *dyrne langað*" (for this dear man a secret longing) (my emphasis, 1879), regards Beowulf as a son he would like to have had as heir. Clark stresses as well the failure of Beowulf to die in battle with his lord Hygelac as heroically necessary because of Hygelac's need for an heir, unlike that of Beowulf in the fight with the dragon, when his retainers abandon him to the fight. Generally, Clark's reading argues that what is at stake is the preservation of this homosocial society through progeny and the loyalty of a lord's *duguð*:

> [T]he ominous comment of the poet at the end that the treasure for which Beowulf gave his life lies in the earth even now 'eldum swa unnyt, swa hyt æror wæs' [as useless to men as it was before] (3168) refers only to fact that it is not being used to cement societal ties, thus strengthening his approbation of homosocial relationships ... the poem undermines the value of treasure ... rather than functioning as an index of moral worth, it falls into the hands of lesser warriors as battlefield loot (as in Hygelac's fatal raid on Frisia), and fails to maintain homosocial loyalties (as with Beowulf's handpicked retainers in the dragon-fight.[18]

The same elegiac note is sounded by Aragorn while the company stops in Rohan—itself constructed as a type of Old English society—in book 3 of *Two Towers*. In particular, Tolkien invokes the famous *ubi sunt* passage from "The Wanderer," in the words of Aragorn: "Where now the horse and rider?/Where is the horn that was blowing?" (*LOTR*, 3:6, 508).[19] Not unexpectedly, it is this kingdom in which the old king has allowed Wormtongue to take over leadership in Rohan, at least until Gandalf exposes the reality of the situation; but even after the king's confidence in himself has been renewed by his hall-guardian Hama and his sister-son Éomer, we hear Théoden, the old king, insist on leading his men into battle while leaving his Valkyrie-like daughter Éowyn behind to care for the women, children, and the elderly Tolkien's criticism of kingship in *The Lord of the Rings* has by now been well documented by readers and scholars; the intent of this chapter is instead to look at how Tolkien exposes the weaknesses in chivalry as a practice and institution that distracts from its essential purpose: the loyal service of the subordinate to the lord in battle while the lord recognizes that loyalty and leads wisely, as many of the extant chivalry manuals have attested, without becoming too absorbed in how success in doing so gratifies the self.

Sir Gawain and the Green Knight: *Tolkien's Three Versions*

Generally the practice of what we understand chivalry to offer is associated with the advent of the Normans into England after the victory of William the Conqueror in 1066, followed by the rise of romance and then courtly love beginning in the twelfth century and continuing at least into the fourteenth century, both in medieval literature and in institutional and social practice.[20] The works par excellence in Middle English include Arthurian romance, most especially *Sir Gawain and the Green Knight*, a fourteenth-century alliterative poem and masterpiece that Tolkien himself spent time teaching, editing, and lecturing about. For graduate students and scholars alike, the magisterial coedition with E.V. Gordon continues to be unmatched in its exacting glossary by Tolkien. Proposed initially to Oxford University Press on 18 January 1921 as a student edition by Kenneth Sisam—for whose *Fourteenth-Century Verse and Prose* Tolkien had also compiled his *Middle-English Vocabulary* (but so delayed it had to be published in a small separate edition)[21]—their edition of *Sir Gawain* was not published until 1925, and then reprinted and finally revised by Norman Davis in 1967.

Tolkien discusses *Sir Gawain* in the essay "Ofermod" mentioned above in this same verse-drama of *The Homecoming of Beorhtnoth*; in his introduction to his *Gawain* translation (compiled from teaching notes by his son Christopher); and in his essay on "Sir Gawain and the Green Knight," based on his W.P. Ker Memorial Lecture on *Sir Gawain and the Green Knight*, delivered at the University of Glasgow on 15 April 1953 and published in *The Monsters and the Critics and Other Essays*. Although *Sir Gawain and the Green Knight* was not added as a set text to the Oxford English School until 1947, Tolkien did teach his first course on the poem during Trinity term at Oxford in 1920. Starting in 1946, he lectured on it every two years starting in 1946, although its sister text and alliterative poem *Pearl*, likely by the same author, as Tom Shippey and others have argued,[22] was required reading at the Oxford English School when he was a student and part of the curriculum when he taught at both Leeds and Oxford.[23] Written in the difficult Northwest Midlands dialect, like *Sir Gawain*, *Pearl*, an elegiac dream vision, was supposed to have been coedited by E.V. Gordon and Tolkien beginning in 1925 but appeared in print only under E.V. Gordon's name in 1953, after his death in 1938, having been revised mostly by his Middle English scholar-wife, Ida, and by Tolkien, to a lesser extent.[24] As Tolkien always did when teaching an Old Norse, Old English, or Middle English work, he translated *Pearl* in 1925–1926 (a translation eventually published posthumously in 1975 along with translations of *Sir Gawain and the Green Knight* and *Sir Orfeo*).[25] Editor Christopher Tolkien has included material garnered from Tolkien's previously unpublished Oxford lectures as brief introductions to each.

How do Tolkien's three treatments of *Sir Gawain and the Green Knight* differ? The first, Tolkien's discussion of *Sir Gawain and the Green Knight* in his introductory essay "Ofermod," accompanied by the verse-drama, and the second, the published lecture on the romance, both touch on pride (or *ofermod*, as in *The Battle of Maldon*). But in the first, Sir Gawain's pride is compared with that of an Anglo-Saxon lord, Byrhtnoth, and in the second, Sir Gawain's pride grow out of his fear of being regarded as unworthy of his fame as Arthur's nephew and best knight. In "Ofermod," this flaw stems from the chivalric necessity for fame in prowess and valor, in contrast to the retainer's heroic obligation of sacrifice of life in battle to serve his lord, as in the case of Byrhtwold in *The Battle of Maldon*. In the third example—Tolkien's introduction to his translation of the poem—the take on the knight's pride seems more appropriately linked with Gawain's honor.

In that introduction to his translation, Tolkien mostly exonerates the knight from what he sees as exaggerated and artificial sins, which explain why the lords and ladies of the court laugh at him when he confesses his failure. For what Tolkien most likes about Gawain is his humanity: "But in terms of literature, undoubtedly this break in the mathematical perfection of an ideal creature, inhuman in flawlessness, is a great improvement. The credibility of Gawain is enormously enhanced by it. He becomes a real man, and we can thus admire his actual virtue."[26] A real man, then, is human. Tolkien goes through each of his alleged sins, stripping away fault with each one, perhaps because he perceives this work as a "romance, a fairy-tale for adults."[27] Tolkien admires this Gawain, with his "exaggerated courtesy of speech, his modesty of bearing, which yet goes with a subtle form of pride: a deep sense of his own honour, not to mention, we might say, a pleasure in his own repute as 'this fine father of breeding' (stanza 38)."[28] Yet in the last scene, Gawain accuses himself of three sins, greed, cowardice, and treachery, the first two of which, Tolkien notes, he is guilty "by a casuistry of Shame."[29] That is, greed for the girdle, or for saving his neck, means that he accepts the girdle; then, he flinches, as well as accepts the girdle, so he is cowardly. The third charge of treachery, "disloyalty, troth-breach, treachery," he is guilty of only "insofar as he had broken the rules of an absurd game imposed on him by his host (after he had rashly promised to do anything his host asked)."[30] In this regard, Sir Gawain most obviously keeps the girdle to save his neck (and, therefore, his reputation for valor) in the contest with the Green Knight at the Green Chapel.

Does Gawain then fail in errantry (and masculinity) because of his cowardice and fear of dying by decapitation by the Green Knight and his act of treachery to his lord Bercilak by not revealing the gift of the magical girdle? In Tolkien's long essay on *Sir Gawain*—his 1953 W.P. Ker Memorial Lecture at the University of Glasgow—he zeros in on the temptation of Gawain in the third fitt, in which Bercilak's wife tempts the knight both through her advances and gifts. Tolkien singles out her "open invitation to adultery," when she says coquettishly, "Ʒe ar welcum to my cors,/ Yowre awen won to wale,/Me behouez of fyne force/ Your seruant be, and schale"(To my body will you welcome be/of delight to take your fill;/for need constraineth me/to serve you, and I will," in the lines as translated by Tolkien.[31] This sexual invitation in fact most troubles the Oxford medievalist in terms of the apparently "chivalric" rather than the "heroic."[32] Chivalry may mediate the conflict between moral law and the requisites of courtesy and the code of honor, [33] but moral law trumps adultery as part of courtesy or knightly honor in keeping his vow.[34] Finally, because Gawain has confessed presumably all his sins, then (according to Tolkien), as a Christian, the knight may view the alleged magic of the green girdle as a trifle not worth a confession.

The Green Knight in his Chapel, for Tolkien, most faults Gawain for not surrendering the green girdle as a gain on the third night, in obedience to the troth he has plighted with Sir Bercilak. Tolkien actually acknowledges the gendered nature of Gawain's fault: "It is as *man to man*, as *opponents in a game*, that he is challenging Gawain. I think that it is plain that in this he expresses the opinion of the author" (my emphasis).[35] Sir Gawain has failed as a man, in his masculinity: as Sheila Fisher has argued: in betraying his own notion of "kynde," Gawain necessarily betrays his masculinity, "for in this poem, knighthood and masculinity are in the end the same things."[36] Clare R. Kinney also notes that Gawain "has both unmanned himself *and*, paradoxically, done what comes all too naturally to men ... in generating alternative accounts of his failing, Gawain feels obliged either to insist that he has completely betrayed his *kynde* (that is, the fellowship of aristocratic male warriors) or to suggest that, if he has kept faith with his *kynde*, that *kynde* is not humankind but *man*kind."[37] However, Tison Pugh, in *Queering Arthurian Romance*, argues that, in flinching before the Green Knight, Gawain's "chivalric identity" is interrogated by the Green Knight and, in the face of death, he loses control of his courtly persona so that the Green Knight accuses him that "Thou art not Gawayn'" (line 2270).[38] Even if the "god-game" that the Green Knight plays ultimately benefits Gawain because of what he learns about himself, as Pugh suggests, nevertheless, "Gawain's chivalric identity as a romance hero is forever altered by his failures in the game," which "also appears to be a practical joke in which the green girdle serves as the punchline, with a masculine and heroic knight adopting a flimsy and feminine accessory."[39]

Tolkien nowhere considers the possibility that if Gawain had succumbed to the lady's advances and consequently needed to offer similar embraces to his lord, the implication would be that Gawain had committed both adultery and treason to his lord. Tolkien never mentions the absurd possibility of sodomy as a result of the contract between the two men, although that would have been the logical and contractual consequence of a sexual gift exchange between the Lady and the knight.[40] The unspoken issue of a gay Gawain that underlies the temptation scenes is made more vivid when the English Arthurian romance is juxtaposed with the French Arthurian lay of *Lanval*, summarized briefly in the Introduction, in which the Breton knight, so uninterested in Guinevere's charms, is accused by Arthur's queen of being homosexual.[41]

> "Lanval," fet ele, "bien le quit,
> Vuz n'amez gueres cel delit;
> Asez le m'ad hum dit sovent
> Que des femmes n'avez talent.
> Vallez avez bien afeitiez,
> Ensemble od eus vus deduiez.
> Vileins cuarz, mauveis failliz.
> Mut est mi sires maubailliz
> Que pres de lui vus ad suffert."

["Lanval," she said, "I am sure you don't care for such pleasure; people have often told me that you have no interest in women. You have fine-looking boys with whom you enjoy {or pleasure} yourself. Base coward, lousy cripple, my lord made a bad mistake when he let you stay with him."]⁴²

By accusing Lanval of being a "Vileins cuars" (Base coward) and also a "mauveis failliz" (lousy cripple) (in line 283), Guinevere strips him of his manhood, in medieval cultural as well as in sexual terms. He likes good-looking boys, and he is not much of a knight in terms of his valor and physical prowess, in the poem as we have it (indeed, from the beginning when Lanval dismounts and lets loose his horse so that he can take a nap, the fairy queen appears and seduces him, an equivalence by which Marie de France deconstructs *chevalerie* and the injustice of its demands). He has been feminized by her seduction, but he has also inmasculated himself. Discussing the same passage, Tison Pugh notes that "If a knight is perceived to fail in his heteronormativity, as famously occurs in Marie de France's 'Lanval,' his overarching male privilege is threatened."⁴³

These two medieval works, when read concurrently, open up discussion of how Tolkien might be queering the homosocial practice of chivalry. Interestingly, both the Breton knight Lanval and the Green Knight while in the Arthurian court in England, and Gawain while at Bercilak's court and the Green Knight's chapel, are literally "strangers in a strange land." A "Gay Gawain" pinpoints the Heinleinian concept of "The Stranger in a Strange Land" to underscore the alterity of these two knights, Gawain and Lanval, within the context of the alien Green Knight's own abrupt transgression of the merry and civilized mood of the English court and its holy festival (the feast of Circumcision, as it is New Year's Day), and coming as he does from a realm possibly that of faërie. Later in the romance, the positions of Gawain and the Green Knight are reversed: Sir Gawain enters as an alien, in his bedraggled finery, over various liminal thresholds into the faërie-like castle, despite wind and snow, while the Green Knight, in the civilized role of host Bercilak de Hautdesert, welcomes him to lodging and a warm fire. Lanval and Gawain are marked by physical and cultural differences from all others: in Lanval's case, one of origin, in that he is from Brittany, as well as a man of great physical beauty, and in Gawain's case, a cultural and social difference in valor and in courtesy toward women.

Tolkien's focus on the "man to man" contest or question, if you will, in his *Sir Gawain and the Green Knight* essay easily leads us into discussion of the feudal relationship of Sam to his "lord" Frodo in *The Lord of the Rings* and, in general, of discussion of other male–male engagements throughout Tolkien's medievalized epic-romance.

"Man to Man" in *The Lord of the Rings*

From the very beginning, Sam's service to his master represents a backdrop against which more minor relationships involving service are replayed. Sam initially serves as gardener before the quest begins, but he becomes a squire to his lord in *The Two Towers* after they are separated from the Fellowship and, eventually, in *The Return of the King*, evolves into a deeply compassionate friend whose love transcends the ordinary. Gollum, also a Hobbit, if degenerate in form, offers a parody of Sam as servant, just as Frodo eventually comes to parody the Dark Lord in Tolkien's version of how self-aggrandizement, greed, and pride pervert masculine relationships. Tolkien portrays their mutual emotional enslavement by the Ring (called the "Precious" by Gollum in an ironic reference both to valuable items and to the beloved) in the most medieval, feudal, scene of oath-swearing in the epic, in "The Taming of Sméagol," when Gollum swears to the Master—Frodo—by the Precious, or tries to: "Sméagol will swear never, never, to let Him have it. Never! Sméagol will save it. But he must swear on the Precious" (*LOTR*, 4:1, 618). At the moment Frodo insists Gollum swear instead *by* the Ring, Sam imagines that "his master had grown and Gollum had shrunk: *a tall stern shadow, a mighty lord who hid his brightness in grey cloud*, and at his feet a little whining dog. Yet the two were in some way akin and not *alien*: they could reach one another's minds" (*LOTR*, 4:1, 618; my emphasis). If Frodo here is lord and Gollum is subject, their feudal relationship can be considered as queer and closeted, just as Sam's relationship to Frodo can be. What is Precious is queer desire—the tough love of queer chivalry, what they are quarreling over, as predicated on mastery and the submission of will, and entirely circular. Indeed, its circularity extends elliptically to other relationships in *The Lord of the Rings*, including that between Sauron and Saruman, Sharkey and Wormtongue.

Tolkien fully rehearses homosocial relationships in scenes that involve the Hobbits as medieval vassals or thanes who serve some lord or master, willingly or no, as a means of suggesting the possibility of the misuse of domination and, therefore, to hint at exaggerated masculinity. In *The Return of the King*, this scene of feudal domination is varied by Hobbit Pippin, who, like Gollum attempting to swear on the Ring, similarly swears to the House of Denethor his allegiance as vassal, but as compensation for the loss of Denethor's son Boromir while defending the Hobbits, in "Minas Tirith": "Here do I swear fealty and service to Gondor, and to the Lord and Steward of the realm, to speak and to be silent, to do and to let be, to come and to go, in need or plenty, in peace or war, in living or dying, from this hour henceforth, until my lord release me, or death take me, or the world end" (*LOTR*, 5:1, 756). After constructing these contrasting scenes of medieval fealty, Tolkien provides a tertium quid when Hobbit Merry willingly and joyfully offers his service to King Théoden of Rohan in "The Passing of the Grey Company": "Filled suddenly with love for this old man, he knelt on one knee, and took his hand and kissed it: 'May I lay the sword of Meriadoc of the Shire on your lap, Théoden King?' he cried. 'Receive my service, if you will!'" (*LOTR*, 5:2, 777).

Throughout *The Lord of the Rings*, Tolkien defines Hobbits in relation to Men, their masculinity representing, according to Holly A. Crocker, an invisible standard of heteronormativity. Aragorn may epitomize the ideal of masculinity, as evidenced by the support he receives from the Free Peoples, yet in what does it inhere, if not in his refusal of dominion over others through "visible gestures?"[44] Hobbits, smaller than Men, the Black Númenóreans, the Ringwraiths, and the Lieutenant of the Tower of Barad-dûr—the Mouth of Sauron identified as a "living man" (*LOTR*, 5:10, 888)—are defined as inversions of Men; so also Orcs, as mutations of Elves, provide what Crocker calls "the distinctions that divide groups."[45] Crocker notes:

> Instead, Aragorn must refashion the masculinity of his kind to avoid their missteps, ultimately by taking a role in the Fellowship that reveals his leadership through gestures of service that avoid visibility. His support of Frodo's errand, therefore, is simply the culmination of a long formation of masculinity that is fostered by contact with groups who protect Middle-earth using quiet modes of dominion.[46]

She also adds, "Before he becomes king, then, the new masculinity that Aragorn realizes is enabled by its ability to pass unseen amongst those it protects ... The central place in field of sight that Aragorn finally assumes, I suggest, asserts masculinity's invisibility by defining it as the standard of identity that will consolidate all kinds in this new reign."[47]

Tolkien's Orcs differ from Men in their broad flat faces, coal-black eyes, and red tongue; they speak their own language, which further isolates them (*LOTR*, 2:5, 325). Bearing yellow fangs, Orcs have "no time to play," meaning that they must work, that is, kill and torture, and they are quarrelsome, dominating, disloyal, and vengeful, differentiated only by a military chain-of-command, not individual personal or temperamental characteristics (*LOTR*, 3:3, 445–46). Cruel—they jeer at Merry when he puts "medicine" on his wound and promise that "We shall have some fun later" (*LOTR*, 3:3, 448)—they are regularly abusive and sadistic verbally, physically, and even sexually. For example, Uglúk, leader of the Uruk-hai of Saruman's Isengard (who have been further mutated so they can march by day), insults Grishnákh of Sauron's Lugbúrz by calling his Orcs swine and maggots: "Don't stand slavering there! Get your rabble together! The other swine are legging it to the forest" (*LOTR*, 3:3, 452). Further, when Grishnákh steals Merry and Pippin away from the other Orcs because he thinks they have the Ring, Tolkien portrays his search for it as disturbingly sexualized. Grishnákh's "long hairy arm" and "foul breath" are apparent when "He began to paw them and feel them. Pippin shuddered as hard cold fingers groped down his back [...]. His fingers continued to grope" (*LOTR*, 3:3, 455). Grishnákh, angry that he has not found the Ring, threatens the Hobbits with torture if he does not find it: "I'll cut you both to quivering shreds" (*LOTR*, 3:3, 457). Ironically, after Sauron's Orc leader is killed by an arrow. Pippin locates Grishnákh's Orc knife and cuts Merry and his bonds. Pippin's acquisition of this phallic weapon—the carved handle of an Orc blade is shaped like a hideous head with "squinting eyes" and "leering mouth" (*LOTR*, 3:3, 489)—represents both his re-arming and masculinization, for it is after this escape that Pippin generously offers his indenture as servant to tyrannical and mad King Denethor of Gondor as compensation for the loss of his son Boromir defending the two Hobbits against the Orcs.

Within this context, Tolkien invests both Orcs and Hobbits with cultural difference. The epithet most descriptive of their mutual alterity is "queer," that is, not like Men. The Orc chieftain is described in *The Two Towers* as "almost manhigh," a phrase Tolkien uses to differentiate the Orc from the human norm (*LOTR*, 2:5, 325). Interestingly, when Men are corrupted they look more like Orcs (*LOTR*, 2:5, 566). The Orcs—mutants bred by Sauron from captured Elves—represent the Other, like the "queer" Hobbits who isolate themselves geographically from Men and all other races. Indeed, "The term 'queer,'" according to Tison Pugh: need not be limited to the sexual, as it also describes relations of power predicated upon relations of sexuality. "[T]o queer" means to disrupt a character's and/or the reader's sense of self by undermining his or her sense of heteronormatively inscribed sexuality, whereas "homosexual" and "homosexuality" are used to describe sexual relationships between members of the same sex (of whatever degree, from kissing to intercourse). Thus, heteronormative identity stands at stake in the queer as much as any specific sexual act.[48]

How this identity stake works depends upon a kind of queer gender paralaxis. Doty observes that "gender" within the queer either mirrors conventional forms of "feminine" and "masculine," parodies external behaviors without complete identification with straight ideology, or resists (or combines) gender codes to transcend straight formulations of female and male; only in the latter two instances does a queer gender identification exist. Doty notes:

> Generally, lesbian- and gay-specific forms of queer identities involve some degree of same-gender identification and desire or a cross-gender identification linked to same-gender desire. The understanding of what "gender" is in these cases can range from accepting conventional straight forms, which naturalize "feminine" and "masculine" by conflating them with essentializing, biology-based conceptions of "woman" and "man"; to imitating the outward forms and behaviors of one gender or the other while not fully subscribing to the straight ideological imperatives that define that gender; to combining or ignoring traditional gender codes in order to reflect attitudes that have little or nothing to do with straight ideas about femininity/women or masculinity/men. These last two positions are the places where queerly reconfigured gender identities begin to be worked out.[49]

The Orc, as repressed sexuality amid brute animality, in queer terms represents the hypermasculine polar opposite of the Hobbit as a form of desexualized and even idealized feminine. Think here of Frodo toward the end of the epic when he is reimagined for the moment as an Orc.

That is, just as Tolkien uses the Orc re-arming of Pippin with Grishnákh's knife in *The Two Towers* to signal the Hobbit's metamorphosis into a being more masculinized and military, his bonds having been cut, our medievalist also changes the costume of Sam and Frodo throughout the epic in their conflicts with other beings, most especially Orcs, to signal the breaking of Hobbit boundaries and borders during their epic quest. Indeed, *who* they are, as they evolve, confuses the enemy, who rely on external signs for racial identity: one small black-skinned tracker Orc quarrels with a larger warrior Orc who bears the sign of the Eye over the object of their search, the two Hobbits: "First they say it's a great Elf in bright armour, then it's a sort of small dwarf-man, then it must be a pack of rebel Uruk-hai; or maybe it's all the lot together" (*LOTR* 6:2, 925).

But the Hobbits are all three, for Frodo's dwarf mithril-coat, given to him by Bilbo, reveals him, in a sense, *as* a Dwarf defending his ancient home, and also protects this newly heroic Hobbit from death in the attack by the Orcs at the Dwarves' abandoned mine at Khazad-dûm when he valiantly stabs the foot of an Orc attempting to break down the door (*LOTR*, 2:5, 324). Later, in Lothlórien, the grey-green and silver Elven hood and cloak Galadriel gives to the Hobbits offer camouflage in any forest setting, near-invisibility from enemies, and lightness and warmth in wearing, but also mark them more symbolically as Elven in their song-making and wisdom. The leader of the Elves tells the Hobbits that "we put the thought of all that we love into all that we make. Yet they are garments, not armour, and they will not turn shaft or blade" (*LOTR* 2:8, 370).

So also when Sam and Frodo put on Orc armor to disguise themselves from Saruman's searching Orcs, the Orcs themselves think Sam is a big Orc. For Frodo, this assumption of Orc armor is necessary because the Orcs who captured him have stripped him of all clothing, including the garments and "armor" given to him by others—the coat of mithril mail from Bilbo and the Elven cloak with the elven-brooch. For Sam, the Elven blade he uses against Shelob has failed (*LOTR*, 4:10, 728), and the short sword he carries has been taken by the Orcs (*LOTR*, 5:10, 889).

This stripping and queered epic re-arming of the hero(es) in *The Return of the King* alerts us to an important stage in their journey together—what might be called a defensive identification of the Other with the Other for self-protection as they cross Mordor, which is indicated by the donning of Orc apparel. The Orc clothing they put on includes long hairy breeches, a dirty leather tunic, a coat of ring-mail, a belt with a sword, and, for Frodo, a black cap on which a red Evil Eye has been painted with iron rim and "beaklike nose-guard" (*LOTR*, 5:1, 913). So effective is this garb that both Hobbits appear to be Orcs: captured Frodo, dazed and dreaming in the chapter "The Tower of Cirith Ungol," in anticipation of Sam's appropriation of Orc costume saw "an orc with a whip, and then it turns into Sam" (*LOTR*, 6:1, 910). After they don the clothing, Sam calls Frodo "a perfect little orc" or would be, if he would cover his face with a mask and if he were longer in arm and bow-legged (*LOTR*, 6:2, 913). Tolkien implies that they have in some way been symbolically transformed into Orcs, but what that means is not explicitly indicated. Further, in the chapter "The Land of Shadow," *before* they meet the Orc company, they divest themselves of some of the armor because Sam is too big and cannot wear Orc-mail over his clothing (he just wears an Orc-helm and a black cloak) and because the Orc-mail is too heavy for Frodo (he borrows Sam's Elven cloak, which he wears over the "orc-rag") (*LOTR*, 6:2, 918).

In "The Land of Shadow," Tolkien parodies the three other medieval comitatus or feudal indenture scenes that I have just described from *The Two Towers* and *The Return of the King* between Hobbit and Hobbit or Hobbit and Man by means of a confrontation between Orcs and Pseudo-Orcs (*LOTR*, 6:2, 916–932). This scene, when compared with the events preceding it in Tolkien, becomes a gloss on the text that reveal the queer underpinnings of the feudal/chivalric bond between lord and thane or knight. The encounter between the Orc company and the Hobbits happens at night, when the Orcs are moving very quickly to reposition themselves for battle. Smaller "breeds" of Orcs who want to get the trip over, even if it means joining Sauron's wars, constitute the group, guided by very large "uruks" (slave-drivers) with whips (*LOTR*, 6:2, 930). Dressed as Orcs in hopes of fitting in, Sam and Frodo do not try to escape—they merely hope they will not be noticed, but of course they are, not as Hobbit imposters, but as deserters. One of the slave-drivers whips and harasses these "slugs" into joining the front of the phalanx: "Now and again the orc-driver fell back and jeered at them. 'There now!' he laughed, flicking at their legs. 'Where there's a whip there's a will, my slugs. Hold up! I'd give you a nice freshener now, only you'll get as much lash as your skins will carry when you come in late to your camp. Do you good'" (*LOTR* 6:2, 931). When the company later meets several Orc companies that converge at the road intersection, during further whippings, scuffles, and confusion Sam falls to the ground with Frodo so that Orcs fall on top and they are able to crawl off in the dark (*LOTR*, 6:2, 932).

In his figuration of the Orcs and Orcish behavior, Tolkien deploys a masculinity theorized as "queer" by Pugh and other critics because of its exaggeration of male physical characteristics and behavior.[50] The symbolic act of Orc re-dressing by the two heroes in this chapter not only enables the next step in the two Hobbits' journey to return the Ring but also situates the couple within a context of extreme and monstrous masculinization necessary for their survival in the savage and warlike world of Mordor. The Orc armor with its metal helmets bearing protective guards for noses and cheeks resembles medieval armor, even if noses and cheeks appear grotesque and deformed. Indeed, this scene parodies a medieval chivalric engagement and feudal relationship: the Orcs savage one another with emotional abuse and demeaning epithets, and their captain brutalizes them with whips and other weapons. For Frodo and Sam to join the group out of survival, even to ensure and protect their progress across Mordor, suggests that they both become—and also fail to become—one with this group. That is, they fail to embrace the ironic Orcish rupture/displacement of the feudal bond between lord and serf, which depends upon a sadomasochistic imbalance between master and slave. Thus they remove the armor afterwards because it—the armor and the Orcish masculinity—is too heavy. In a sense, they remain children, they do not "grow up" to become "men" in the bizarrely Orc parody of masculinity. They remain non-men—different, queer.

Within this context of multicultural and multiracial difference, one of the major moral points of *The Lord of the Rings* is that all four of the Hobbit heroes (or antiheroes) are described as different from the other Hobbits. Of all these queer and unnatural Hobbits, Gollum is the most disgusting and least sympathetic. Both Sam and Frodo regard Gollum as queer and unnatural. For Frodo, Gollum is the Shire equivalent of a Brandybuck living across the river, so that the Ringbearer initially reacts to Gollum's strangeness—his "queerness"—as Sandyman did to him—with suspicion and indignation. Early on, after learning from Gandalf of how the Ring was found and what power it wreaks on others, Frodo, not understanding the mercy or pity that stayed Bilbo's hand, wishes he had killed Gollum long ago (*LOTR* 1.2, 58). But, as Tolkien himself says, in letter 181, to Michael Straits, about the end of the quest in *The Lord of the Rings*:

> [T]he "salvation" of the world and Frodo's own "salvation" is achieved by his previous pity and forgiveness of injury. At any point any prudent person would have told Frodo that Gollum would certainly betray him, and could rob him in the end. To "pity" him, to forbear to kill him, was a piece of folly, or a mystical belief in the ultimate value in itself of pity and generosity even if disastrous in the world of time. He did rob him and injure him in the end—but by a "grace," that last betrayal was at a precise juncture when the final evil deed was the most beneficial thing any one cd. have done for Frodo! By a situation created by his "forgiveness," [Frodo] was saved himself, and relieved of his burden. (*Letters*, 234)

Because of Gollum the quest is completed. As Gandalf reminded Frodo, forgiveness is the way to grace and peace of mind, because we simply do not know enough to judge others who are different from us, in person, race, or culture. Further, despite seeming initially different, Gollum is merely a much diminished Hobbit. Descended from the wandering, matriarchal Stoor branch of the Gladden Fields, he is not a typical Harfoot Hobbit, from the Shire or Bree, or a fair, adventuresome Fallohide from the upper Anduin or Eriador (the branch of the Hobbits from which leaders often come, and the line from which the Tooks, Brandybucks, and Bolgars descended). In this sense Gollum represents a Hobbit alter-ego for Bilbo–Frodo, both of the Bagginses so queer and different from others in the Shire because of their Fallohide–Harfoot mixed ancestry.

Aside from the considerably diminished figure of Hobbit Gollum—definitely abject—Tolkien considers the role of the insignificant Hobbits Frodo and Sam as metaphorically crucial to the saving of Middle-earth. In relation to the events of World Wars I and II that appeared to cast ordinary humankind as insignificant in the shaping of their outcome, Tolkien declares, "Anyway I myself saw the value of Hobbits, in putting earth under the feet of 'romance', and in providing subjects for 'ennoblement' and heroes more praiseworthy than the professionals: *nolo heroizari* is as good a start for a hero, as *nolo episcopari* for a bishop."[51] That Tolkien would then create lifelong friendships similar to his own with his childhood and college friends among his fictional Hobbits in *The Lord of the Rings*, written from the thirties and continuing during World War II, more or less finished by 1950, is no surprise. And all his humble figures, historical or mythical, are not unlike Tolkien himself, wounded spiritually by his own participation in the Battle of the Somme during World War I—a battle in which he lost many school friends.

Tolkien recast the medieval hero in this world of *The Lord of the Ring* in new, unlikely, and multiple forms. These forms include, in addition to small Hobbits, suspicious dark Rangers like Strider, sisters and sister-daughters (nieces) like Éowyn, sister of Éomer and niece to King Théoden (brother of her mother, Théodwyn), and second sons like Faramir, younger brother of Boromir. In the medieval romance the quest-hero frequently appears as the nephew to the king—the son of the king's sister, or "sister-son"—as was Gawain, nephew to King Arthur in the fourteenth-century *Gawain and the Green Knight* and son of Morgan le Fay and her half-brother, Arthur, and of Morgause in the fifteenth-century Sir Thomas Malory's *Morte Darthur*. Most importantly, Tolkien changed the nature of the epic quest from a journey to join in the war of nations to an *anti*-quest, a *non*-battle, and a lonely trip to a place of death (Mordor).

That same mercy or pity toward Gollum will grow in Frodo and eventually but ironically save the Ringbearer on the lip of Mount Doom. Here, in explaining Frodo's pity and Gollum's service, Levinas might be helpful: in *Totality and the Other* he remarks, "The poor one, the stranger, presents himself as an equal ... But he joins me to himself for service; he commands me as a Master. This command can concern me only inasmuch as I am master myself; consequently this command commands me to command. The *thou* is posited in front of a *we*."[52] Gollum's disobedience toward his "Master" Frodo at Mount Doom—only in a greater and providential sense to be construed as service—saves Frodo when this "Master" betrays himself, in no way to be construed as mercy or pity.

And it is not that Gollum's (or Frodo's) hand is stayed—again, only Frodo's finger is bitten off, with the Ring still attached, which saves Middle-earth and also, ironically, Frodo, given his intention to keep the Ring after all—but not Gollum, whatever his intended role, as sacrificial servant to his master or alien usurper, at the last moment.

Notes

1. Emmanuel Levinas, *Totality and Infinity: An Essay on Exteriority*, trans. Alphonso Lingis, Duquesne Studies Philosophical Series, vol. 24 (Pittsburgh, PA: Duquesne University Press, 1969), 215.
2. See Tison Pugh, *Queer Chivalry: Medievalism and the Myth of White Masculinity in Southern Literature* (Baton Rouge: Louisiana State University, 2013), 6–7.
3. Holly A. Crocker, "Masculinity," in *Reading the Lord of the Rings: New Writings on Tolkien's Classic*, ed. Robert Eaglestone, 111–23 (London and New York: Continuum, 2005), 122–23. Her citation from Homi K. Bhabha comes from "Are You a Man or a Mouse?" in *Constructing Masculinity*, ed. Maurice Berger, Brian Wallis, and Simon Watson (New York: Routledge, 1995), 58.
4. "Sir Gawain and the Green Knight," in *The Monsters and the Critics and Other Essays* (London: George Allen & Unwin, 1983), 72–108; and E[ric].V[alentine]. Gordon, ed. *The Battle of Maldon* (London: Methuen, 1937).
5. See the *Oxford University Gazette*, 59 (1928–1929): 55, cited in Thomas Honegger, "*The Homecoming of Beorhtnoth*: Philology and the Literary Muse," *Tolkien Studies* 4 (2007): 189–99. Tolkien's lectures were presented at Oxford in Michaelmas Term, 1928, starting on 16 October (Honegger, 189). Honegger believes Tolkien was composing modern English word-lists from the Old English drawn from *The Battle of Maldon*

as early as 1920, evident in Oxford Bodleian Special Collections MS Tolkien A21/5 (Honegger, 189, 196n4). Tolkien's notes and material on Old English meter and translations from *The Battle of Maldon* are contained in MS Tolkien 30/2 (n.d.) (Honegger, 196n4).

6. See J.R.R. Tolkien, "The Homecoming of Beorhtnoth Beorhthelm's Son," *Essays and Studies by Members of the English Association*, n.s., 6 (1953):1–18; repr. in *The Tolkien Reader* (New York: Ballantine, 1966), 1–28, with just the verse-drama on 7–20 (from which citations in this chapter will come); Scull, *Reader's Guide*, 407; and Humphrey Carpenter, *Biography*, 214. Christopher Tolkien and Scull believe there exists an even earlier text of "The Homecoming of Beorhtnoth, Beorhthelm's Son" extant in the Bodleian Library Department of Special Collections (*Reader's Guide*, 408). Following this hint, Honegger indicates a scribbled headnote identifies the earliest copy as MS Tolkien 5, version A, followed by nine drafts beginning with B, I, being the most recent and complete version, and K, the final typescript, although J is a fragment; an eleventh version, what Honegger adds as "α," is merely a brief dramatic dialogue between Danish Pudda and Tibba (later on, Totta and Tudda) (196n6).
7. *The Battle of Maldon*, lines 310–12, 61; my translation, based on Gordon's excellent glossary and notes. But see also the (somewhat less than literal) translation contemporary with young Tolkien by Cosette Faust and Stith Thompson (1918), in Turgon (David Smith) [aka Douglas A. Anderson], ed. *The Tolkien Fan's Medieval Reader*, 69–76 (Cold Spring Harbor, NY: Cold Spring Books, 2004), 76. Gordon believes Byrhtwold might be the same Brihtwold as the "cniht" of Byrthnoð's sister-in-law, Æðelflæd (84).
8. Tolkien, "The Homecoming of Beorhtnoth," 19.
9. See Wayne G. Hammond and Christina Scull, *The Lord of the Rings: A Reader's Companion* (Boston: Houghton Mifflin, 2005), 498.
10. Scull, *Reader's Guide*, 408, citing Tolkien's letter to Rayner Unwin, 25 April 1966, in the Tolkien-George Allen & Unwin archive, HarperCollins.
11. For the history of the complicated composition of "Errantry," see Christopher Tolkien, ed. *The Treason of Isengard*, The History of Middle-earth, vol. 7 (London: HarperCollins, 1989), 106–17. Christopher includes the edited MS Tolkien 5/α, described in the above note, also on 106–7, which he dates to the early twenties or thirties (*Treason*, 106). "Errantry" first appeared in print in *Oxford Magazine*, 52(5) (9 November 1933): 180; and later in J.R.R. Tolkien, *The Adventures of Tom Bombadil and Other Verses From the Red Book* (London: Allen & Unwin, 1962), 24–27.
12. See Scull, *Reader's Guide*, 262–64.
13. Tolkien, *The Adventures of Tom Bombadil*, repr. in *The Tolkien Reader*, 8; also in Tolkien, *The Adventures of Tom Bombadil and Other Verses From the*

Red Book, ed. Christina Scull and Wayne Hammond (London: HarperCollins, 2014), 31.
14. See *The Book of Lost Tales, Part Two* (1984), 267–79; "The Voyage of Éarendel the Evening Star." (Carpenter, *Biography*, 71); and *The Book of Lost Tales, Part Two*, 268.
15. Scull, *Reader's Guide*, 234.
16. These lines from *The Battle of Maldon* (lines 89–90) are quoted and translated by Tolkien in "Ofermod," 19 (my emphasis).
17. Tolkien, "The Homecoming of Beorhthelm Beorhtnoth's Son," 17.
18. David Clark, *Between Medieval Men: Male Friendship and Desire in Early Medieval Literature* (Oxford: Oxford University Press, 2009), 134. See also Clare A. Lees, who examines maleness, masculinism, and manhood in "Men in Beowulf," in *Medieval Masculinities: Regarding Men in the Middle Ages*, ed. Lees, 129–48 (Minneapolis: University of Minnesota Press, 1994).
19. See also my previous discussion in Jane Chance (Nitzsche), *Tolkien's Art: A "Mythology for England"* (London, Macmillan Press, 1978; New York: St. Martin's Press, 1979, repr. Papermac Editions, 1980; rev. edn. Lexington: University of Kentucky Press, 2001), 169–71.
20. There are many histories of the development of chivalry; see, for example, Maurice Keen, *Chivalry* (New Haven: Yale University Press, 1984).
21. See J.R.R. Tolkien, *A Middle English Vocabulary, Designed for Use with Sisam's Fourteenth Century Verse and Prose* (Oxford: Clarendon Press, 1922; repr. 1925).
22. See Tom Shippey, "Tolkien and the *Gawain*-poet," in *Proceedings of the J.R.R. Tolkien Centenary Conference*, Keble College, Oxford, 1992, ed. Patricia Reynolds and Glen H. GoodKnight, 213–20, *Mythlore* 80/*Mallorn* 30 (Winter 1996) (Milton Keynes: Tolkien Society; Altadena, CA: The Mythopoeic Press, 1995); repr. in Tom Shippey, *Roots and Branches: Selected Papers on Tolkien*, Cormarië Series no. 11 (Jena, Germany: Walking Tree Publishers, 2007). See also A.C. Spearing, *The Gawain-Poet: A Critical Study* (Cambridge: University Press, 1970), 237.
23. See Scull, *Reader's Guide*, 924, 748.
24. See *Pearl*, ed. E.V. Gordon, pref. by Ida Gordon (Oxford: Clarendon Press, 1953). Also see Scull, *Reader's Guide*, 748–52; and Douglas A. Anderson, "An industrious little devil": E.V. Gordon as Friend and Collaborator with Tolkien," in *Tolkien the Medievalist*, ed. Jane Chance, 15–25 (London: Routledge, 2003). For the coedited *Sir Gawain and the Green Knight*, see J.R.R. Tolkien and E.V. Gordon, eds., *Sir Gawain and the Green Knight*, 2nd edn., rev. Norman Davis (Oxford: Clarendon Press, 1968).

25. See J.R.R. Tolkien, trans. *Sir Gawain and the Green Knight, Pearl, Sir Orfeo*, ed. Christopher Tolkien (London: George Allen & Unwin, 1973). References are to page number(s).
26. All citations in this paragraph come from Tolkien, trans. *Sir Gawain and the Green Knight*, 11.
27. Tolkien, trans. *Sir Gawain and the Green Knight*, 14.
28. Tolkien, trans. *Sir Gawain and the Green Knight*, 15.
29. Tolkien, trans. *Sir Gawain and the Green Knight*, 5.
30. Tolkien, trans. *Sir Gawain and the Green Knight*, 5.
31. *Sir Gawain and the Green Knight*, eds. J.R.R. Tolkien and E.V. Gordon, 2nd edn., ed. Norman Davis (Oxford: Clarendon Press, 1968), lines 1237–40; Tolkien, trans. *Sir Gawain and the Green Knight*, 55–56.
32. Tolkien, "Sir Gawain and the Green Knight," 91.
33. Tolkien, "Sir Gawain and the Green Knight," 84, 86.
34. Tolkien, "Sir Gawain and the Green Knight," 91.
35. Tolkien, "Sir Gawain and the Green Knight," 93.
36. Sheila Fisher, "Leaving Morgan Aside: Women, History, and Revisionism in *Sir Gawain and the Green Knight*," in *The Passing of Arthur: New Essays on the Arthurian Tradition*, ed. Christopher Baswell and William Sharpe, 129–51 (New York: Garland, 1988), 141.
37. See Clare R. Kinney, "The (Dis)Embodied Hero and the Signs of Manhood in *Sir Gawain and the Green Knight*," in *Medieval Masculinities: Regarding Men in the Middle Ages*, ed. Clare A. Lees, 47–57 (Minneapolis: University of Minnesota Press, 1994), 55.
38. Tison Pugh, *Queering Medieval Genres* (New York: Palgrave, 2004), 124.
39. Pugh, *Queering Medieval Genres*, 124, 127.
40. See Carolyn Dinshaw, "A Kiss is Just a Kiss: Heterosexuality and Its Consolation in *Sir Gawain and the Green Knight*," *Diacritics* 24 (1994): 205–26.
41. The connection between the homoerotic and French romance in the latter half of the twelfth century has been noted, especially in relation to the *Roman d'Enéas*, a French vernacular translation of Virgil's *Aeneid*, in articles by Simon Gaunt, "From Epic to Romance: Gender and Sexuality in the *Roman d'Eneas*," *Romanic Review* 83 (1992): 1–27; and by Christopher Baswell, "Men in the *Roman d'Eneas*: The Construction of Empire, in *Medieval Masculinities: Regarding Men in the Middle Ages*, ed. Claire Lees, 149–68 (Minneapolis: University of Minnesota Press, 1994). The connection has also been made between the *Roman d'Enéas* and Marie de France's *Lanval*, as well as other romances, by Anna Klosowska, *Queer Love in the Middle Ages* (New York: Palgrave Macmillan, 2005), chapter 3, 117–44. See also Jane Chance, "Marie de France versus King Arthur: Lanval's

Gender Inversion as Breton Subversion," in *The Literary Subversions of Medieval Women* (New York: Palgrave Macmillan, 2007), 41–62.
42. See *Marie de France: Lais*. ed. Alfred Ewert (1944; repr. Bristol: Bristol Classical Press and London: Gerald Duckworth, Ltd.; Newburyport, MA: Focus Information Group, 1995), 65 (lines 277–285); and Marie de France, *The Lais*, trans. Robert Hanning and Joan Ferrante (Grand Rapids, MI: Baker Books, 1978), 196.
43. Pugh, discussing the same passage in *Lanval*, acknowledges that the queen's weapon is "the threat of homosexuality," a rhetorical one, in *Queering Medieval Genres* (New York: Palgrave Macmillan, 2004), 3. See also Glen Johnson, who perceives that "Queering appears especially in how [gay] novelists take familiar genres and subvert their conventions," in "Queering the Genre," *Harvard Gay and Lesbian Review*, 2(2) (Spring 1995), 21 [21–23].
44. Crocker, "Masculinity," 121.
45. Crocker, "Masculinity," 111.
46. Crocker, Masculinity," 117
47. Crocker, "Masculinity," 117, 122.
48. Tison Pugh, *Queering Medieval Genres*, 5.
49. Alexander Doty, *Making Things Perfectly Queer: Interpreting Mass Culture* (Minneapolis and London: University of Minnesota Press, 1993), 5.
50. See Tison Pugh, "Queering the Medieval Dead: History, Horror, and Masculinity in Sam Raimi's *Evil Dead* Trilogy," in *Race, Class, and Gender in "Medieval" Cinema*, ed. Lynn Ramey and Tison Pugh, 123–36 (New York and London: Palgrave Macmillan, 2007); also, Lee Edelman, *No Future: Queer Theory and the Death Drive* (Durham, NC: Duke University Press, 2004).
51. Ardenne, "The Man and the Scholar," 215.
52. Levinas, *Totality and Infinity*, 213. See also Joseph Tadie, "'That the World Not Be Usurped': Emmanuel Levinas and J.R.R. Tolkien on Serving the Other as Release From Bondage," in *Tolkien Among the Moderns*, ed. Ralph C. Woods, 219–45 (Notre Dame, IN: University of Notre Dame Press, 2015).

CHAPTER 9

Conclusion: The Ennoblement of the Humble: The History of Middle-earth

> "There are of course certain things and themes that move me specially. The inter-relations between the 'noble' and the 'simple' (or common, vulgar), for instance. The ennoblement of the ignoble I find specially moving."—Tolkien, letter 165 to Houghton Mifflin Co., 30 June 1955

> "The very status of the human implies fraternity and the idea of the human race. Fraternity is radically opposed to the conception of a humanity united by resemblance, a multiplicity of diverse families arisen from the stones cast behind by Deucalion, and which, across the struggle of egoisms, results in a human city."—Emmanuel Levinas, *Totality and Infinity*[1]

In the fantastic world of Middle-earth depicted in Tolkien's modern epic-romances—or fairy-stories (as he describes *The Lord of the Rings* in a draft of letter 181, 232, written in January or February 1956 to Michael Straights, editor of the *New Republic*)—he queers the nature of the questor and the purpose of the quest. The questor is an ill-equipped, middle-aged Hobbit, not unlike Tolkien in age (given the fantasy's difference in year-calculations)[2]—and like Bilbo, whose unlikely task is to steal something that had been previously stolen from the Dwarves or simply to return a ring to its source—like Frodo. Bilbo's band of helpers either consists of the Dwarves themselves, or Frodo's Hobbits, equally unused to fighting—Merry, Pippin, and Sam—and their human comrades. The latter include Éowyn, a shield-maiden from Anglo-Saxon-like Rohan, prohibited by her uncle-king from participating in the battle but, nevertheless, in violation of that ban, dons armor as the warrior Dernhelm to kill a Nazgûl lord. Faramir is a second son of the Steward of Gondor who has been cast away to police outlying territory. And Aragorn, Tolkien's most important human hero, he depicts as a dirty Ranger who stands revealed as the King of Gondor only at the end of the entire fairy-story. Meanwhile, epic battles do rage in the background, but Tolkien seems more interested in those individuals who exist at the margins of battle, if at all, in ways and forms and for reasons that differ from those in the conventional epic-romance.

Those reasons Tolkien explains in the appendices to *The Lord of the Rings* by means of the love of Arwen and Aragorn, which is not just a romantic story. What Tolkien has to say in that letter to Michael Straight cited above is most important for understanding his postmodern anti-epic of *The Lord of the Rings*: "I regard the role of Arwen and Aragorn as the most important of the Appendices; it is part of the essential story, and is only placed so, because it could not be worked into the main narrative without destroying its structure: which is planned to be 'hobbito-centric,' that is, primarily a study of the ennoblement (or sanctification) of the humble" (letter 181, 237). To understand the role's significance is to grasp the point of his entire mythological history of Middle-earth and much of his approach throughout his scholarship and translation. That mythological history evolves over time through war, division, and violence—Levinas's "struggle of egoisms"—until Middle-earth attains a peace attained in part through the most ignoble and hobbitocentric of all—the Hobbit. But the peace will depend upon and be maintained by a human city whose leaders are united despite and through difference: they have "arisen from the stones cast behind by Deucalion."

Arwen, the wise beloved of Aragorn, chooses to sacrifice her near-immortality as Half-elf to live side-by-side in Middle-earth with the human Aragorn until death.[3] At the end of the trilogy, it is Galadriel and her Elves and not Arwen who departs for the Undying Lands when the Third Age melds into the Fourth, the Age of Man; Arwen gives away her passage to Frodo (*LOTR* 6:6, 975). This departure, earned by Galadriel's rejection of Frodo's proffered Ring, represents forgiveness for her own role as half-niece to Fëanor and participant in the revolt of the Noldor (as described in *The Silmarillion*). Because of Galadriel's disobedience, she was banned from joining the other Elves in Valinor for long years.[4] This fact's importance for Tolkien cannot be underestimated, for the harmony that will exist at the beginning of that Fourth Age, of Man, following the ending of the bellicose Third Age, of Elves, will be symbolized by the marriage of the Man Aragorn and Half-elf Arwen, as this conclusion will show.

The love story of Aragorn and Arwen mirrors the pattern of the quest of their ancestors, the Man Beren and the Half-elf/half Maia Lúthien in *The Silmarillion* (and in the appendices to the novel). Aragorn and Arwen must similarly overcome an obstacle set by her father, here, Elrond: Aragorn must be found worthy of marrying his daughter, which he does by earning the right to be crowned king. Beren and Lúthien were initially prohibited from marriage by her father, Thingol, when he demanded an extraordinary boon of Beren in return for his daughter's hand—the retrieval of one of Fëanor's captured jewels, the Silmarils, from Morgoth's crown. During Beren's quest for the Silmaril, Lúthien functions as hero equally with her male lover, in fact transcending him in her artistic and heroic roles (*Silm*, chap. 19). For example, Rapunzel-like, Lúthien escapes imprisonment by her father by braiding her hair into a rope; further, her singing has a power that stuns her enamored adversaries. Indeed, through her efforts and those of her magical wolfhound, Huan, she escapes capture by Celegorm, conquers Sauron (whose form she wrests from him), and rescues Beren from imprisonment. Finally, loyal Lúthien offers Beren the choice either of relinquishing the quest and wandering the earth or of challenging the power of darkness, although she promises that "on either road I shall go with you, and our doom shall be alike" (*Silm*, 214). Lúthien matches in knowledge or artistry whatever Beren accomplishes in brave feats: for example, when Curufin, brother of Celegorm, tries to shoot her with an arrow, Beren steps in front and is himself wounded—but then Lúthien heals him. She sings for Morgoth, which blinds him, so that Beren can steal the Silmaril. Lúthien sucks out the venom from Beren after the wolf Carcharoth has bitten off Beren's hand holding the Silmaril (*Silm*, 182). Although Beren also dies upon the successful completion of the quest, Lúthien sings to him and they meet again "beyond the Western Sea," where she is offered the choice of mortal life with Beren without certainty of joy, which she accepts.

Tolkien finds his ideal union in the match of Beren and Lúthien,[5] not only romantic paradigms for himself and Edith and antecedents for Aragorn and Arwen, but also the latter couple's ancestors. Significant in this respect is the ennoblement of the Man Aragorn through his Elven-Maian blood and also the fact that he is related as a first cousin to Halfelven Arwen, who according to the appendices spent time in Lothlórien both before she met Aragorn and then after he died and left her behind. I say "first cousin," but many times removed, given the generations that have intervened between the Half-elf Elros, the brother of Arwen's father, the Half-elf Elrond, and Aragorn, as opposed to none at all between Elrond and his daughter, Arwen. Arwen was born in the Third Age, in 241, but Aragorn, in 2931, making her 2690 years older than he when he first sees her.[6]

Arwen herself mixes the blood of different branches of Elves. She is the daughter of Celebrían and Elrond and granddaughter of Galadriel and Celeborn. Through Galadriel's father, Finarfin—the half-brother of the important Noldo antihero Fëanor—Arwen is connected to both the Noldor and the Vanyar. Her father Finarfin's mother, Indis of the Vanyar, was the second wife of the Noldo Finwë. Her grandmother Galadriel descends from three Elven families: the Noldorin Vanyarin Elves united with the Teleri through her mother, Eärwen, daughter of the Teleri's Olwë of Alqualondë.[7] Lúthien's ancestry is even more impressive than Arwen's in its symbolic uniting of differing peoples: her mother was Melian the Maia (servant to the Valar), and her father was Thingol (or Elwë), the brother of Olwë of the Teleri.

The long history of the Elves dramatizes the division of the three branches, the Noldor (joined by Men), the Teleri, and the Vanyar, at various times alienated or geographically separated from each other. Specifically, in *The Silmarillion* the Noldor, headed by Fëanor, are exiled from the Blessed Realm because of the Kinslaying; from them and their alliance with the Edain—Men of the Three Houses of the Elf friends who came to the West because they were attracted to the light and joined the Eldar against Morgoth—descends Tolkien's ultimate and first hero, Eärendil the Mariner. As the son of the Man Tuor and the Elf Idril (the third important union in Tolkien's mythology), Eärendil the Mariner represents both the Elves and the Men. Idril, an Elda and daughter of Turgon, king of Gondolin, marries Tuor, human son of Huor of the House of Hador (Third House of the Edain) and gives birth to Eärendil the Mariner. Through this special position of mariner, ideal hero Eärendil sails to the Uttermost West as "ambassador of both Elves and Men" to obtain the help that will defeat Morgoth. He and his ship are thereafter transformed into a star to provide hope to voyagers (*LOTR* 1034; App. A:I:i). From Eärendil spring the Halfelven sons Elros and Elrond—the latter, father of Arwen.

Tolkien models these intermarriages and mixed blood progeny on the classical prototype of the hero as half god, half human, but nevertheless mortal, with all the problems attendant on a mixed marriage that ultimately separates the lovers by the death of one of them. The unification of

Man, Elf (all the branches), and Maia through the marriage of Aragorn and Arwen comes about only through the sacrifice and suffering of the lovers, chiefly because of what Tolkien terms the Doom of Men (his euphemism for death, also called a "Gift"). In the appendices (*LOTR* 1057; app. A:I:v), where much of their love story is relayed, after the death of Aragorn's own father, Arathorn, when he is two years old (recall that Tolkien was four when his own father died), his mother takes him to live in the House of Elrond, where he is called Estel, "Hope," to disguise his true identity from the Enemy. On the very next day, when Aragorn turns twenty—after his foster-father, Elrond, reveals Aragorn's true identity as the Heir of Isildur— the future king first sees Arwen (who has been living in Lothlórien with her mother's kin) and, thinking she is Tinúviel (Lúthien), falls in love with her. He does so even though his mother, Gilraen, warns him that "it is not fit that mortal should wed with the Elfkin" (*LOTR* 1059; app. A:I:v) and even though Elrond informs Aragorn that he will not have any bride until he is found worthy (Aragorn will be over eighty years old when he earns that honor) (*LOTR* 1061; app. A:I;v). In these relatively mild twin obstacles—a parallel to those to the marriage of Beren and Lúthien— is an additional "doom" laid upon Elrond and Arwen (exile, because of the Kinslaying) to remain with the youth of the Eldar until Elrond must depart, when Arwen can choose to accompany him or not. Although Arwen accepts human mortality in order to marry Aragorn, she must also accept parting from her father and her people—and, along with that parting, the demise of Aragorn before her.

The family backgrounds of Arwen, Galadriel, and Lúthien are important to Tolkien's mythology. All three family lines blend the blood of different kindreds or tribes, Maia, Elf, and Man, symbolic of Tolkien's appropriation of the ideal of peace-weaving embodied by Anglo-Saxon noble women[8] and the utopian goal of the reconciliation of all social differences through peace and harmony in marriage among differing cultures. In the appendices Tolkien explains that only three such unions of Eldar and Edain have existed in the history of Middle-earth—those of Tuor and Idril, Beren and Lúthien, and Aragorn and Arwen. All three couples, but especially Aragorn and Arwen, symbolize the unification of alienated, diverse, or separated peoples: Tolkien declares, "By the last the long-sundered branches of the Halfelven were reunited and their line was restored" (*LOTR* 1034; app. A:I:i).

Through such past and present love of other members of different species, the future of Middle-earth is guaranteed in the Fourth Age. Although the lovers Beren and Lúthien suffer mutilation and even death, in Beren's case, in the quest to win her hand from her father, and although Lúthien will sacrifice her world-long stay in Valimar to share a possibly joyless mortality with Beren in Middle-earth, in Tolkienian terms their literal union is fruitful and symbolically expressive of their deep and loyal love for one another. In the last line of their tale in *The Silmarillion* Tolkien affirms that "in her choice the Two Kindreds have been joined; and she is the forerunner of many in whom the Eldar see yet, though all the world is changed, the likeness of Lúthien the beloved, whom they have lost" (*Silm*, 187). This union of two kindred (families, tribes, races, nations) can indeed go far to create a world in which peace predominates.

What Tolkien has done, in his remaking of the Middle Ages, is to imbue his post-World War II fantasy with modern reality and to suggest its recovery from prejudice, discrimination, selfishness, and insensitivity toward those different from others by means of love and toleration of difference. He understands how dangerous the strategies of separation and division can be, the major focus in *The Lord of the Rings*. Within the larger context of Middle-earth, the agenda of both Maia Sauron and wizard Saruman is similar: to erase difference, by installing one point of view. Tolkien achieves the making of his most successful fairy-story through the harbinger of peace to come through this symbolic union of Aragorn and Arwen, long in coming through thousands of years.

Notes

1. Emmanuel Levinas, *Totality and Infinity: An Essay on Exteriority*, trans. Alphonso Lingis, Duquesne Studies Philosophical Series, vol. 24 (Pittsburgh, PA: Duquesne University Press, 1969), 214.
2. The equivalence of Bilbo with Tolkien is acknowledged by the translation into English of the runes on the original dust jacket for *The Hobbit*, which reads "The Hobbit or There and Back Again Being the Record of a Year's Journey Made by Bilbo Baggins of Hobbiton Compiled From His Memoirs by J.R.R. Tolkien and Published by George Allen Unwin Ltd." See *The Annotated Hobbit*, ed. Douglas A. Anderson, 2nd edn. (Boston: Houghton Mifflin, 2003), 180n11.
3. See the discussion by Richard C. West, "'Her Choice Was Made and Her Doom Appointed': Tragedy and Divine Comedy in the Tale of Aragorn and Arwen," in *The Lord of the Rings 1954–2004: Scholarship in Honor of Richard E. Blackwelder*, ed. Wayne G. Hammond and Christina Scull, 317–29 (Milwaukee, WI: University of Marquette Press, 2006).

4. See the different unused texts that appear in J.R.R. Tolkien, *Unfinished Tales of Númenor and Middle-earth*, ed. Christopher Tolkien (London: Allen & Unwin, 1979; Boston: Houghton Mifflin, 1980).
5. See the important story in *Silm*, 195–228, chapter 19, "Of Beren and Lúthien." Richard C. West has written an excellent analysis of the story of Beren and Lúthien in "Real World Myth in a Secondary World: Mythological Aspects in the Story of Beren and Lúthien," in *Tolkien the Medievalist*, ed. Jane Chance, 259–67 (London and New York: Routledge, 2002, 2003); see also Jen Stevens's emphasis on another "real world myth" in their tale, in "From Catastrophe to Eucatastrophe: J.R.R. Tolkien's Transformation of Ovid's Mythic Pyramus and Thisbe into Beren and Lúthien," in *Tolkien and the Invention of Myth: A Reader*, ed. Jane Chance, 119–132 (Lexington: University Press of Kentucky, 2004).
6. See Tolkien, Appendix B to *LOTR*, 1085, 1089, discussed by West, "Her Choice Was Made," 323.
7. See the genealogical tables—for the Noldo Finwë, the Teleri brothers Olwë and Elwë, Bëor the Old, and the tribes of the Elves—that appear at the end of the text, in *Silm*, 379–83.
8. See the discussion of Anglo-Saxon gender roles in Chance, "The Structural Unity of *Beowulf*: The Problem of Grendel's Mother," 287–303, and also "Peace-Weaver, Peace Pledge: The Conventional Queen and *Ides*," chapter 1 of Chance, *Woman as Hero in Old English Literature*, 1–12; and Helen Damico and Alexandra Hennessey Olsen, eds., *New Readings on Old English Women* (Bloomington, IN: Indiana University Press, 1990).

Works Cited

Åberg, Magnus. "An Analysis of Dwarvish." Accessed on 23 August 2015. http:www.forodrim.org/daeron/md_kuzdul.pdf
Ancrene Wisse. See J.R.R. Tolkien. "Preface." Mary Salu's translation.
Anderson, Douglas A. "'An industrious little devil': E.V. Gordon as Friend and Collaborator with Tolkien." In *Tolkien the Medievalist*. Ed. Jane Chance, 15–25. London: Routledge, 2003.
Ardenne, S[imonne] R[osalie] Th[érèse] O[dile], d'. (either S.R.T.O., or S.T.R.O.). "The Man and the Scholar." In *Tolkien: Scholar and Storyteller: Essays in Memoriam*. Eds. Mary Salu and Robert T. Farrell, 33–37. Ithaca and London: Cornell University Press, 1979.

———. "A Neglected Manuscript of British History." In *English and Medieval Studies Presented to J.R.R. Tolkien on the Occasion of His Seventieth Birthday*. Eds. Norman Davis and C. L. Wrenn, 84–93. London: George Allen and Unwin, 1962.

———, ed. *An edition of Þe liflade ant te passiun of seinte Iuliene*. Bibliothèque de la Faculté de philosophie et lettres de l'Université de Liège, fasc. 61. Liège: Faculté de philosophie et lettres. Paris: E. Droz, 1936. Rev. edn., *Þe Liflade ant te Passiun of Seinte Iuliene*. EETS no. 248. London: Oxford University Press, 1961.

———, ed. *The Katharine Group, edited from MS. Bodley 34*. Bibliothèque de la Faculté de philosophie et lettres de l'Université de Liège, fasc. 215. Paris: Société d'Edition Les Belles Lettres, 1977.

———, and E.J. Dobson, eds. *Seinte Katerine, re-edited from MS. Bodley 34 and the Other Manuscripts*. EETS no. 7. Oxford: Oxford University Press, 1981.

———, and J.R.R. Tolkien. "'Iþþlen' in *Sawles Warde*." *English Studies* (Amsterdam) 28 (1947): 68–70.

———, and J.R.R. Tolkien. "MS. Bodley 34: A Re-Collation of a Collation." *Studia Neophilologica* 20 (1947–48): 65–72.

Arul, Melissa Ruth. "A Critical Study of the Self and the Other in Selected Texts of Tolkien." M.A. thesis. University of Malaya-Kuala Lumpur, 2009.

———. "Elvish Identity: A Journey." The Festival on the Shire Conference, Aberystwyth, Wales, 13 August 2010.

Bartlett, Neil. *Who Was That Man? A Present for Mr. Oscar Wilde*. London: Serpent's Tail, 1988.

Baswell, Christopher. "Men in the *Roman d'Eneas*: The Construction of Empire." In *Medieval Masculinities: Regarding Men in the Middle Ages*. Ed. Claire A. Lees, 149–68. Minneapolis: University of Minnesota Press, 1994.

Battis, Jes. "Gazing upon Sauron: Hobbits, Elves, and the Queering of the Postcolonial Optic." In *J.R.R. Tolkien Special Issue*. Guest ed. Shaun Hughes. *Modern Fiction Studies* 50 (4) (Winter 2004): 908–26.

Benson, Larry D., ed. *King Arthur's Death: The Middle English "Stanzaic Morte Arthur" and "Alliterative Morte Arthure."* TEAMS Middle English Texts Series. Rev. Edward E. Foster. Kalamazoo, MI: Medieval Institute/Western Michigan University, 1994.

Bhabha, Homi K. "Are You a Man or a Mouse?" In *Constructing Masculinity*. Eds. Maurice Berger, Brian Wallis, and Simon Watson, 57–65. New York: Routledge, 1995.

Bolintineau, Alexandra. "On the Borders of Old Stories: Enacting the Past in *Beowulf* and *The Lord of the Rings*." In *Tolkien and the Invention of Myth*. Ed. Jane Chance, 263–73. Lexington: University Press of Kentucky, 2004.

Bosworth, Joseph. *An Anglo-Saxon Dictionary*. Ed. T. Northcote Toller. London: Oxford University Press, 1898. Repr. 1976.

Brackmann, Rebecca. "Dwarves are not Heroes: Antisemitism and the Dwarves in J.R.R. Tolkien's Writing." *Mythlore* 109/110 28 (3–4) (2010): 85–106.

Bradley, S.A.J., trans. and ed. *Anglo-Saxon Poetry*. London: Dent, 1982.

Brunsdale, Mitzi M. "Norse Mythological Elements in *The Hobbit*." *Mythlore* 9 (1983): 49–50.

Bryce, Lynn. "The Influence of Scandinavian Mythology in the Works of J.R.R. Tolkien." *Edda* 7 (1983): 113–19.

Burger, Glenn. *Queering the Middle Ages*. Minneapolis: University of Minnesota Press, 2001.

Burns, Marjorie J. "Gandalf and Odin." In *Tolkien's 'Legendarium': Essays on The History of Middle-earth*. Eds. Verlyn Flieger and Carl F. Hostetter. 219–32. Westport, CT and London: Greenwood Press, 2000.

———. "Norse and Christian Gods: The Integrative Theology of J.R.R. Tolkien." In *Tolkien and the Invention of Myth: A Reader*. Ed. Jane Chance, 163–78. Lexington, KY: University Press of Kentucky, 2004.

———. *Perilous Realms: Celtic and Norse in Tolkien's Middle-earth*. Toronto: University of Toronto Press, 2005.

Callahan, Patrick J. "Tolkien's Dwarfs and the Eddas." *Tolkien Journal* 15 (1972): 20.

Carpenter, Humphrey. *The Inklings: C.S. Lewis, J.R.R. Tolkien, Charles Williams, and Their Friends*. London: George Allen & Unwin, 1978.

———. *Tolkien: A Biography*. London: Allen and Unwin; New York: Houghton Mifflin, 1977.

Chance, Jane. "Cognitive Alterities: From Cultural Studies to Neuroscience and Back Again." In *Cognitive Alterities/Neuromedievalism*. Eds. Jane Chance and Antony D. Passaro. *Postmedieval: A Journal of Medieval Cultural Studies* 3 (3) (Fall 2012): 247–61.

———. Interview and Consultation. In and for *Beyond The Lord of the Rings*. National Geographic TV. DVD, 2002. Directed by Lisa Kors.

———. *The Literary Subversions of Medieval Women*. Eds. Jane Chance, 41–62. New York and London: Palgrave Macmillan, 2007.

———. *The Lord of the Rings: The Mythology of Power*. Twayne Masterwork Studies, vol. 99. New York: Twayne/Maxwell Macmillan, 1992. Rev. edn. Lexington, KY: University Press of Kentucky, 2001.

———. "The Structural Unity of *Beowulf*: The Problem of Grendel's Mother." *Texas Studies in Literature and Language* 22 (Fall 1980): 287–303.

———. "Subversive Fantasist: Tolkien on Class Difference." In *The Lord of the Rings, 1954–2004: Scholarship in Honor of Richard E. Blackwelder*. Eds. Wayne G. Hammond and Christina Scull, 153–68. Milwaukee, WI: Marquette University Press, 2006.

———. "Tolkien and the Other: Race and Gender in Middle-earth." In *Tolkien's Modern Middle Ages*. Eds. Jane Chance and Alfred Siewers, 171–86. New York and London: Palgrave Macmillan, 2005.

———. *Tolkien's Art: A "Mythology for England."* London: Macmillan Press, 1978; New York: St. Martin's Press, 1979. Rev. edn. Lexington: University of Kentucky Press, 2001.

———. "Tolkien's Hybrid Mythology: *The Hobbit* as Old Norse 'Fairy-Story'." In *The Hobbit and Tolkien's Mythology: Essays on Revisions and Influences*. Ed. Bradford Lee Eden, 78–96. Jefferson, NC: McFarland, 2014.

———. "Tolkien's Women (and Men): The Film and the Book." In *Tolkien on Film: Essays on Peter Jackson's "The Lord of the Rings."* Ed. Janet Brennan Croft, 175–93. Altadena, CA: The Mythopoeic Press, 2004.

———. "Tough Love: Teaching the New Medievalisms." In *Defining Medievalism(s) II: Some More Perspectives*. Ed. Karl Fugelso, *Studies in Medievalism* 18 (2010): 76–98.

———. "Why Teach *The Silmarillion*? The Mythology of the Abject Hero." In *Approaches to Teaching Tolkien's Lord of the Rings and Other Works*. Ed. Leslie A. Donovan, 56–64. New York: Modern Language Association, 2015.

———. *Woman as Hero in Old English Literature*. Syracuse: Syracuse University Press, 1986. Repr. Eugene, OR: Wipf and Stock, 2005.

———, ed. *Tolkien and the Invention of Myth: A Reader*. Lexington, KY: University Press of Kentucky, 2004.

———, ed. *Tolkien the Medievalist*. Routledge Studies in Medieval Culture and Religion, vol. 3. London: Routledge, 2002; New York: Routledge, 2003.

———, and David Day. "Medievalism in Tolkien: Two Decades of Criticism in Review." In *Medievalism: Inklings and Others* (special issue). Ed. Jane Chance. *Studies in Medievalism* 3 (3) (1991): 375–88.

———, and Alfred Siewers, eds. *Tolkien's Modern Middle Ages*. New Middle Ages Series. New York and London: Palgrave Macmillan, 2005.

Christiansen, Bonniejean. "*Beowulf* and *The Hobbit*: Elegy into Fantasy in J.R.R. Tolkien's Creative Technique." Ph.D. diss. University of Southern California, 1970.

———. "Tolkien's Creative Technique: *Beowulf* and the *Hobbit*." *Orcrist* 7 (1972–1973): 16–20.

———. "Gollum's Character Transformation in *The Hobbit*." In *A Tolkien Compass*. Ed. Jared Lobdell. 9–28. LaSalle, IL: Open Court Press. Repr. New York: Ballantine Books, 1980.

Churchill, Winston. *My Early Life, 1874–1904*. New York: Scribners, 1996.

Clark, David. *Between Medieval Men: Male Friendship and Desire in Early Medieval English Literature*. Oxford: University Press, 2009.

Clark, George. "J.R.R. Tolkien and the True Hero." In *J.R.R. Tolkien and His Literary Resonances*. Ed. George Clark, 39–52. Westport, CT, and London: Greenwood Press, 2000.

Clark-Hall, John R., trans. *Beowulf and the Finnesburg Fragment*. With prefatory remarks by J.R.R. Tolkien. London: George Allen & Unwin, 1911; rev. edn. 1940, 1950.

Clute, John, and John Grant, eds. *The Encyclopedia of Fantasy*. London: Orbit, 1997.

Cohen, Jeffrey Jerome, and Bonnie Wheeler, eds. *Becoming Male in the Middle Ages*. New York: Garland, 1997.

Compact Edition of the Oxford English Dictionary, Complete Text Reproduced Micrographically. 2 vols. Oxford: University Press, 1971.

Crocker, Holly A. *Chaucer's Visions of Manhood*. New York and Houndmills, Basingstoke, and Hampshire, UK: Palgrave Macmillan, 2007.

———. "Masculinity." In *Reading the Lord of the Rings: New Writings on Tolkien's Classic.* Ed. Robert Eaglestone, 111–23.

Croft, Janet Brennan. "Walter E. Haigh, Author of *A New Glossary of the Huddersfield Dialect.*" *Tolkien Studies* 4 (2007): 184–88.

———, and Leslie A. Donovan, eds. *Perilous and Fair: Women in the Works and Life of J.R.R. Tolkien.* Altadena, CA: Mythographic Press, 2015.

Curry, Patrick. "Tolkien and His Critics: A Critique." In *Root and Branch—Approaches Towards Understanding Tolkien.* Cormarë Series 2. Ed. Thomas Honegger, 81–148. Zürich: Walking Tree, 1999.

Damico, Helen. *Beowulf's Wealtheow and the Valkyrie Tradition.* Madison: University of Wisconsin Press, 1984.

———, and Alexandra Hennessey Olsen, eds. *New Readings on Old English Women.* Bloomington, IN: Indiana University Press, 1990.

Davis, Norman. "Man and Monsters at Sutton Hoo." In *English and Medieval Studies Presented to J.R.R. Tolkien on the Occasion of his Seventieth Birthday.* Eds. Norman Davis and C. L. Wrenn, 321–29. London: Allen and Unwin, 1962.

Dimond, Andy. "The Twilight of the Elves: Ragnarök and the End of the Third Age." In *Tolkien and the Invention of Myth.* Ed. Chance, 179–89. Lexington, KY: University Press of Kentucky, 2004.

Dinshaw, Carolyn. "A Kiss is Just a Kiss: Heterosexuality and Its Consolation in *Sir Gawain and the Green Knight.*" *Diacritics* 24 (1994): 205–26.

Donovan, Leslie A. "The Valkyrie Reflex in J.R.R. Tolkien's *The Lord of the Rings*: Galadriel, Shelob, Éowyn, and Arwen." In *Tolkien the Medievalist*, vol. 3. Ed. Chance, 106–32. London: Routledge, 2002; New York: Routledge, 2003.

Doty, Alexander. *Making Things Perfectly Queer: Interpreting Mass Culture.* Minneapolis and London: University of Minnesota Press, 1993.

Drout, Michael D.C. "A Mythology for Anglo-Saxon England." In *Tolkien and the Invention of Myth.* Ed. Chance, 229–47. Lexington, KY: University Press of Kentucky, 2004.

Eaglestone, Robert, ed. *The Lord of the Rings: New Writings on Tolkien's Classic.* London and New York: Continuum, 2005.

Edelman, Lee. *No Future: Queer Theory and the Death Drive.* Durham and London: Duke University Press, 2004.

Eilmann, Julian and Allan Turner, eds. *Tolkien's Poetry.* Zurich, Switzerland, and Jena, Germany: Walking Tree Press, 2013.

Emery, Elizabeth. "Medievalism and the Middle Ages." *Studies in Medievalism* 17 (2009): 106–17.

Evans, Jonathan. "The Dragon-Lore of Middle-earth: Tolkien and Old English and Old Norse Tradition." In *J.R.R. Tolkien and His Literary Resonances: Views of Middle-earth.* Ed. George Clark and Daniel Timmons, 21–38. Westport, CT, and London: Greenwood Press, 2000.

Fehrenbacher, Richard W. "*Beowulf* as Fairy-story: Enchanting the Elegiac in *The Two Towers*." *Tolkien Studies* 3 (2006): 101–15.
Fimi, Dimitra. *Tolkien, Race, and Cultural History: From Fairies to Hobbits*. London: Palgrave Macmillan, 2009.
Fisher, Sheila. "Leaving Morgan Aside: Women, History, and Revisionism in *Sir Gawain and the Green Knight*." In *The Passing of Arthur: New Essays on the Arthurian Tradition*. Eds. Christopher Baswell and William Sharpe, 129–51. New York: Garland, 1988.
Flieger, Verlyn. "A Mythology for Finland: Tolkien and Lönnrot as Mythmakers." In *Tolkien and the Invention of Myth*. Ed. Chance, 277–83. Lexington, KY: University Press of Kentucky, 2004.
———. "Naming the Unnamable: The Neoplatonic 'One' in Tolkien's *Silmarillion*." In *Diakonia: Studies in Honor of Robert T. Meyer*. Eds. Thomas Halton and Joseph P. Williman, 127–33. Washington, DC: Catholic University of America Press, 1986.
———. "'There Would Always Be a Fairy-Tale': J.R.R. Tolkien and the Folklore Controversy." In *Tolkien the Medievalist*. Ed. Jane Chance, 26–35.
———, and Carl F. Hostetter, eds. *Tolkien's Legendarium: Essays on the History of Middle-earth*. Westport, CT, and London: Greenwood Press, 2000.
Garth, John. "'The road from adaptation to invention': How Tolkien Came to the Brink of Middle-earth in 1914." *Tolkien Studies* 11 (2014): 1–44.
———. *Tolkien and the Great War: The Threshold of Middle-earth*. London: HarperCollins, 2003.
———. *Tolkien at Exeter College: How an Oxford Undergraduate Created Middle-earth*. Oxford: Privately printed by Exeter College, 2014.
Gaunt, Simon. "From Epic to Romance: Gender and Sexuality in the *Roman d'Eneas*." *Romanic Review* 83 (1992): 1–27.
Gay, David Elton. "J.R.R. Tolkien and the *Kalevala*: Some Thoughts on the Finnish Origins of Tom Bombadil and Treebeard." In *Tolkien and the Invention of Myth*. Ed. Jane Chance, 295–304.
Giddings, Robert, ed. *J.R.R. Tolkien: This Far Land*. London: Vision Press; Totowa, NJ: Barnes & Noble Books, 1983.
Gilliver, Peter, Jeremy Marshall, and Edmund Weiner. *The Ring of Words: Tolkien and the Oxford English Dictionary*. Oxford: University Press, 2006.
Goldberg, Jonathan and Madhavi Menon. "Queering History." *PMLA* 120 (2005): 1608–17.
Gordon, E[ric].V[alentine], ed. *The Battle of Maldon*. London: Methuen, 1937.
———, ed. *Pearl*. Pref. by Ida Gordon. Oxford: Clarendon Press, 1953.
Gueroult, Denys. "'Now Read On.' Radio Interview with J.R.R. Tolkien." 16 December 1970. London: BBC Radio 4. BBC Cassettes: 1980.
———. "J.R.R. Tolkien, An Interview." Transcript of BBC Radio Interview. *News From Bree* (19 November 1974): 3–5.

Haigh, Walter E. *A New Glossary of the Dialect of the Huddersfield District*, with Foreword by J.R.R. Tolkien. London: Oxford University Press, 1928.

Hammond, Wayne G., and Douglas A. Anderson. *J.R.R. Tolkien: A Descriptive Bibliography*. Winchester, UK: St. Paul's Bibliographies; New Castle, Delaware: Oak Knoll Books, 1993.

———, and Christina Scull. *The Lord of the Rings: A Reader's Companion*. London: HarperCollins, 2005; repr. Boston: Houghton Mifflin, 2008.

Helms, Randel. *Tolkien's World*. Boston: Houghton Mifflin, 1974.

Hiley, Margaret, and Frank Weinreich, eds. *Tolkien's Shorter Works: Essays of the Jena Conference 2007*. Conmarë Series 17. Zurich, Switzerland, and Jena, Germany: Walking Tree Publishers, 2008.

Hogan, Patrick Colm. *Understanding Nationalism: On Narrative, Neuroscience, and Identity*. Columbus, OH: Ohio State University, 2009.

Hollander, Lee M., ed. *The Poetic Edda*. Austin: University of Texas Press, 1962.

Holmes, John R. "Oaths and Oath-Breaking: Analogues of the Old English Comitatus in Tolkien's Myth." In *Tolkien and the Invention of Myth*. Ed. Jane Chance, 249–61. Lexington, KY: University Press of Kentucky, 2004.

Holsinger, Bruce. *The Premodern Condition*. Chicago: University of Chicago Press, 2005.

Honegger, Thomas. "*The Homecoming of Beorhtnoth*: Philology and the Literary Muse." *Tolkien Studies* 4 (2007): 189–99.

Hostetter, Carl J., and Arden R. Smith. "A Mythology for England." *Proceedings of the J.R.R. Tolkien Centenary Conference*, Keble College, Oxford, 1992. Ed. Patricia Reynolds and Glen H. GoodKnight. *Mythlore* 80/*Mallorn* 30 (Winter 1996): 281–90.

Hughes, Shaun F. D., guest ed. *J.R.R. Tolkien Special Issue. Modern Fiction Studies* 50 (4) (Winter 2004).

Inglis, Fred. "Gentility and Powerlessness: Tolkien and the New Class." In *J.R.R. Tolkien: This Far Land*. Ed. Robert Giddings, 25–41. London: Vision Press; Totowa, NJ: Barnes & Noble Books, 1983.

Johnson, Glen. "Queering the Genre." *Harvard Gay and Lesbian Review* 2 (2) (Spring 1995): 21–23.

Jones, Garrett. *Alfred and Arthur: An Historic Friendship*. Hertford, UK: Authors Online, 2001.

Jónsson, Finnur. *Atlakviða*. Copenhagen: Thieles Bogtrykkeri, 1912.

Kane, Douglas Charles. *Arda Reconstructed: The Creation of the Published Silmarillon*. Bethlehem, PA: Lehigh University Press, 2009.

Keen, Maurice. *Chivalry*. New Haven: Yale University Press, 1984.

Kendrick, T.D. "The Sutton Hoo Finds. VI. Sutton Hoo and Anglo-Saxon Archaeology." *British Museum Quarterly* 13 (1939): 116–28.

Kinney, Clare R. "The (Dis)Embodied Hero and the Signs of Manhood in *Sir Gawain and the Green Knight*." In *Medieval Masculinities: Regarding Men in the Middle Ages.* Ed. Clare A. Lees, 47–57. Minneapolis: University of Minnesota Press, 1994.

Klaeber, Fr[iedrich], ed. *Beowulf and the Fight at Finnsburg.* 3rd edn. Boston: D.C. Heath, 1950.

———. 4th edn. With supplemental materials by R. D. Fulk, Robert E. Bjork, and John D. Niles. Toronto: University of Toronto Press, 2008.

Klosowska, Anna. *Queer Love in the Middle Ages.* New York: Palgrave Macmillan, 2005.

Kristeva, Julia. *Pouvoirs de l'horreur. Essai sur l'abjection.* Paris: Le Seuil, 1980.

———. *Powers of Horror: An Essay on Abjection.* Trans. Leon S. Roudiez. European Perspectives. New York: Columbia University Press, 1982.

Lafontaine, David. "Sex and Subtext in Tolkien's World." *The Gay and Lesbian Review/Worldwide* (November–December 2015): 14–17.

Lang, Andrew. *The Lilac Fairy Book.* London: Longmans, Green, 1910; repr. New York: Dover Books, 1968.

———. "The Story of Sigurd." In *The Red Fairy Book*, 1890. Repr. New York: Dover, 1966. 357–67.

Lees, Clare A., "Men and Beowulf." In *Medieval Masculinities: Regarding Men in the Middle Ages.* Ed. Lees, 129–48. Medieval Cultures 7. Minnesota: University of Minnesota Press, 1994.

Lévinas, Emmanuel. *God, Death, and Time.* Trans. Bertina Bergo. Stanford: Stanford University Press, 2000.

———. *Time and the Other* [and additional essays]. Trans. Richard A. Cohen. Pittsburgh, PA: Duquesne University Press, 1987.

———. *Totality and Infinity: An Essay on Exteriority.* Trans. Alphonso Lingis. Duquesne Studies Philosophical Series, vol. 24. Pittsburgh, PA: Duquesne University Press, 1969.

Lönnrot, Elias, comp. *Kalevala: The Land of Heroes.* 1849. Trans. W. F. Kirby. London: J. M. Dent, 1907.

———. *The Kalevala.* Trans. Keith Bosley. Oxford and New York: Oxford University Press, 1989.

Macaulay, Thomas Babington, *The Lays of Ancient Rome.* London: Longman, 1847.

———. http://www.victorianweb.org/authors/macaulay/lays/4.html

Macdonald, Helen. *H is for Hawk.* London: Grove Press, 2015.

Magnússon, Eiríkr, and William Morris, trans. *Völsunga Saga: The Story of the Volsungs and Niblungs, with Certain Songs from the Elder Edda.* Ed. H. Halliday Sparling. London: Walter Scott, 1870; repr. 1888.

Marie de France. *Lais.* Ed. Alfred Ewert. 1944; repr. Bristol: Bristol Classical Press and London: Gerald Duckworth; Newburyport, MA: Focus Information Press, 1995.

———. *The Lais.* Trans. Robert Hanning and Joan Ferrante. Grand Rapids, MI: Baker Books, 1978.

Matthews, Dorothy. "The Psychological Journey of Bilbo Baggins." In *A Tolkien Compass.* Ed. Jared Lobdell, 29–42. Lasalle, IL: Open Court Press, 1975. Repr. New York: Ballantine Books, 1980.

McFadden, Brian. "Fear of Difference, Fear of Death: The *Sigelwara*, Tolkien's Swertings, and Racial Difference." In *Tolkien's Modern Middle Ages.* Ed. Jane Chance, 155–69. New Middle Ages Series. New York and London: Palgrave Macmillan, 2005.

McGatch, Milton. "The Medievalist and Cultural Literacy." *Speculum* 66 (1991): 591–604.

Michel, Laura. "Politically Incorrect: Tolkien, Women, and Feminism." In *Tolkien and Modernity.* Eds. Frank Weinreich and Thomas Honegger, 55–76. Bochum and Jena, Germany: Walking Tree Publishers, 2006.

Mitchell, Bruce. "J.R.R. Tolkien and Old English Studies." In *Proceedings of the J.R.R. Tolkien Centenary Conference*, Keble College, Oxford, 1992. Eds. Patricia Reynolds and Glen H. GoodKnight, 206–11. *Mythlore* 80/*Mallorn* 30 (Winter 1996).

Moffat, Wendy. "The Narrative Case for Queer Biography." In *Narrative Theory Unbound: Queer and Feminist Interventions.* Ed. Robyn R. Warhol, 210–26. Columbus: Ohio State University Press, 2015.

Morland, Iain and Annabelle Wilcox, eds. *Queer Theory.* Houndmills, UK, and New York: Palgrave Macmillan. 2004–5.

Morris, William. *The Defence of Guenevere and Other Poems.* Ed. Robert Steele. London: Alexander Moring/The De La More Press, 1904.

———. Trans. *Volsunga Saga: The Story of the Volsungs and the Niblungs.* 1870. Repr. with an Intro. and Glossary by Robert W. Gutman. New York: Collier Books, 1962.

Morson, Gary Saul. *Narrative and Freedom: The Shadows of Time.* New Haven and London: Yale University Press, 1994.

Müllenhof, Karl. "Der Mythus von Beóvulf." *Zeitschrift für deutsches Altertum und deutsche Literatur* 7 (1849): 419–41.

———. "Sceáf und seine Nachkommen." *Zeitschrift für deutsches Altertum und deutsche Literatur* 7 (1849): 410–19.

Nagy, Gergely. "The 'Lost' Subject of Middle-earth: The Constitution of the Subject in the Figure of Gollum in *The Lord of the Rings.*" *Tolkien Studies* 3 (2006): 57–80.

———. "Saving the Myths: The Re-Creation of Mythology in Plato and Tolkien." In *Tolkien and the Invention of Myth.* Ed. Jane Chance, 81–100. Lexington, KY: University Press of Kentucky, 2004.

Newton, Sam. "*Beowulf* and the East Anglian Royal Pedigree." In *The Age of Sutton Hoo: The Seventh Century in Northwestern Europe.* Ed. M.O.H Carver, 65–74. Woodbridge, Suffolk, UK: Boydell, 1992.

———. "*Beowulf* and Sutton Hoo." *Saxon: The Newsletter of the Sutton Hoo Society* 21 (1994): 1–8.
———. *The Origins of Beowulf and the Pre-Viking Kingdom of East Anglia*. Cambridge: D.S. Brewer, 1993.
Nitzsche, Jane Chance. *See* Jane Chance.
Norman, Philip. "The Prevalence of Hobbits." *New York Times Magazine*. 15 January 1967. 100.
O'Neill, Timothy R. *The Individuated Hobbit: Jung, Tolkien, and the Archetypes of Middle-Earth*. Boston: Houghton Mifflin, 1979.
Orchard, Andy. "Tolkien, the Monsters, and the Critics: Back to *Beowulf*." In *Scholarship and Fantasy: Proceedings of the Tolkien Phenomenon, May 1992, Turku, Finland, Anglicana Turkuensia* no. 12. Ed. K. J. Battarbee, 73–84. Turku: University of Turku, 1992.
O'Rourke, Michael. "Becoming (Queer) Medieval: Queer Methodologies in Medieval Studies: Where Are We Now." In *Roundtable: Queer Methodologies and/or Queers in Medieval Studies: Where Are We Now?*, 9–14. UK: International Congress of the European Middle Ages, University of Leeds, July 2002. http://ir.uiowa.edu/cgi/viewcontent.cgi?article=1200&context=mff. Accessed 21 September 2015.
Otty, Nick. "The Structuralist's Guide to Middle-earth." In *J.R.R. Tolkien: This Far Land*. Ed. Giddings, 154–78.
Priestman, Judith, ed. *Life and Legend. An Exhibition to Commemorate the Centenary of the Birth of J.R.R. Tolkien* (1892–1973). Oxford: Bodleian Library, 1992.
Pugh, Tison. *Queer Chivalry: Medievalism and the Myth of White Masculinity in Southern Literature*. Baton Rouge: Louisiana State University Press, 2013.
———. "Queering the Medieval Dead: History, Horror, and Masculinity in Sam Raimi's *Evil Dead* Trilogy." In *Race, Class, and Gender in "Medieval" Cinema*. Eds. Lynn Ramey and Tison Pugh, 123–36. New York and London: Palgrave Macmillan, 2007.
———. *Queering Medieval Genres*. New York: Palgrave Macmillan, 2004.
———, ed. *Sexuality and its Queer Discontents in Middle English Literature*. New York: Palgrave Macmillan, 2008.
———, and Angela Jane Weisl, eds. *Medievalisms: Making the Past the Present*. London: Routledge, 2012.
———, and Kathleen Coyne Kelly, eds. *Queer Movie Medievalisms*. Queer Interventions Series. Farnham, Surrey, UK, and Burlington, VT: Ashgate Press, 2009.
Rateliff, John D. "'And All The Days of Her Life Are Forgotten': *The Lord of the Rings* as Mythic Prehistory." In *The Lord of the Rings, 1954–2004: Scholarship*

in *Honor of Richard E. Blackwelder*. Ed. Wayne G. Hammond and Christina Scull, 67–100. Milwaukee: Marquette University Press, 2006.

———. *The History of the Hobbit*: Part 1, *Mr. Baggins*; Part 2: *Return to Bag-End*. 2 vols. London: HarperCollins, 2007–2008.

———. "The Missing Women: J.R.R. Tolkien's Lifelong Support for Women's Higher Education." In *Perilous and Fair: Women in the Works and Life of J.R.R. Tolkien*. Ed. Janet Brennan Croft and Leslie A. Donovan, 41–69. Altadena, CA: Mythopoeic Press, 2015.

Rearick III, Anderson. "Why is the Only Good Orc a Dead Orc? The Dark Face of Racism Examined in Tolkien's World." *Modern Fiction Studies* 50 (2004): 861–75.

Reilly, R. J. "Tolkien and the Fairy-Story." In *Tolkien and the Critics*. Ed. Isaacs and Zimbardo, 128–50.1968. Repr. as *Understanding "The Lord of the Rings."* Ed. Isaacs and Zimbardo. 2004. *See* Isaacs.

Ripley, William Z. *The Races of Europe*. London: Kegan Paul, 1899.

Rosebury, Brian. *Tolkien: A Cultural Phenomenon*. Houndmills, Basingstoke, Hampshire: Palgrave Macmillan, 2003. rev. edn. of *Tolkien: A Critical Assessment*, 1992.

Ryan, J. S. "Folktale, Fairy Tale, and the Creation of a Story." In *Tolkien: New Critical Perspectives*. Ed. Isaacs and Zimbardo, 19–39. Repr. in *Understanding "The Lord of the Rings."* Ed. Zimbardo and Isaacs, 106–21.

Salu, Mary, and Robert T. Farrell, eds. *J.R.R. Tolkien: Scholar and Storyteller: Essays in Memoriam*. Ithaca and London: Cornell University Press, 1979.

Saxton, Benjamin. "Tolkien and Bakhtin on Authorship, Literary Freedom, and Alterity." *Tolkien Studies* 10 (2013): 167–84.

Scull, Christina, and Wayne G. Hammond. *The J.R.R. Tolkien Companion and Guide: Chronology; Reader's Guide*. 2 vols. London: HarperCollins, 2006.

Sedgwick, Eve Kosofsky. *Touching Feeling: Affect, Pedagogy, Performativity*. Durham: Duke University Press, 2003.

Selling, Kim. "'Fantastic Neo-Medievalism': The Images of the Middle Ages in Popular Fantasy." In *Flashes of the Fantastic: International Conference on the Fantastic in the Arts*. Ed. David Ketterer, 211–18. Westport, CT: Praeger, 2004.

Shippey, T[om] A. "Grimm, Grundtvig, Tolkien: Nationalisms and the Invention of Mythologies." In *The Ways of Creative Mythologies: Imagined Worlds and Their Makers*. 2 vols. Ed. Maria Kateeva, 1:1–17. Telford: Tolkien Society Press, 2000. Repr. in Tom Shippey, *Roots and Branches: Selected Papers on Tolkien*. Zollikofen, Switzerland Walking Tree Press, 2007. 79–96.

———. *J.R.R. Tolkien: Author of the Century*. London: HarperCollins, 2000.

———. "Light-elves, Dark-elves, and Others: Tolkien's Elvish Problem." *Tolkien Studies* 1 (2004): 1–15.

———. "Medievalisms and Why They Matter." *Studies in Medievalism* 17 (2009): 63–75.

———. *The Road to Middle-earth.* 1982. Rev. edn. London: Allen and Unwin, 1992.

———. "Tolkien and the Appeal of the Pagan: *Edda* and *Kalevala*." In *Tolkien and the Invention of Myth*. Ed. Chance, 145–61.

———. "Tolkien and the *Gawain*-poet." In *Proceedings of the J.R.R. Tolkien Centenary Conference, Keble College, Oxford, 1992.* Ed. Reynolds, 213–20. Repr. in Shippey, *Roots and Branches,* 61–78.

———. "Tolkien and Iceland: The Philology of Envy." In *Roots and Branches*. Ed. Shippey, 187–202.

———. "Writer of Alliterative Poetry in Modern English." In *Tolkien's Poetry*. Ed. Julian Eilmann and Allen Turner, 11–28. Zurich, Switzerland, and Jena, Germany: Walking Tree Publishers, 2013.

———, ed. *The Shadow-Walkers: Jacob Grimm's Mythology of the Monstrous*. Tempe, AZ: Arizona Center for the Study of Medieval and Renaissance Studies/Brepols, 2005.

Sibley, Brian, presenter. *J.R.R. Tolkien: An Audio Portrait*. London: BBC, 2001.

Sinex, Margaret. "'Monsterized Saracens,' Tolkien's Haradrim, and Other Medieval 'Fantasy Products.'" *Tolkien Studies* 7 (2010): 175–96.

Smol, Anna. "Frodo's Body: Liminality and The Experience of War." In *The Body in Tolkien's Legendarium*. Ed. Christopher Vaccaro, 39–63. Jefferson, NC: McFarland, 2013.

———. "'Oh ... oh ... Frodo!' Readings of Male Intimacy in *The Lord of the Rings*." In Hughes, *Tolkien Special Issue, Modern Fiction Studies* 50 (4) (Winter 2004): 949–79.

Spearing, A.C. *The Gawain-Poet: A Critical Study*. Cambridge: University Press, 1970.

Stenström, Anders. "A Mythology? For England?" In *Proceedings of the J.R.R. Tolkien Centenary*. Ed. Reynolds, 310–14.

Stevens, Jen. "From Catastrophe to Eucatastrophe: Tolkien's Transformation of Ovid's Mythic Pyramus and Thisbe into Beren and Lúthien." In *Tolkien and the Invention of Myth*. Ed. Chance, 119–32.

Strong, Andrew. *Beowulf, translated into Modern English Rhyming Verse*. London: Constable, 1925.

Tadie, Joseph. "'That the World Not Be Usurped': Emmanuel Levinas and J.R.R. Tolkien on Serving the Other as Release From Bondage." In *Tolkien Among the Moderns*. Ed. Ralph C. Woods, 219–45. Notre Dame, IN: University of Notre Dame Press, 2015.

Tennyson, Alfred Lord. *Idylls of the King*. Ed. J. M. Gray. London: Penguin, 1983.

Tolkien, J.R.R. *The Adventures of Tom Bombadil and Other Verses From the Red Book*. London: Allen & Unwin, 1962. Repr. in Tolkien, *The Tolkien Reader*. New York: Ballantine Books, 1966, 6–64. Rev. edn., *The Adventures of Tom Bombadil and Other Verses From the Red Book*. Ed. Christina Scull and Wayne Hammond. London: HarperCollins, 2014.

———. "*Ancrene Wisse* and *Hali Meiðhad*." *Essays and Studies by Members of the English Association* 14 (1929): 104–26.

———. *The Annotated Hobbit*. Ed. Douglas A. Anderson. London: HarperCollins, 1988. 2nd edn. Boston: Houghton Mifflin, 2003.

———. "The Battle of the Eastern Field." *King Edward's School Chronicle*, 26 (186) (March 1911): 22–26. Repr. in *Mallorn*, 12 (1978): 24–28.

———. *Beowulf and the Critics*. Ed. Michael D.C. Drout. Medieval and Renaissance Texts and Studies, vol. 248. Tempe: Arizona Center for Medieval and Renaissance Studies, 2002. Rev. edn., 2011.

———. "Beowulf: The Monsters and the Critics." *Proceedings of the British Academy* 22 (1937): 245–95. Repr. in *The Monsters and the Critics and Other Essays*. Ed. Christopher Tolkien, 5–48. London: Allen & Unwin, 1983; Boston: Houghton Mifflin, 1984. Also in *Beowulf: A Verse Translation*. Trans. Seamus Heaney. Ed. Daniel Donoghue, 103–29. New York: W.W. Norton. 2002.

———. *Beowulf: A Translation and Commentary, Together with Sellic Spell*. Ed. Christopher Tolkien. Boston and New York: Houghton Mifflin Harcourt, 2014.

———. *The Book of Lost Tales, Part 1*. Ed. Christopher Tolkien. *The History of Middle-earth*, vol. 1. London: George Allen & Unwin, 1983; Boston: Houghton Mifflin, 1984.

———. *The Book of Lost Tales, Part 2*. Ed. Christopher Tolkien. *The History of Middle-earth*, vol. 2. London: Allen & Unwin; Boston: Houghton Mifflin, 1984.

———. "Chaucer as a Philologist: *The Reeve's Tale*." *Transactions of the Philological Society* (1934): 1–70.

———. *The Children of Hurin*. Ed. Christopher Tolkien. London: HarperCollins, 2007.

———. "The Devil's Coach-Horses." *Review of English Studies* 1 (1925): 331–36.

———. "English and Welsh." In *The Monsters and the Critics and Other Essays*. Ed. Christopher Tolkien, 162–97. London: George Allen & Unwin, 1983.

———. "Errantry." *Oxford Magazine* 52 (5) (9 November 1933): 180.

———. *The Fall of Arthur*. Ed. Christopher Tolkien. Boston and London: Houghton Mifflin Harcourt, 2013.

———. *Farmer Giles of Ham*. London: George Allen & Unwin, 1949; Boston: Houghton Mifflin, 1950. Repr. in *The Tolkien Reader*. 1966.

———. *Finn and Hengest: The Fragment and the Episode*. Ed. Alan Bliss. London: George Allen & Unwin, 1982.

———. Foreword to Walter E. Haigh, *A New Glossary of the Dialect of the Huddersfield District*. London: Oxford University Press, 1928, xiii–xviii.

———. "Goblin Feet." *Oxford Poetry 1914–1916*. Oxford: B.H. Blackwell, 1917. 120–21.

———. *The History of Middle-earth*. Ed. Christopher Tolkien. 12 vols. London: Allen and Unwin and HarperCollins; Boston: Houghton Mifflin, 1983–1996.

———. "The Hoard." Repr. in Tolkien, *The Adventures of Tom Bombadil*. Eds. Christina Scull and Wayne Hammond, 98–102. London: HarperCollins, 2014.

———. *The Hobbit; or There and Back Again*. 3rd edn. London: Allen & Unwin, 1937, 1966; Boston: Houghton Mifflin, 1938, 1967; repr. Boston: Houghton Mifflin, 1997.

———. "The Homecoming of Beorhtnoth Beorhthelm's Son." *Essays and Studies by Members of the English Association*, 6 (1953): 1–18. Repr. in *The Tolkien Reader*. New York: Ballantine, 1966, 1–28; and Tolkien. *The Monsters and the Critics and Other Essays*. Ed. Christopher Tolkien, 72–108.

———. Interview with Denys Gueroult, "Now Read On." BBC Radio 4 (1964). Transcript printed in "J.R.R. Tolkien, An Interview." *News From Bree* (19 November, 1974): 3–5. London: BBC Cassettes: 1980.

———. "Iúmonna Gold Galdre Bewunden." *Gryphon* 4 (4) (January 1923): 123; repr. in Tolkien. *The Annotated Hobbit*. Ed. Douglas Anderson, 288–89 (A3dd-ee).

———. "The Istari." In *Unfinished Tales of Númenor and Middle-earth*. Ed. Christopher Tolkien. London: Allen & Unwin, 1979; Boston: Houghton Mifflin, 1980.

———. *The Lays of Beleriand*. Ed. Christopher Tolkien. *The History of Middle-Earth*, vol. 3. London: HarperCollins, 1985.

———. *The Legend of Sigurd and Gudrún*. Ed. Christopher Tolkien. London: HarperCollins; Boston: Houghton Mifflin, 2009.

———. "Letter to the Editor." *The Observer*, 20 February 1938: 9.

———. *The Letters of J.R.R. Tolkien: A Selection*. Ed. Humphrey Carpenter with assistance from Christopher Tolkien. London: George Allen and Unwin, 1981; Boston and New York: Houghton Mifflin, 1981; London: HarperCollins, 1995.

———. *The Lord of the Rings*. 1954–1955. 2nd edn. with Note on the Text by Douglas A. Anderson. London: HarperCollins, 1994.

———. "Middle English 'Losenger': Sketch of an Etymological and Semantic Enquiry." *Essais de philologie moderne* 129 (1951): 63–76.

———. *A Middle English Vocabulary, Designed for Use With Sisam's Fourteenth-Century Verse and Prose*. Oxford: Clarendon Press, 1922. Repr. 1925.

———. *The Monsters and the Critics and Other Essays*. Ed. Christopher Tolkien. London: Allen & Unwin, 1983. Boston: Houghton Mifflin, 1984.

———. *Morgoth's Ring*. Ed. Christopher Tolkien. *The History of Middle-earth*, vol. 10. London: HarperCollins, 1990.

———. "The Name 'Nodens'." Appendix I. In R.E.M. Wheeler and T.V. Wheeler. *Report on the Excavation of the Prehistoric, Roman, and Post-Roman Site in Lydney Park, Gloucestershire*. 132–37. Reports of the Research Committee of the Society of Antiquaries of London, no. 9. London: Oxford University Press, 1932. Repr. *Tolkien Studies* 4 (2007): 177–83.

———. *The Old English Exodus: Text, Translation, and Commentary by J.R.R.Tolkien*, editorial apparatus by Joan Turville Petre. Oxford: Oxford University Press, 1981.

———. "On Fairy-Stories." In *Essays Presented to Charles Williams*. Ed. C.S. Lewis. London: Oxford University Press, 1945.

———. "On Translating *Beowulf*." In *The Monsters and the Critics*. Ed. Christopher Tolkien, 49–72.

———. *The Peoples of Middle-earth*. Ed. Christopher Tolkien. *The History of Middle-earth*, vol. 12. London: HarperCollins, 1996.

———. Preface to *The Ancrene Riwle* (The Corpus MS: Ancrene Wisse). Trans. M.B. Salu. London: Burns & Oates, 1955; Notre Dame, IN: University of Notre Dame Press, 1956.

———. "Prefatory Remarks on a Prose Translation of *Beowulf*." In *Beowulf and the Finnsburg Fragment*. Trans. John R. Clark Hall. 1911. Rev. edn. London: Allen & Unwin, 1972.

———. "A Secret Vice." In *The Monsters and the Critics and Other Essays*. Ed. Christopher Tolkien, 198–223. Boston: Houghton Mifflin, 1983.

———. *A Secret Vice*. Eds. Dimitra Fimi and Andrews Higgens. London: HarperCollins, 2016.

———. *The Shaping of Middle Earth*. Ed. Christopher Tolkien. *The History of Middle-earth*, vol. 4. London: HarperCollins, 1986.

———. "Sigelwara Land. pts. 1 and 2." *Medium Aevum* 1 (1932): 183–96; and 3 (1934): 1–70.

———. *The Silmarillion*. Ed. Christopher Tolkien. 1976; 2nd edn. London: HarperCollins, 1999; Boston: Houghton Mifflin, 2001.

———. "Sir Gawain and the Green Knight." In *The Monsters and the Critics*. Ed. Christopher Tolkien, 72–108.

———. *Smith of Wootton Major*. London: George Allen & Unwin; Boston: Houghton Mifflin, 1967.

———. *Smith of Wootton Major*. Ed. Verlyn Flieger. London: HarperCollins, 2005.

———. "'The Story of Kullervo' and Essays on *Kalevala*." Ed. Verlyn Flieger. *Tolkien Studies* 7 (2010): 211–78. Repr. in *The Story of Kullervo*. Ed. Verlyn Flieger. London: Harper Collins, 2015.

———. *Tolkien on Fairy-stories: Expanded Edition, with Commentary and Notes*. Eds. Verlyn Flieger and Douglas A. Anderson. London: HarperCollins, 2008.

———. *The Tolkien Reader*. 2nd edn. New York: Ballantine, 1966.

———. *Tree and Leaf, Including the Poem "Mythopoeia."* Intro. Christopher Tolkien. Rev. edn. London: Allen & Unwin, 1988; Boston: Houghton Mifflin, 1989.

———. *The Treason of Isengard.* Ed. Christopher Tolkien. *The History of Middle-earth,* vol. 7. London: HarperCollins, 1989.

———. *Unfinished Tales of Númenor and Middle-earth.* Ed. Christopher Tolkien. London: Allen and Unwin, 1979; Boston: Houghton Mifflin, 1980.

———. "Valedictory Address to the University of Oxford, 5 June 1959." In *The Monsters and the Critics.* Ed. Christopher Tolkien, 224–40. Also in Salu and Farrell, *J.RR. Tolkien: Scholar and Storyteller: Essays in Memoriam.* 16–32.

———, ed. *The English Text of the Ancrene Riwle: Ancrene Wisse, edited from MS Corpus Christi College Cambridge 402.* Early English Text Society 249. London: Oxford University Press, 1962.

———. Trans. *Sir Gawain and the Green Knight, Pearl, Sir Orfeo.* Ed. Christopher Tolkien. London: George Allen & Unwin, 1975.

———, and E.V. Gordon, eds. *Sir Gawain and the Green Knight.* 1925. 2nd edn. Rev. Norman Davis. Oxford: Clarendon Press, 1968.

Tolkien, John, and Priscilla. *The Tolkien Family Album.* London: HarperCollins, 1992.

Tolkien Remembered. DVD video (38 minutes). Princeton, NJ: Films for the Humanities and Sciences, 2005.

Toller, T. Northcote. *An Anglo-Saxon Dictionary Based on the Manuscript Collections of the Late Joseph Bosworth. Supplement.* London: Oxford University Press, 1921. Repr. 1966.

Traub, Valerie, "The New Unhistoricism in Queer Studies." *PMLA* 128 (2013): 21–39.

Turgon (David E. Smith) [aka Douglas A. Anderson]. Ed. *The Tolkien Fan's Medieval Reader.* Cold Spring Harbor, NY: Cold Spring Books, 2004.

Vaccaro, Christopher, ed. *The Body in Tolkien's Legendarium: Essays on Middle-earth Corporeality.* Jefferson, NC: McFarland, 2013.

———. "To All My Elf Friends and Wizard Pupils, 'It Gets Better': Medieval Queer in Modern Categories of Tolkien's *Lord of the Rings.*" Queer Tolkien Session. Forty-Eighth International Congress on the Middle Ages. Kalamazoo, MI: Western Michigan University. 10 May 2013.

Vink, Renée. "'Jewish' Dwarves: Tolkien and Anti-Semitic Stereotyping." *Tolkien Studies* 10 (2013): 123–46.

Webster's New Universal Unabridged Dictionary. New York: Barnes and Noble, 1996.

West, Richard C. "'Her Choice Was Made and Her Doom Appointed': Tragedy and Divine Comedy in the Tale of Aragorn and Arwen." In *The Lord of the Rings 1954–2004.* Ed. Hammond, 317–29.

———. "Real World Myth in a Secondary World: Mythological Aspects in the Story of Beren and Lúthien." In *Tolkien the Medievalist*. Ed. Chance, 259–67.
———. "Setting the Rocket Off in Story: The *Kalevala* as the Germ of Tolkien's *Legendarium*." In *Tolkien and the Invention of Myth*. Ed. Chance, 285–94.
———. "Turin's Ofermod: An Old English Theme in the Development of the Story of Túrin." In *Tolkien's Legendarium*. Ed. Flieger, 233–45.
White, T. H. *Goshawk*. London: Cape, 1939.
———. *The Once and Future King*. London: G.P. Putnam's, 1938–58.
Wilcox, Miranda. "Exilic Imagining in *The Seafarer* and *The Lord of the Rings*." In *Tolkien the Medievalist*. Ed. Chance, 133–54.
Yandell, Stephen. "Niggle, Smith, and Giles: Medieval as Queer." Queer Tolkien Session. Forty-Eighth International Congress on the Middle Ages. Kalamazoo, MI: Western Michigan University. 10 May 2013.
Yates, Jessica. "'The Battle of the Eastern Field': A Commentary." *Mallorn* 13 (1979): 3–5.
Zaleski, Philip, and Carol Zaleski. *The Fellowship: The Literary Lives of the Inklings, J.R.R. Tolkien, C.S. Lewis, Owen Barfield, and Charles Williams*. New York: Farrar, Straus, and Giroux, 2015.
Zettersten, Arne. "The AB Language Lives." In *The Lord of the Rings, 1954–2004: Scholarship in Honor of Richard E. Blackweld*. Ed. Hammond, 13–24.
Zimbardo, Rose A., and Neil D. Isaacs, eds. *Understanding The Lord of the Rings: The Best of Tolkien Criticism*. Boston: Houghton Mifflin, 2004.
Zipes, Jack. *Breaking the Magic Spell: Radical Themes of Folk and Fairy Tales*, 1979. Rev. edn., Lexington: University of Kentucky Press, 2002.
———. *Fairy Tales and the Art of Subversion: The Classical Genre for Children and the Forces of Civilization*. London: Methuen, 1988. Rev. edn., 2011.
Žižek, Slavoj, Eric L. Santner, and Kenneth Reinhard. *The Neighbor: Three Inquiries in Political Theology*. Chicago and London: University of Chicago Press, 2005.
Zunshine, Lisa. *Strange Concepts and the Stories They Make Possible: Cognition, Culture, Narrative*. Baltimore, MD: Johns Hopkins University Press, 2008.

INDEX[1]

A

Åberg, Magnus, 13
abjection, 19–20; *Beowulf* and, 92, 96–97, 191–92, 205; Bilbo Baggins and, 49, 62–66; in "Cottage of Lost Play," 25–26; in *Fall of Arthur*, 113; female characters and, 190, 208; Frodo and, 38; in "Goblin Feet," 24–25; Gollum and, 45n67, 234; heroes and, 49, 101; *Kalevala* and, 25, 45n64, 78n36; Kristeva's definition of, 19, 38; Kullervo and, 78n36; queerness and, 122; in *Sellic Spell*, 92; Sigurd and, 49, 59; *Silmarillion* and, 20–21, 45n65; Tolkien and, 19–23, 25, 29–30, 87, 101, 139, 179, 191; Túrin Turambar and, 37–39; in "You and Me," 25. *See also* exile; Other; *wraecca*
Abraham (son of Noah, in Tolkien's *Exodus*), 145

Adventures of Tom Bombadil, The (Tolkien), xxxii, 84–86, 219, 236n11. *See also Red Book*
Æsir (Tolkien's Óðin, Loki, and Hœnir), 54, 59
Ælfwine of England (Tolkien), xxv, 27, 42n28, 126
Æðelflæd (Byrhtnoð's sister-in-law), 236n7
Agravain (*Fall of Arthur*), 115, 118
Agravaine (*The Once and Future King*), 115
AIDS, 122
"Ainulindäle" (*Silm.*), 71
Ainur (*Silm.*), 71–75. *See also* Elves
Alcuin (ca. 797), 197
Allen & Unwin, 79n44, 138
Alliterative Morte Arthure, 111–12, 114, 119, 125, 228, 242–45
Alliterative Revival, 142
Ancrene Riwle (*Ancrene Wisse*) (Tolkien), xv, xxix, 148, 175n51, 179, 184–89

[1]Note: Page numbers followed by 'n' denote notes.

Anderson, Douglas, xviii, xxi, 29, 76n10, 94, 105n6, 183–84, 187
Andreas (Old English poem), 144
Andrew Lang Lecture (1939), xiii, xxx, 49–51, 76n3, 91, 96, 107n31, 112. *See also* "On Fairy-Stories"
Andvari, 54, 57, 59, 66, 73, 134, 201–2. *See also* Dwarves; *Legend of Sigurd*; *Völsunga Saga*
"Andvari's Gold" (Tolkien), 54, 57–60
antihero(es): Beowulf, xiii, 104; Bilbo Baggins, xiii, 49; *Fall of Arthur* and, 113; fantasy literature and, 7; "Farmer Giles of Ham" and, 12; Fëanor, 244; Gollum and, 171; *Hobbit* and, 49, 165; Kullervo, xiii, 28–38; *Lord of the Rings, The*, and, 140, 158, 171, 233; Sigurd and, xiii, 49, 56–61, 75; Tolkien and, xii–xiii, 28, 49. *See also* heroes, abject and flawed
anti-Semitism, 133–34
apartheid/apartness, 140–58, 160–65, 167–72. *See also* neocolonialism; queerness; Other; "Sigelwara Land"
Apolausticks, 23, 180
Apollo (god), 94
Aragorn (*LOTR*), 113, 137, 165, 207, 221, 228, 242–46. *See also The Lord of the Rings*
Arathorn (Aragorn's father), 245
Arkenstone (*The Hobbit*), 64, 66, 74. *See also* Dwarves; Smaug; treasure
Arthur, King (*Lanval*), 9–10. *See also Fall of Arthur*
Arthur's Grave, 125
Arul, Melissa Ruth, 20, 40n7
Arwen (*LOTR*), xv, 169, 242–46
Aryan ideal, 137

Āsemo (Tolkien, "Story of Kullervo"), 35
Ashwood (Æschere), 102
asterisk philology, 141
Atani heroes, 80n51
Atli (Attila), 202–4
Auden, W.H., vii, 3, 31, 39, 48, 138–39
Aulë (*Silm*), 38, 70, 72, 134
Avalon, 113, 125–26, 128. *See also The Fall of Arthur*; Tol Eressëa

B

Bag End and Hobbiton, 158–60
Baggins family, 78n37, 159, 165, 169
Bakhtin, Mikhail, 4
Baldwin (Briton; *Fall of Arthur*), 119
Barber, E.A., 180
Bartlett, Nick, 5
Baswell, Christopher, 238n41
Battis, Jes, 11
"The Battle of Brunanburh," 169
Battle of Camlann, 125
Battle of Maldon, The/"Battle of Maldon, The," xii, 39, 84, 113, 124, 168, 217–18, 220–21, 223, 235–36n5, 236n7
"Battle of the Eastern Field, The" (Tolkien), xxiv, 86–88
Baynes, Pauline, 84, 105n6, 151, 175n56
Bediver (Briton; *Fall of Arthur*), 119
Beewolf (*Sellic Spell*), 101–4
Beleg (Sindarin Elf slain by Túrin), 37–38
Benson, Larry D., 129n10
Beorhtwold ("The Homecoming of Beorhtnoth"), 168
Beorn (*The Hobbit*), 51, 69
Beow (*Beowulf*), 92–93, 97–98, 101–4, 196

INDEX 269

Beowulf (character), xii, xiii, 50, 57, 63–64, 84–85, 90–92, 177, 179, 198–99
Beowulf (poem): "Doom" in, 50; Dragon in, xiii, 50, 54, 64, 84–85, 90, 92, 96, 98, 100–1, 117, 120, 121, 191–92; "Elegy of the Last Survivor," 85; *Exodus, Andreas*, and, 144; fairy-stories and, 66–67; *Fall of Arthur* and, xiv, 113–14, 117, 119–22; Geat hero, 96–101; genealogy in, 86; gender in, 5; Grendel's Mother and, 195–96; Hengest in, 27; influence of on Tolkien's fantasies, xii, 57, 83–84, 104n1; *Legend of Gudrún* and, 204–5; *The Lord of the Rings* and, 50, 207; masculinity in, 215, 217, 221; Merry and Pippin and, 169; *Sellic Spell* and, xiii, xxx; and Shield Sheafing, Beow(ulf), and Beewolf, 101–4; Sigurd and, 56–57; *Silmarillion* and, 66; Tolkien and, 27, 64, 67; Tolkien's teaching commentary on, 90–93, 101, 196–98; treasure in, 54, 57, 84–85, 221; women in, 177, 179, 189–93. *See also* "Beowulf and the Monsters"; "Beowulf: The Monsters and the Critics"; *See also* Grendel; Grendel's Mother; treasure
Beowulf, Tolkien's translation of, xiii–xiv, xxvii, xxx, 48, 56, 83–84, 88–99, 109n57, 112, 193–96
"Beowulf and the Critics," A and B Drafts, 213n91
Beowulf and the Finnsburg Fragment (Klaeber), xxx
"Beowulf and the Monsters," 198–99

"Beowulf: The Monsters and the Critics," xxviii–xxix, 56, 64, 83–84, 112, 120, 126; reprints of, 104n2; title of, 104n2
Bercilak de Hautdesert (*Sir Gawain*), 224
Beren (*Silm.*), 33; Aragorn/Arwen love story and, 243; death of, 36–37; first version of tale of, xxv, xxvii; *Kalevala* and, 36, 45n64; relationship with Lúthien, 20, 36–37, 243, 245–46; Sauron and, 36
Bhabha, Homi, 12, 216, 235n3
Bilbo Baggins: as abject hero, 49, 62–66; as alter-ego for Tolkien, 5, 21, 241, 246n2; ancestry of, 61–63; as antihero, 101, 113; avarice of, 64; Bag End and, 155–56, 158; birthday party of, 156; as burglar, 62, 66, 68; Dwarves and, 54; Elves and, 73–75; errantry of, 219–20; fairy-stories and, 49; family of, 62, 113, 158–59, 165–67; as flawed, 38; Frodo and, 62, 78n37, 159; Gandalf and, 68–69, 74–75; gender and, 216; "Goblin Feet" and, 24; Gollum and, 63, 172, 233–34; humility of, 74–75, luck and, 61, 63, 68, 74; magic and, 71, 73; major feats of, 63; masculinity of, 216; mithril coat of, 231; morality of, 155; multiculturalism and, 233–34; One Ring and, 63–65, 74, 154–55, 157–58; political skills of, 155–56, 158; queerness of, 49, 154, 158–59, 162–63; *Red Book* of, 86; Samwise Gamgee and, 155, 168–69; *Sellic Spell* and, 101; Shire and, 154–58, 162; and

Sigurd, 49, 57, 61–64, 74; and Smaug, 63–66, 74; social status of, 166–69; treasure and, 54, 57, 64. *See also* Hobbits
Birmingham, xiii, xxiii, 20–23, 29, 40n8, 47, 86. *See also* King Edward's School
Bliss, A.J., xxx–xxxi
Bolintineanu, Alexandra, 16n38
Bombadil, Tom, 43n54, 151
Book of Lost Tales, Parts 1 and 2 (Tolkien), xii, xxv, 5, 25, 27, 37, 41n19, 42n29, 68, 219
Borghild (wife of King Siggeir), 55
Boromir (brother of Faramir), 4, 227, 229, 234
Bosworth, Joseph, xxvii, 41n25, 48, 50
Bowers, John, 175n47, 211n26
Brackmann, Rebecca, 172n3
Brandybuck, Primula, 62, 159, 165
Brandybucks and Tooks, 161
Bratt, Edith: *see* Tolkien, Edith Bratt
Bretherton, Christopher, 28
Brian of Ireland (*Fall of Arthur*), 119
Brothers Grimm, 67, 95
Brunsdale, Mitzi, 16n39
Bryce, Lynn, 16n39
Brynhild (Valkyrie), 52–53, 56, 58–59, 61, 178, 189, 199–202, 204
Budli (Atli's father), 202, 204
Burne-Jones, Edward, 180
Burns, Marjorie J., 68, 76n5
Byrhtwold (old retainer, *The Battle of Maldon*), 218, 236n7

C

Cador, Briton (*Fall of Arthur*), 119
Cain (in *Beowulf*), 193, 212n63
Calaquendi ("Elves of the Light"), 72

Callahan, Patrick, 16n39
Candle in the Wind, The (White), 114
Canterbury Tales, The (Chaucer), xi, 146, 149
Carcharoth (wolf in *Silm.*), 36, 243
Carey, John, 138
Carpenter, Humphrey, xxi, xxiii, 20, 48, 79n44, 217
Castor and Pollux (Macauley, *Lay of Lake Regillus*), 87, 88
"Cauldron of Story" (Tolkien, "On Fairy-Stories"), 94
Celeborn (husband of Galdriel), 5, 244
Celebrían (mother of Arwen), 244
Celegorm (Noldorin Elf), 36, 243
Chambers, R.W., 112–13, 128n6
Chaucer, Geoffrey, xxiii, xxvi–xxvii, 42n37, 135–36, 139, 146–51, 185, 211n26
"Chaucer as a Philologist" (Tolkien), xxviii, 147–48
Chaucer's Works II (Skeat), 42n37
Children of Húrin, The (Tolkien), xxvi, xxvii, 37, 113
chivalry: Arthurian legend and, 87–88; Beorhtnoth and, 218, 220; Beowulf and, 104; Gawain and, 218, 222–26; Hobbits and, 161, 165, 169; identity in, 225; in *Lanval*, 9–10; in *Lord of the Rings*, 152, 161, 165, 169, 215–16, 227, 232; Merry and Pippin and, 169, 215–16, 227; Orcs and, 232; queer desire and, 227; queerness and, 216, 227; *Sir Gawain and the Green Knight* and, 222–27; Tolkien's fairy-stories and, 84; weaknesses in, 222. *See also* "Errantry"; *The Homecoming of Beorhtnoth, Beorhthelm's Son*; *Lanval*; *The*

Lord of the Rings; masculinity; "Ofermod"; *Sir Gawain and the Green Knight*
Christiansen, Bonniejean, 63, 80n49
Churchill, Winston, 86
Círdan (Master of Grey Havens), 70
Clarendon Chaucer anthology, 139, 146–47, 175n47, 185
Clark, David, 221, 237n18
Clark-Hall, John, xxx, 83
Clute, John, 136
Cohen, Richard A., 130n26
commemoratio ("Lay of Lake Regillus" as), 87
"*Cottage of Lost Play, The*" (Tolkien), xxiv, xxv, 24–27
Corpus Christi College's Sundial Society, xxiv, 29
Cradoc (*Fall of Arthur*), 115, 119
Craigie, William, 180
Crist (Old English poem), 26, 219
Critical Race theory, 6
Crocker, Holly, 15n37, 177, 216, 228
Croft, Janet Brennan, and Leslie A. Donovan, 178
Cults of the Greek States (Farnell), 180
Curry, Patrick, 11
Curufin (brother of Celegorm), 36, 243
Curumo: *see* Saruman
Curunír: *see* Saruman

D

Daddy Twofoot (Hobbit), 158
Damico, Helen, 212n49, 247n8
d'Ardenne, Simonne T.R.O., xxx, 86, 106n13, 149, 183–84, 187, 210n20, 210n22
Dark Riders (*LOTR*), 140, 154, 216. *See also* Nazgûl
Davin, D.M., 147

Davis, Norman, 86, 146, 222
De Chirico, Giorgio, xix
"Death of Sinfjötli, The," 58, 60
Deleuze, Gilles, 12
Denethor (*LOTR*), 4, 170–71, 215–16, 227, 229. *See also* Boromir; Faramir
Dernhelm (*LOTR*), 242
Deucalion, 241–42
"Devil's Coach-Horses, The" (Tolkien), 147
Dialectical Society, 189
Dimond, Andy, 17n39
Dinshaw, Carolyn, 238n40
Dobson, E.J., 184
Donovan, Leslie A., 178, 208
Doty, Alexander, xii, 6, 12, 122, 230
Dragon(s): in "Andvari's Gold," 54, 59–61; antihero and, 49; in *Beowulf*, 198–99, 205, 221; Beowulf's death and, 84–85, 90, 92, 121, 126; Bilbo and, 63–66, 74; fairy-stories and, 49–51; Gandalf's stories of, 69; Glaurung, 38; heroes and, 50–51; influence on Tolkien's writings, 64; Last Survivor and, 100–1; in *Legend of Gudrún*, 201, 203; in *Legend of Sigurd*, 54, 57–58, 64, 201, 203, prophecy and, 53, slaying of, 63; as "monstrous adversary," 63–64, 120; slaying of, 50, 120, 205, 221; Smaug, xiii, 49, 54, 64–65, 74; in "Story of Sigurd," 57–62, 71; as symbol of death, 92, 96, 126; Tolkien's fascination with, 191–93; Tolkien's teaching commentary and, 197–98; treasure and, 54, 57, 64–65, 74, 84–85, 117; Túrin Turambar and, 37–38; venom of,

198–99. *See also* Andvari; Fáfnir; Smaug
Dream of the Rood, 221
Drogo (Dwarf), 78n37, 159, 165, 169
Dronke, Ursula, 183
Drout, Michael, xvi, 16n38, 42n28, 105n6, 212n46
duguð (Tolkien's comitatus), 146
Dwarves: in "*Andvari's Gold*," 54; Bilbo and, 158, 231, 241; dragons and, 63–64; Elves and, 165; fairy-stories and, 50, 74; as forces of good, 68–69; greed of, for gold, 64, 85; in *Hobbit*, 63, 71, 73–74; Hobbits and, 166; Jews and, 133–34; language of, 134; "On Fairy-Stories" and, 50; queerness and, 154; rings of power and, 150; in *Silm.*, 72–73; Smaug and, 64–66; treasure and, 63–66, 74. *See also* "Andvari's Gold"; Arkenstone; Gimli; Thorin Oakenshield
dyscatastrophe, 92, 101, 120. *See also* "On Fairy-Stories"

E

Eaglestone, Robert, 15n37, 235n3
"Éalá Éarendel Engla Beorhtast" (poem), xxiv, 219
Eanmund (Onela's nephew), 196, 213n70
Eärendel (Eärendil), 21, 24–27, 36, 38, 41n19, 125–26, 219–20, 244; "son of," 41n20. *See also Crist*; *Silmarillion*; "Voyage of Éarendel"
Eärwen (daughter of Olwë), 244
Ecgtheow/Ecgþeow (*Beowulf*), 93, 100

Edelman, Lee, xii, xiv, xvi, 9, 12–13, 122, 126–27
Eileen Elgar, 168
Eitill (son of Atli), 203
Eldar (*Silm.*) ,26, 70, 72, 244–46
Elder Edda, xxviii, 48, 52, 54, 78n28, 204
Eliot, Charles N.E., 29, 42n37
Eliot, T.S., 11
Elrond (*LOTR*), 73, 137, 243–45
Elros (Half-Elf, brother of Elrond), 243–44
Elves: in *Beowulf*, 194; Bilbo and, 73–75; in "Cottage of Lost Play," 25, 28; dark vs. light and, 151; departure to Undying Lands, 242; Dwarves and, 165; Ents and, 206; Eriol and, 27; fairies and, 50–51, 67–68; and the Fourth Age, 75; Gandalf and, 68, 70; in *Hobbit*, 166; Istari and, 70; in "Iúmonna Gold Galdre Bewunden," 85; languages of, 1–2; Lórien and, 151–52; and magic, 51; Merry and Pippin and, 167; Orcs as mutations of, 140, 228–29; queerness and, 126; Rings of Power and, 158; Rivendell and, 167; Sam Gamgee and, 163, 168–69; Took family and, 62; Túrin Turambar and, 38; weapons/cloaks given to Hobbits, 231; Wood-, 73; in *Silmarillion*, 67–68, 71–74, 244. *See also* Quenya; Sindarin
Emery, Elizabeth, 7
"English and Welsh" (Tolkien), 144
English Dialect Grammar (Joseph Wright), 180
Ents (*LOTR*), 205–6, 215
Entwives (*LOTR*), xv, 205, 206, 207

Éomer (*LOTR*), 207, 221, 234. See also Théoden
Éowyn (*LOTR*), 170, 205, 207, 208, 214n94, 215, 221, 234, 241. See also Théoden
Epicurus (Greek philosopher, fl. 307 B.C.), 111
Eriador (region from which Hobbit leaders come), 167, 172, 234
Eriol (Ælfwine, "Elf-Friend"), 21, 24–27, 42n28. See also Eärendel the Mariner; "The Story of Eriol's Life"; Tol Eressëa
Erp and Eitill (Gudrún's sons with Atli), 203
"Errantry" (poem), 219–20, 236n11
Esperanto ("A Secret Vice"), 2
Ethiopians, 142–44
eucatastrophe, 51, 92, 103, 120. See also "On Fairy-Stories"
Evans, Deann Delmar, xvi
Evans, Jonathan, 15n38
Everett, Caroline, 138
Exeter College Essay Club, 180
Exeter College Oxford, xxiii, xxviii, 23, 29, 32, 48, 112, 137, 139, 180–81, 191, 209n6, 220
exile: of Abraham, 145; of Cain, 193; of Celeborn and Galadriel, 244; of Ecgþeow, 93; of Elrond and Guenever, 118; of Grendel and Grendel's Mother, 193–94; of the Israelites, xiv, 142, 144–45; of Lancelot, 117; of Moses, 144–45; of the Noldor, 20, 26–27, 36, of Sigurd, 192; soul's, 143; Tolkien's, 5, 25, 39; in "The Wanderer," 145; in "Valedictory Address," 145–46. See also *wraecca*

Exodus (Old English, Tolkien's), xiv, xxvii, xxviii, 5, 142–47
Eylimi (king; father of Hjørdis), 55

F
faërie, 10, 24, 26, 27, 28, 57, 71, 93, 153, 226
Fáfnir: in "Andvari's Gold," 54, 59; curse of, 61, 64; death of, 58, 63, 192, 201; Dragon in *Beowulf* and, 191; fairy-stories and, 57; Ódin and, 52–53; Regin and, 59–61; Smaug and, 64; in "Story of Sigurd," 57–58; as symbol of greed, 203; treasure and, 57, 61. See also Dragon(s)
fairy-stories: *Beowulf* and, 66–67; defined, 49, 91–93; *Legend of Sigurd* and, 49–52; *Lord of the Rings* and, 67–68, 75, 241–42; *Silmarillion* and, 57, 66–75; three faces of, in "On Fairy-Stories," 51, 71; *Völsunga Saga* and, 95–96. See also "On Fairy-Stories"
"Fairy Stories" (Andrew Lang Lecture), 67, 85, 91. See also Andrew Lang Lecture; "On Fairy-Stories"
Fall of Arthur, The (Tolkien), 111–31; alliterative meter in, 112; Arthur and his men in, 114–19; Arthur in as "gloomy depressive," 119; and *Arthur's Grave*, 125; *Beowulf* and, 97, 119–22; and "chronicle tradition," 115; composing of, 96, 111–12; dating of, 112; Guinever as cold and dissembling in, 116; influence on by

Alliterative Morte Arthure and Malory's tales, 111, 119; interruptions in Tolkien's completion of, 112; "no future" in, 124–25; and queer endings, 122–28; *Sellic Spell* and, 103; unfinished ending of, 96, 113–14; and White's *Once and Future King*, 112, 113–14, 115, 124, 125, 130n28; and William Morris, "Defence of Guenevere," 112, 116–17

Fall of Gondolin, "The Fall of Gondolin" (event, work, essay), xxv, 27

fantasy: "Battle of the Eastern Field" as, 86; character, and Tolkien, 4–5; Christianity in, 51, 94–95; and *Fall of Arthur*, death as, 128; in films and video games, 7; hero in, as knight, 7; and Lee Edelman, 127; and the medieval, xii, 13; present real and, 127; queer, *LOTR* as, 152–53; reworking of Chaucer in, 149; *Sellic Spell* as, 95; subversive, 136, 217; suspension of disbelief in, 94; and Tennyson's *Idylls of the King*, 112, 116, 121; world of, as Middle-earth, 26

Faramir, 4, 41n19, 165, 170, 234, 242. *See also* Boromir; Denethor

Farmer Giles of Ham (Tolkien), xxx, 12, 51, 92, 152–53

Farmer Maggot, 163–64

Farnell, Lewis R., 180

fascism, xi, 137–38, 152–53

Faust, Cosette, 236n7

Fëanor (*Silm.*), 20, 38, 61, 80n51, 101, 177, 242, 243, 244

Fehrenbacher, Richard W., 103

Ferdinand, Franz, Archduke, 180

Fimi, Dimitra, 13n1, 66–68, 144

Finarfin (*Silm.*), 244

Finnish Grammar (Eliot), 29, 42n37

Finwë (*Silm.*), 20

Fisher, Sheila, 224

Flieger, Verlyn, xix, 29, 37, 42n35, 43n45, 44n58, 45n64, 71, 76n10, 94

Forster, E.M., 5

Fosco (father of Drogo Baggins), 78n37

Foucault, Michel, xvi, 12, 15n37

Frazer, James, 94–95, 97

Freawaru (*Beowulf*), 109n59, 191, 196–99, 203, 207

Freccero, Carla, 8

Freud, Sigmund, 19

Frodo Baggins: abjection of, 101; ancestry of, 62; as antihero, 113, 140; Baggins family and, 155–56, 159, 165–66; Beewolf and, 103; Bilbo and, 62, 155–59, 78n37; Brandybucks and, 158, 161, 165; class and, 164–65; disguise of, 231–32; Dwarves and, 231; Farmer Maggot and, 163–64; as flawed hero, 38; Gollum, oppositional figure to, 4, 171–72, 233–35; journey of, 159–60; loyalty of, 226–28; "man to man" and, 226–28; masculinity and, 216; Merry and Pippin and, 162–63, 169–71; monsters and, 140; nobility of, 62, 241; One Ring and, 157; queerness of, 133, 154–55, 159, 163, 208, 230–31; salvation and, 233–35; Sam Gamgee and, 160–61, 167–69, 218, 226; Shelob and, 218–19; Shire and, 138, 154, 166–67; Tolkien's identification with, 5, 21, 24, 39; and the Tooks, 161,

165; Valinor and, 242. *See also* Bilbo; Hobbits

G

Gaffer (Sam's father), 155, 156, 159–61
Gaheris (brother of Gawain), 115, 118
Galadriel, 5, 168, 177, 219, 231, 242, 244–45
Gandalf: analysis of Gollum, 38, 172, 233; Bilbo and, 62, 68–69, 74–75; class and, 163, 170; Elves and, 68, 70; as force of good, 57, 68; Frodo and, 157–58, 233; Gondor and, 170; Hobbits and, 62, 153–54, 158; Hobbits' view of, 69, 158; Istari and, 70; magic of, 57, 68–69, 70; Pippin and, 170; Sackville-Bagginses and, 159; Óðin and, 68; One Ring and, 157, 233; other names for, 70; prophecy and, 74; queerness and, 69, 158, 165; Rohan and, 207, 221; Sam Gamgee and, 160, 163; Saruman and, 4, 70; Sauron and, 70; stories told, 69, 163
Gareth (brother of Gawain), 115, 118
Garth, John, xvi, 32, 42n37, 43n48, 180–81, 209n6
Gatekeeper at Bree, 164–65
Gaunt, Simon, 238n41
Gawain, Sir: battle with Mordred and, 123–24; chivalry and, 218; in *Fall of Arthur*, 114–15, 118–20, 124–26; grave of, 125; in *History of the Kings of Britain*, 115; Lancelot and, 123; in *Once and Future King*, 115; queerness and, 123; ship of, 126. *See also Sir Gawain and the Green Knight*;

"Sir Gawain and the Green Knight" (W.P. Ker Lecture)
Gay, David Elton, 43n54
gender: difference and, 12, 170, 181; Elves and, 20; Ents and, 205–6; Gawain and, 224; identity and, 230; medievalism and, 8, 24n25; Middle-earth and, 5; prejudice and, 217; queerness and, 6, 11, 230; women and, 177–78, 190, 208
Geoffrey of Monmouth, 114–15
Giddings, Robert, 15n37, 173n15
Gilliver, Peter, 41n19
Gilraen (Aragorn's mother), 245
Gilson, Robert Quilter, xxiv, 23, 28
Gimli (*LOTR*), 165, 207. *See also* Dwarves
Glaurung (dragon) (*Silm.*), 38
Glastonbury (Engl.), 125
"Goblin Feet" (Tolkien), xxiv, 24–25
God, Death, and Time (Levinas), 122
Goldberg, Jonathan, and Menon Madhavi, 8
The Golden Bough (Frazer), 94
Golden Hall, 102
Golden Key, The (MacDonald), xxxii, 51
Gollum (Sméagol): abjection of, 234; antihero, 171; Bilbo and, 63, 172, 233–34; Merry and Pippin and, 229; oppositional figure to Frodo, 4, 160, 171–72, 233–35; queer, 171–72, 208, 233; and the Ring, 38, 64–65, 160–61, 227, 235; Sauron and, 63, 161
Gordon, E.V., xxvii, xxviii, xxix–xxxi, 137, 146, 217, 222–23, 236n7
Gordon, George S., xxvi, xxvii, 146
Gram (Sigurd's sword), 60, 201
Grani (Sigurd's horse), 57, 58, 60, 200, 201

Grant, John, 136
Grendel (*Beowulf*), 90, 99–100, 120–21, 145, 198, 204; ancestry of, 193; in "Beowulf and Grendel," xxviii, 89–90; in "Beowulf and the Monsters" (lay), 198; in "Beowulf: The Monsters and the Critics" (article), 189, 192–93; curses of, 198; "Doom" and, 50; *Exodus* and, 145; family and, 121; as marred human, 192, 194, 196; as "monstrous adversary," 63; *Sellic Spell* and, 102–3; in Tolkien's *Beowulf* translation, 89–91, 99–100, 193, 195–96. *See also* abjection; *Beowulf*; Grendel's Mother
Grendel's Mother, 90–91, 121, 177, 179, 190–96, 198–99, 204–5. *See also Beowulf*; "Beowulf and Grendel"; "Beowulf and the Monsters"; Grendel; "Lay of Beowulf"
Grey Annals, 44n63
Grímhild (*Legend of Gudrún*), 200–2
Grímnir, Sigmund's sword, 60
Grimm, Jacob, 67, 95
Grimm, Wilhelm, 67, 94, 95
Grinder (*Sellic Spell*), 99, 102–3. *See also* Grendel
Grishnákh (Orc, *LOTR*), 229, 230. *See also* Orcs
Gryphon (Leeds), 84
Guattari, Félix, 12
Gudrún: Atli and, 202–4; Attila and, 204; Brynhild and, 58–59, 199–200; *Hobbit* and, 65; influence of on Tolkien's other writing, 178–79, 199–200; Sigurd's death and, 202; Sigurd's love for, 201; Tolkien's lays and,
48, 101; "woe of Gudrún," 202. *See also Legend of Gudrún*; *Legend of Sigurd*; Sigurd
Gueroult, Denys, 45n69, 133
Guenevere: in Morris, "Defence of Guenevere," 48–58, 116; in White, *Idylls of the King*, 200–4
Guinever: differing versions of, 115; in *Fall of Arthur*, 115–20, 123–26, 151–52; in *Lanval* and, 9–10, 226. *See also* King Arthur; Lancelot
Gunnar (*Legend of Gudrún*), 48, 58, 200–3
Guðrúnarkviðaenforna (Eddaic), 178
Guðrúnarkviðaennýja (Eddaic), 199–200
Gymir (enemy of Frey; father of Gerðr), 197

H
Haigh, Walter E., xxviii, 141, 144. *See also* Huddersfield Dialect
Hali Meiðhad, 187
Hall, John Clark, xxx, 83, 105n3
Hallam, Arthur, 130n28. *See also* Alfred Lord Tennyson
Háma (Rohan hall-guardian), 165, 207, 221
Hammond, Wayne, xvi, xxi, xxiii, 29, 85, 105n6, 219
Handshoe (Hondscióh), 102
Haradrim (*LOTR*), 144
Harfoots, 62, 63, 78n37
Helm of Dread (Sigurd's, Lang), 58
Helm of Horror (Sigurd's, Tolkien), 61
Helms, Randel, 81n72
Hengest (*Beowulf*), 27
Heorrenda (son of Eriol), 27

heroes, abject and flawed, anti-, 38; aristocracy and, 169–71; Bilbo as, 61–66; Beewulf as, 101; *Beowulf* and, 205; childhood and, 21; chivalry and, 7, 84, 215, 224–25; Christianity and, 121, 144; class and, 162, 165; death and, 111, 113, 223; fairy-stories and, 49, 84, 153, 208; feminized, 10; gender and, 180, 189–91, 216–18; half-god nature of, 244; Hobbits as, 165–68; hybrid, 165; loneliness and, 96; magic and, 50–52, 57; medieval, 28–29, 39; monsters and, 190–92, 19; names and, 93; ordinary characters as, 158, 160; power and, 10; progeny and, 113; queerness of, 49, 231–33; and Sigurd, 49; Tolkien's self-projection into, 35, 101–2; weakness and, 58; WWII and, 39. *See also* antiheroes, individual, Beowulf; Bilbo; Kullervo; Sigurd; Túrin Turambar

Hesse, Hermann, 5

heteronormativity, 6, 8, 11–12, 226, 228–29

"Hiawatha": see "Song of Hiawatha"

Hickes, George, 189

Higgens, Andrews, 13n1

Hiley, Margaret, 77n15

"History of Eriol, or Aelfwine and the End of the Tales" (Tolkien), xxv

History of Middle-earth, The (Tolkien), 25, 67–68. *See also middangeard*; Middle-earth, history of

Hitler, Adolf, 121, 137

Hjalprek (father of Alf and king of Denmark), 56

Hjørdis (*Völsunga Saga*), 55–56

"Hoard, The" (Tolkien), 84–86

Hobbit, The (Tolkien): *Beowulf* and, 83, 85, 197; Bilbo in, 49, 61, 63–66; Christianity and, 75; dating of, 76n9; Dwarves in, 54, 63, 65–66, 68, 71, 73–74; Elves in, 73; as fairy-story, 50–52, 66–67, 76n10; Gandalf, role of in, 68; Gollum in, 63–65, 80n49; goodness in, 75; heroes, abject, in, 61–62; heroes, flawed, in, 38–39; as hybrid story, 66–68; inheritance of Bag End in, 155; *Legend of Sigurd* and, 54, 57; *Lord of the Rings* and, 138–40, 205; luck in, 61; magic in, 59, 65–66, 71; mythology and, 21, 27, 47, 66; nobility in, 62; One Ring in, 65; origin of, 138; psychology and, 75; publication of, 91, 96, 112, 186; second edition of, 80n49; *Sellic Spell* and, 91, 103; *Silm.* and, 73–74; Smaug and, 54, 63–65, 68, 74; Tolkien's childhood and, 21; treasure in, 54, 66; *Völsunga Saga* and, 48–49, 56; writing of, 48, 137–38. *See also* Bilbo; *Legend of Sigurd* (Tolkien); "On Fairy-Stories"; Smaug; "The Story of Sigurd" (Lang)

Hobbits, 39, 49, 138; Bag End, Hobbiton, and Brandybucks, 158–60; Bilbo and, 154–58; branches of, 62–63, 166; Brandybucks and Tooks of Buckland, 161; class structure of, 156, 161, 168–71; definition of, 228; difference and, 140, 158–59, 229–30; Ents and, 205–7; Fallowhide, 62, 146, 161; Farmer Maggot, 133, 163–64; farming and, 138, 153; Gandalf; and, 69,

153; gender and, 205–8; Gollum and, 160–61, 171–72, 227, 234; Harfoot, 146; and Hobbiton, 151, 160; homosocial relationships of, 227–28; masculinity and, 216–17, 229–33; "normal," 158–59; Orcs and, 229–31; and Otherness, 151–53; politics among, 156–58; queerness and, 133, 154–55; Shire and, 68–69, 153–54; Stoor, 146; taxonomy of, 146, 165–67; Tolkien on, 154; Tolkien's identification with, 5, 21, 39, 241, 246n2. *See also individual*; Bilbo; Frodo; Merry and Pippin; Samwise Gamgee
"Hobby for the Home" (Tolkien, "A Secret Vice"), 1
Hogan, Patrick Cohn, 153
Högni (*Legend of Sigurd and Gudrún*), 200–3
Hollander, Lee, 213n91
Hollywood, Amy, 8
Holmes, John R., xvii, 16n38
Holsinger, Bruce, 7
Homecoming of Beorhtnoth Beorhthelm's Son, The/"The Homecoming of Beorhtnoth Beorhthelm's Son" (Tolkien), xv, xxix–xxxi, 16n38, 39, 84, 113, 124–25, 215, 217–20, 222, 236n6
homoeroticism, 238n41. *See also* homosocial bonds; *Fall of Arthur*; *Lanval*; *Roman d'Eneas*
homophobia, 5
homosexuality, 6, 9–10, 122–23, 127, 137, 225, 229, 239n43
homosocial bonds, xv, 10, 123, 181, 218, 221, 226–27
Honegger, Thomas, 16n38, 209n3, 235n5, 236n6

Horatius: A Lay Made About the Year Of The City CCCLX, 87
Horsa (*Beowulf*), 27
Hostetter, Carl, 16n39, 79n44, 81n53
House of the Wolfings (Morris), 180
Hreidmar (father of sons Fáfnir, Regan, Otr), 53, 54, 56, 59, 60
Hrothgar (*Beowulf*), 50, 93, 98–99, 191, 193, 195–96, 204, 207, 215, 221. *See also Beowulf*
Huan (*Silm.*), 36, 243
Huddersfield Dialect, xxviii, 141–42, 144
Hugh of St. Victor, 187
Hughes, Shaun, 10–11, 15n37
Huor (father of Tuor), 244
Húrin (*Silm.*), 37
Hygd (wife of Hygelac; *Beowulf*), 101, 191
Hygelac (Geat king, *Beowulf*), 101–2, 191, 221

I

ides (Anglo-Saxon peace-pledge), 109n58
Idril (Elda, married to Tuor), 244, 245
Idylls of the King (Tennyson), 112, 116, 121
Iliad, The (Homer), 87
Ill-Made Knight, The (White), 114
Ilúvatar (*Silm.*), 37, 71, 73, 75, 134
Indis (Finarfin's Vanyar mother), 244
Ingeld (married to Freawaru, *Beowulf*), 109n59, 191, 196–99, 203
Inglis, Fred, 137
intimacy, 3, 98, 188
invention of languages, Tolkien's, 1–2. *See also* "Secret Vice, A"

invisibility, 58, 65–66, 155–56, 177, 216, 228, 231
Istari, xxxi, 70, 74. See also Gandalf; Saruman
"Iúmonna Gold Galdre Bewunden" (Tolkien), xxvi, 84, 85, 86, 105n6, 117. See also "Hoard, The"
Ivor (Mordred's squire, Fall of Arthur), 119
Ivy Bush and Green Dragon, 160

J

Jackson, Peter, xvi, xviii, 5, 10, 151
Jews, 133–34, 137
Johnson, Glen, 239n43
Jones, Garrett, 130n28
Jones, J. Morris, 180
Jónsson, Finnur, 213n91
jouissance, 127
Joyce, James, 11
Juliana, St., xv, 187. See also *Seinte Julienne*, 184

K

Kalevala: The Land of Heroes (Lönnrot's compilation), 43n43; animism in, 35; cycles in, 30; fairy tales and, 33, 67, 95; influence on Tolkien's work, 28–29, 67; *Sellic Spell* and, 86; Tolkien's writings on, 28–29, 35, 37; translation of, 31–32. See also Kullervo (character); Tolkien's "Story of Kullervo"
Kane, Douglas Charles, 44n63, 172–73n5
Katherine, St., xv, 187. See also *Seinte Katerine*, 184
Keen, Morris, 237n20
Kelly, Katherine Coyne, 14n25

Kendrick, T.D., 106n10
Ker, Walter Paton, xxxi, 222, 224
Khuzdul (*LOTR*), 134; and Semitic languages, 172n4
King Arthur: "Battle of the Eastern Fields" and, 87; Beewolf and, 102; Beowulf and, 98–99; chivalric code and, 87–88; Christlike imagery of, 97; death of, 98, 111; in *Lanval*, 9–10; *Sellic Spell* and, 103; Shield Sheafing and, 97. See also *Fall of Arthur*; *Idylls of the King*; *Morte Darthur*; *Once and Future King, The*
King Edward's School, 22–23, 29, 47, 86, 88, 137, 139, 180–81
Kinney, Clare R., 224
Kirby, W.F., 29, 32, 42n35, 43n43, 43n48
Klaeber, Friedrich, 89, 96–97, 99–100, 130n22, 194
Klosowska, Anna, 238n41
Kolbítar Reading Group, xxvii-xxviii, 48, 181
"Kortirion among the Trees" (Tolkien), 28, 42n29
Kristeva, Julia, xiii, 4, 12, 19–20, 38
Kullervo (*Kalevala*), 28, 30–31
Kullervo (Tolkien, "Story of Kullervo"), 30–36, 42n35, 56, 78n36, 101; as antihero, 34, 179; as Sākehonto, 34–35; Sigurd and, 59; Tolkien's identification with, 45n64, 101; and Túrin Turambar, 38. See also *Kalevala*

L

Lafontaine, David, 14n19
Lalaith (*Silm.*), 37
Lancashire Fusiliers, xxiv, 21, 180

Lancelot (Breton; *Fall of Arthur*), 111, 113–19, 123–26, 131n33. *See also* Alfred Tennyson; Guinever; King Arthur; Mordred; William Morris

Lang, Andrew, xiii, xviii, xxix, 47–53, 55–57, 59–61, 66–68, 74–75, 91, 93–96, 108n45, 112

Lanval (Marie de France), 9–10, 225–26, 238n41

Lay of Lake Regillus (Macauley), 86, 87, 106n21

"Lay of Regin" (Eddlaic), 54

Lays (Tolkien): "Beowulf and Grendel," xxviii, 90, 198; "Beowulf and the Monsters," 198–99; "Lay of Atli," 204; "Lay of Beowulf," 89–90; *Lay of Leithian*, 36, 44n57, 112; *Lay of Sigurd*, 52; *Lay of Sigurd and Gudrún*, 101; *Lay of the Children of Húrin, The*, 37, 113; *The Lays of Beleriand*, 37; "New Lay of the Volsungs," 48. *See also* "Andvari's Gold"

Lays of Ancient Rome (William Macauley), 87

"Leaf by Niggle" (Tolkien), xxx, 12, 51, 84, 92, 95

LeCarré, John, 137

Leeds University, courses at, 108n40

Lees, Clare A., 190–91, 237n18

Legend of Good Women (Chaucer), 150

Legend of Gudrún (Tolkien), 58, 199, 202

Legend of Sigurd (Tolkien): cosmic frame of, 52–56; as fairy-story, 49–52; and the Poetic *Edda*, 76n8; prophecy in, 200; Tolkien's adaptation of, 48–49, 199; *Völsunga Saga* and, 49, 54, 59–60. *See also* Gudrún; Sigurd; "Story of Sigurd" (Lang)

Legend of Sigurd and Gudrún, The (Tolkien), 39, 48, 58, 103, 112–13

Legolas (*LOTR*), 165, 207. *See also* Elves

"Lemminkäinen" (Tolkien, "On 'The Kalevala' or Land of Heroes"), 43n51. *See also* Kullervo; *Kalevala*

Letters (Tolkien), 48, 133, 233; letter 43 to Michael Tolkien, 181; letter 54 to son Michael Tolkien, 22; letter 131 to Milton Waldman, 79n44, 168; letter 163 to W.H. Auden, 31–32, 39–40, 138; letter 165 to Houghton Mifflin, 179, 205, 241; letter 181 to Michael Straights, 233, 241, 242; letter 213 to Deborah Webster, 39; letter 246 to Mrs. Eileen Elgar, 85, 168; letter 261 to Anne Barrett, 84; letter 294 to Charlotte and Denis Plimer, 13n1, 39; letter to Mr. Rang, 220; letter to Rayner Unwin, unpublished, 25 April 1966, 219, 236n10

Levinas, Emmanuel, 12, 111, 122, 130n25, 130n26, 151–52, 215, 235, 241–42

Lewis, C.S., xxviii, 140, 183

Life and Death of Jason (William Morris), 180

Lilac Fairy Book, The (Andrew Lang), 47, 95

Lindo ("Cottage of Lost Play"), 25

Lobelia Sackville-Baggins (Hobbit), 156, 214n94

Loki (Norse mischief-maker), 52–54, 59–60, 202. *See also Legend of Sigurd*; Norse mythology; Ódin

Lonely Isle: *see* Tol Eressëa
Longfellow, Henry Wadsworth, 32, 43n48
Lönnrot, Elias, 29, 43n42, 43n43, 67, 95
Lord of the Rings, The (Tolkien): Chaucer and, 136, 148; Christianity and, 51; composition of, 27, 38, 70, 138–40; difference in and: class, 162–64; conflict in, 150; discrimination in, 165–67, 246; Elven languages in, 1–2; fairy-stories and, 67–68, 75, 241–42; *Fall of Arthur* and, 112; Farmer Maggot's wife in, 214n94; film adaptations of, 10–11; flawed heroes and, 38–39; gender in, 205–8; geography in, 146, 165; Gollum and, 171–72; Hobbits in, differences among, 158–59, 165–67, 229–30; homely and alien in, 151–54; influences on, 5, 21; map of a copy of latitudes between Oxford and Hobbiton, etc., 175n56; masculinity in, 215–21, 226–35; Otherness in, 151–53; politics in, 156–58; relationships and, 227–28; safety of Shire, 153–54; taxonomy in, 165–66; Middle-earth in, 41n19; monsters in, 63; multiculturalism in, 158–59; Norse mythology and, 59, 62; postmodern theory and, 10–11; *Sellic Spell* and, 103; women in, 177–79, 185–86, 205–8, 214n94; World War II and, 138–39
losenge, lozenge (in Tolkien's "Middle-English 'Losenger'"), 149–50, 210n22
Lucius, Emperor of Rome, 114, 115

Lúthien, 20, 33, 36–37, 45n64, 177, 182, 208, 243–46. *See also* Beren; *Silmarillion*

M

Macaulay, Thomas Babington, xxiv, 86–87, 106n21
MacDonald, George, xxxii, 51
Macdonald, Helen, 130n28
Magnússon, Eiríkr, 93
Maiar (*Silm.*), 70–72, 74, 140
Malory, Thomas, 111, 114–15, 125, 234
manuscripts: "Beowulf," Oxford Bodley Junius 11, 76n8; "Hali Meiðhad" Group, Oxford Bodley 34, 187–88; Liège, University Library 369 C, 210n22; Oxford Bodleian Special Collections Tolkien a21/5, 236n5; Poetic (or Elder) Edda, Codex Regius, Copenhagen Royal Collection no.2365.4, 76n8; "Rule for Nunnes," Corpus Christi College Cambridge 402, xxvi, 185–87, 236n5
Manwë (*Silm.*), 36, 68, 70, 72
Margaret, St., 187
Marie de France (*Lanval*), 9–10, 226
Marx, Karl, 138
masculinity: in *Battle of Maldon* and, 218–22; *Beowulf* and, 215, 217, 221, 237n18; Bilbo Baggins and, 216; chivalry and, 215–16, 218, 220, 222–27; *Homecoming of Beorhtnoth* and, 218–22; in *Lanval*, 9–10; *Lord of the Rings* and, 215–21, 226–35; medieval errantry and, 217–26; queerness and, 10, 227–34; Saruman and, 215–16, 227, 229, 231; Sauron and, 216, 227–29, 232; in *Sir*

Gawain and the Green Knight, 217–19, 222–26
Masti (dog; Tolkien, "Story of Kullervo"), 33, 35, 36
Matthews, Dorothy, 81n72
Matthews, W.R., 133
McFadden, Brian, 16n38, 174n37
McGatch, Milton, 7
medievalism, xiii, xviii, 5–12, 14n25, 15–16n38, 135–36, 216
Melian (*Silm.*), 244
Melkor (*Silm.*), 20, 72, 73
Mellyagraunce (Morris), 117
Menon, Madhavi, 8
Merry and Pippin (*LOTR*): aristocracy and, 161, 169–71; class and, 138, 162; Ents and, 205–6; as flawed heroes, 38; Frodo and, 159, 162–63, 169–71; Gatekeeper at Bree and, 164; masculinity and, 216–17, 227; Orcs and, 229–30. *See also* Hobbits
Michel, Laura, 178
Michelet, Jules, 7
middangeard (Middle-earth), 41n19
Middle-earth, history of, 27, 41n19, 70, 241–47. *See also History of Middle-earth*
Míriel (*Silm.*), 20, 177
misogyny, Tolkien's, alleged, xv, 9, 177, 205
Mitchell, Bruce, 15n38
Mitchison, Naomi, 133
Mithrandír (Gandalf), 70
Moffat, Wendy, 5
Mordred (*Fall of Arthur*), 97, 113–20, 123–25
Morgan, Father Francis Xavier, xxiii, 22
Morgan le Fay, la Fée, 126, 234
Morgause (T.H. White), 114–15
Morgoth (*Silm.*), 36, 37, 38, 72, 243
Morris, William, 76n5, 108n45; "Defence of Guenevere" by, 112, 116–17, 129n14; "House of the Wolfings" by, 180; influenced by Tennyson, 129n14; *Völsunga Saga of*, 47–49, 53–56, 59–60, 93, 95–96, 180
Morson, Gary Saul, 4
Morte Darthur (Malory), 115, 234
Morwen (*Silm.*), 37
Moses (Old English *Exodus*), 144–45
Müller, F. Max, 94–95
"Mythology for England, A," 79n44. *See also* letter 131 to Milton Waldman

N

Nagy, Gergely, 15n37, 38, 45n67
"Name Nodens, The" (Tolkien), xxviii
"Narn I Chin Húrin" (Tolkien), 37, 44n63
Nazgûl, 170–71, 242. *See also* Dark Riders
Neave, Edwin, xxiii, 20
Neave, Jane, 20, 183
neocolonialism, 140. *See also* postcolonial theory
Nevbosh (Tolkien language), 2
New Criticism, 190–91
"new essentialism," 8. *See also* Valerie Traub
A New Glossary of the Dialect of the Huddersfield District (Haigh), 141, 144
Newton, Sam, 86
Nienor (*Silm.*), 37–38
"No Future" concept, 120, 122, 124, 126. *See also* Lee Edelman
Noah (in Old English *Exodus*), 145
Nokes (*Smith of Wootton Major*), 103
Norman, Philip, 40n10, 176n61
Norse mythology: Frey, 52, 197; Loki, 52–54, 59–60, 202; Óðin, 52–60, 62–63, 68, 199–202, 216; Thor,

52. See also Legend of Sigurd and Gudrún; Völsunga Saga
Númenórean myths, 80n51

O

Ódin, in "Andvari's Gold," 54, 59; anointing of Sigurd as hero by, 53–55; Brynhild and, 199–201; Gandalf and, 68; horse of, 63; in Lang's "Story of Sigurd," 57–58; in Legend of Sigurd, 52–53, 59–60; Sigurd's ancestry and, 55–56, 60, 62, 202; treasure and, 54, 59; William Morris on, 55
"Ofermod" (Tolkien), 215, 217, 219–20, 222–23, 237n16
Olórin (Gandalf), 70
Olsen, Alexandra Hennessey, 247n8
On Fairy-Stories/"On Fairy-Stories" (Tolkien), xii, xxx, 24, 26, 67, 75, 76n3, 76n10, 90–96, 107n31, 136; Andrew Lang Lecture and, 51, 67; Beowulf and, 90–96, 120; "Beowulf: The Monsters and the Critics" and, 84; composing of, 107n31; "Cottage of Lost Play" and, 26; Draft (Manuscript) A of, 50; Draft (Manuscript) B of, 51, 71, 73; Elves and, 50, 73; and fantasy, 136; and "The Homecoming of Beorhtnoth," 84; Legend of Sigurd and, 47, 49–51; mythology and, 75; publication of, xxx; "secondary world" in, 24, 94; Sellic Spell and, 95; Silmarillion and, 50; tale-teller in, 94; "tragedy" in, 120; Völsunga Saga and, 49. See also fairy-stories
"On 'The Kalevala' or Land of Heroes" (Tolkien), 29, 43n48, 43n51

"Once and Future King, The" (White), 113, 114, 115, 124, 125, 130n28
One Ring, The: Bilbo and, 63–65, 74, 154–55, 157; desire and, 156; destruction of, 235; effect on self, 154–55; Frodo and, 157–58, 162, 164, 171–72, 241; Galadriel and, 242; Gandalf and, 157, 233; Gollum and, 38, 63–65, 160–61, 171, 227, 229, 233, 235; hierarchy of power and, 150; invisibility granted by, 65; origin of, 67; power and, 156–57; queerness and, 159, 232; Sam Gamgee and, 167, 218; Sauron and, 150; Smaug's lair and, 65; War of the Ring, 167. See also Lord of the Rings, The
O'Neill, Timothy R., 81n72
Orchard, Andy, 15n38
Orcs: in Hobbit, 69; Hobbits and, 137–38, 166; in Lord of the Rings, 140, 206–7, 216, 218, 228–32. See also Uruk-hai
Ormulum, 187
O'Rourke, Michael, 6, 14n24
Orwell, George, 11
Other: in Beowulf, 190; Hobbits as, 140, 207; Levinas on, 215; medievalism and, 7–8, 11; monstrous, 4; Orcs as, 229; Other Other, 7; past as, 8–9; Sam and Frodo as, 231; Tolkien on, 12; Žižek on, 4, 152. See also "Secret Vice, A"
Otho Baggins (LOTR), 156
Otr (Völsunga Saga), 52–54, 57, 59
Otty, Nick, 137–38
Oxford: Tolkien's lectures on The Battle of Maldon, 1928, 235n5; Tolkien's undergraduate courses taken at, 108n40

P

Paradise (Elven), 126–28. *See also* Tol Eressëa

Pearl (trans. Tolkien), xxvii, xxxi-xxxii, 113, 137, 142, 222–23

Philological Society, xxviii, 147–48

Plimmer, Charlotte and Denis, 39

Poesis (personification in "*Beowulf*" essay), 189–91

postcolonial theory, 6, 10–12, 20, 215–16

postmedievalism, 10–11

postmodernism: *Lord of the Rings* and, 242; medievalism and, 8; Other and, xv; queerness and, 5–6, 8–9, 122; Tolkien's medievalist works and, 10–11

Powers of Horror (Kristeva), 19

Praell and Pi'r ("Sigelwara Land"), 144

Prentice (*Smith of Wootton Major*), 103

Priestman, Judith, 40n2

Primer of the Gothic Language (Joseph Wright), 23, 180

Prose Edda, xxviii, 48, 59. *See also Lay of Sigurd*; *Völsunga Saga*

Pugh, Tison, xii, xvi, 6, 8, 11, 14n25, 216, 225–26, 229, 232, 239n42

Pugh, Tison, and Angela Weisl, 135–36

Pugh, Tison, and Kathleen Coyne Kelly, 14n25

Purcel, John, 185

Pym, Barbara, 183

Q

"queer creature," xv, 1–2, 6

queer endings: of Arthur and Beowulf, 119–22; Edelman on, 122–28; of King Arthur and his men, 114–19

queer historicism, 8–9

queer medievalism, 5–6, 9–11, 14n25

queerness, 14n24, 122; *Ancrene Wisse* and, 187; biography and, 5; chivalry and, 226–27; death and, 122; definitions of, by Battis/Smol, 11; Doty, 6; Edelman, 9; O'Rourke, 14n24; Pugh, 229; difference and, 152–54; Elves and, 126; in *Fall of Arthur*, 123; Gandalf and, 69; Gollum and, 171–72, 208, 233–34; in *Hobbit*, 49, 69; Hobbits and, 229, 233–34; in *Kalevala*, 30; in *Lord of the Rings*, 152, 54–59, 165, 227, 229–31, 233–34; masculinity and, 10, 227–34; of Merry and Pippin, 162–63; modernism and, 9–13; Orcs and, 229–33; self/identity and, 4–5, 8–9, 12–13; separation and, 133, 135, 140; the Shire and, 163–64; studies of, 6–7; Tolkien and, 3–5, 49, 122, 165, 241; women and, 178–79

Quendi, 72

Quenya (language), 1, 29, 70. *See also* Elves; Sindarin

R

Radagast (wizard, Istar), 70

Rædwald (East Anglian king), 86

Rateliff, John, 134, 183

Red Book of Westmarch (Bilbo's diary), 86, 105n6, 161, 167, 219. *See also Adventures of Tom Bombadil*

Red Fairy Book (Lang), xviii, 47, 51, 56, 95, 96

Reeve's Tale (Chaucer), 147, 148

Regin, dwarf and son of Hreidmar, 53–61, 68, 71, 73, 200. *See also Legend of Sigurd*; "Story of Sigurd"

Reid, Robin, 209n4
Reilly, R.J., 51
Renault, Mary, 183
Reynolds, R.W., xxvii, 45n65
rings, magic: in "Andvari's Gold," 54, 59; Brynhild and, 201; fairy-stories and, 51, 57; in *Hobbit*, 49, 51, 61; in *Legend of Gudrún*, 202; in *Legend of Sigurd*, 201; in rings of power, 70, 150; and *Sellic Spell*, 103; Sigurd and, 55–58, 66; Sigurd's mother and, 61–62; Tolkien's writings and, 48. *See also* One Ring
Rivendell, 167, 219. *See also* Elves
Rohan, 103, 151, 165, 167, 170, 205, 207, 215, 221, 228, 241. *See also* Éomer; Éowyn; Théoden
Roman Catholicism, 7, 22, 39, 50, 64, 75, 137, 139
Roman d'Enéas, 238n41
Rosebury, Brian, 137–38
Rosie Cotton (*LOTR*), 214n94
Roverandom (Tolkien), 51
Ruskin, John, 138
Ryan, J.S., 51

S
Sackville-Baggins, Camellia (*LOTR*), 78n37
St. Andrews Citizen, The (review of Tolkien's Andrew Lang Lecture), 50
St. Julienne, 184
Salu, Mary B., xxxi, 175n51, 184, 186
Samwise Gamgee (*LOTR*), 140, 155, 160, 162, 163, 167–69, 227, 230, 232, 233, 234
Sandyman (*LOTR*), 153, 154, 156, 160, 168, 169, 171–72
Saracens (*LOTR*), 144

Saruman (*LOTR*): difference and, 246; Ents and, 206; Gandalf and, 4, 70; Hobbits and, 153, 171; Istari and, 70; masculinity and, 215–16; monstrosity of, 140; Orcs and, 229, 231; queerness of, 227; Sauron and, 227
Sauron (*LOTR*): difference and, 153, 246; Eye of/disembodiment, 140, 156; Free Peoples versus, 172; Gandalf and, 70; Gollum/Sméagol and, 63, 161; Hobbits and, 153; identity and, 155; Lúthien and, 243; masculinity and, 216, 227–29, 232; monstrosity of, 63, 140; Norse mythology and, 59; One Ring and, 150, 155–56, 158; servants of, 153; in *Silmarillion*, 36, 72, 243
Sawles Warde, 184, 187
Saxton, Benjamin, 4
Scull, Christina, xvi, xxi, xxiii, 29, 85, 105n6, 217, 219, 236n6
Scotsman, The (review of Tolkien's Andrew Lang lecture), 50
Scyld Scefing (*Beowulf*), 93, 97, 101. *See also* Shield Sheafing
"Secret Vice, A" (Tolkien), xii, 1–3, 13n1
Sedgwick, Eve, 5
Seinte Katerine, 184. *See also* St. Katherine
self-projection, authorial, and identity: and abject characters, 179; *Ancrene Wisse* and, 189; Aragorn and, 245; assumptions about, 5; *Beowulf* and, 191–92; chivalry and, 225; difference and, 145, 153, 230; folk-tales and, 94; as Hobbit, 39, 168; masculinity and, 228–29; normative, 8; One Ring and, 155; and the Other, 231;

queerness and, 6, 9, 11–12, 126–27, 228–30; shifts in, 38; twin, 12; "Wanderer" and, 135; Yandell on, 12. *See also* "sideshadowing"

Sellic Spell (Tolkien): Beewolf in, 93, 101–4; *Beowulf* translation and, 96–99; comic tone of, 91–93; fantasy elements in, 95; "Iúmonna Gold Galdre Bewunden" and, 86; manuscripts of, 89; Tolkien on, 83; Tolkien's translation into Anglo-Saxon, 89

Selling, Kim, 7

Sharkey (*LOTR*), 153, 171, 227

Shelob (*LOTR*), 38, 216, 218–19, 231

Shield Sheafing (Tolkien *Beowulf* translation), 97, 101–4

Shipman's Tale (Chaucer), 147

Shippey, Thomas, 7, 76n8, 16n39, 141, 210n18, 222

Sibley, Brian, 173n19

"sideshadowing," 4. *See also* Ben Saxton; Gary Saul Morson

"Sigelwara Land" article (Tolkien), xxviii, 142–43

Sigemund (*Beowulf; Völsunga Saga*), 50, 98

Siggeir (king of Gautland), 55, 60

Sigmund (Sigurd's father), 50, 55–56, 59, 60

Signy (Sigmund's sister), 55, 56, 58–60

Sigurd, xiii, 38–39, 93, 101, 113, 178, 179, 192, 199–204; as antihero, 56–61; Bilbo as, in *Hobbit*, 47–81; genealogy of, in William Morris, 55; love for Gudrún, 201. *See also Legend of Sigurd* (Tolkien); "The Story of Sigurd" (Lang); *Völsunga Saga*

"Sigurd Born," 58, 60

Silmarillion, The (Tolkien): abject hero in, 45n65, 61; earliest writings of, 45n65, 80n51; fairy-stories and, 57, 66–75; *Fall of Arthur* and, 126; *Homecoming of Beorhtnoth* and, 219; *Lord of the Rings* and, 242–44, 246; mythology of, 85, 113, 185–86; postcolonial analysis of, 20; queer medievalism and, 5, 11; "Story of Kullervo" and, 33, 36; *Völsunga Saga* and, 49; women and, 178, 194, 208; writing of, 25, 48, 138. *See also* Túrin Turambar

Sindarin (language), 1, 37–38, 72–73, 151. *See also* Elves; Quenya

Sinex, Margaret, 144, 174n37

*sinhomo*sexuality, 127. *See also* Lee Edelman

Sir Gawain and the Green Knight (Middle-English poem, coedited Tolkien), 146: apartness and, 142; *Fall of Arthur* and, 124–26; *Lord of the Rings* and, 139, 234; three incarnations of, 222–26. *See also* Gawain

"Sir Gawain and the Green Knight" (Tolkien lecture), 217–19

Sir Gawain and the Green Knight (trans. Tolkien), 113, 137, 146

Sir Israel Gollancz Lecture (1936), xxix, 56. *See also* "Beowulf: The Monsters and the Critics" (article)

Sir Orfeo (Tolkien's translation), xxx, xxxi-xxxii, 113, 223

Sisam, Kenneth, xxvi, 56, 89, 180, 185, 222

Sitwel, Dom Gerard, 188, 189

Skeat, W.W., 42n37, 81

Smith, David E., 42n35

Smith, G.B., xxv, 23, 28, 236n7

INDEX   287

Smith of Wootton Major (Tolkien), xxxii, 12, 51, 95, 102–3, 152–53
Smol, Anna, 11, 38
"Song of Hiawatha, The" (Longfellow poem), 32, 43n48
"Songs for the Philologists" (Tolkien), xxviii
Spearing, A.C., 237n22
Speratus (bishop of Lindisfarne), 197
Stanzaic Morte Arthur, 114
Stapledon Society, 180
Stenström, Anders, 79n44
Steppenwolf (Hermann Hesse), 5
Stevens, Jen, 247n5
"Story of Eriol's Life," 27
"Story of Kullervo, The" (Tolkien), 29, 31, 33, 36–37, 42n35, 61, 67; and Tom Bombadil, 43n54
"Story of Sigurd" (Lang): adaptation of, 47; fairy-stories and, 75, 91, 96; *Hobbit* and, 61, 73–75; magical elements in, 57, 71; mystical in, 51–52, 65; Regin in, 57. *See also* Andvari; *Legend of Sigurd*; Sigurd
Story of the Volsungs (Morris), 180
"Straight Path" myth, 112, 126
Straights, Michael, 233, 241–42
Strong, Archibald, 193
Sutton Hoo, 85–86
Sword and the Stone, The, 114

T
Tadie, Joseph, 239n52
"Tale of the Children of Húrin" (Tolkien), 44n63
"Tale of Tinúviel" (Tolkien), 27, 44n57
Taylor, Samuel Coleridge, 32
TCBS (Tea Club Barrovian Society), 23, 28, 180, 183

teleoscepticism, 8
Teleri (*Silm.*), 36, 72, 151, 244
temporal normativity, 8
Tennyson, Alfred, Lord, 112, 114–16, 118, 121, 123, 130n28
Théoden *(LOTR)*, 4, 70, 205, 207, 215, 221, 228, 234
Thingol (*Silm.*), 36–38, 243–44
Thompson, Stith, 236n7
Thorin Oakenshield (*Hobbit*), 54, 57, 64, 66
Tídwald ("Homecoming of Beorhtnoth"), 218, 220
Time and the Other (Levinas), 111
Tol Eressëa (England), 25, 27, 42n28, 126–28. *See also* Avalon; Elves; Paradise
Tolkien, Arthur Reuel, 21
Tolkien, Christopher: alterations and styling of *Beowulf* translation, 90, 107n24, 193, 198; on Arthurian sources of *Fall of Arthur*, 111, 115; "Commentary on *The Cottage of Lost Play*," 27; compiling of "Of Aulë and Yavanna" (*Silm.*, ch. 2), 172–73n5; on dating of "Errantry," 236n11; on Dwarves in *Silm.*, 173n5; editing of father's works, 48, 77n26, 173n5; on ending of *Fall of Arthur*, 124; on publication of father's works, 12, 184; recollections of father's writings, xxviii, 2, 13n1, 25, 47–48, 89; relation with father, 90, 139; scholars' debt to, xvi, 104n1; on *Silm.* and *Fall of Arthur*, 113, 126; titling of "A Secret Vice"; on a voice for Guinever, 116
Tolkien, Edith Bratt, xxiv, 20–22, 24–25, 28, 177, 181–83, 243

Tolkien, Hilary, 21, 22
Tolkien, J.R.R.: abjection of, 19–24, 139, 191; allegorization of identity of, 3–5; and early life of, 19–22; education of, 22–23; early writings of, 19–40; creation of mythology, 27–28; invention of languages by, 1–3; *Kalevala* and, 28–37; on Kullervo and Túrin Turambar, 37–40; "oppositional figures," creation of, 4; Otherness, 6–7, 12–13, 23; queerness of, 5–6; and relationship with and loss of his mother, 19–22; scholarship on medieval works, 11–12; self-projection of, in characters, 5; wife of, 20–22, 177. *See also* Christopher Tolkien; "Cottage of Lost Play"; Edith Bratt Tolkien; "Goblin Feet"; "The Story of Kullervo"; "You and Me," 24–25
Tolkien, John, Father, 76n9
Tolkien, Mabel Suffield, xxiii, 19–22, 33
Tolkien, Michael, xxvi, 22, 76n9, 181, 182, 208
Tolkien, Priscilla, 177
Tolkien, Ronald: *see* J.R.R. Tolkien
Tolkien Remembered (video), 76n9, 173n11, 210n18
Toller, T. Northcote, 41n25, 77n12, 214n93
Took family: background of, 62, 165–67; Belladonna, 78n37, 159; Bilbo and, 62, 165–66; Buckland and, 161; Bullroarer, 62, 161, 166; noble class of, 62, 165, 170, 172; Frodo and, 62; of Great Smials, 62, 166–67; Lady Took in, 169; Old Took, 68–69, 159; Peregrin (Pippin), 159, 161, 169–70; queerness and, 162, 164. *See also* Merry and Pippin
Torhthelm (*Homecoming of Beorhthelm*), 218, 220
Totality and the Other (Emmanuel Levinas), 25
Traub, Valerie, 8–9
treasure, 50, 54, 56–58, 63, 84–85, 98, 100–1, 117, 144–45, 195–96, 221. *See also* Dragons; Dwarves; *Hobbit*; *Legend of Sigurd*; *Völsunga Saga*
Treebeard (*LOTR*), 205–7. *See also* Ents; Entwives
Tuor (kinsman of Túrin Turambar), 244
Turgon (king of Gondolin), 244
Túrin Turambar: in *Silm.*, 37–38, 50; as abject, xiv, 61; "doom" of, 50; lack of children of, 113; like Kullervo, 37–38, 44n63; in "Túrin Turambar and the Dragon," 37
Tyndall, Denis, Reverend, 45n65

U

Uglúk (Orc, *LOTR*), 229
Unfinished Tales (Tolkien), xii, xxii, xxxi, 37, 70
Unfriend (Unferth), 102
Untamo (*Kalevala*), 30, 31
Untamo (Tolkien, "Story of Kullervo"), 32, 33, 34
Unwin, Rayner, 186, 219
Upphaf (Tolkien), 52, 58
Uruk-hai, 229–30. *See also* Orcs

V

Vaccaro, Christopher, xix
Väinämöinen (*Kalevala*), 30, 31

Vairë ("Cottage of Lost Play"), 25, 26
Valar (*Silm.*), 20, 70–72, 128, 244
"Valedictory Address to the University of Oxford" (Tolkien), xxxii, 23, 133–35, 145
Valhöllu, 60
Valinor (*Silm.*), 126–28
Valkyries, 60–61, 199–200, 208, 221. *See also* Brynhild; *The Legend of Gudrún*
Vanyar (*Silm.*), 72
Varda (*Silm.*), 70, 72
Vinaver, Eugène, xxviii
Vingi (*Legend of Gudrún*), 202, 203
Vink, Renée, 172n3, 172n4
Völsung (father of Signy), 60
Völsunga Saga: Andvari in, 134; antihero in, 56; Brynhild in, 199; Dwarves in, 134; Fáfnir in, 191–92; fairy-stories and, 95–96; *Legend of Gudrún* and, 58, 199–203, 213n90; *Legend of Sigurd* and, 49, 54, 59–60; and *Lord of the Rings, The*, 134, 179; monsters and, 64; *Sellic Spell* and, 101; *Silmarillion* and, 50; Tolkien's identification with, 180; translations of, 47–49, 52, 93, 95–96; women and, 189
"Voyage of Éarendel the Evening Star, The" (Tolkien), xxiv, 219

W

Wagner, Richard, 7, 137
"Wanderer, The" (Old English poem), 135, 145, 169
Wanley, Humphrey, 189–90
Wānōna (Tolkien, "Story of Kullervo"), 32–33, 35
Wars of Alexander, The, 142
Warwick (Engl.), 28
Wealhtheow, 86, 191, 197, 207. *See also Beowulf*
Webster, Deborah, 39
Welsh Grammar, A (Jones), 180
Weohstan (Wiglaf's father), 196
West, Richard C., 247n5
White, T.H., 97, 112–15, 121, 123–25, 130n28
Widsith, 86
Wíglaf the Wægmunding (*Beowulf*), 113, 119, 192–93, 195–96
Wilcox, Miranda, 16n38
Wingelot (Foam-Flower), in *Gawain*, 126
Wiseman, Christopher, 23
Witch in the Wood, The (T.H. White), 114
wizards: *see* Istari
Woden, 106n13, 210n22
Women: in *Ancrene Wisse*, 185–89; in *Beowulf*, 189–93, 198–99; Brynhild and Gudrún, 189–93, 199–205; and gender, 177–78, 190, 208; in *Lord of the Rings, The*, 205–8, 240–42; in *Silm.*, 242–47; students of Tolkien, 140, 177, 183–84, 187, 189; and Tolkien's alleged misogyny, 177; in Tolkien's *Beowulf* teaching translation, 193–96; and Tolkien's early life, 180–81; Tolkien's identification with, 179; Tolkien's representation and views of, 178, 181–82; in Tolkien's teaching commentary on *Beowulf*, 196–98. *See also* Arwen; Brynhild; Elizabeth Mary Wright; Entwives; Éowyn; Freawaru; Gudrún; Lúthien; Mary Salu; Simonne T.R.O. d'Ardenne; Ursula Dronke

World War I, xi, xxiv, 1, 21, 28, 41n16, 68, 139, 179–80, 234
World War II, xi, xv, 39, 138–39, 210n20, 234, 246
Wormtongue, 207, 215, 216, 221, 227
W.P. Ker Memorial Lecture ("Sir Gawain and the Green Knight"), xxxi, 217–19
wraecca (in *Beowulf*), 145, 192–93, 198. *See also* exile
Wrenn, C.L., 105n3
Wright, Elizabeth Mary, 183
Wright, Joseph, 23, 180, 183

X
xenophobia, 153, 160, 165

Y
Yandell, Steve, 12, 17n41
Yavanna (*Silm.*), 70, 134
"You and Me" (Tolkien), 24–25
Young, Brigham, 182
Young, K.J., 86

Z
Zaleski, Philip and Carol, 209n14
Zettersten, Arne, 211n40
Zipes, Jack, 67, 94
Žižek, Slavoj, 4, 151–52
Zunshine, Lisa, 153

The manufacturer's authorised representative in the EU is Springer Nature Customer Service Centre GmbH, Europaplatz 3, 69115 Heidelberg, Germany. If you have any concerns regarding our products, please contact ProductSafety@springernature.com

Printed and bound by CPI Group (UK) Ltd, Croydon, CR0 4YY

23/03/2026

02076459-0005